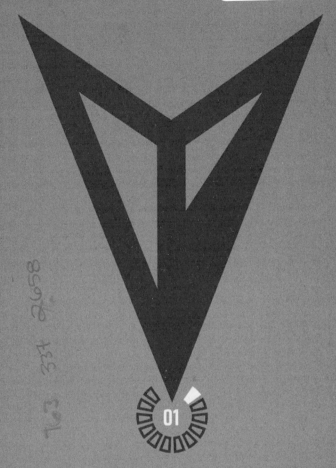

01

# TAKEN

**01**

# TIM LaHAYE
# JERRY B. JENKINS

 TYNDALE HOUSE PUBLISHERS, INC., CAROL STREAM, ILLINOIS

Visit Tyndale online at www.tyndale.com.

Discover the latest Left Behind news at www.leftbehind.com.

*Taken* is a special edition compilation of the following Left Behind: The Kids titles:

Cover designed by Mark Anthony Lane II

Interior designed by Jenny Swanson

Published in association with the literary agency of Alive Communications, Inc., 7680 Goddard Street, Suite 200, Colorado Springs, CO 80920.

*Taken* is a work of fiction. Where real people, events, establishments, organizations, or locales appear, they are used fictitiously. All other elements of the novels are drawn from the authors' imaginations.

For manufacturing information regarding this product, please call 1-800-323-9400.

**Library of Congress Cataloging-in-Publication Data**

Jenkins, Jerry B.
    Taken / Jerry B. Jenkins, Tim LaHaye.
        p. cm.
Contents: The vanishings—Second chance—Through the flames—Facing the future.
    ISBN 978-0-8423-8351-6
    1. Children's stories, American. [1. End of the world—Fiction.  2. Christian life—Fiction.]
I. LaHaye, Tim F.   II. Title.
    PZ7.J4138 Tak 2003
    [Fic]—dc21                                                                                2003007987

ISBN 978-1-4143-9950-8 (sc)

Printed in the United States of America

21   20   19   18   17   16   15
 7    6    5    4    3    2    1

**1**

**JUDD** Thompson Jr. had always hated having the same name as his father. Until now.

Every time the phone rang and someone asked for Judd, it was "Which one? Big Judd or Little Judd?" The funny thing was, Little Judd was already taller than his father. He had just gotten his driver's license, and the whiskers on his chin formed a thin goatee. He was tired of being called *Junior*, and if he were never called Little Judd again for the rest of his life, it would be too soon.

But now, for once, being Judd Thompson Jr. was working in Judd's favor.

This break was meant to be, Judd decided. After days of fighting with his parents about where he was going, who he was with, what he was doing, and how late he would be in, he had just happened to be home one afternoon. And his mother picked that day to ask him to bring in the mail. If that didn't prove this was meant to be, Judd didn't know what did.

Judd sighed loudly at his mother's request. She said he acted like any small chore or favor was the biggest burden in the world. That was exactly how he felt. He didn't want to be told to do anything.

"Why can't *you* get it?" he asked her.

"Because I asked you to," she said.

"Why do *I* have to do everything?"

"Would you like to compare what you do around here with what I do?" she asked, and that began the usual argument. Only when his mother threatened to ground him did he stomp out to the mailbox. He was glad he did.

On the way back to the house, idly flipping through catalogs and letters and magazines, he had found it—an envelope addressed to him. It was clearly a mistake—obviously intended for his father. He knew that as soon as he saw it. It was business mail. He didn't recognize the return address.

Just to be ornery, he slipped it inside his jacket and gave the rest of the mail to his mother. Well, he didn't actually give it to her. He tossed it onto the kitchen table in front of her, and half of it slid to the floor. He headed to his room.

"Just a minute, young man," she said, using another of his least favorite names. "Get back here and give me this mail properly."

"In a minute," he said, jogging up the steps.

"Oh, never mind," she said. "By the time you get back here, I'll have it picked up, read, and answered."

"You're welcome!" he hollered.

"A job not finished is not worthy of a thank-you," she said. "But thanks anyway."

Judd took off his jacket, cranked up his music, and lay on his bed, opening the envelope. Onto his chest dropped a credit card in his name, Judd Thompson Jr. A sticker on it told him to call a toll-free number and answer a few questions so he could begin using the card. The letter told him they had honored his request. He could spend tens of thousands of dollars using that card alone.

Judd couldn't believe his luck. He dialed the number and was asked his mother's maiden name and his date of birth. He knew enough to use his grandmother's maiden name and his father's birthday. This was, after all, really his father's card, wrong name or not. The automated voice told Judd he could begin using the card immediately.

It was then that he planned his escape.

Judd felt desperate to get away. He wasn't sure what had happened or why, but he was sure his family was the problem.

Judd's father owned a business in Chicago and was wealthy. His mother had never had to work outside the home. Judd's little brother and sister, nine-year-old twins Marc and Marcie, were young enough to stay out of his hair. They were OK, he guessed.

Marc's and Marcie's rooms were full of trophies from church, the same as Judd's had once been. He had really been into that stuff, memorizing Bible verses, going to camp every summer, all that.

But when Judd had gone from the junior high to the senior high youth group at New Hope Village Church in Mount Prospect, Illinois, he seemed to lose interest overnight. He used to invite his friends to church and youth group. Now he was embarrassed to say his parents made him go.

Judd felt he had outgrown church. It had been OK when he was a kid, but now nobody wanted to dress like he did, listen to his kind of music, or have a little fun. At school he hung with kids who got to make their own decisions and do what they wanted to do. That was all he wanted. A little freedom.

Even though they could afford it, Judd's parents refused to buy him his own car. How many other high school juniors still rode the bus to school? When Judd did get to drive one of his parents' cars, one of them told him where he could go, whom he could go with, what he could do, and when he had to be back.

If only his parents knew what he was doing when they thought he was "just out with the guys," Judd thought. How he hated his curfew, his parents' constant watch over his schoolwork, their criticizing his hair, his clothes, and his friends.

Worst of all, he was grounded if he didn't get up for Sunday school and church every Sunday. Just the Sunday before, he had put up such a fuss that his mother had come into his room and sat on his bed. "Don't you love Jesus anymore?" she asked.

*What a stupid question*, Judd thought. He didn't remember ever really loving Jesus. Oh, he had liked all the stories and knew a lot of verses. But loving Jesus? Loving God? That was for little kids and old ladies. But what could he say to his mother?

"If you want the truth, I only go to church so I can go out on weekends and use the car."

That was clearly not what she had wanted to hear. "All right then, just forget it!" she said.

"I can stay home from church?"

"If you don't want to go anywhere for a week."

Judd swore under his breath. It was a good thing his mother hadn't heard *that.* He'd have been grounded for life.

In Sunday school, Judd copped an attitude. He wore clothes his parents only barely approved of, and he stayed as far away as possible from the "good" kids. What losers! They never had any fun. Judd didn't smile, didn't carry a Bible, didn't look at the teacher, didn't say anything. When the teacher asked his opinion of something, he shrugged. He wanted everyone to know he was there only because he had to be.

In church, he slouched when his father wasn't looking. He wanted to burrow within himself and just make it through to the end of the service. He didn't sing along, he didn't bow his head during prayer, he didn't shut his eyes. No one had ever said those were rules; Judd was simply trying to be different from everyone else. He was way too cool for this stuff.

As usual, Pastor Vernon Billings got off on his kick about what he called the Rapture. "Someday," he said, "Jesus will return to take his followers to heaven. Those who have received him will disappear in the time it takes to blink your eye. We will disappear right in front of disbelieving people. Won't that be a great day for us and a horrifying one for them?"

The kindly old pastor talked about how important it was for everyone to be sure of his own standing before God and to think and pray about friends and loved ones who might not be ready. Judd's little secret was that he had never really believed any of that.

He'd had enough chances. At vacation Bible school, his friends had prayed and received Christ. He was embarrassed. He told them he had already done that at home. At camp a few years later, Judd felt guilty and sinful when a young speaker talked about church kids who weren't really Christian believers. He had wanted to go forward; he really had. But he had also just been named Camper of the Week for memorizing a bunch of Bible verses and being the fastest to look up some others. What would people say?

Judd knew he didn't have to go forward or talk with anyone to receive Christ. He knew he could do it by himself. He could pray sincerely and ask God to forgive his sins and make Jesus the Lord of his life. But later, when the meeting was over and the emotion wore off, he told himself that was something he could do anytime.

Judd felt the most guilty when he was twelve years old and many of his Sunday school classmates signed up to be baptized. Their teacher and Pastor Billings made clear to them that this was an act of obeying Christ, a step taken by Christians to declare themselves followers of Jesus.

As the students were baptized, they were asked to tell about when they had received Christ. Judd had done the unthinkable. He had quoted Scripture and made up a story about when he had become a Christian "once by myself at camp."

He felt guilty about that for weeks, never having the guts to tell his parents or his Sunday school teacher. Yet something kept him from confessing to God and getting things right with Christ. Now he was sixteen and had feelings and thoughts he believed no one would understand. He was bored with his church, frustrated with his parents, and secretly proud that he wasn't really part of the church crowd. He went because he had to, but someday soon he would make his own decisions.

With the small error on that credit card, Judd Thompson Jr. had his ticket to freedom. He had seen his dad get cash with his credit card at the bank and at the automatic teller machines. And he knew that almost anything could be paid for with that magic card.

Of course, one day the bill would come and his parents would be able to trace where he had been. But he could put a lot of miles between himself and them in the meantime.

For several days, Judd saved cash, withdrawing as much as he could each day from the automatic teller machine. He hid the money with the passport he had gotten the year before when his father took him along on a business trip to Asia. He had been miserable on that trip and let his dad know it every chance he got. Judd Sr. had finally given up trying to convince Judd Jr. that this was "the opportunity of a lifetime."

Secretly Judd had to admit that he enjoyed the hotels, the meals, and even learning how to get around in foreign cities with different cultures and languages. But he wasn't about to tell his dad that. Judd knew Dad had dragged him along only to get him away from his new friends, the ones his mother called the "evil influences." It was also supposed to be a time for him and his dad to bond—whatever that meant. Dad had tried, Judd had to give him that, but there had been no bonding. Mostly it was just Judd scowling, complaining, arguing, and begging to go home.

At least he got a passport out of the deal. That, along with his new driver's license and the credit card, gave him what he thought was complete freedom. A friend had told him he looked old enough to pass for twenty-one and that he should get a fake identification card that would allow him to buy liquor in Illinois. It was cheaper and easier than he thought to get both his driver's license and his passport copied with a new birth date.

His plan was to take his stash of cash and go to O'Hare International Airport some night. He would take the first flight he could get to another English-speaking country. Beyond that, his plan was not clear. One thing was sure: He wasn't going to bum around begging for a place to stay. He would live first-class all the way.

Now Judd was a criminal. He told himself he wasn't scared. Breaking the law only made him bolder about his plan, and he began making up reasons why he had to get away from home as soon as possible.

As he made his plans, Judd became more and more angry.

He disagreed with everything his parents did or said. He was mean and sarcastic.

One day after school his little brother came into his room.

"What do *you* want?" Judd asked Marc.

"I just wanted to ask you a question. Are you still a Christian?"

Judd lied. "Of course," he said. "What's it to you?"

"I was just wonderin' because it doesn't seem like you're happy or acting like one."

"Why don't you get out of here and mind your own business!"

"Will you be mad at me if I pray for you?"

"Don't waste your breath."

"You're makin' Mom cry, you know that?"

"She shouldn't waste her tears either."

"Judd, what's the matter? You used to care—"

"Out! Get out!"

Marc looked pale and tearful as he left. Judd shook his head, disgusted, and told himself Marc would be a lot better off when he outgrew his stupidity. *I used to be just like that,* Judd thought. *What a wuss!*

Judd stuffed some of his favorite clothes in his book bag and jogged downstairs. "And where do you think you're going, mister?" his mother said. Did she always have to talk like that? Couldn't she just ask a simple question?

"I'm going to the library to study," Judd said. "I'll be there till closing, so don't wait up for me."

"Since when did you get interested in studying?" his mother asked.

"You said you wanted my grades to improve!"

"You don't need to go to the library to study, Judd. Why don't you stay here and—"

"I need some peace and quiet, all right?"

"What will you do for dinner?"

"I'll get something out."

"Do you need some money?"

"No! Now leave me alone!"

"All right! Just go! But don't be late!"

"Mom! I already told you! I'm staying till closing, so—"

"Don't wait up, yeah, I know. Are you meeting someone there?"

"No!"

"I'd better not find out you've been out with your friends, young man. . . ."

But Judd was already out the door.

---

At O'Hare, Judd found a flight on Pan-Continental Airlines that left early in the evening and was scheduled to arrive in London the following morning. His phony identification cards worked perfectly, and he enjoyed being referred to as Mr. Thompson. His first-class ticket was very expensive, but it was the only seat left on the 747.

Judd knew it wouldn't be long before his parents started looking for him. They would discover his car at the airport, and they would quickly find his name on the passenger list of the Pan-Con flight. He'd better enjoy this freedom while he could, he decided. He would try to hide in England for as long as possible, but even if he was found and hauled back to the United States, he hoped he would have made his point.

What was his point, exactly, he wondered. That he needed his freedom. Yeah, that was it. He needed to be able to make some decisions on his own, to be treated like an adult. He didn't want to be told what to do all the time. He wanted the Thompson family to know that he was able to get along in the world on his own. Going to London by himself, based on his own plans, ought to prove that.

Judd sat on the aisle. On the other side of the aisle sat a middle-aged man who had three drinks set before him. Beyond him, in the window seat, a younger man sat hunched over his laptop computer.

Judd was stunned at the beauty of the flight attendant, whose name badge read "Hattie." He'd never known anyone with that name, but he couldn't work up the courage to say so. He was excited and pleased with himself when she didn't even ask to see any identification when she offered him champagne.

"How much?" he asked.

"It's free in first class, Mr. Thompson," she said.

He had tried champagne a few times and didn't like it, but he liked the idea of its sitting on the tray table in front of him. He would pretend to be on business, on his way to London for important meetings.

Captain Rayford Steele came over the intercom, announcing their flight path and altitude and saying he expected to arrive at Heathrow Airport at six in the morning.

Judd Thompson Jr. couldn't wait. This was already the most exciting night of his life.

**2**

**VICKI** Byrne was fourteen and looked eighteen. Tall and slender, she had fiery red hair and had recently learned to dress in a way that drew attention, from girls and guys. She liked leather. Low cut black boots, short skirts, flashy tops, lots of jewelry, and a different hairstyle almost every day.

She was tough. She had to be. Other kids at school considered kids who lived in trailer parks lower class. Vicki's friends were her "own kind," as her enemies liked to say. When she and her trailer park neighbors boarded the bus on Vicki's first day of high school, they quickly realized how it was going to be.

The bus was full. It was obvious the trailer park was the last stop on the route. Only the first two kids of the twelve boarding from the trailer park found a seat even to share. Every morning they jostled for position to be one of the lucky first ones aboard. Vicki had given up trying. Two senior boys, smelling of tobacco and bad breath and never, ever, carrying schoolbooks, muscled their way to the front of the line.

No one on the bus looked at the trailer park kids. They seemed to be afraid that if they made eye contact, they might have to slide over and make room for a third person in their seat. And, of course, no one wanted to sit next to "trailer trash." Vicki had seen them hold their noses when she and her neighbors boarded, and she had heard the whispers.

How was a freshman girl supposed to feel when people pretended not to see her, pretended she didn't exist, acted as if she were scum?

The bus driver refused to pull away from the trailer park until everyone was seated, so the two senior trailer boys—who had already found seats—rose and scowled and insisted that people make room. Some "rich kids," which they all seemed to be if they didn't live near Vicki, begrudgingly made room.

The first day, Vicki had found herself the last to find a seat. She looked in the front, where most of the black kids sat. They had to be among the first on the bus, because no one seemed to want to sit with them either—especially the trailer park kids. In fact, Vicki's friends called the black kids horrible names and wouldn't sit with them even if they offered a seat.

Vicki had been raised to believe black kids were beneath her too. No black people lived in the trailer park, and she didn't know why they were supposed to be inferior, other than that they were a different color. Her father had said they were lazy, criminal, stupid. And yet that was how Vicki saw her father himself. At least until two years before.

When she was twelve, something had happened to her parents. Before that they had seemed the same as most of their neighbors. Every Friday night there was a community dance where drunk and jealous husbands fought over their wives and girlfriends. It was not unusual for the dances to be broken up by the police, with one or more of the fighters being hauled off to jail for the night. Often, her mother bailed out Vicki's dad, and then they would fight over that for the rest of the weekend.

Vicki's father had trouble keeping a job, and her mother's waitressing didn't pay enough to cover their bills. Vicki's dad had been a mechanic, a construction worker, a short-order cook, and a cashier at a convenience store. Being arrested or late or absent from work one too many times always cost him his job, and then they would live on welfare for a few months until he could find something else.

Vicki had wished her parents would stay away from the community dance every Friday night, but they seemed to look forward to it as the highlight of their week. She had to admit she used to love hanging around with her older brother Eddie and little sister Jeanni and their friends during those dances. They were always off sneaking around and getting into mischief while their parents danced, sang, drank, and fought. It was while running with those kids that Vicki learned to smoke and drink. When Eddie graduated from high school, he moved out on his own to Michigan.

There were a few trailer park families who never came to the dances. They, Vicki's father said, were the "religious types. The goody-goodies. The churchgoers."

Vicki's mother often reminded him, "Don't forget, Tom, that was the way I was raised. And it's not all bad. We could do with some church around here."

"I rescued you from all that superstitious mumbo jumbo," he had said.

That became Vicki's view of church. She believed there was a God out there somewhere, and her mother told her he had created the world and created her and loved her. She couldn't make that make sense. If God created this lousy world and her lousy life, how could he love her?

One Friday night when Vicki was in seventh grade, the family heard the loud music signaling the weekly dance and began moseying to the parking lot to hear the band. Vicki's plan was to ditch Jeanni as soon as the party started and run off somewhere with her friends to sneak some cigarettes and maybe some beer.

But before she could do that, the music stopped and everyone looked toward the small stage in surprise. "Uh, 'scuse me," the lead singer said. "One of our neighbors here has asked if he can introduce a guest who'd like to speak to us for a few minutes."

Sometimes local politicians said a few words at the dances, or the police reminded people to behave, or the landlord reminded everyone that "this is a privilege and can be ended if there are more fights."

But the neighbor with a guest speaker had never been seen at one of these dances. He was one of those church people Vicki's dad made fun of. And his guest was a preacher. As soon as he began to speak, people groaned and began shouting to "get on with the music."

But the speaker said, "If you'll just indulge me for a few moments, I promise not to take more than five minutes of your time. And I plead with you to let your children hear this too."

Somehow, that quieted the crowd. The man launched into a very fast, very brief message that included verses from the Bible and a good bit of shouting. Vicki had been to church only once with a friend, and she had no idea what he was talking about. She was struck, however, that everyone, even the bartenders and musicians, seemed to stop and listen. No one ran around, no one spoke, no one moved.

The speaking didn't seem all that great, but there was a feeling, an atmosphere. The man seemed to know what he was talking about and spoke with confidence and authority. The best Vicki could figure out, he was saying that everyone was

14

a sinner and needed God. God loved them and wanted to forgive their sins and promise to take them to heaven when they died.

She didn't believe him. She hated her life, and if she did things wrong, they weren't any worse than what her own parents did. They smoked and drank and fought. What was the big deal? And if God loved them, why were they living in a trailer park?

Vicki wanted to get going, to run with her friends, but she didn't want to be the only one moving. Everyone else seemed frozen in place. Vicki didn't understand it. She hadn't heard too much of this religious talk, and she didn't care to hear any more. When she turned to complain to her parents, she was shocked to see her mother standing there with her eyes closed, silently moving her lips. Could she be praying?

And her father! Usually something like this would make him nervous and fidgety. It wouldn't have surprised her if he had tried to shout down the speaker or cause some other disturbance. But there he stood, staring at the preacher, not moving. "Daddy?" she whispered.

He held up a hand to shush her. What was so interesting? What was keeping all these party people quiet? The preacher asked his listeners to bow their heads and close their eyes. Now *there* was something they would never do. If there was anything Vicki's dad and his friends hated more than being told what to do, she didn't know what it was.

When she looked around, however, almost everyone was doing it! Some just stared at the ground, but most had their eyes closed. The preacher told them how they could receive Christ. "Tell God you realize you're a sinner," he said. "Thank him for sending Jesus to die for you, and accept his offer of forgiveness."

Vicki still didn't understand. The whole thing made her uneasy, but something was happening here. She looked to her dad and was stunned to see he had fallen to his knees and was crying. Her mother crouched next to him, hugging him and praying with him.

Vicki was embarrassed. As soon as the preacher finished and the music started again, she slipped away with her friends. "What was that all about?" she asked them.

"Who knows?" a boy said, pulling cans of beer from a paper bag and passing them around. "You ought to ask your old man. He really seemed into it. Your mom too."

Vicki shrugged. Her girlfriend added, "They left the dance, you know."

"What do you mean?" Vicki asked.

"Your mom was leading your dad back to the trailer, and your little sister was tagging along behind them. They must've got religion or something."

"Whatever that means," Vicki said, hoping to change the subject. "I need a cigarette."

Vicki didn't really need a cigarette. It was just something to say that made her feel older. She smoked, yes, but she didn't carry a pack with her. She just bummed smokes off her friends once in a while.

At the end of the evening, when she and her friends had had enough beer and cigarettes to make her feel wasted, she filled her mouth with gum to try to hide the smell and made her way back home. She walked through the parking lot where the music and the dancing were still going on.

Some of the people she had seen with their eyes closed and seeming to pray were now drinking and carrying on as usual, but there didn't seem to be any fights or any reason for anyone to call the police.

Vicki was half an hour past her curfew, but her parents had never been home this early from a weekend dance before. She expected a loud chewing out, the usual threats of grounding (which were rarely followed through), and charges that she had been involved in all kinds of awful things. All she and her friends had done was to put firecrackers in a few mailboxes and run away, and they tipped over a few garbage cans. Her father always accused her of much worse than that, but his promised punishments were nearly always forgotten.

This night was strange. Her little sister, Jeanni, was already in bed, but her parents were as awake as she had ever seen them. Her mother sat at the tiny kitchen table, her dusty old Bible in front of her. Vicki's father was excited, beaming, smiling, pacing. "I want to quit smoking and drinking, Dawn," he said, as Vicki came in. "I want to clean up my whole act."

"Now, Tom," Vicki's mother cautioned, "nobody says you can't be a Christian if you smoke and drink. Let's find a good church and start living for God and let him do the work in our lives."

Vicki shook her head and started for her bedroom, but her father called her back. "I became a Christian tonight, honey," he said, a name he hadn't called her since she was a preschooler.

"What were you before?" Vicki asked.

"I was a nothing," he said. "Your mom was a Christian, but I—"

"I knew the Lord," Vicki's mother said, "but I haven't lived for him for years. I was pretty much a nothing myself. But I came back to the Lord tonight. We're going to start going to church and—"

"Church?" Vicki said. "*I'm* not going!"

"Of course you are," her dad said. "When you get saved, you'll *want* to go to church. I can't wait."

"I can," Vicki said. "And when I get saved from what?"

"Saved from hell, saved from your sin. You'll be safe in the arms of Jesus, and you'll go to heaven when you die."

"You really believe that?" Vicki said.

"You bet I do," Mr. Byrne said.

"I'll tell you what I bet," Vicki said. "I bet you'll be drinking and cussing and fighting and losing your job again."

Her father's smile froze. She knew she had made him mad, and she could tell he wanted to hit her. She had spoken what she believed was the truth, but she hadn't really wanted to hurt him.

He approached and reached for her, and she flinched. "Don't you touch me!" she screamed.

He took her gently by the shoulders and spoke softly. "I'm not going to hit you, Vicki," he said. "Let me hug you." She couldn't remember how long it had been since he had done that. "I know this all has to sound strange to you, but something happened to me tonight. It was as if God spoke to me. I don't know why I listened or how he got through, but he did. And things are going to change around here."

*That'll be the day*, Vicki thought.

"I know you have no reason to believe me, hon," her dad said. "I don't blame you for not understanding. I've never given you any reason to trust me, so I guess I'll just have to prove it."

"Let's let God work on her," her mom said. "We have enough work to do on ourselves, and he's going to help us with that too."

Vicki finally pulled away from her dad. "Well, I'm glad if this works for you two," she said, "but don't expect me to be part of it. It sounds weird. You hear a crazy preacher for five minutes and now all of a sudden you're holy?"

"We're not holy," her mother said. "We're just giving ourselves to God."

"And you don't think that sounds strange?"

"When God gets through to you," her dad said, "you won't think it sounds so strange."

Vicki finally made it to the little bedroom she shared with Jeanni and flopped into bed. She was scared about what was happening with her parents. She decided that if this really kept her dad from drinking and fighting and being a lazy worker, it would be all right. But this much of a change in such a short time was too much to handle.

Jeanni stirred. "Is that you, Vick?"

"It's me."

"Did you hear what happened tonight?"

"I heard. Go back to sleep."

"Then you know I'm a Christian now?"

"You too?"

"Yup. I got Jesus in my heart."

Vicki sat up. Now her parents were brainwashing her little sister! "Jesus in your heart? What does that mean?"

"Well," she said, "he's not really inside me, but I took him into my life. I'm going to go to heaven someday."

"Oh, brother!"

"You'd better do it too, Vicki. You don't want to go to hell."

"You'd better get one thing straight, Jeanni. Everybody in this trailer park is going to hell, and that includes you and me."

Vicki regretted it as soon as she'd said it. Who was she to be dumping on her little sister? Maybe church would be good for Jeanni, too, as long as they didn't make Vicki go. Jeanni's response proved she had not been bothered by what Vicki said.

"Not me," she said brightly. "I'm going to heaven with Jesus!"

*Good for you,* Vicki thought. *Just leave me out of it.*

**3**

**LIONEL** Washington's parents had moved him out of the inner city of Chicago when he was six years old. His mother, Lucinda, had been a reporter for the Chicago office of *Global Weekly* magazine. When she was promoted to bureau chief, the family could afford to move to the suburbs. They were among the first blacks to live in their Mount Prospect neighborhood.

Now, seven years later, thirteen-year-old Lionel was having trouble deciding where he fit. When he visited his relatives in Chicago, or when his other relatives visited him from the South, his cousins criticized him for "losing your blackness. It's like you're white now."

It was nice to live in a neighborhood where he didn't have to be afraid to ride his bike anywhere or run with his friends, even after dark. And Lionel enjoyed having more things than he was used to having when he was smaller. His cousins, probably to cover their jealousy of his nicer clothes and shoes and the fact that his parents had two cars, called him "rich boy" and "whitey" and said he might as well not even be black.

Lucinda Washington was a no-nonsense woman. She had

become a well-paid executive with the leading newsmagazine in the country, despite her being black and a woman. She laughed when her nieces and nephews teased Lionel. "He's as black as you are and always will be," she said. "Now you just go on and leave him alone."

Still, Lionel didn't like it. No way did he want to give up what he thought was a better and safer life than he had known. But neither did he want to be different from his relatives. There were few other black kids in his junior high, and none of them went to his church. His older sister, Clarice, went to Prospect High School, and his younger brother and sister, Ronnie and Talia, were still in elementary school.

That made him feel all the more alone at his school. He grew quieter there and at home, and he could tell his mother was worried about him. Lionel didn't like the changes in his body and his mind as he became a teenager. It was too strange. He found himself thinking more. He thought about everything.

Mostly, he thought about his Uncle André. André was the bad apple of the family. He was a drunk and had been known to use and abuse drugs. He'd been in and out of jail for years and once even served a short term at Stateville Penitentiary in Joliet, Illinois.

The thing about Uncle André was that he was a charming guy. When he was sober and out of trouble and working, everybody loved him. He was fun and funny and great to be around. When he was "sick," which was the family term for when he was doing drugs or drinking or running with the wrong crowd, they all worried about him and prayed for him and tried to get him to come back to church.

Uncle André was a great storyteller. He loved to regale the family with exaggerated tales that made them all laugh. He told the stories in a high-pitched whine, making up new things as he went along, and each story grew funnier each time he told it. He would throw his head back and grab his belly and laugh until he could barely catch his breath. Tears would stream down his face until everyone else laughed right along.

That was puzzling to Lionel. How could Uncle André be everyone's favorite half the time and everyone's worry the other half? Lionel's mother told him it was all about understanding and forgiveness. "I don't excuse what he does when he's weak and goes back to doing things he knows he shouldn't," she said, "but when he comes back to church and asks forgiveness and tries to live for the Lord, well, we have to accept him and help him if we can. I believe he's really trying."

Lionel was proud of his mother, but for reasons other than that she seemed wise in the areas of forgiveness and acceptance. The truth was, with her job, she was the star of the family. Not just Lionel's family, but the whole Washington clan. They traced their roots to the freedom riders on the Underground Railroad during the days of slavery, and many of his ancestors had been active in the civil rights movement, fighting for equal opportunities among the races. His mother was one who had proved that a person, regardless of the color of her skin or the housing project she had grown up in, could achieve and make something of herself if she really committed herself to it.

Lucinda Washington told Lionel she had been born and raised in a Cleveland ghetto, but "I loved to study. And that was going to be my way out of the projects." She said she fell in love with journalism, reporting, and writing. She graduated from journalism school and worked her way up finally to *Global Weekly* magazine.

She made good money, even more than her husband, Charles, who was a heavy-equipment operator. He was as proud of her as anyone, and secretly Lionel was proud of her too.

23

But Lionel had another secret, and it caused him no end of anxiety. Lionel knew something no one else in the family except André even suspected. Neither he nor André were really Christians, even though the whole family history revolved around church.

Church was something that had not changed when Charles and Lucinda Washington had moved to the suburbs. They had been able to somehow fit in to the strange white culture, though many people made it clear they were not happy about a black family's moving in, wealthy or not. The Washingtons had quickly befriended those homeowners who had not moved out and convinced them they were good neighbors.

Finding a church they were comfortable in was another story. Lionel could not remember when he had not been attending church. Family legends said his mother took him to church when he was less than a week old, but his mother told him that was slightly exaggerated. "But you weren't two weeks old," she said, grinning. "You might as well have been born in the church and grown up there."

Actually, he liked church a lot. Lionel was glad that his parents drove all the way back into the city to attend their old church. Some of the people who criticized them for "moving out and moving up" were glad to see they had not forgotten their roots. And even if they were jealous of the Washingtons' ability to move out of a high-crime area, they were glad to see them come back every Sunday morning and evening and every Wednesday night.

Church was what the Washington family was about, but Lionel knew it went deeper than that. His mother not only loved church, she truly loved God. And Jesus. And the Holy Spirit. They had visited a few churches in the suburbs, including a couple that had both white and black members. Lionel had been a young boy then, but even he could see that these just were not the same as his home church in Chicago.

Those people didn't seem to have any spirit. His mother assured him, "They are certainly true believers, and I don't question their salvation for a second. But I need to go to a church where people don't mind expressing themselves. If I was to jump and shout praises or sing at the top of my lungs, or sway to the music or even dance in the aisles, I wouldn't want to worry about what someone thinks."

Lionel knew what she was talking about. He loved to clap and sing and sway, and while he had not danced in the aisle, he enjoyed watching people who did. The services at his church were long and loud and enthusiastic. People were happy and joyful. He was as happy as anyone when his parents finally realized they would not find their kind of church in their new neighborhood.

So Lionel had the best of both worlds. He lived in a safe place, went to good schools, learned to work and earn and save but also had whatever he really needed, and he got to go back "home" for church twice a week. Every Sunday, his family stayed with relatives between the morning and evening services.

One week while staying with his grandparents, Lionel got to spend a lot of time with Uncle André. Lionel rode along while André picked something up at the store. When André came out, Lionel was surprised to see him followed closely and quickly by two other men about André's age. Obviously not noticing Lionel at first, one of them said to André, "You hear what I'm saying? You get us that money by Friday or you disappear."

André immediately smiled and slapped hands with them, nervously introducing them to "my big sister's little boy." Lionel shook hands with them, but he was scared. He pretended not to have heard, but those guys had clearly just threatened Uncle André. As they drove back to the neighborhood, Lionel asked him about it.

"Them?" André said. "Oh, they're just friends. They were havin' fun with me."

"It didn't sound like it," Lionel said. "I don't like them. They scare me."

André pulled to the curb, several blocks from his parents' home. He took a deep breath and told Lionel, "You're right. They're bad guys. I borrowed some money from them for a deal that went bad, and I don't know how I'm ever gonna pay them back. I'll figure out somethin', or I'll just have to hide out for a while."

"Aren't you scared?" Lionel said.

" 'Course I am. But that's my life, Lionel. That's why it's good you're a Christian and bein' raised by my sister. She'll keep you on the straight and narrow path."

"Uh-huh," Lionel said.

"What's that mean?" Uncle André said. "You in trouble already?"

"No, but I was just wondering. I mean, you're a Christian too, aren't you?"

Uncle André looked surprised. "Me? Do I seem like a Christian to you?"

"When you're not, um, I mean—"

"When I'm not gettin' in trouble, you mean?"

"Yeah."

André chuckled, but he looked sad. "You've seen me come back to the Lord lots of times, huh?"

Lionel nodded.

"I'm gonna tell you the truth about that, Nephew, but you can't be tellin' anyone, you hear?"

Lionel nodded again.

"I mean, I don't even want you tellin' your mama. Now listen, those people care about me, I know they do. And I need a place to crash and people to help me get back on my feet now and then. And when I get myself cleaned up and try to start over, I'm serious about it. But the truth is, I tell 'em whatever they want to hear so they'll take me back. If they knew I was serious about surviving but not serious about God, I'd have nobody."

Lionel sat stunned. "So, you're not really a Christian then?"

André sighed as if he hated to admit it. "No, I'm not. Truth is, I don't believe God would forgive somebody like me. I just keep messing up. And every time I go straight, I know I'm gonna mess up again."

"But doesn't God forgive you every time?"

"I don't ever feel forgiven. My family forgives me, but that's because they believe I'm either tryin' or I'm sick."

"But my mom says that's how God forgives people. He uses the people who love them to show them his forgiveness."

"Well, I can't deny my family has done that. But the truth is, I've never been a true believer, a real Christian, and I really believe it's too late for me."

Lionel sat shaking his head. This was sad, but it was also scary.

"So, Lionel, tell me I'm wrong."

"That's the trouble," Lionel said. "I don't know, because I think I agree with you."

"That's not what I wanted to hear," André said. "I was kind of hopin' you were still young enough to believe."

"Well, Mama says you're never too young or too old, and you're never too good or too bad to become a Christian."

"I know she does. Remember, I grew up with her. But what'd you mean by sayin' you agree with me?"

Lionel wasn't sure how to say it without coming right out with it. "I've never really become a Christian either."

André squinted at him and smiled. "So we're the two secret heathens in the Washington family?"

Lionel did not find it funny. "It's a secret all right. Everybody thinks you're a Christian who has bad spells once in a while. They think I might become a preacher or a missionary someday."

André pulled away from the curb. "You ought to talk with your mother about this," he said. "I'd rather see you grow up like her than like me."

"I can't talk to her," Lionel said. "It'd kill her. She thinks I'm one of the best young Christians she knows. You won't say anything to her, will you?"

"Not if you don't want me to. You could spill the beans about me too, so we'll just keep each other's secrets, OK?"

Lionel nodded, but he didn't feel good about it. He wondered if André was as worried about Lionel's not being a Christian as Lionel was about Andre. "Aren't you afraid it might all be true?" Lionel said. "And that we might end up in hell?"

André parked in the alley behind his parents' home. He threw back his head and cackled that crazy laugh of his. "Now that," he said, "I do not believe. I may have once, but I've outgrown that. Some of these stories and legends about what's goin' to happen at the end of the world, I don't know where the preachers get them. I can't imagine they're in the Bible."

"My mom says they are."

"Well, maybe someday she can show me, and then I'll think about it. Meantime, I'm not goin' to worry about fairy tales, and you shouldn't either."

But Lionel did worry. When they got back to the rest of the family, everyone was gathered around the piano and singing old hymns. Lionel liked that. He sang well and enjoyed blending harmonies. Uncle André sang right along with the rest of them, but once he winked at Lionel. Then he worked his way near him and whispered, "This stuff makes for good singing, but remember, half of it's a good way to live and the other is just fairy tales."

Lionel wondered if Uncle André really believed that. He was a cool guy and older and seemed wise in the ways of the world. If anybody should worry about what happened to him when he died or when the end of the world came, it should be André. But he didn't seem worried. He had a plan, a scheme. He had convinced himself he could play the game well enough to keep his loving family around him.

Lionel would rather have been like his mother than like his uncle, but he knew he and André were pretty much the same. André did a lot worse things, but if what Lionel's mother and the rest of the family believed was true, Lionel knew that he and André were in the same boat.

André began dancing to the music, and his relatives clapped and urged him on. Lionel couldn't help but smile, seeing his joyous uncle entertaining everyone. Lionel's mother put her arm around him as she watched André. She pulled Lionel to herself and said, "Isn't the Lord wonderful? Don't we have a good God?"

Lionel tried to ignore her, but she noticed. "Hm?" she said. "Aren't you glad to serve a God who loves you so much?"

"Um-hm," Lionel lied. "Sure, Mama. 'Course I am."

He felt terrible. Like a hypocrite. Like the liar he was.

**"YOUR** real name's Rayford?" Ryan Daley squealed at his best friend. "We've known each other how long, and I never knew that!"

Raymie Steele smiled and shook his head. "Don't make such a big deal about it. Otherwise I'll tell everybody your middle name!"

The boys had grown up on the same street, one living on each end. They had begun kindergarten together, and now they were both twelve and in the sixth grade. They were as close as brothers. Ryan was an only child, and Raymie may as well have been. His only sister, Chloe, was eight years older and had been away at college two years already.

Ryan and Raymie had a lot in common. Each had a father who was too busy for him. These guys needed each other. Ryan was a little shorter and thicker than Raymie, who was slender and tall and dark like his father. Ryan was a blond and the better athlete of the two.

Like any close friends, they squabbled a lot. Once in a while they even said nasty things to each other and vowed never to talk to each other again. The next day one would call the other or just go to his house, and they would start in where they had left off, best friends. No apologies, no mention of the argument. Just friends again.

They had always gotten a kick out of how close their first names were. That was what had started the discussion of their real full names. Ryan said he had been named after three famous Chicagoans. "My first name comes from Dan Ryan. I don't even know who he was, but there's an expressway named after him. And my middle name, promise you'll never tell a soul, comes from some old mayor from way back when who got assassinated."

"What's his name?"

"I don't want to tell you. I don't trust you."

"If you can't trust *me*—"

"OK, I trust you. But you gotta promise."

"I promise."

"And you've got to tell me a secret you don't want anybody to know."

"I will."

"All right," Ryan said. "The mayor's name was Anton Cermak."

Raymie Steele had doubled over laughing. Ryan couldn't resist laughing too. "So," Raymie said when he caught his breath, "is your middle name Anton or Cermak?"

"Cermak," Ryan mumbled.

"No!"

"Yes! Isn't that awful? And my last name's the same as a former Chicago mayor too."

"I know. How'd your middle-name guy get assassinated?"

"My mom made me look it up. For some reason he was in a parade in Florida with President Roosevelt when some guy tried to shoot the president, missed, and hit Cermak."

"Which Roosevelt?"

"I don't know. Was there more than one?"

" 'Course," Raymie said. "Teddy and Franklin."

"Probably Teddy, I guess."

"When was this?"

"In the 1930s, I think."

"Then it had to be Franklin."

"Whatever, Raymie. How do you know all that stuff?"

"I don't know. I just like to study, and I remember a lot of it."

"So it's your turn to tell me something you don't want anybody else to know."

"All right, Ryan, as long as we're talking about names, I'm actually a 'junior.' "

"Your name is the same as your dad's?"

"Yup."

"So his name is Raymond? You're actually Raymond Steele?"

"Nope. It's Rayford."

Now it was Ryan's turn to laugh. They swore to each other that they would never tell anyone else. But when they were alone, they started calling each other Rayford and Cermak. It usually made them smile.

One of the reasons their friendship worked so well was that in spite of all their similarities, they also had individual strengths and weaknesses. Raymie was the student, the one who seemed to know everything and was usually right. It drove Ryan crazy that Raymie actually enjoyed school.

Ryan went to school mostly to play. He was the athlete of the two. You name the sport, he enjoyed it and was good at it and played with all his might. He was the fastest runner, the highest jumper, the best hitter and thrower and even the best basketball shot in his class. Raymie said he considered himself a klutz in sports but that he enjoyed watching Ryan and was proud to be his friend.

Ryan liked it when Raymie stayed overnight at his house or he stayed at Raymie's. Secretly, Ryan believed Raymie had the best dad. Raymie's dad was Rayford Steele Sr., an airline pilot. He always called it "driving" the planes, and the planes he drove were the big ones, the 747s.

Ryan had gotten to go into the cockpit of a 747 once when Mr. Steele had taken him and Raymie to O'Hare. They watched the planes take off and land, and Captain Steele gave them pilot caps, wing pins, and even old computer printouts of weather conditions and route logs.

Whenever Ryan stayed at Raymie's, he hoped Captain Steele was home and would tell him airplane stories. Mr. Steele insisted that his job was actually quite routine and boring. "The important thing is that we do it right and do it safely," he said. He had never crashed, which disappointed Ryan because he thought there would be a great story behind something like that.

The only thing Ryan didn't like about being at Raymie's house was that Mrs. Steele seemed so religious. She always made them pray before they ate, and she often talked about God and even told Bible stories. Ryan enjoyed some of those, but it made him nervous when Mrs. Steele made Raymie say his prayers before going to sleep. Church and prayer and Bible stories had never been part of Ryan's life.

His father was nothing quite as dramatic as an airline pilot. Ryan's dad was a sales manager for a big plumbing fixture company. Ryan was proud that his dad was successful and seemed to make good money. His dad seemed a little upset that, as he said, "I probably don't make as much as your friend's dad, the pilot, but I'm not far behind."

Ryan's mother also worked, so he often came home alone after school. He wasn't supposed to have anyone in the house when his parents weren't there, but for many years he and Raymie cheated on that. They would play and eat and watch television, always keeping an eye out for Mrs. Daley. When she pulled into the driveway, Raymie would hurry to the front door and slip out as she came in the back. Once she was in the house, he knew it was safe to ring the doorbell as if he had just gotten there.

That kept Ryan out of trouble. But one day, a few months before, that had all changed. For a few days, Raymie had excuses for why he couldn't come over after school. Finally Ryan asked him right out. "What's the deal, Raymie?"

"Well, you're not supposed to have anybody over without one of your parents there, right?"

"Hello!" Ryan said. "We've been breaking that rule for a long time. My mom has never even suspected."

"That still doesn't make it right."

"We'll never get caught, Raymie!"

"I'm not talking about getting caught. I'm talking about whether it's right."

"So, if she catches us, we'll tell her it was the first and only time."

Raymie had shaken his head and Ryan was frustrated. "So you'd make it worse by lying," Raymie said.

"Who cares?"

"I do!" Raymie said.

"Why all of a sudden?"

"I need to talk to you about that."

"Then come on over and we'll talk about it."

"Ryan, you just don't get it. I'm not going to your house anymore when your mom isn't there, OK? You don't have to agree, but that's how it's going to be."

"You're right. I don't get it. What's got into you?"

"Why don't you come to my house and I'll tell you? Didn't your mom say that if you weren't home when she got home, the only other place you were allowed to be was my house?"

Ryan agreed. A few minutes later they were talking in Raymie's garage. Both Raymie's parents happened to be home. Raymie started right in.

"We started going to a new church, and we've been learning a lot of new things."

"Oh no, not this again! Are we gonna wind up prayin'?"

"No," Raymie said. "This is different. Really. At our old church we believed in God and the Bible and everything—"

"Don't I know it!"

"Yeah, but we were getting kind of bored, especially my mom."

"Your Mom? I thought she liked all that stuff."

"She did, but she said something was missing. Somebody invited her to this new church, and we started going, and we learned a lot more."

"Like what?"

"You really want to know?"

"No, but something tells me you're going to tell me anyway, so let's get it over with."

Ryan had hoped that would insult Raymie just a little and they could get on to playing, but Raymie plunged ahead. "At this new church, New Hope right here in town, they have this really nice old pastor—"

"Wait, the church is called what?"

"New Hope Village Church."

"Weird name for a church."

"Anyway, Pastor Billings is a really nice old guy, but he doesn't just read out of the Bible and then talk about stuff in general like the guy at our other church. Pastor Billings has everybody look up the verses and follow along with him, and he tells us we should read the Bible every day at home, too."

"Every day? Yuck!"

"No, it's great. It's like we can check up on him and make sure we understand and agree and all that."

"But all that boring religious stuff!"

"That's what I used to think too, Ryan. I liked the stories in Sunday school, but when I had to sit in the service, I hated it. I thought I would hate it here, too, but I don't. Pastor Billings says there's more to being a Christian than just going to church and trying to be good. You want to know what he says?"

"No, but keep going. You're gonna be a preacher yourself someday!"

"He says we can know God."

"Oh, come on!"

"No! That's what he says. He showed us from the Bible that God loves everyone and wants them to know him. That's the reason Jesus came to earth. He was actually God and—"

"Yeah, and he taught us how to live and everything, I know."

"No, it's more than that. He wants people to become true Christians by following him, not just doing what he said but letting him live in our lives."

"Now you've lost me."

"I wish I could explain it like he does. You have to come with me sometime."

"I don't think so."

"Come on! If you told me something was great and important, I'd at least listen."

"Good for you. You think I'm going to follow Jesus or let him, what did you say, live in . . . ?"

"Live in your life."

"Too strange."

"I'm just not explaining it right. My mom knows. Let's ask her."

"No! I've heard enough, OK? You know God now, is that it?"

"Well, yeah . . ."

"And that makes you want to follow all the rules and do everything right. Why? So you can get to heaven?"

"No! That's what I used to think. When I'd do something I knew was wrong—like breaking your mom's rules and everything—I felt bad because I thought that might be enough to send me to hell. I thought if I did enough right things to make up for the wrong things, maybe I'd make it to heaven. But I never knew for sure."

"Now I'm really not getting it."

"That's why you should talk to my mom. We've both received Christ and—"

"*Received* Christ? You're not gonna be like those people that go around knocking on everybody's door, are you?"

"Sometimes I'd like to, Ryan. I want everybody to know."

"So, if doing everything right is not how you get to heaven, why did you all of a sudden become so perfect?"

"I didn't. I want to do right things because I know that's what God wants. But I'm just doing that to thank him for forgiving me and saving me and promising me heaven someday. Know what I mean?"

"No!"

"And you don't want to talk to my mom?"

"No, thanks. What about your dad?"

"Well, we're praying for him."

"So he doesn't go for all this stuff?"

Raymie looked embarrassed. "Not really."

"Well, maybe somebody in this family still has a brain. What about your big sister?"

"We're praying for Chloe too."

"So I'm not the only person you know who thinks this is a lot of baloney."

"That's what you think?"

"Not really, Raymie. It just sounds weird, that's all. And I don't think you even understand it much."

Raymie shrugged. "That's true, but I understand enough."

"Are we done now?"

"I guess."

"Can we play with that model of your dad's plane?"

"I'll get it."

When Raymie left the garage and trotted up the stairs to his room, he left the door that led into the house open. Suddenly Ryan found himself listening in on a strange conversation. Mr. and Mrs. Steele were talking about something even weirder than Raymie had. "Can you imagine, Rafe?" she was saying, "Jesus coming back to get us before we die?"

Ryan heard the rattle of a newspaper. Mr. Steele said, "Yeah, boy, that would kill me."

Now Mrs. Steele sounded mad. "If I didn't know what would happen to me," she said, "I wouldn't be so glib about it."

"I *do* know what would happen to me," Mr. Steele said. "I'd be dead and gone. But you, of course, would fly right up to heaven."

That seemed to shut her up. Ryan heard Mr. Steele rise. "Come on, Irene," he said. "Tell me thousands of people wouldn't just keel over if they saw Jesus coming back for all the good people."

Now she was crying. "I've told you and told you. Saved people aren't good people, they're—"

"Just forgiven, yeah, I know."

Ryan heard Raymie bounding back down the stairs, just as Mr. Steele was saying, "If it makes you feel any better, I'm happy for you that you can be so sure."

Raymie's mother answered softly. "I only believe what the Bible says."

These people were crazy, Ryan decided. He wanted to ask Raymie what his parents meant, talking about Jesus coming back for people before they died. But he just wanted to play and think about something else.

He thought that maybe someday he *would* go along with Raymie to that new church and see what all the excitement was about.

But he never did.

# 5

**THE** evening before the event that would change the lives of Judd Thompson, Vicki Byrne, Lionel Washington, and Ryan Daley, they didn't know each other. Oh, Judd Thompson had seen Vicki Byrne at New Hope Village Church on those few occasions when she was dragged there, all but kicking and screaming, by her parents. But he couldn't have told you her name.

He knew she went to his school, Prospect High. But she was trailer trash. They would not have been seen together. He didn't know, any better than Lionel Washington did, that Lionel's sister Clarice shared a seat on the school bus with Vicki. Judd and Clarice didn't run in the same circles either.

It didn't register with Judd, even when the pilot's name was announced on the 747 flight to London, that the captain also occasionally attended New Hope Village Church. Judd had seen Raymie Steele at church. Raymie was part of the middle school youth group. But Judd didn't know Raymie's name. And he certainly had no knowledge of Raymie's best friend, Ryan Daley.

In truth, the four kids were entwined in a web of connections they knew nothing about. Only the events of that night, mainly *the* event late in the evening, Chicago time, would push them together, a strange mix of most different people and personalities.

---

Judd Thompson Jr. took a bigger gulp of the champagne than he should have and had to cover his mouth to keep from spitting it out. Some of it came out through his nose, which burned as he coughed. He looked around sheepishly and was relieved to notice that no one had paid any attention. *Ick!* He would just pretend to sip from the glass until the beautiful flight attendant took it away.

Judd had his eye on the two seats ahead of the men across the aisle from him. A rather large man had squeezed his way past Judd to sit in the window seat next to him, and as roomy as first class seats were, Judd decided he would rather sit alone if he had a choice. He had been told at the counter that he had bought the last seat on the plane, but those two seats on the other side were still empty. He hoped whoever had reserved them had changed their mind or would miss takeoff for some reason.

But just as the flight attendants were gathering up glasses and napkins and telling passengers to stow their tray tables, a stooped, old couple boarded and headed for those seats. The flight attendants had helped the other first-class passengers store their belongings, but all were busy as the couple made their way up the aisle.

The young man sitting in the window seat across the aisle from Judd was shutting down his laptop computer when he seemed to notice the old couple. He turned to the man on his right, the one who had already loosened his tie and downed three small bottles of liquor. "Sir, that elderly gentleman could use a little help, I think."

"So?" the man on the aisle said. "What do I look like, a stewardess?"

"Would you let me by, then, so I can help him?"

The drinking man cursed and turned in his seat to let the younger man pass. Judd watched as the old man took off his sport jacket and felt hat and reached for the overhead bin, which was too high for him. The younger man said, "May I help you with that, sir?"

"Why, thank you, son. You're very kind."

"Not a problem."

"What's your name?"

"Cameron Williams," he told the old man. "Call me Buck."

"Peterson," the old man said, extending his hand. "Call me Harold."

Judd was fascinated. Harold Peterson introduced his wife to Buck, and as they all sat down Mrs. Peterson told Buck her husband was a retired businessman and asked what Buck did for a living.

"I'm a writer," Buck said. "With *Global Weekly.*"

*Wow*, Judd thought. *A big shot. And not that old.*

After takeoff, dinner, and a movie, Judd tried to relax. Most passengers put away their reading material and curled up with blankets and pillows. Soon the interior lights went off, and when Judd headed toward the tiny bathroom, he noticed only the occasional reading lamp here and there. By the time he was back in his seat, the plane was a dark, quiet, humming chamber. He wished he could sleep, but he couldn't get his mind off his family.

When would they discover he was gone? How would they feel? What would they do? Was it too late to just catch a plane back home, apologize, and beg for mercy? No, he was going to see this through. He was going to prove he could be independent.

But boy, he thought, he was going to be tired. When that plane hit the ground in London, he was going to have to find a place to stay. Nervous energy left him weak and drowsy, but there was no way he could keep his eyes shut. Too much to think about.

———————————————

For two years since her parents had become Christians in the most bizarre way at that trailer park dance, Vicki Byrne had watched for them to fail. She was embarrassed by what they called "witnessing"—telling other people about Christ. They said they were "sharing their faith" with the people they cared about.

That sounded so much like a cult, like the weirdos who tried to talk to people in airports, that Vicki wanted nothing to do with it. Her little sister was so excited about Sunday school and church that Vicki decided not to hassle Jeanni about it. Her older brother, Eddie, wrote and told her he had begun going to church up in Michigan.

Vicki felt surrounded by idiots. She admitted to herself that she was impressed that her father had quit drinking. He still smoked, but he was trying to quit. He always said he felt bad about that, but she never saw him smoke at church, and he didn't even smoke in the trailer anymore. He often said, "Someday God is going to give me the strength to beat this thing."

Vicki's mother pleaded with her, to the point of tears, to go to church with them once in a while. Vicki finally gave in and asked if they would get off her back if she went to one service a month. They agreed, but she really had gone only three or four times in all. Every time her mother or father reminded her that she was not upholding her end of the bargain, the arguing began. She would swear she had just been to church with them the month before. They would show her on the calendar that she had not. She would yell and scream and walk out. They would plead and cry and pray for her.

When she went to church, she hated it. Sometimes her mother looked at her to see if she had listened to what the pastor had just said, and at other times her mother leaned over and whispered the pastor's last sentence. "Get out of my face!" Vicki hissed at her. Again, her mother fought tears.

Vicki didn't understand herself. Often she asked herself why she had to be so mean, so angry. It was obvious that this . . . this thing, whatever it was, was working. Her dad was a new man. He never missed work, was always on time, got promoted, had more friends. He was always sober. He looked happier. The only sore point in his life, besides his smoking, was Vicki. She could see him getting more and more frustrated with her, and she had to admit her goal was to make him explode in anger. Why? So she wouldn't feel so bad about herself.

She had always hated it when he had blown up at her in the past, but this new obsession with church and God was worse. The one time she pushed her dad past his limit, rather than yell, he broke down. "I think the devil's got hold of your soul and he won't let go!" her father exclaimed.

Vicki laughed in his face. "What?!" she said. "You really believe that, don't you? You think we're living in the dark ages and maybe I'm a witch, is that it?"

"I didn't say that," her father said, moaning.

"Don't you see how crazy you all are? Please, just leave me out of this!"

"We don't want you to go to hell!" her mother pleaded.

"At least I'll be with my friends," Vicki said. She had heard people say before that they wanted to spend eternity where all their friends were. She thought it was a pretty sassy line. Her parents just cried all the more. That didn't reach her. It made her sick. After a year or so they couldn't get her to go to church at all.

The only control Vicki's parents had over her was grounding her. She was not allowed to go anywhere or do anything if she stayed out too late. They didn't know where she was or what she was doing, but they had an idea who she was with, and they didn't approve of her friends.

Vicki considered herself lucky that the last two times she had been out past her curfew, only twenty minutes each time, she had been able to slip into the trailer and tiptoe past her sleeping parents' bedroom undetected.

On this evening, though, the same night Judd Thompson Jr. was making his escape from boredom on a flight to London, Vicki Byrne was going out. Her parents would have a fit, she realized, if they knew what she and her friends were up to. They had scored some pot and were smoking and riding around with older kids who had cars.

By the time her friends dropped her off at the entrance to the trailer park, far enough from her trailer so the car wouldn't wake anybody, Vicki was already more than an hour late. Her mother had told her she would be waiting up for her in the little living room. Vicki felt wasted, and she didn't want the lecture, the grounding, the tears, the prayers.

As she came into view of the trailer, she noticed the only

light on was a small reading lamp in the living room. If her mother was dozing there, she would surely awaken if Vicki tried to sneak past. She knew what she would do. She would slip in the back door. If her mother discovered her in her bed, she would swear she had come home on time and had even tried to wake her mother.

Vicki crept around back, trying not to make noise in the gravel. She slowly opened the little-used door and did her best to keep it from creaking. She held her breath and pulled it softly closed behind her. She could see the light on in the living room. She undressed in the dark and slipped into the bedroom she shared with Jeanni.

As Vicki lay on her back in bed, she allowed herself to breathe again. But something was strange. Maybe the pot had done something to her mind, or her hearing. Normally she could hear her father snoring from down the hall. And she could always hear Jeanni's deep breathing.

Now she heard nothing. Not a thing.

*So much the better*, she thought. She felt as tired as she'd ever been and was grateful for the peace and quiet that allowed her to drift into a deep sleep.

---

Lionel Washington always looked forward to the times when Uncle André would come to Mount Prospect and stay overnight. He might be in town for an Alcoholics Anonymous meeting or one of the other half-dozen or so support groups he belonged to. Other times he might just be in the area "on business," though Lionel's mother often asked him not to share what that business might be.

The night Judd Thompson Jr. sat on the 747, unable to

sleep, and Vicki Byrne crept into her bed, unable to stay awake, Lionel Washington grew bleary-eyed in his own home.

Lionel's older sister, Clarice, had helped her mother put the younger kids to bed a few hours before. Then she and Lionel and their mother and father sat in the family room as Uncle André told story after story, making them laugh and cry and laugh some more.

Clarice was the first to beg off. "I've got to get up early tomorrow," she said.

Lionel's mother was next. "We're expecting a story to be filed from our London office tomorrow. I can't be late for work. Lionel, when André finally runs out of steam, which I hope is real soon, you two can sleep on the couch in the basement as usual."

"Thank you, Sis," André said. "I won't keep your man up much longer."

He was referring to Lionel's dad, who loved André and his stories. There he sat in his easy chair, trying to listen, trying not to doze. He looked comfortable, a big old working man in a terry cloth robe three sizes too big. He rubbed the corners of his eyes. "Should have taken these contacts out hours ago," he said.

"I'm gonna let you go to bed, bro-in-law," André told him. "Lionel and me will head downstairs."

"Good idea," Mr. Washington said. "I'll just sit here a few more minutes before going up to bed myself. G'night, boys."

Lionel found himself falling asleep next to his uncle in the basement even though André was still telling some story. Lionel was half listening for his father's footsteps above them, which would let Lionel know he had gone off to bed.

But he couldn't keep his eyes open any longer. He fell asleep listening to his uncle's whispering, whiny laugh and

only hoped André wouldn't be insulted when he realized
Lionel was asleep.

---

Ryan Daley had very nearly been allowed to stay at his best
friend's house that night. His mother had to take the next
morning off so she could pick up Ryan's dad at O'Hare
Airport. Ryan was to walk to school with Raymie Steele just
before his mother was to leave. Both boys thought it might be
a good idea if he just stayed overnight with Raymie.

But Mrs. Steele apologized for not being able to have a
guest that night. Ryan's mother told him that Mrs. Steele had
said that her husband had a flight and that she preferred they
do this some other night. "In fact, she suggested this weekend
and asked if it was all right if you went to church with them.
I told Mrs. Steele that that would be fine."

"Oh, Mom!"

"It won't be so bad, honey. I went to church a few times
when I was a kid, and it didn't hurt me any. Just act nice, and
they'll be nice to you."

Ryan dreaded even the thought of that, and he wished he
could have stayed at Raymie's that night. But he would see
Raymie in the morning, and they would have fun this weekend—even if he did have to go to church.

With his dad away on business, Ryan knew his mother
would stay up watching television longer than normal. He let
her see him in bed and turn off his light, then waited until he
was sure she was settled in downstairs. He shut his door all the
way and stayed up reading and listening to music.

Ryan was getting drowsy when he thought he heard something. He lifted one earphone, listening for his mother. If she

was coming up to bed, she would be able to see the light streaming under his door. He rolled over and flicked off his light, but he heard no footsteps on the stairs. What he heard was a siren, maybe more than one.

He tiptoed to the window and peered out. On the horizon he saw the pink glow of a fire in the distance. Way to his left was another. Then he heard closer sirens. This was a crazy night for some reason. He wanted to see if there was anything on the news, and he wondered if he could convince his mother the sirens had woken him when he padded downstairs.

Ryan carefully opened the door and went down the carpeted steps. He peeked into the television room, where his mother's movie was ending. She was sound asleep. He waited until the credits had rolled and the commercials came on, hoping there might be some news. But as soon as the last commercial played, the national anthem came on, signaling the end of the broadcast day.

He thought about changing the channel, but he knew that would awaken his mother. When the station signed off the air, the static roused his mother, and Ryan hurried back upstairs before she noticed him. He climbed under the covers in the dark and pretended to be asleep when she peeked in on him, as usual.

He was going to put his headphones back on and try to tune in some radio news. But now he was really tired. The sirens seemed farther away, so he just closed his eyes.

**JUDD** was so keyed up, so excited, and yet so worried about what his parents were going to do when they discovered he had disappeared, he couldn't imagine having fallen asleep. Yet he had. He figured out how to make the seat back recline, and he was soon staring at the dark ceiling, his eyes beginning to grow accustomed to the low light. He folded his arms across his chest and forced himself to breathe more and more slowly. He had to relax, needed to get some rest if he was going to succeed in finding a place to hide out in London.

Hattie, the flight attendant, glided by every half hour or so, and Judd realized he was finally starting to unwind when he quit looking forward to watching her. Eventually, the slow blinking began, then he turned sideways and curled up. Now he had to close his eyes or he would appear to stare at the large man in the window seat next to him.

The man had said not one word the entire flight, but Judd noticed he had bowed his head before eating. That Judd would never do, not even in private, unless he was with his family. That was another reason he needed to be out on his own—so he wouldn't be embarrassed by all their religious rituals. His mother hated when Judd referred to her faith as a religion. She had told him so many times he had memorized it, "Christianity is not a religion, it's a relationship with God through Christ."

*Yeah, OK*, Judd thought.

Judd had no idea how long he had been sleeping. In fact, he wasn't sure he had slept at all. And if he had slept, was he really awake now? He was disoriented, in the same position he had curled into, how long ago? He felt as if he had been sleeping and had not moved. But his eyes were open.

Something was different. A blanket! The flight attendant must have draped it over him. He looked at his watch. Not quite eleven at night, four in the morning out over the Atlantic. He knew the plane had to be nearly halfway between England and the States now.

The man next to him had a blanket too, but it was folded neatly in his lap. The air flow above him was directed on his face, and Judd imagined him sweating in his sleep. He was spread out over that seat, hands at his sides, head back, mouth open. Judd was grateful the man was not snoring.

With his chin on his shoulder, Judd was just inches from the big man. But that was the way with airplanes. Strangers had to sit close to each other. He looked across the aisle to where the drinker seemed to have collapsed onto his tray table. Beyond him the magazine writer, the one who had introduced himself to the old man, sat sleeping with his back straight, his head down, chin on his chest.

Ahead of those two was the elderly couple, the Petersons. Judd couldn't see the woman. She was small and hidden in her seat. Her husband had tucked a pillow behind him and slept with his head poking out into the aisle. Judd was still barely awake when Hattie came by. She had to avoid the old man as she slipped past. Judd mustered his courage and whispered, "Thanks for the blanket."

She flashed him a smile. "Oh, you're welcome, hon," she said. "My partner, Tony, brought you that. Need anything else?"

He was too tongue-tied to say any more. He shook his head, turned back to face the big man on his right, and drifted off to sleep again.

Activity behind him nagged Judd to semiconsciousness. How long had he slept this time? It seemed only a few minutes, but it could have been hours. He didn't want to rouse, didn't want to open his eyes. He fought to stay asleep. Someone had said something. Another person was up and about. Someone walked by quickly. Surely it wasn't dawn yet. Sunlight peeking through the window coverings surely would have awakened him.

For a minute Judd heard nothing and was grateful. He brought his watch up to his face and peeked ever so slightly at it. He couldn't make it out. It seemed nearly the same time as the last time he checked. He took a deep breath, then opened his eyes.

The man next to him must have gone to the bathroom. Why hadn't Judd felt him get by? Judd's long legs were stretched under the seat in front of him. No way was that man agile enough to have climbed over him without his knowing. He squinted and stared in the darkness, wondering if he was dreaming.

The flight attended hurried past. No, she more than hurried. She was nearly sprinting up the aisle toward the cockpit. This was no dream. Judd sat straight up and noticed a few others doing the same. He craned his neck and looked back toward the circular stairway that led to coach class. He heard too much activity for the middle of the night. Someone shrieked and another called out, but he couldn't make it out.

Just as Hattie reached the cockpit, Judd saw the door open and one of the pilots mosey out. Hattie nearly bowled him over. Judd couldn't hear them, but it was clear she was upset, maybe scared. Did she know something the pilot didn't? Was something wrong with the plane? Wouldn't that be a kick in the teeth, Judd dying in a plane crash on his first night of freedom! His parents would never understand.

Hattie pulled the pilot out of the aisle and into the cooking compartments. Judd was desperate to know what was going on. He heard a noise up there, as if she had fallen. He leaned into the aisle and saw her on her knees, whimpering. The captain seemed to be trying to comfort her, and she held on to him as if scared to death.

Judd suddenly felt very young and very afraid.

Behind him more people were crying out. What was going on? What were they saying? The young man and the drunk across the aisle were both sound asleep. Judd could no longer see the old man. And the two people in front of Judd must have slid down in their seats too.

The pilot left Hattie in the galley area and stepped out into the aisle, as if studying the seats in first class. Judd pulled off his blanket and tried to catch the captain's eye, to read something on his face. But it was too dark. And the pilot was distracted.

From the seat ahead of him and to the left, he heard the voice of the old woman. "What in the world?" she said. "Harold?"

Was something wrong with the old man? Judd couldn't resist standing to look. Everyone else in first class seemed to be sleeping. He unfastened his seat belt and rose to look at the old couple. The woman sat there with her husband's sweater and dress pants in her hands!

Judd shook his head, trying to clear his mind. What was she doing with her husband's clothes? And where was he? Obviously, that's what she was wondering too.

The pilot hurried past before Judd could think how to phrase a question. All he wanted to know was what was going on, but the pilot and certainly the flight attendant didn't seem to know either. When the pilot reached the stairs, Mrs. Peterson stood and called out to him. "Sir, my husband—"

Judd saw the pilot put a finger to his lips and whisper, "I know. We'll find him. I'll be right back."

And now here came Hattie. Judd said, "Ma'am?" but she didn't answer.

She grabbed the pilot by the shoulders from behind. "Should I turn on the cabin lights?" she asked.

"No," the pilot whispered. "The less people know right now, the better."

What did that mean? Judd watched the two hurry down the stairs. He turned back to see the old woman talking to the writer behind her. He was dragging his fingers through his long blond hair.

"Trouble, ma'am?" Buck said.

"It's my Harold," she said.

"Does he need something?" Buck asked, stretching.

"He's gone!"

"I'm sorry?"

"He's disappeared!"

"Well," Buck said, "I'm sure he slipped off to the washroom while you were sleeping."

"Would you mind checking for me? And take a blanket."

"Ma'am?"

"I'm afraid he's gone off naked. He's a religious person, and he'll be terribly embarrassed."

Judd still stood, as if glued to the floor in front of his seat. He watched Buck Williams climb over the sleeping drunk in the aisle seat and move up to take a blanket from the old woman. Buck crouched and studied the clothes Mr. Peterson had left in his seat. "Does your husband have epilepsy?"

"No."

"Sleepwalking?"

"No."

"I'll be right back."

Judd didn't want to look down into the seats in front of him, and he certainly didn't want to look to his right where the big man had been. But he forced himself to. Over the backs of the seats ahead of him he saw blankets, pillows, and full sets of clothes. Glasses, jewelry, even a man's wig lay on his seat.

His heart racing, Judd looked next to him. That neatly folded blanket now lay atop flat trousers that led to empty socks and shoes. On the back of the seat lay the limp, still-buttoned white shirt, the still-knotted tie, and little bits of metal. Judd's knees were weak. Other passengers woke up and discovered their seatmates missing, their clothes left behind.

Judd leaned close to the big man's pile of clothes and turned on the overhead light. He could still smell the man's cologne. And those tiny bits of metal were dental fillings!

Buck Williams moved past Judd's seat. "Excuse me," he said to another passenger. "I'm looking for someone."

"Who isn't?" a woman said.

The pilot rushed back toward the cockpit, followed by his flight attendant. She told Buck, "Sir, I need to ask you to return to your seat and fasten your belt." Hattie turned and gave Judd a look as if she expected the same from him. He sat quickly and refused to look at the clothes his seatmate had left behind.

Buck tried to explain. "I'm looking for—"

"Everybody is looking for someone," Hattie said. "We hope to have some information for you in a few minutes. Now, please."

When Hattie passed him, Judd quickly left his seat and ran to the stairway. Halfway down he saw the cabin lights finally come on. All over the plane people held up clothes and gasped or shrieked that someone was missing. Judd walked stiff-legged back to his seat and heard Buck tell Mrs. Peterson, "Apparently many people are missing." She looked afraid and puzzled.

Judd was afraid too, but he wasn't puzzled. As the pilot came over the intercom, pleading for people to remain calm, the full realization of what had happened hit Judd. He didn't know how many other people on the plane had any idea, but he sure did. Christ had come as he promised and raptured his church. Judd lowered his face into his hands and shuddered. It was the worst nightmare imaginable, and he was wide awake. He, and most of the passengers on that plane, had been left behind.

Judd raised his head when Hattie approached again. Her face was red and puffy, and she breathed fast, seeming to fight for control. She stopped in the aisle, right next to him, and put her hand on his seat back to steady herself. Draped over her arm was a sweater-vest with a shirt and tie still in it. The name-plate dangling in front of Judd read "Tony."

The pilot's voice came over the intercom and announced that cards would be passed out to determine who and how many were missing. Hattie roused the sleeping drunk on the aisle and asked if any in his party were missing. He drooled, his eyes heavy. "Missing? No. And there's nobody in this party but me." He closed his eyes again, and Judd knew he had no idea what had happened.

Later, when the captain announced they were turning around and heading back to Chicago, Judd led the cheering. Home had never sounded so good. His plan—his crazy, stupid, selfish plan—was out the window now. He would pay his dad back for the money he had already taken with the card, and if it wasn't too late, he would get right with God. It seemed strange to even think that way, and he suddenly realized that if he was right about what had happened, he would be going home to an empty house.

Judd dropped his head again and felt the tears come. From across the aisle he heard Buck say to the sleeping drunk, "I'm sorry, friend, but you're going to want to be awake for this."

The drunk said, "If we're not crashin', don't bother me."

In spite of their terror, passengers seemed to settle down for the long flight back to Chicago. Judd refused all offers of food and beverage, unable to think of anything but what he might find at home.

As the heavy plane retraced its route across the Atlantic, it retreated from the rising sun. The pilot announced that they were going all the way back to Chicago because most other airports were jammed and closed. He also said to expect chaos on the ground because these disappearances had happened everywhere around the world at the same time.

Judd saw Hattie and Buck talking. She told him that even more bizarre than the vanishings was the fact that every single little child on the plane had disappeared. Many adults and some teenagers, but *all* the babies. That awakened the sleeping man on the aisle. "What in blazes are you two talking about?" he said.

"We're about to land in Chicago," Hattie said. "I've got to run."

"*Chicago?*" the man demanded.

"You don't want to know," Buck said.

Judd looked out the window as the plane cut through the clouds and offered a view of the Chicago area. Smoke. Fire. Cars off the road and smashed into each other and trees and guardrails. Planes in pieces on the ground. Emergency vehicles, lights flashing, picking their way around the debris.

As the airport came into view, it was obvious no one was going anywhere soon. There were planes as far as the eye could see, some crashed, some burning, the others gridlocked in line. People trudged through the grass toward the terminals. Cranes and wreckers tried to clear a path through the front of the terminal so traffic could move, but that would take hours, if not days.

The pilot announced that he would have to land the plane two miles from the terminal and that passengers would have to slide down inflatable emergency chutes to get to the ground. All Judd cared about was getting on the ground. He would run all the way to the terminal, where he could call home. He would ask someone how he could get home, and he was willing to pay any amount. He had that credit card and wads of cash in his pocket.

Half an hour later, when Judd came huffing and puffing past the crowds and into bigger crowds in the terminal, he saw lines a hundred long waiting for the phones. On TVs throughout the terminal he watched news stories from around the world of people disappearing right out of their clothes in front of the camera. A nurse vanished as a woman was about to give birth, and the baby disappeared before it was born. A groom disappeared as he was putting his bride's ring on her finger. Pallbearers at a funeral disappeared while carrying a casket, which fell and popped open, revealing that the corpse had vanished too.

Judd raced outside and through the jammed cars, following lines of people to cabs and limousines. He sprinted to the front and stuffed a huge roll of bills into the driver's hand. Judd told him his address, and the man pulled away.

It took two hours to pick their way through the results of crashes and fires. The limo driver said, "Some people disappeared with stuff cooking on the stove, and there was no one there to turn it off. That's why you see so many homes burned or burning."

When they finally reached Judd's street in Mount Prospect, the driver stopped and said, "There you go, son. Sure hope you find what you're expecting."

"I hope I don't," Judd said.

# 7

**DAWN** came way too soon for Vicki Byrne. The morning sun poured through the slatted window at the back of the house trailer where she shared a tiny bedroom with her little sister.

Vicki lay on her stomach and felt as if she hadn't moved since shortly after she had collapsed into bed. The buzz from the marijuana was long gone, but she still tasted the stale tobacco from the cigarettes and was hung over from several too many beers. She wondered how soon her mother would come to get her up. Vicki had purposely not set her alarm. Her mother usually roused her just before she left for work and just in time for Vicki to dress, eat, and make the school bus.

That usually happened shortly after Vicki smelled breakfast, or at least coffee coming from the kitchen situated just this side of the living room. This morning she smelled something metallic, but not food. She heard nothing. Was it still too early? Usually after a night like she'd had, her mother would have to shake her to wake her.

She felt as if she could sleep a few more hours. What time was it, anyway? Vicki lifted the covers and rolled to her back.

Jeanni was already up. Why couldn't she hear her? Vicki sat up and stretched, rubbing her eyes. Strange. Jeanni's school clothes were still set neatly on her chair. *She must be in the bathroom,* Vicki decided. She lay back down and waited for her mother.

Half an hour later, Vicki awoke quickly and looked at the clock for the first time. What was this? Had her parents given up on her altogether? They both had to be gone to work by now. Had Jeanni gone off to school in her play clothes?

Vicki dragged herself out of bed. She didn't know what it felt like to be an old woman, but it couldn't be much different from this. She was stiff, and her whole body ached. She padded down the hall to the bathroom, realizing she was the only one in the trailer. On her way back to the bedroom she suddenly stopped. Something was wrong. She backed up two steps and looked out the window to the asphalt apron.

Vicki squinted and shook her head. What in the world? Her dad's pickup and her mom's little rattletrap of a car were still there! Occasionally one of them would drive the other to work if one of the vehicles wasn't running. And once in a while one of them might get a ride to work with someone else. But both of them? On the same day? Vicki stood staring out the window, trying to make it compute.

Finally, she was convinced, she had figured it out. She hadn't heard anything because she had slept too deeply. Her sister probably dressed for a field trip. And for some reason, something was wrong with both cars on the same day. No big deal. Her mother had not tried to awaken her because she was mad at her. Mom had probably fallen asleep in the living room waiting for her to get home, knew Vicki was late but somehow missed her sneaking in. Just for that, Mom wouldn't get her up in time for school.

*So what?* Vicki thought. *I can blame it on Mom for not getting me up, and I can get more sleep.*

Then she smelled it. Something acrid. Something burning. And it was *in* the trailer! She hurried into the kitchen, where the teapot was smoking on the stove. The ceramic paint was black, the pot misshapen and clearly dry. Vicki's mother often liked tea late at night, but it wasn't like her to leave the pot on the stove until the water had evaporated away.

Vicki grabbed a pot holder before reaching for the handle, which had nearly melted. Even through the thick cloth the pot was searing hot. She dropped it in the sink, where it hissed in the water. What was water doing in the sink? Her mother never let dishes soak. She drew water only when she was ready to do all the dishes, and she always did them all and emptied the sink.

Vicki turned off the burner and looked around. Her mother had not even gotten out her teacup yet. She had never known Mom to forget water she had put on to boil, and certainly not overnight. What was going on?

Something out the window caught Vicki's eye. It was one of her friends, an older girl, wandering between trailers. Vicki swung open the door. "Shelly! Shelly, what's up?"

But Shelly didn't even turn. She just kept walking, as if in a trance. Still in her pajamas, Vicki stepped outside and yelled at her friend. Still she didn't turn. Vicki darted back in and threw on a top, shorts, and slip-on shoes. She trotted down the road until she was right behind Shelly. "Hey, girl!" she said. "What's the matter with you?"

Shelly turned and faced her, pale and trembling. "Shel, what happened? Are you all right?"

"Haven't you heard?" Shelly said, looking at Vicki as if she were a stranger.

"Heard what? What's going on?"

"People are missing," she said. "Disappeared. Vanished. Right out of their clothes. Watch the news. It's all over the world. Three trailers here burned to the ground. Lots of people lost family. Mrs. Johnson vanished late last night drivin' her husband home from the bus stop. He couldn't grab the wheel in time, and the car hit a tree. He's hurt real bad."

"Shelly, are you high? drunk? walking in your sleep? What?"

Shelly turned and walked away. Vicki called after her, but Shelly didn't respond. Vicki looked down the road to the cluster of trailers at the end of her area. People milled about, talking. Were all these people off work? She stepped off the road as a fire truck left the area. Could Shelly be right?

Vicki hurried back to her trailer and stood on the top step to survey the area. She saw two trailers that were now just charred remains, one with smoke still rising. People held each other, crying. She didn't want to go back inside, afraid of what she might find. But she had to.

She pulled the door closed behind her as she stepped back into the living room. Where was the remote? Her mother didn't like late-night TV. She would have stayed up reading. For the first time, Vicki looked at the chair where her mother would have been waiting for her the night before. Her mother's slippers were on the floor in front of the chair. Curlers and hairpins were strewn about, as if they had been dropped. Her mother's flannel nightie and thin robe were draped over the chair. Her Bible appeared to have fallen, hit the chair, and flipped over, landing page-side down on the floor, forming a little black tent.

What was that in the middle of the chair, atop her nightclothes? Vicki slowly moved closer. It was her mother's dental plate, the metal bridge with a porcelain tooth she was so self-conscious about. She never took it out in front of anybody, thinking it made her look old to have bridgework in her mouth from a childhood bike accident.

Vicki could barely breathe. Hands shaking, her whole body shuddered as she turned on the television. ". . . these grisly scenes from around the world," the announcer was saying, "evidence of the mass disappearances that occurred in every country at approximately midnight, Eastern Standard Time. . . ."

She was light-headed, and her stomach churned. This had to be a dream. She felt her way to a chair, unable to take her eyes from the screen. She pinched her arm and winced. No dream. "Here again," the newsman said, "is one of the strangest images we have received from this phenomenon no one can explain. This video was shot by the uncle of a soccer player at a missionary boarding school in Indonesia. Watch as the players race down the field. In slow motion now, watch as all but one player disappears. Their uniforms float to the ground as the ball bounds away and the sole remaining player stops and stares in horror. Watch as the cameraman keeps the video rolling and turns from side to side, showing he is one of few adults remaining, the rest having also disappeared right out of their clothes."

Vicki heard a throaty moan and realized it was her own. As the TV droned on and bizarre images came from everywhere, she made her way to her parents' bedroom. Her father's leather necklace, the one that so embarrassed her, lay on his pillow. The necklace had the initials W. W. J. D. carved into it, which her father proudly told her reminded him that in every situation he was to ask himself, "What Would Jesus Do?"

An empty drinking glass lay on the bed in a drying circle of water. Dad liked a glass of ice water in bed almost every night. Vicki forced herself to squeeze between the foot of the bed and the wall and moved to her dad's side of the bed. She pulled the covers back to reveal his T-shirt and boxers, the only things he ever wore to bed.

Where were her mom and dad? Where *could* they be? What had happened to everyone? What would she do? Had Jeanni discovered them missing? And if she had, why hadn't she awakened Vicki? *Oh, no!* she thought. *Not Jeanni too!*

Vicki scrambled over her parents' bed and headed down the hall to her and Jeanni's room. A sob rose in her throat, and she felt dizzy. She whipped the covers off Jeanni's bed and saw Jeanni's goofy little kangaroo pajamas.

What was she going to do? Where could she go? She had been so awful to her parents, and now they were gone. Vanished. Would they be back? *Why them and not me?*

And suddenly it hit her. Was it possible? Could it be? Had they been right? Had she been as stubborn and stupid as a person could be? Had she seen the dramatic changes in their lives and still not believed any of the God stuff? Had they gone to heaven and left her behind?

Vicki moved to the phone and speed dialed her brother in Michigan. "I'm sorry," she heard, "all circuits are busy now. Please try your call again later."

Vicki pulled up a chair and hit the redial button a hundred times in a row, crying but trying to keep from becoming hysterical. How close had she come to being burned up in a fire just like the one that had cost her neighbors their trailers? The TV showed picture after picture of huge chain-reaction car crashes, plane crashes, ships running aground. There were reports of suicides, including the only soccer player who had been left on that field in Indonesia. Others had been killed in accidents caused by drivers disappearing.

Finally, Vicki's call got through. She nearly lost control when her brother's phone rang four times and the answering machine picked up. She waited through the message and then pleaded with him, in tears, to answer. "Eddie, are you there? It's Vicki! Please pick up if you're there! Please be there! Eddie, please!"

Someone came on the line. "Vicki?"

"Eddie?!"

"No, this is Bub." Vicki knew the name but had never met Eddie's roommate.

"Is Eddie there?"

"Uh, no. No, he's not."

"Have you seen what's going on, Bub?"

"Who hasn't, kid?"

"Then you know what I want to know."

"Are you sure, Vicki? I could just as easily tell you I have no idea where he is, just that he's not here."

Vicki sobbed. "But that isn't true, is it? You found his clothes or something, didn't you? He disappeared along with all those other people, didn't he?"

"You'd better let me talk to your mom or dad."

"Bub! They're not here! They're gone, right out of their clothes. My little sister too! Now tell me about Eddie!"

"OK, listen, honey, I didn't see this myself, all right? This is all secondhand, but Eddie was working second shift last night, three in the afternoon to eleven. I was off and we were going to meet at an all-night diner at midnight. I waited for him for about twenty minutes, and I never knew him to be late for a meal. I called the plant, and they said he had left there at about eleven-thirty."

"Wait," Vicki said, "what time is it there now?"

"We're on Eastern Time, sweetie. An hour ahead of you."

"Oh. And please quit calling me little girl names. I'm four-teen!"

"Sorry, Vicki. The picture Eddie showed me must have been when you were little."

"He showed you a picture of me?"

"He bragged on you all the time. So, anyway, a guy comes in the diner who knows us, and he asks me am I waiting for Eddie. I say yeah, and he says Eddie was in a wreck a couple miles up the road. I ask him is Eddie all right, and he says they couldn't find him. All his clothes and stuff were in the car, but he was gone."

Vicki was crying.

"The guy tells the diner guy to get the TV on, that people have disappeared all over the world. The waitress runs to a booth in the back and screams. She says, 'I thought those guys had sneaked out on their bill! Their suits are all still here!' She about fainted. Anyway, we all watched TV for a while, then I came home. You know where all these people are, don't you?"

"I think I *do*, Bub. Do you?"

"Eddie talked about it all the time. He told me about your mom and dad getting religion—'saved' he called it. He starts going to church, and he gets saved. Dragged me along a couple of times, but it wasn't my thing, you know. You think that could be it? They're all in heaven?"

"I don't know what else to think," Vicki managed. "What else could it be?"

"You gonna be all right?"

"I don't know what I'm going to do."

"You want me to come down there and look after you? Far as I know I didn't lose any family but maybe a couple of other friends."

"Don't worry about me, Bub. I usually ride the school bus with a black girl who knows all about this stuff. I'm going to try to find her. I hope she's still around."

"Good luck," Bub said. "This is really wacky, you know?"

That seemed to Vicki a pretty mild thing to say about the craziest thing that ever could have happened in history. She hung up and turned all the way around. From where she stood she could see her mother's bedclothes in the chair, her father's T-shirt in the bed, and the door to her and Jeanni's bedroom down the hall.

Vicki didn't know what to think. Part of her was glad her family was right. She wouldn't wish her own feelings on anyone, especially on people she loved. Loved. Yes, she realized, she loved them. Each of them. All of them. She only hoped they *were* in heaven. It wasn't like they were dead.

But they might as well have been. She had become an orphan overnight. And all of a sudden all those so-called friends of hers, the waste-oids who hid from their feelings and their problems behind a buzz of booze and pot, didn't interest her in the least. The girl she wanted to find was the one she often sat with on the bus, the one who had tried to explain to her what had happened to Vicki's parents when they "got saved."

Vicki looked in the phone book under Washington. There were dozens of them, and she didn't know Clarice's father's name. She dialed every Washington whose name began with an A or a B and about half of them whose names began with a C, but none knew a Clarice Washington. Then she remembered that Clarice had said her mother worked at *Global Weekly* magazine.

Vicki looked up that number and dialed. She was told that Mrs. Washington was not in yet and that no, they could not give out her home number. "Is it an emergency, young lady?"

"It sort of is," Vicki said. "I'm a friend of her daughter Clarice, and I need to talk to her."

The woman at the magazine told Vicki she would call the Washington home and pass on her message. "I'm sure she'll call you," the woman said.

# 8

**THERE** was no clock in the basement of the Washington home where Lionel and his uncle slept soundly. Lionel never had to worry about getting up on time. His father made some racket before he pulled out at six every morning. Then Lionel's mother made sure everybody was up and in the process of getting ready for school by the time she left at seven. "I don't know what you kids are going to do when you're out on your own," she often said. "I'm creating monsters who don't move till they're told."

It seemed too bright, too late when Lionel awoke. He had always been a slow riser, in a cloud until he got up and moved around, went to the bathroom, got breakfast. This morning he didn't feel like moving. He merely opened his eyes, squinted at the sun rays that had somehow found their way through the tiny basement windows, and watched the dust dance in the columns of light.

Lionel was on his back, staring at the floorboards, wiring, and ductwork in the basement ceiling. This was a scary place in the dark of night. He never slept here alone.

Lionel had a vague recollection of André slipping out of bed, sometime after midnight, he guessed. André sometimes sneaked out of the house for a smoke. Because André always slept so soundly after that, Lionel's father once wondered aloud if André was smoking something stronger than tobacco. And when André spent more time than necessary in the tiny bathroom in the basement, even Lionel wondered if he was taking drugs.

When André came back from whatever he was doing, he would collapse onto the sofa bed with Lionel and wouldn't seem to move a muscle for hours. It was not uncommon for Uncle André to still be sleeping, in the same position, even after Lionel's mother had come down to roust Lionel out of bed. They might argue or crab at each other—usually just in fun—and they were never quiet. But Uncle André would remain dead to the world.

Once, Lionel's mother had made the mistake of trying to rouse André too. He was so out of it and so angry that she just apologized and never tried again. He got up when he got up, and that was often very late in the morning. This morning Lionel couldn't even hear André breathing. He turned to make sure his uncle was alive.

There he lay, on his stomach, his face turned away from Lionel. The slow, rhythmic heaving of his back told Lionel that André was fine. But he sure was quiet.

Lionel heard the phone ring upstairs. His mother or Clarice would answer it. They always did. Lionel's father often urged his wife to let the answering machine screen calls when they were trying to get ready for work and school or when they were having a meal or sleeping. But Lucinda Washington made it clear to the family that she hated answering machines. Theirs was off as long as anyone was in the house. The last one out could turn it on "so it can serve the purpose it was designed for," she would say. "Not so we can screen calls or get lazy. It's for catching calls when we're away, period."

This morning the phone kept ringing, and Lionel heard no footsteps upstairs. Maybe it was earlier than he thought. He sat up, feeling that fogginess and heaviness that made him move so slowly every morning. No one was answering the phone. What time was it, anyway?

Lionel groaned and whipped off the blankets. Uncle André did not stir. Lionel felt the chill of the basement as he moved stiff-legged toward the stairs. Passing a window, he noticed his father's pickup truck in the driveway, blocking the garage door where his mother's car was parked. *It is early*, Lionel decided. *Who'd be calling at this time of the morning?*

Lionel was in his underwear, and his mother didn't want him "parading around that way, now that you're a teenager," but he thought she might forgive him if he answered the phone for her. But why wasn't she or Dad answering it? They had an extension phone on their bed table.

The phone rang and rang, but Lionel was in no hurry. The phone was never for him anyway. He would answer it only because it woke him and there was nothing else to do. Anyway, he was curious.

The kitchen was at the top of the stairs. The lights were off. No one was up. He reached for the phone. It was Verna Zee from his mother's office. "Hi, hon," she said. "Lionel, isn't it?"

"Yes, ma'am."

"Is she there?"

"Who?"

"Your mother, of course."

"Um, I think so. She's not up yet."

"Not up? She's usually the first one here."

Lionel glanced at the wall clock, stunned. It was late morning. "Uh, I'm pretty sure her car's still here. You want me to wake her?"

"No. I work for her, not the other way around. The only reason I let the phone ring for so long is that I know someone's always there if the machine doesn't pick up."

"Um-hm." Lionel wished he were still in bed.

"It's just that on a big news day like this, I'd expect her before now."

"Um-hm." Lionel had no idea what Verna was talking about, and neither did he care. Big news for adults was rarely big news for him. "You want me to tell her you called?"

"Please. Oh, and I also have a message for your sister."

"Which one?"

"Clarice. Her friend Vicki called and wants Clarice to call her. You know her?"

"No, but I've heard 'Reece talk about her."

"Well, she sounds real anxious to talk to Clarice." Verna gave him the number, and Lionel promised to pass along the message.

Lionel didn't want to know why everyone was sleeping in. He just wanted to enjoy it. He could head back downstairs and catch some more sleep. If the phone didn't wake anyone, why shouldn't he? He glanced at the calendar. It was no holiday. Nothing was planned but work and school. He had started back downstairs when he stopped and turned around.

*Wait,* he thought. *I could be a hero. I could be the one who keeps everybody from being even* more *late.*

Lionel went from the kitchen through the dining room toward the stairs that led to the upstairs bedrooms. He opened the door when he noticed something in his peripheral vision. On his dad's easy chair lay the oversized terry cloth robe.

Lionel stopped and turned, staring at it. He had never known his father to take his robe off outside the bedroom. Though he slept in pajamas, he considered it impolite to "walk around in public in them," he always said, referring to his own family as the public.

Maybe he had been warm. André and Lionel had gone to the basement while Dad was still sitting there, nearly dozing. Maybe he shed his robe while half asleep, not thinking. But that wasn't like him. He had always taken great pride in "not being one of those husbands whose wife always has to trail him, picking up after him."

Lionel moved into the living room, where he noticed his father's slippers on the floor in front of the chair. The robe lay there neatly, arms draped on the sides of the chair almost as if Dad's elbows still rested there. When Lionel saw the pajama legs extending from the bottom of the robe and hanging just above the slippers, it was obvious his father had disappeared right out of his pajamas and robe.

Though Lionel was always unhurried and deliberate in the logy mornings, now it was as if life itself had switched to slow motion. He was not aware of his body as he carefully advanced, holding his breath and feeling only the pounding of his heart. The harsh sunlight shone on the robe and picked up sparkling glints of something where Dad's lap should have been.

Lionel knelt and stared at his father's tiny contact lenses, his wristwatch, his wedding ring, dental fillings, his dark brown hearing aid, the one he was so proud of because he had saved until he could afford one that would truly blend with his skin color.

Lionel's hands shook as he forced himself to exhale before he exploded. He felt his lips quiver and was aware of screams he could not let out. He crept forward on his knees and opened the robe to find Dad's pajamas still buttoned all the way up. Lionel recoiled and sat back, his feet under him. Suddenly it hit him. He lowered his face to between his knees and sobbed. If this was what he feared it was, he knew what was upstairs. Empty beds. Nightclothes.

But would everyone be gone? He didn't want to horrify himself. He didn't want to see everything that had been left behind, just as he was. He just wanted to know whether he was alone. Lionel ran to the stairs and bounded up two at a time. Little Luci's bed was empty. So was Ronnie's.

Lionel was out of breath. He didn't want to panic, but he couldn't control his emotions. It was too perfect that in Clarice's tiny room, her open Bible lay on her pillow. He imagined her there, as he had noticed so many times, lying on her stomach, reading.

The master bedroom was more than he could bear. His parents' bed was still made, his mother's bedclothes draped on one side where it was clear she had been kneeling in prayer. How Lionel wished he had been taken to heaven with his family and that he had been found reading his Bible or praying when Jesus came.

Only for the briefest instant did Lionel wonder if he were dreaming. He knew better. This was real. This was the truth. All doubt and question had disappeared. His family had been raptured as his church, his pastor, and his parents had taught. And he had been left behind.

He had wanted to believe his Uncle André when he said that living a good life was one thing but that all this about pie-in-the-sky by-and-by and heaven and the Rapture was just so much mumbo jumbo. Lionel realized that he believed even more than André did, but since he had never done anything about it, he had missed out.

Uncle André! He was still in the basement, and for all Lionel knew, was still sound asleep. Tears streaming down his face, Lionel hurried back down, forcing himself not to look at his dad's empty clothes on the chair on his way to the kitchen and the basement stairs. On the table he noticed the message he had just written to Clarice from her friend Vicki. He grabbed it and bounded down the steps.

Lionel yanked on jeans and a shirt and was lacing up his sneakers as he called out to André. "You'd better get up, man," he whined, feeling the sobs in his throat. "We're in big trouble."

But André didn't stir. Lionel sat on the edge of the couch and stared at his unconscious uncle. How he would like to blame André, anybody, for his own failure. But he couldn't. He knew everything his family knew. He had simply not bought into it. The question now was, was it too late? Was there any hope for someone who had been left behind?

He suddenly felt older and wiser than his uncle. And André didn't seem all that cool and wise anymore. Lionel knew something André didn't, that they had both been wrong, dead wrong. What was the use of waking André now? He would learn the truth soon enough. Let him sleep in ignorance, Lionel decided. This news would ruin the rest of his life.

Lionel trudged back up to the kitchen and slumped into a chair near the phone. Was anyone from his church left behind besides him and André? He called the church, and the answering machine picked up, the pastor's voice announcing when Sunday's and Wednesday's services were scheduled. He concluded, "And remember: Keep looking up, watching and waiting, for the time of the Lord draweth nigh."

Lionel stood to hang up the phone as the announcement continued about leaving a message after the tone, but suddenly someone picked up the phone. "Hello? Hello? Is anyone there?"

"Yes!" Lionel said. "Who's this?"

"This is Freddie."

"Freddie, this is Lionel. Who else is there?"

Freddie was chairman of the trustee board, the committee that took care of the church and also supervised the ushers. Freddie was often at the church, working or organizing the maintenance.

"Nobody, Lionel. Nobody else is here but me. Old Mr. Hazel's clothes are here, but he was the only one in the building last night, playing night watchman when the trumpet sounded."

"When the *what?*"

"Oh, I didn't hear it, Lionel. If I'da heard it, I'd be gone and so would you. But you're calling just like everybody else who's calling this morning. You missed it just like me, didn't you? And you're the only one in your family left, aren't you?"

"I am. Well, except André."

"Is he there?"

"He's still sleeping."

"Get him up and let me talk to him!"

"No, I'm going to let him sleep, Freddie." Lionel didn't dare ask how a man so dedicated to the church could have missed the Rapture.

"I'm coming over there then," Freddie said. "We, you and I, we both learned a hard lesson today, didn't we, boy?"

"Yes, sir."

"I'm going to talk some sense into that uncle of yours, and we're going to be ready for all the people who come to this little lighthouse looking for answers."

Everybody in Lionel's church referred to it as the little

lighthouse at one time or another. "So nobody else from the church got left behind but us three?" Lionel asked.

"Oh, there'll be more," Freddie said. "So far all I've heard from are neighborhood people. I'm praying everybody else who knew the truth acted on it before it was too late, but I imagine there'll be more of us turning up."

"What do we do now, Freddie? Are we going to hell?"

"I don't know for sure, boy, but I aim to find out. And for starters I'm coming to talk to that uncle of yours."

It would be at least an hour before Freddie could get to Mount Prospect, Lionel knew. He wanted to turn on the TV and see what the news said about the disappearances. It must have caused all sorts of chaos. But first he dialed the number Verna Zee had given him for Vicki Byrne.

Lionel heard desperation in her voice. He identified himself and she immediately said, "Clarice is gone, isn't she? Disappeared."

"Yes."

"And your parents and, what, a couple of younger kids?"

"All gone."

"Oh, God."

"That's what I think too. It was God."

"There's no doubt about that. What are you going to do, Lionel?"

"I don't know. My uncle's here, and a guy's coming from church. I'll be all right. What are you going to do?"

"I'm going to go to my parents' church. I called there, and a guy named Bruce Barnes is waiting for me. He says there's still hope."

"Hope?"

"For us, for everybody left behind."

"Really?"

"That's what he said. He didn't want to talk about it on the phone. But I'm going there. It's not far from your house."

"The white church?"

"I think it's brick."

"No, I mean the white people's church?"

"I guess. I'm going this afternoon. Why don't you come too?"

"I might."

Later, after Freddie arrived and roused André, Lionel answered yet another call.

"Washingtons," he said.

"Cameron Williams of *Global Weekly* calling for Lucinda Washington."

"My mom's not here."

"Is she still at the office? I need a recommendation for where to stay near Waukegan."

"She's nowhere," Lionel said. "I'm the only one left. Mama, Daddy, everybody else is gone. Disappeared."

"Are you sure?"

"Their clothes are here, right where they were sitting. My daddy's contact lenses are still on top of his bathrobe."

"Oh, man! I'm sorry, son."

"That's all right. I know where they are, and I can't even say I'm surprised."

"You know where they are?"

"If you know my mama, you know where she is too. She's in heaven."

The man sounded unconvinced. "Yeah, well, are you all right? Is there someone to look after you?"

"My uncle's here. And a guy from our church. Probably the only one who's still around."

"You're all right then?"

"I'm all right."

From the basement Lionel heard first the laughter from his uncle, who accused Freddie of pulling a practical joke on him. Freddie assured him it was no joke, and André began to cry, then to scream. He raced up the steps, pushing past Lionel. "Tell me it isn't true, Lionel!"

"It's true, Uncle André."

In the living room Andre shrieked at the sight of his brother-in-law's pajamas, robe, and other material items. Lionel poked his head in. "You don't want to go upstairs, André."

But André ignored him and charged up there. Lionel heard loud sobbing, swearing, and doors opened and slammed shut. André barged back down.

"Where's your daddy keep his truck keys?" he demanded.

"Why? Your car is still—"

"My car is trash! Now where are they?"

Andre's eyes were wild.

"On the hook next to the refrigerator, but—"

André grabbed the keys, dropped them, scooped them up again, and hurried out. "Aren't you going to get dressed?" Lionel called after him, apparently making Andre remember he didn't even have his wallet.

André ran back in, gathered up his pants and wallet and shoes, and bounded back out in his underwear. He roared away in the truck, and Lionel wondered if he would ever see him again.

Freddie asked if Lionel wanted to go back to the church with him. "No, sir. I'm going to stay here and watch the news. Then I'm going to meet a friend of Clarice's."

"I'll check on you later," Freddie said, and Lionel thanked him.

He made his way slowly into the living room and sat on the couch, watching the horrible news from around the world. Sitting across from his father's empty bedclothes, Lionel had never felt so alone.

# 9

**RYAN** Daley awoke early that fateful morning. He had a fading recollection of noise in the middle of the night. It had not been enough to wake him fully, but he remembered thinking his dad had come home. But then he remembered that his dad was not expected until morning. His mother was to pick up his dad after Ryan headed toward the Steeles' to walk to school with Raymie.

Ryan didn't hear his mother and assumed he had risen before her. He took his shower and dressed, then finished his homework before heading down to breakfast. Surely she would be up by now.

But she wasn't there. A note awaited Ryan. It read: "Honey, please stay here until I call you. I'm going to try to get to O'Hare. I'm not sure I'll get through because of everything that's been happening, so please don't worry. And if the stuff on television bothers you, just turn it off. Dad and I'll be home as soon as I can find him. I couldn't get an answer at the Steeles, so don't go there unless you talk to Mrs. Steele or Raymie first. And don't walk to school alone. There may not even be school today. They should say on the news. I'll call you sometime this morning. Don't go anywhere until you hear from me, please. Love, Mom."

Ryan had no idea what she was talking about, but that didn't keep him from worrying.

He got himself some cereal and turned on the little TV his mom kept on the kitchen counter. None of the stations would come in, so he turned it off. When he finished eating, he decided he would call Raymie. The phones weren't working, but he noticed the message light blinking on the answering machine. He pressed the button. His mother had called at four-thirty in the morning. So that was what he had heard. She had left in the middle of the night. And this call came long after she had written the note and left.

"Ryan," his mother's recorded voice said, "I'm stuck in some unbelievable traffic here, and I don't know if I can get to O'Hare or back home. I'll just keep trying. When you get this message, call me on my car phone. You know the number. I can't get through to O'Hare by phone either, and the first time I tried to call you all the circuits were busy. So if it doesn't work, keep trying. And remember, don't worry. I'll find Dad and we'll get home as soon as we can."

His mother had sounded worried herself. How could he not worry? Ryan still couldn't bring in any TV stations, so he turned on the radio and hooked up his video games. He was immersed in his favorite game when he realized what was happening. It was like a scary science-fiction movie, the kind he had not been allowed to watch until he turned twelve and which still scared him if he was honest with himself.

Something had happened. Millions of people all over the world had disappeared at the same time. They left everything behind but flesh and bone. Driverless cars, trucks, and buses had crashed, ships ran aground, planes crashed. Wherever someone was in charge of something important and they disappeared, something terrible went wrong.

Ryan yanked his video game controller out of the TV and began searching for any good channel. Finally every channel was suddenly crystal clear, and the newsmen even talked about that. They said that service providers were finding that power, water, and communications were sometimes good, sometimes bad. "If you must make a phone call, be sure it's an emergency and get off quickly to keep lines open as much as possible."

Now Ryan was scared. What if his dad had been on a plane where the pilot disappeared? This had happened just before eleven, when he had first heard the sirens! The news reports told of fires throughout the suburbs and the city of Chicago. In fact, there were fires all over the world where people had put something on the stove, then disappeared and never came back to turn it off. Ryan imagined his mother trying to drive through impossibly blocked neighborhoods. He saw a helicopter view of the expressways, which were like huge parking lots. The only luck some people had was when they were able to get off the highways and try the side streets.

Ryan knew his mother had expected to be home by now and not leave him there alone to see this. He was fascinated by the reports from around the world, and he sat wide-eyed, his mouth hanging open, as video shots showed people disappearing and their clothes floating to the ground.

A tape broadcast from Hawaii showed a birthday party where the birthday girl, her two brothers, and her parents vanished as a neighbor videotaped her blowing out her candles. She leaned close to the cake and took a breath, then she disappeared, and her party hat fell into the candles and erupted into flames. The woman doing the videotaping saw only the flames and quickly doused the fire, then realized that she and another couple were the only people still there. Ryan heard her gasping and trying to talk as she taped the scenes of little piles of clothes all around the room.

When the station replayed the tape in slow motion, Ryan saw what the video camera woman had not seen. Just before the little girl's hat fell into the candles, the girl had disappeared, and her dress dropped out of the picture.

A video from a helicopter on the West Coast showed cops pulling over a motorist. As one patrolman approached the driver's side and the other backed him up at the right rear of the car, the driver and one of his two passengers disappeared, and so did the backup cop! The patrolman assumed the driver and one of his passengers had ducked down in the seat, so he pulled his weapon and warned his partner, who was no longer there.

The cop put both hands on his revolver and skipped to the back of the car to check on his backup and discovered his cap, shirt, badge, trousers, belt, gun, cuffs, ammunition, and shoes right where he had been standing. The patrolman panicked, screaming at the occupants of the car to come out with their hands up while he scampered behind his own patrol car for cover.

As he crouched there, one woman in the backseat of the car came out in hysterics, screaming that the driver and the other passenger had disappeared. The cop made her lie face down on the pavement, and he cuffed her before searching the car. He pulled empty clothes from the seats, then released her from the cuffs and comforted her as they tried to make sense of it.

By the time the cameraman in the chopper realized what had happened, several accidents had occurred on the same stretch of highway. He pulled back and panned wide to see tractor-trailer trucks hung up on guard rails, cars having plunged down ravines, and even the clothes of a utility worker hanging from a ladder that led to the top of a light pole.

Ryan wished his mother was home, but he didn't think he could speak even if someone was there to listen. This couldn't be real! He changed channels and found the same thing on every one. People were urged to stay in their homes as long as they were safe, and to stay tuned for more information. Ryan tried Raymie's phone again and reached only the answering machine. He did not leave a message. Later, if he dared, he would walk down to the Steele home and see what was going on. He wondered if anyone he knew had disappeared.

Ryan tried his mother's car phone. It rang and rang, but no one answered. He didn't get that usual recording about the cell phone customer having driven outside the service area or already being on the phone, so he knew he was getting through. It wasn't like his mother to leave the phone in the car if she wasn't there, and she always left it on when she had it with her. Ryan couldn't figure it out, and now he was really worried.

He found a station that listed all the crashes of planes that had been due into O'Hare that morning. His father had been coming in from Asia, which was all he knew. One of the crashed planes was coming from there, but Ryan didn't know the time or the number or even the airline. He just hoped against hope his father had not been on that plane.

News helicopters showed scenes from above O'Hare where big jets were parked up and down the runways. People walked from the planes as far as two miles to the terminal, and once there, it was nearly impossible for them to get out of the airport. Traffic gridlocked the road that led into and out of the airport. Ryan watched as thousands of stranded passengers walked through the zigzagged cars and down the overpasses and exits until they found taxis and limousines that would carry them toward their homes, if they could make it through the tangled mess.

Somewhere out there Ryan's mother was either trying to get to O'Hare to learn some news about her husband's flight, or she had already picked him up and was trying to make her way home. From what Ryan could see on the news, he didn't expect her for a long time. He dialed and redialed her cell phone number, but she never answered. He hoped with all his might it was just part of the communications breakdown caused by so many people disappearing.

Ryan grew panicky, unable to reach anyone by phone and not having any idea whether his parents were safe. He hated to think his mother might try to call him while he was gone, but he had to get out of there. He had to get to Raymie's house and see what was going on.

Ryan tried his mother again, then Raymie's line. Still just the machine. He hung up and ran from the house, down the block, and to the edge of Raymie's property. People were outside their homes, talking with neighbors. Many were crying. They watched as he approached the front porch of the Steele home. He didn't want to appear to be up to anything, so he just sat on the front step as if waiting for his friend, until people seemed to forget about him.

Ryan was going to ring the bell when he realized the drapes were open, the door was unlocked, and it stood open about an inch. There was no car in the driveway, but someone must have been home. He slipped inside to the bitter smell of burnt coffee. He tiptoed into the kitchen and saw the coffeepot in the sink, still hot.

Ryan knew someone was home, but who? He opened the door that led to the garage. Only Mr. Steele's BMW was missing. Mrs. Steele's car was there, and so was the one Raymie's sister drove when she was home. Raymie's four-wheeler was there, of course, and his snowmobile and his bike. So who was here and who wasn't? He checked the hall closet where Raymie's father's trench coat, flight bag, and cap were stored. Captain Steele was supposed to have been on some long trip to England or somewhere.

Ryan tiptoed upstairs to the bedrooms, past a bunch of family photos on the walls. Raymie's door was shut. Ryan knocked lightly. No answer. He pushed the door open. Raymie's nightclothes were in a neat pile on the bed, and Ryan looked enviously at the picture on the bedside table of Mr. Steele in uniform near his plane.

As Ryan left Raymie's room, he held his breath. He heard something coming from the master bedroom suite. What was it? Someone was home!

From the hall, Ryan could see all the way into the suite. There, lying face down on the bed, his uniform in a pile on the floor beside him, was Raymie's dad. He appeared to be sleeping, except that his shoulders heaved as if he were crying. Ryan didn't dare disturb him. He slipped back down the hall, down the stairs, and headed for home.

Ryan had a sinking feeling as he entered his quiet house. He turned on the TV and saw lists of people who had been on board the flights that crashed on their way to O'Hare. "We repeat," the announcer said, "it has never been our policy to release names of missing or presumed-dead passengers before next of kin can be notified. However, with such massive tragedies and the impossibility of local law enforcement agencies being able to keep up with the grisly business of informing families, we have been asked to make these names public as tastefully as possible. Remember, if someone you know appears on these lists, it means only that they held reservations

89

on these flights and that their whereabouts are currently unknown."

Ryan covered his eyes and peeked through his fingers as the names slowly scrolled by. He recognized one as the father of a friend of his. Another one or two looked familiar, and all he could do was wonder how many friends had lost family members. Then he saw his dad's name, and he burst into tears.

He turned off the TV and shook his head. It couldn't be. He tried to make himself believe that his dad had somehow survived and would be calling him. But that wasn't going to happen, and he knew it. It would be just he and his mom now. Did she know already? There was no message light blinking on the answering machine. Maybe she wanted to tell him in person. Maybe she didn't even know yet!

He dialed her cell phone for what seemed the hundredth time. It rang and rang, and finally someone answered. It was a gruff male voice. "Hello! Who's this?"

"This is Ryan Daley, and I thought I was dialing my mother's cell phone."

"Uh, you are, son, if your mother's full name is, ah, Marjorie Louise Daley."

"Yes!"

"Where are you?"

"Who is this?"

"I'm sorry, son. This is Sergeant Flanigan, Des Plaines police."

"What happened? Is my mom all right?"

"I'm afraid she's not, Ryan. There was a gas-main leak we didn't know about, and it blew while several cars were in an intersection here. Your mother's been taken to Lutheran General in Park Ridge. You know where that is?"

"No, sir."

"Well, it's—jes' a minute, son. . . . Yeah, OK. . . . Listen, Ryan, you have friends or relatives there that can look after you for a while?"

Ryan wanted to blurt that he had just seen his dad's name on a list of air crash victims, but he didn't. "Why?"

"Son, I hate like everything to tell you this over the phone, but your mother didn't make it. The county morgues are full, so one is being set up at Maine East High School in Park Ridge, not far from the hospital. You'll want to get someone to get you over here in a day or two for identification, but don't try to come right away."

Ryan couldn't speak.

Sergeant Flanigan apologized again. "I'm sorry, son. You're sure you've got someone there to take care of you?"

But Ryan hung up. Was it possible that the people who had believed in Jesus had been taken to heaven, just like Raymie had tried to tell him? He and his parents and Captain Steele had been left behind, but now both his parents were dead. What was he going to do?

Ryan had no idea, but he was going to try one thing. Raymie's church was less than a mile away. Ryan wasn't in a hurry. He just wanted to walk and think and cry. If anyone was left at that church, Ryan might be able to find some help.

# 10

"**EVERYTHING** all right at your place, Judd?" a neighbor called out as Judd Thompson headed around to the back of the house.

"Don't know yet," Judd hollered.

In truth, of course, he did know. He knew exactly what he would find in that house. The buzz of the champagne was long gone, and he felt suddenly foolish with his scraggly goatee, his wallet full of cash, and that top-of-the-line credit card. *Aren't I something?* He asked himself. *Big man. Big criminal. Big shot. Now I'm an orphan.* He felt like a child, despite his sixteen years.

Judd ran upstairs and checked Marcie's room first. She was the persnickety one, the one who always kept her room just so, dolls lined up in a row, her schoolbooks and the next day's clothes laid out neatly. Two tiny barrettes lay in the dent in the pillow her dark-haired head had left. Judd pulled back the covers, revealing her nightie.

In Marc's room, was which almost as messy as Judd's own, he found socks and underpants in the bed.

He glanced at his own room before heading down to the master bedroom. His parents had been in there, that was clear. They had gone through his stuff, looking for clues to where he might be. Maybe they had called the library to check on him. Somehow, they had figured it out, but he had left no clues in his bedroom. Fooling them, tricking them, putting one over on them had seemed so cool when he was on his way to O'Hare. Now he felt like an idiot.

Judd had a sinking feeling in the pit of his stomach as he descended the stairs. He wanted his little brother and sister and his parents to be with Jesus, of course. That was what they wanted, what they talked about, what they looked forward to. But he didn't want to be alone, either.

He slipped into his parents' bedroom, where the curtains were closed and it was dark. He didn't turn the light on, letting his eyes grow accustomed to the darkness. Judd shut the door and leaned back against it, feeling weak. He hadn't slept much on the plane, and now he was paying for the nervous energy that had kept him awake.

Judd was stunned to see that his parents' bed was still made. Could it be? Was it possible they had not been taken? No! It couldn't be! He whipped the covers back and saw no bedclothes. He looked around the room, now turning on the light. His mother's robe was draped over a chair. This made no sense. He found his father's robe in the closet and held out a flicker of hope. But what was he hoping? That his little brother and sister had been taken and his parents had not?

He ran to the living room, where the truth quickly became clear. The phone receiver was on the floor. From the positions of his parents' sets of clothes, it was obvious they had changed back into them when they realized they might have to drive somewhere to look for him. His dad's jeans and pullover shirt and shoes were in a pile near the phone. His mother's casual outfit lay in a chair where she had been sitting.

Judd returned the phone to its cradle and scooped up the clothes. He sat with them in his lap and smelled the faint scent of his dad's cologne and his mother's perfume. And he cried. They loved him so much, cared for him, worried about him. And look how he had treated them. He held their clothes close to his chest and closed his eyes, realizing he had gotten just what he deserved.

His mother had told him and told him that Jesus was coming again and that it could happen in Judd's lifetime. He knew that was what his church taught, but it had seemed so preposterous. Well, not any more. It had happened, and he had been left behind. What was he going to do?

Judd knew there would be no sleeping, tired as he was. He had to think about how he was going to get the car back from O'Hare. When would that be possible?

What he should do, he knew, was go to his church. His church. He hadn't called New Hope Village Church his own church since he was in elementary school. Who would be left there? Was he the only member who didn't go to heaven? He felt alone in the world, not just in this house. He decided to call the church, just to see if anyone else was around.

The voice on the New Hope answering machine was the visitation pastor's, a man named Bruce Barnes, who had been there for several years. It was clear from the message that he had been left behind too!

"You have reached New Hope Village Church. We are planning a weekly Bible study, but for the time being we will meet just once each Sunday at 10 A.M. While our entire staff, except me, and most of our congregation are gone, the few of us left are maintaining the building and distributing a videotape our senior pastor prepared for a time such as this. You may come by the church office anytime to pick up a free copy, and we look forward to seeing you Sunday morning."

Judd didn't want to wait. He looked for his mother's keys and backed her car out of the garage, only to go a couple of blocks and find all the roads blocked. He returned to get his little brother's bike. He was way past feeling self-conscious. He was on his way to church, and for the first time in as far back as he could remember, he really wanted to get there.

---

When Ryan Daley came within view of New Hope Village Church, he didn't know what to think. He had been in a church a couple of times in his twelve years, but not this one. A big, dark-haired kid on a small bike came pedaling past him. They looked at each other but didn't speak. Ryan had never seen him before.

The big kid let his bike fall near the front door and hurried in. Ryan was in no hurry. He didn't know who or what he was looking for. By the time he got into the building, the kid who had been on the bike was talking to a man in his thirties with curly hair and wire-rimmed glasses.

"Can I help you, son?" the man asked, seeing Ryan over Judd's shoulder.

Ryan couldn't get the words out. How were you supposed to ask if it was true, if Jesus had taken his people to heaven?

"Did you lose some family?" the man said.

Ryan nodded. "They died," he managed.

"No, they are in heaven with Jesus."

"They didn't get taken," Ryan insisted. "My dad died in a plane crash and my mom in a car accident."

Bruce approached and reached for Ryan. The boy felt self-conscious, but he let the man hug him. "My name is Bruce Barnes," he said. "I'm the only person left from the staff of this church, and I know exactly what happened. I'm going to teach a small group of young people here soon, and you're welcome to stay."

"You're going to teach?"

Bruce nodded. "I know what happened because I missed it. I have a tape from the senior pastor that will help explain. Is that something you'd be interested in?"

Ryan nodded. So did the big kid, whom Bruce introduced as someone from the church family named Judd Thompson. They shook hands. Ryan didn't know any other kids as old as Judd, except for a few cousins in California.

Bruce said he was expecting two more kids to show up. "I got a call from a girl named Vicki Byrne. I invited her, and she called back later to say she had invited a boy named Lionel Washington. When we're all here, we'll get started. I want to tell you my story."

---

When Vicki and Lionel arrived, Bruce took the four of them into a small office where he had set up a VCR and a TV. "You're not going to understand everything the pastor says," Bruce said, "but still you'll be astounded that he knows what's going on, even though he's gone. More important, you need to know that I have the same story you do.

"I lost my wife and my young children. They disappeared from their beds, and I knew immediately that I had been living a lie. I had been to Bible college and was a pastor, but I always thought I could get by, living for myself and never making the

97

decision to receive Christ. Judd, I know you and your family. I'm surprised to see you here, but I'm not surprised the rest of your family is gone. You know what happened, don't you?"

Judd nodded miserably. Bruce asked the others to share their stories. They cried when they spoke, and they cried when they listened. They had been thrust together by a tragedy none of them could have ever expected.

"I know it's hard for you to grasp right now," Bruce said, "but I have good news for you. The question you all must have now is whether there is any hope for you. You missed Christ when he came, but you are not lost forever. We're going to live through some awful days and years, but the Bible is clear that there will be a great soul harvest during this time. People can still become believers and be assured of heaven when they die.

"That won't take away your sorrow, your grief, or your loneliness. I can't even imagine a day when I won't cry over what I've lost. But now I don't apologize for telling everybody who comes in here how they can receive Christ. It's really quite simple. God made it easy. If you want to hear this, just say so, and I'll walk you through it."

Vicki raised a hand. "Are you saying that if we had done this before, we wouldn't have been left behind?"

Bruce nodded.

"And now we can still get to heaven when we die?"

He nodded again. "Everybody want to hear this?" They all nodded. "First," he said, "we have to see ourselves as God sees us. The Bible says all have sinned, that there is none righteous, no, not one. It also says we can't save ourselves. Lots of people thought they could earn their way to God or to heaven by doing good things, but that's the biggest misunderstanding ever. The Bible says it's not by works we have done, but by his mercy that God saves us. We are saved by grace through Christ, not of ourselves, so we can't brag about our goodness."

"But I didn't do anything good," Vicki said. "I didn't even *try* to get to heaven because I didn't really believe any of this."

"What do you think now?" Bruce said kindly.

"I think I was wrong."

"Me too," Judd said.

"Me three," Lionel said.

Ryan said nothing, but it was clear to Bruce he was listening. This was all brand-new to him, except for what Raymie had tried to tell him.

"The punishment for sin is death," Bruce continued. "Jesus took our sins and paid the penalty for them by dying so we wouldn't have to. He died in our place because he loves us. When we tell Christ that we know we are sinners and lost and then we receive his gift of salvation, he saves us. A transaction takes place, a deal. We go from darkness to light, from lost to found. We're saved. The Bible says that to those who receive him he gives the power to become sons of God. That's what Jesus is—the Son of God. When we become sons of God, we have what Jesus has: We become part of God's family, we have forgiveness for our sins, and we have eternal life.

"After you watch this video our pastor left behind, I'm going to ask you something I never wanted to ask people before. I want to know if you're ready to receive Christ right now. I'll pray with you and help you talk to God about it. It may seem too fast for you. This may be new to you. I don't want you to make a hasty decision when you're still in shock over what has happened. But neither do I want you to wait too long, to put this off when the world is a more dangerous place than it's ever been. Maybe you missed Christ the first time around because you didn't know any better. But now you know. What could be worse than knowing and then still dying without Christ?"

The four kids sat there, each grieving in his or her own way. Judd had been humbled. Vicki felt a fool. Lionel felt a sadness so deep he didn't know if it would ever go away. Ryan was puzzled. Raymie had told him all this, and Ryan had thought it was stupid. He didn't think so anymore.

As they watched the video of the senior pastor, now in heaven, telling what was going on and how they could come to Christ, each felt a sudden closeness to the other. Bruce told them that if they became believers, they would be brothers and sisters in Christ. They could become each other's family.

They would discover their connections later. Judd would one day realize that Ryan was the best friend of the son of the pilot of the plane he had been on. Vicki knew Lionel through his sister, but she didn't know that his mother had worked for the same magazine as a man who had been on the plane with Judd.

For now they were simply four kids from the same town who shared a common horror and grief. Bruce seemed to have in mind for them a future as a small group. That sounded good to each, especially in their gnawing loneliness.

When the video ended, each sat stunned that the pastor had known in advance all that was now taking place. Clearly this was truth. Certainly this demanded their attention and a decision. Each sat staring as Bruce posed the question of the ages.

"Are you ready?" he said. "Will you receive Christ?"

# 11

**JUDD** Thompson Jr. had always sized up situations quickly. It was clear to him that of the four kids who had fled to nearby New Hope Village Church during the greatest crisis the world would ever see, he was the oldest. The redhead, the only girl, had a hard, bitter edge to her. But still, if Judd had to guess, he would have said she was younger than he was.

Ah, what did he care. How could he ever care about anything anymore? The end of the world, at least the world as he knew it, had come. Millions all over the world had disappeared right out of their clothes, leaving everything but flesh and bone behind.

It wasn't that Judd didn't know what had happened. He knew all too well. As he had heard in church and Sunday school and at home his whole life, Jesus Christ had come back to rapture his church, and Judd had been left behind.

He even knew why. It didn't take the earnest visitation pastor of New Hope Village Church, Bruce Barnes, to explain that. Of all things, Pastor Barnes himself had been left behind.

Bruce Barnes had spent the last several minutes telling

Judd and the three other shell-shocked kids his own story. He
finished by telling them there was still hope. Life would be
miserable from now on, of course, and they would be alone
except for other new believers, but it was not too late for them
to come to Christ.

Bruce had urged them to think about it and not to waste
much time. The world had become dangerous overnight. With
so many Christians disappearing from important jobs, the
result was chaos. No one had any guarantees. Life was fragile.
Judd was impressed that Bruce seemed so eager to convince
them that their only hope now was to trust Christ.

Judd knew it was the truth. He had to face himself, and he
didn't like what he saw. His whole look, the way he carried
himself, the me-first attitude, the secret that he had never
really become a Christian—all those things sickened him now.

Why had he wanted to appear so old? Why was it so
important to him to know where he fit in every crowd? Everything that ever mattered to him now seemed ridiculous. He
had been a tough guy, a big shot, the one with all the plans
and schemes. He had stolen his dad's credit card and bought
phony identification papers that said he was old enough to
travel on his own. *Yeah*, Judd thought, *I was a real player.*

But though Judd had come to some hard realizations
about himself, he still had a major problem. There was no
question Bruce was right. Judd didn't want to live without his
family and without Christ. Though he knew he had had every
chance and could have been in heaven with his parents and
brother and sister right then, everything in him still fought to
blame somebody else. But whom could he blame?

His parents had been wonderful examples to him. Even his
little brother had recently asked Judd if he still loved Jesus. If
he couldn't blame his family and he didn't want to blame

himself, that left only God. He knew there was no future in blaming a perfect and holy God, but right then he had to admit that he didn't much care for God's plan.

Whatever happened to the idea that God loved everybody and didn't want anybody to die and go to hell? What kind of a God would leave a sixteen-year-old kid without his family?

Judd knew he wasn't thinking straight. In fact, he had to admit he was being ridiculous. But just then he didn't like God very much. He was mad at God because there was no one else to be mad at.

Besides, Judd was grieving. No, his family had not died. But they might as well have. He was glad for them, he guessed, that they had gotten their reward for believing. But that was of little comfort to him.

Bruce Barnes asked the four kids to introduce themselves and talk about themselves a bit. Judd didn't see the point of that. Bruce began with the youngest boy, the little blond who appeared stocky and athletic.

Judd was reminded of his own little brother, Marc. Marc and Marcie were twins, nine years old. Both had been tremendously athletic. While Judd had lost interest in sports after Little League, Marc and Marcie had seemed interested in every sport imaginable. They had both been dark-haired and younger and smaller than Ryan Daley, but still Judd found it hard to listen to the boy without thinking of them both. Already he missed them more than he could say. Just being around someone even near their age cut like a knife deep into his heart.

Ryan was telling his story at just above a whisper. Judd could tell the boy had spent a lot of time crying that day. No doubt there would be more tears until he could cry no more.

"I don't know what I think about all this stuff you've been saying, Mr. Barnes. If it's true, I don't think either of my parents went to heaven. For sure my mom didn't because she was killed on the road sometime this morning. My dad was listed with the passengers that went down in a plane crash. I don't think he would have been one of those who disappeared. I mean, he was great and I loved him, but he never said anything about being a Christian or even going to church."

Ryan told about waking up to find his mother's note and then hearing from the police about her death. When he stopped and buried his head in his hands, Bruce Barnes leaned forward and put a hand on his shoulder. "So you've never, ever been in church before?"

"Well, not never," Ryan managed, raising his head. "Somebody invited me to one of those Bible school things they have in the summertime at church once—"

"Vacation Bible School?" Bruce said.

"Yeah, that's it. But I was really little then and I don't remember much about it. My friend—his dad's an airline pilot—wanted me to go to church with him here. I never did."

"And who was that?"

"His name was Raymie Steele. He tried to tell me all about this, the way you just did. I thought he was nuts."

"What do you think now, Ryan?"

With that, Ryan buried his face in his hands again and sobbed. Bruce began to ask him something, but Ryan wrenched away and shook his head. Judd thought he knew exactly how Ryan felt.

Bruce turned to Lionel Washington. Judd noticed that the lanky young boy with the smooth face and chocolate complexion had sat expressionless since they had begun. His wide, dark eyes seemed to rarely blink. He merely sat forward, his chin resting on his fist, listening. Judd couldn't tell if he was interested or not, but something had brought him there.

Bruce asked Lionel if he knew any of the others. "No, but my sister Clarice knew Vicki here. They rode the school bus together."

"How do you feel about all this?" Bruce said.

"Oh," Lionel said, "this is nothing new to me. I know exactly what happened. You're right, we all missed it. The real Christians have gone to heaven, and we've all been left behind."

Ryan leaped from his seat and ran out, shouting through his sobs, "It's not fair! It's not fair! This is crazy! Why would God do this?"

Judd, Bruce, Vicki, and Lionel watched him go. "Aren't you going to stop him?" Judd asked Bruce.

Bruce shook his head. "He'll be back. Where else does he have to go?"

Lionel, who seemed to Judd to have been shaken by Ryan's quick exit, finished his own story of having grown up in a Christian family and gone to church all his life, only to never have made a true decision himself to become a follower of Christ. "I don't know how the rest of you feel, but I can't say I'm surprised or that I didn't get exactly what I deserved. I don't know if I believe there's really still a second chance, but if there is, I want it."

"Believe me, there is a second chance," Bruce said, "and I think it's something you'll want to take advantage of right away, don't you?"

"You better believe I already prayed the prayer," Lionel said. "If that's what you mean. I told God I was sorry, begged his forgiveness, and asked him to save me once and for all. You're saying it's not too late?"

"That's what I'm saying. Welcome to the family."

"To tell you the truth, sir," Lionel said, "I'd rather be in heaven with my own family right now."

"You and me both," Bruce said.

Judd was stunned at how much he and Lionel had in common, though they had never even seen each other before. Lionel, like Judd, also had a younger brother and sister. And Judd and Lionel had been raised in the church by Christian families.

Now it was Vicki's turn. "Well," she began with a quavery voice, "I guess I should have known better too."

Judd noticed how young and scared she sounded for someone who said she was fourteen years old. Of course, he felt very young and scared himself just then, but she looked like a tough girl. Whatever edge there had been to her seemed to have been stolen away when her mother, father, and little sister had been raptured. She told her story about growing up in the trailer park, about the weekend beer brawls and dances that had one time, seemingly out of the blue, begun with an evangelist preaching for just a few minutes and resulted in her parents becoming Christians.

"I saw big changes in their lives," Vicki admitted, "but actually I hated it. I hated church, and I didn't want to have anything to do with religion. They kept telling me it wasn't religion, it was Jesus, but I didn't see the difference."

"Now you do, of course," Bruce said.

"Of course," she said.

"Forgive me for being pushy," Bruce said, "but what are you going to do about it now?"

Vicki looked down and busied herself tracing a pattern on the floor with the toe of her shoe. "Actually, even though I know you're right, I just don't want to make a decision like this while I'm still in shock."

Bruce seemed to be trying gently to push her into seeing that, despite the trauma she had just been through, she really shouldn't take more time. "You know the truth. That makes it your responsibility to act upon it."

"I know," she whispered. But she would not return his gaze. Her body seemed rigid. To Judd it seemed as if she was through listening or talking about it. He was surprised when she looked up and appeared to be listening when it was his turn to tell his story.

Judd kept his account short. He merely mentioned that he too had been raised in a Christian home and knew exactly what had happened. He told of his plan to run away from home and be his own person, and how it had all come crashing down on him when the Rapture occurred while he was on a plane over the Atlantic on the way to London.

"I have to say, though, Pastor Barnes, I feel like Vicki here. I know what I'm *supposed* to do, what I *should* do, and what I'm sure I *will* do. But I just feel too much pressure. I can hardly get my mind around the fact that I'll never see my family again."

Bruce stood and moved near to Judd. "Don't you kids see? That's my point! If I'm right and a seven-year period of tribulation begins soon, it's unlikely any of us will live through it. We had better be prepared to see God, or we'll wind up without him for all of eternity."

Judd knew Bruce was right, but he caught Vicki's glance and knew the two of them were still determined not to be pushed. He only hoped that it wasn't simply a pride thing. He was pretty sure it wasn't. He was way past pride now.

"I'm sorry, Pastor Barnes, but I just need more time to deal with all of this," Judd said.

"Me too," Vicki said.

"Don't be waiting too long now," Lionel said. "I waited way too long as it is."

"I couldn't have said that better myself," Bruce said.

**IF** THERE was one thing Vicki Byrne was sure of when she left New Hope Village Church that day, it was what she was feeling. No way around it, she decided. She felt guilty.

She stopped at the door and looked back to see Bruce Barnes sitting wearily, hands atop his head, fingers entwined. He was almost imperceptibly shaking his head.

"I'm going to go look for that little kid," Lionel said, excusing himself as he slipped past her and out of the church.

"We'll be back, I'm sure," Judd Thompson was telling Bruce. Vicki was certain of that too, and she felt bad because she understood how much Bruce Barnes cared and how urgent he felt it was that they make their decisions for Christ now.

Vicki started toward home, though it was the last place she wanted to go. That empty trailer would only remind her how truly alone she was. She hesitated on the sidewalk, noticing the small bicycle someone had left out front. She assumed it was Ryan's. There was nowhere else to go, nothing else to do. She headed on foot for the trailer park.

Judd Thompson called to her from the door of the church. "So, what are you going to do?" he said.

"Same as you," she said. "Think it over. Do the right thing. We both know what that means. I just don't want to do it when I'm so exhausted and keyed up at the same time."

"I know what you mean," Judd said. "But I meant what are you going to do right now?"

"Just go home I guess," she said.

"You want to go somewhere with me?"

"Like where?"

"I've got to go get my father's car. I left it at O'Hare."

Vicki shrugged. "Why not? How are we getting there? We gonna ride double on Ryan's bike?"

"That's my little brother's bike. I'm going to see if Bruce will let me leave that here. I was thinking of taking a cab."

"You must have a lot more money than I do," Vicki said.

"That's one thing I'm not short of," Judd said. "But I'd trade it all to be in heaven right now."

"I know," Vicki said. "This is awful."

A few minutes later, Marc Thompson's bike was stored just inside the front door of the church and Judd was on the phone to a cab company. It took forever to get a connection and then for someone to answer. He was told there would be a premium on the fare. "What does that mean?" he asked.

"That it's going to cost you triple the normal amount. And we don't recommend trying to get into O'Hare. It's still a mess."

"I need to get my car out of there," Judd said.

"That parking garage is a disaster. A bunch of people disappeared while driving out of there, and their crashed cars left a gridlock that's going to take days to untangle."

"I still have to try," Judd said. "I want to make sure it's OK and get it before someone steals it."

"Suit yourself. Somebody should be there for you within the hour."

Vicki and Judd sat on the curb, waiting. She didn't recall having seen this boy before. Despite his scruffy look, it was clear to her Judd was a rich kid. Their paths would not have crossed for long, had they ever met. Vicki felt an unexplained need to keep some sort of conversation going. Though she hated the idea of facing that trailer, what she really wanted was to get home to her own bed and bury her face in the pillow and cry over all that she had lost. What a waste her life had been, she decided.

Still, she was grateful for something to do, somewhere to go, someone to be with. She asked Judd to tell her more about his family. He cried as he told her, and that made her cry too. "We're both going to have to do the right thing here soon, aren't we?" she said.

"I know," Judd said.

The cab arrived nearly two hours later. "Sorry it took me so long," the cabby said. He was a burly man in a sleeveless T-shirt. He looked as if he could use some sleep. "It's hard for us to get to our call-ins because we're not allowed to pass by anyone who's trying to flag us down on the way."

"And a lot of people are doing that?" Vicki said.

"I had three other rides before I got here," the cabby said. "And I even told another guy to wait for another cab. He wanted to pay me to take him all the way to Wisconsin."

"Wow!"

"You're telling me! I don't think he could have afforded it anyway, but I don't have to take somebody that far when I've got a call-in. You kids aren't really going to O'Hare, are you? You know there's nothing flying out of there—"

"I'm just going to try to get my car out of there," Judd said.

"That's gonna be no picnic either, son," the cabby said.

"I know. But I have to try. I've got nothing else to do."

Vicki was amazed to see so many fires as the cab snaked its way through the remains of car wrecks, traffic gridlocks, even fights. It was clear there would never be enough local police to go around. *So this is what it's like at the end of the world,* she thought.

Where were all these people going? All Vicki had noticed near the church were sirens in the distance and the glow of distant fires on the horizon. Now she could see that those fires were not so distant. "Why is everything burning?" she asked.

"You don't know?" the cabby said. "Nobody knows yet how many people disappeared late last night, but any of them who had anything on the stove just left it there. You leave something on the stove overnight, eventually the food burns up, the water turns to steam, the pan gets hotter than blazes, and before you know it your kitchen's on fire. With nobody there to fight it or report it, boom, there goes your house."

Vicki saw looks of jealousy on the faces of people waving at the cab from street corners, disappointed to see that it was already hired. What a mess. Were all these people just trying to find somewhere, anywhere, that wasn't turning to rubble?

As the night grew dark and the cab slowly picked its way through side streets and back roads toward Interstate 294, Vicki noticed that Judd had seemed to lose interest in talking. He sat with his chin resting in his hands. He had turned away from her and appeared to stare out the window as they slowly rode along. When would it sink in? she wondered. When would she feel her own fatigue and exhaustion and finally be able to sleep? And how would all this feel when she finally woke up and realized it was not a dream, not a nightmare, but reality? How do you go from being part of a family to becom-

ing an orphan overnight? She sighed. She hadn't even liked
being in her family. She didn't like it when her parents were
loud drunks, and she liked it even less when they became
Christians.

Now she realized, of course, that for at least the last two
years—since her parents had become believers—she herself
had been the problem. She had somehow realized that her
life would not be her own if she became a Christian like her
parents. They had told her and told her that she didn't need
to clean up her life before she came to Christ. "Jesus accepts
you just the way you are," her mother had told her. "He'll
start showing you what needs to be changed and will help
you change."

The problem was, Vicki knew her mother was right. She
simply didn't want to change, whether she herself was making
the changes or God was. She had liked her life just the way it
was because it was just that—her life. Why had it taken this,
something so huge, so cosmic, so disastrous to show her how
foolish she had been? She had been such a rebel, so mean to
her parents and even to her sweet little sister, Jeanni.

And what was with this dolt sitting next to her? Judd
Thompson seemed like a nice enough guy, having made the
same huge life-and-death mistakes she had made. But had he
even once asked her about herself or her family? Sure, she had
told her story in the little meeting at New Hope, just like he
had. But how was it that she knew to ask for more details, even
if just to be polite, and he didn't? Wasn't that just like a rich
kid to not care about anybody else? She had a bad feeling that
she wasn't going to like this guy very much, despite what they
were going through together. Well, she concluded, at least he
had asked her to go with him on his errand. That was better
than being alone just now.

Of course, she decided, that was the real reason he had invited her anyway. He didn't want to be alone any more than she did. Vicki was finally doing a little something for somebody other than herself. She could serve that purpose. She could keep this poor rich kid from being alone during the worst night of his life.

The tollway to O'Hare was stop-and-go when it was moving at all. Vicki simply didn't understand where all these people were going. But then, she and Judd were going somewhere, so why couldn't everyone else?

The cabby had fallen silent long ago. He kept taking huge swigs from a mug of coffee and opened his window so the cool night air filled the car. Vicki shivered and wished he would shut it, but didn't say anything. The way he looked, he had probably been driving for twenty-four hours. She was not about to discourage anything that would keep him awake.

Within a couple of miles of the airport, the traffic stopped dead. With Judd seemingly still more interested in staring out the window than talking to her and the cab driver appearing to concentrate on simply staying awake, Vicki was alone with her thoughts. It was, she knew, time to talk to God. It would be the first time she had done that in as long as she could remember.

As Vicki rested her face in her hands, she felt movement next to her. She peeked at Judd, who was still turned away from her. His shoulders heaved, and she knew he was sobbing, though he was somehow able to muffle the sounds.

Vicki was suddenly overcome with an emotion she hadn't felt in years. She felt desperately, overwhelmingly sorry for this boy. Maybe he was a rich kid, maybe he was insensitive, maybe he was so selfish he couldn't even be polite. But he was suffering the way she was suffering. She knew exactly how he felt.

Almost without thinking, Vicki put her hand gently on his

shoulder. Judd lowered his head to his hands and sobbed aloud. Vicki saw the cab driver's sympathetic glance through the rearview mirror. Judd whispered hoarsely, "I was so stupid. So stupid." Judd moved slightly, and Vicki worried that he might be embarrassed. She pulled her hand away and retreated to her own thoughts.

Fighting a sob in her own throat, she prayed silently. "God," she said, "I don't even know how to talk to you, let alone what to say. Bruce Barnes said you loved us and cared about us and didn't want to leave us behind. I hope that's true because I want to believe in you. I'm sorry for having been such a bad person, and I'm sorry that it took something like this to make me come to you. I wish I could say I would have done this eventually anyway, but I can't. I had enough chances, but I didn't want to give you my life. If you can forgive me for that and still accept me, you can have whatever is left of my life. For a long time I hoped you weren't real and that I wouldn't have to answer to you someday, but I always knew down deep you were there. And if nothing else convinced me, this mess sure has. I know it can't be as good to believe now when I have no choice, but if you'll accept me, I will live for you for as long as you let me stay alive."

Vicki and Judd sat in silence for almost another two hours while the cab slowly inched its way toward the international airport. Suddenly the cabby pulled off the road and sat on the shoulder, shifting into park. He turned to Judd. "I'm sorry, son, but you can see if I take that exit ramp to O'Hare right there, we might not get out of there for days. You're still a couple of miles from the parking garage, but I think this is as close as I can get you."

Vicki could see he was right. Nothing was moving on that ramp. Judd looked at her, and they both shrugged. Judd paid the driver and thanked him.

Suddenly Vicki found herself alone with a strange boy on a chilly night, on foot in a world that had come apart at the seams.

It was while walking with Judd that fatigue overcame Vicki. She didn't want to say so, but she wondered with each step if she could take another. This had been one long, grueling, horrifying day. Now, she thought, maybe she could finally rest in her own bed. The memories and her loss would still haunt her, but she believed God would allow her to sleep. She knew she didn't deserve to have him in her life, but she could do nothing less now than to trust him and believe in him and depend upon him.

Finally, walking in the grass next to the shoulder of the road, which was filled with cars barely moving, Judd broke his long silence. "Vicki, I've been thinking and praying."

"Me too," she said.

"Really?"

She nodded.

"That's good," he said, "because I don't think we're smart to put off our decision any longer. Who knows what might happen?"

"So you already became a Christian?" she asked.

He nodded. "I just figured it was really dumb to wait any longer. Not that I'm saying you're dumb, you know."

"I did the same thing a little while ago, Judd. If what Bruce said is true, then I guess that puts us in the same family. We're brother and sister now."

Judd nodded again. "I guess we are," he said. "I could use a sister."

"I could use a brother."

"Yeah, didn't you say your big brother was living in Michigan and you thought he was raptured too?"

"I thought you'd never ask."

116

**LIONEL** Washington had sprinted down the street away from New Hope Village Church, looking both ways for any sign of Ryan Daley. He knew the little guy had gotten quite a head start on him and only hoped that Ryan was not still running. If he was, Lionel would never catch him.

Lionel was a fast runner, but this was ridiculous. He huffed and puffed and sucked air, running in the general direction of his own house. He hoped Ryan's home was somewhere on the way. Maybe the kid had to stop and catch his breath himself.

Lionel slowed to a walk and put his hands on his hips, allowing his chest to expand and his lungs to drink in more air.

He squinted at a small form huddled under a street lamp two blocks ahead. It could have been anybody, of course, as people just like him—people who had lost loved ones and were scared to death and wondering what was going on—wandered about hoping to see someone they knew.

When Lionel was within a block of the streetlight, the form rose and began to walk. It was Ryan Daley. This time, fortunately, he was not running. At least not until he turned and looked behind him. When he saw Lionel, he began to jog.

"Hey! Hey, kid!" Lionel called. For the moment, he had forgotten the boy's name. "Wait up!"

At first Ryan seemed to speed up, but then it appeared he had resigned himself to the fact that there was nowhere to go anyway. He stepped off the sidewalk into the grass and thrust his hands deep in his pockets, his chin tucked to his chest. Lionel figured he had been crying. Maybe he still was. He sure didn't have to be ashamed of that, Lionel thought.

Lionel hurried to the boy and stood next to him, matching his posture, pushing his hands into his pockets and looking down. "What are you gonna do?" Lionel said. In his peripheral vision, Lionel saw Ryan shrug. "Ryan, isn't it?" Lionel said. "That's your name, right?" Lionel looked up in time to see Ryan nod slightly. "Ryan, I know how you feel. This is terrible, and we all hate it."

"How could you know how I feel?" Ryan blurted. "Your family's in heaven. For all I know, my parents aren't just dead, they're in hell."

Lionel didn't know what to say. He believed that was true. Nothing he said could make that any better. "The important thing now is," he finally managed, "what are *you* gonna do?"

Ryan sat in the grass in the darkness and put his face between his knees. Though his voice was muffled, Lionel could make out what he was saying. "I have no idea what I'm gonna do. I'm not going to be able to stand being in that house all by myself, I know that. I thought maybe I'd just gather up a bunch of stuff and pitch my tent in the backyard. I guess I can stand going in there for food and the bathroom, but I wouldn't want to live in there. And I sure wouldn't want to sleep in there."

"Me either," Lionel said. "My house has my family's

clothes all over the place, right where they left them when they disappeared."

"I wish mine did," Ryan said. "Then I wouldn't have to believe all this stuff about everybody who disappeared going to heaven."

Lionel nodded, but said nothing.

"I don't s'pose you'd want to help me get my tent set up?"

"Sure I would," Lionel said. "I've got nothing else to do."

"It's just a couple of blocks from here," Ryan said. "Thanks, Lyle."

"It's Lionel."

"Sorry. Like the train?"

"Uh-huh."

A few minutes later Lionel and Ryan were digging around in the garage at Ryan's house. Lionel saw Ryan occasionally looking at the door that led into the kitchen. "You want something in there?" Lionel said. "I'll get it for you."

"I *am* getting a little hungry," Ryan said. "It's just that I don't want to go in there yet."

"I'll get you whatever you want," Lionel said. "You want me to just find whatever I can in the refrigerator and the cupboards?"

The Daleys' kitchen was similar to Lionel's own. He could hear Ryan dragging stuff from the garage to the backyard, and he hoped the boy would invite him to stay. Lionel would have to go home and get some of his stuff, but he didn't want to be in his house any more than Ryan wanted to be in this one.

Lionel found a bunch of snacks and soft drinks and went directly into the backyard from the kitchen. He wondered if Ryan would be too shy to invite him. "You want some company tonight?" Lionel offered.

"You'd stay with me?"

"Sure! I don't want to be alone tonight any more than you do."

Once the tent was set up—snacks, flashlights and all—the boys headed toward Lionel's house, just over a mile away. Ryan wasn't saying much. Lionel had never been a big talker either, but when he wasn't talking he felt like crying, and he assumed Ryan felt the same. "I guess we don't have to worry about going to school tomorrow," Lionel said.

"Yeah. I heard on the news that enough students and teachers and parents disappeared that it might be a long time before school opens again."

Lionel snorted. "So we can be thankful for a little good news in all this mess." That wasn't really funny, of course. This was a nightmare from which neither of them would awaken.

Lionel figured Ryan was just as tired as he was by the time they reached Lionel's house. "You want to come in for a minute while I get my stuff?"

"It beats being outside alone, I guess."

The first thing Lionel noticed in the kitchen was that the answering machine was emitting a steady tone that indicated the tape was completely full of messages. Ryan followed him upstairs as Lionel ignored his parents' and his sisters' bedrooms and grabbed a backpack that he stuffed with clothes. On the way down he turned toward the kitchen to listen to the messages, noticing that Ryan was no longer behind him. Lionel turned to see Ryan staring at Lionel's father's nightclothes draped over the chair in the living room. "C'mon, man," Lionel said. "That gives me the creeps just as much as it does you."

White people were nothing new to Lionel, of course, and he wasn't surprised that a blond boy was paler than most. But he had never seen a face as ghostlike as Ryan's when he turned away from those empty clothes in the living room. Ryan appeared to be gasping for breath. Lionel wanted to get Ryan's mind off what he had just seen. "Let me listen to these messages," he said, "and then we'll go."

Lionel played the answering machine tape for several minutes before getting past the messages he had already heard that morning. He was stunned then to hear that the entire rest of the tape was just one long, rambling message from none other than his uncle André.

As soon as Lionel began listening to it, he wished he hadn't turned it on. He wished even more that Ryan was not there to hear it. It was clear Uncle André was either drunk or high or both. His grief and his horror were obvious. "Lionel, man," he said, "I done you wrong. I led you down the wrong path, boy. I just called to tell you I'm sorry and to say good-bye. I never meant to do wrong by you. I hope you'll find it in yourself to forgive me someday. I should have been there for you, and I should stay here and be here for you now, but I just can't. I can't live with myself."

Lionel had never heard anything like that before, but it sure sounded like André was planning to kill himself. Lionel listened with urgency, hoping and praying he would hear some clue about where André was calling from.

A couple of times Lionel thought he heard voices in the background and wondered if André's enemies—the ones he owed money to—had put him up to this. Maybe they wanted it to sound like he was planning suicide when actually they were going to kill him. Lionel didn't want his imagination to run away with itself. This was bad enough. André was serious. Dead serious.

Lionel sneaked a glance at Ryan, who still appeared ashen and seemed to be barely breathing. Lionel turned the machine off. "Maybe you don't want to hear this," he said.

"No, it's all right. You'd better find out where he's calling from or we'll never be able to help him."

"I'm not going to drag you into this. This guy is my uncle, and I'll need to handle it myself."

"Don't keep me out of this, Lionel!" Ryan said. "I got to keep myself busy or I'll be thinking about the same thing your uncle is thinking about."

"Let's hope he's still just thinking about it."

Lionel turned the machine on again and could hear what sounded like a bottle being poured into a glass. Also, if he had to guess, he would have assumed André was downing some pills. André's voice became slower and more slurred, and he cried more as he spoke. "Lionel, don't make the same mistakes I made. I was wrong, totally wrong. I heard all my life that God loved me and that Jesus died for me and that I was a sinner. I knew it. I believed it. I just never bought into it for myself. I told you a lot of it was fairy tales, and I hoped I was right. But I was wrong. I was wrong."

Lionel didn't think he had any more tears to shed, but he could feel them welling up again. André sounded so lost, so empty. Lionel thought about whom he could call, where he could possibly find André. He wondered if anyone left behind at the church might have any idea where André was. He flipped off the machine and dialed the church. The line was busy. He tried time and again, but always it was busy. He asked Ryan to take over and keep dialing. Meanwhile, he listened to the rest of the tape, which went on for more than twenty minutes. In it, his uncle André simply repeated how sorry he was, how sick he was of himself, how much he hated his life, and what a waste it had been. In the end, he resorted to simply apologizing over and over and saying good-bye. He was still talking, mumbling, rambling, when the tape ran out.

Ryan said, "It's ringing!"

Lionel grabbed the phone. When the machine at the church picked up, however, it merely signaled a long tone as well. The tape was full, and no one was there to answer either.

"I've got to get to André's place," Lionel said.

"Where's that?" Ryan said.

"In Chicago."

"How are you going to get there?"

"On my bike, I guess," Lionel said. "You want to go with me?"

"Sure. But I've never ridden a bike to Chicago."

"You can use my sister's bike," Lionel said.

"No, I've got my own. Just give me a ride back to my house and I'll get mine."

Half an hour later, Lionel and Ryan were pedaling quickly out of Mount Prospect, heading toward Chicago. Lionel hoped he would recognize the same landmarks he did while riding in the car. It seemed to take so long to get to each one while riding bikes. He soon realized he was going too fast to keep up his endurance. "Let's slow down," he hollered. "Let's save our strength. It's going to be a long trip."

The boys reached André's neighborhood around eleven o'clock. Lionel had never been out that late alone before, and he was intrigued that no one seemed to mind. He couldn't imagine riding his bike through cordoned-off expressways and side streets on his way to the inner city of Chicago without being stopped by the police. It simply seemed too strange that two young boys would be out on their bikes in Chicago at this time of the night.

Had it not been for his grief and his fear and his anxiety over Uncle André, Lionel might have enjoyed an adventure like this. But just then he couldn't imagine ever enjoying anything again. He sure hoped Bruce Barnes was right and that he was still eligible to become a Christian, even at this late date. It was awful that he had missed the truth the first time around, especially when he knew better. He sure didn't want to live through a period like this and lose out on heaven altogether.

"How do your legs feel?" Lionel asked Ryan. "Tight and heavy?"

"Yeah," Ryan said. "I can't imagine riding all the way back to Mount Prospect tonight."

"But we have to," Lionel said. "The only people I would want to stay with down here are all gone. I wouldn't feel safe with the ones who are left."

When Lionel and Ryan came within sight of the tacky little hotel where André rented a room, a couple of policemen were getting back into their cruiser. The one getting in the passenger side noticed the boys. "No time to even deal with you two tonight," he said. "Why don't you just run along home?"

"I'm looking for someone," Lionel said.

"Who isn't?" the cop said.

"My uncle lives in this building," Lionel said. He gave the officer André's full name.

The cops glanced at each other with what Lionel sensed was a knowing look. "Should I tell him?" the one cop said to the other.

The driver shrugged. "Why not?"

"Son, your uncle is the reason we were called off traffic duty, where we've been all day. He was found in his apartment a couple of hours ago. His body was just loaded onto an ambulance and taken to one of the morgues set up at a high school about seven blocks down the street here."

"A morgue?" Lionel said, his voice tight.

"Yeah. Sorry."

"How did he die?"

"I'm not at liberty to tell you that, son. You can take it up with the people at the morgue. I'm real sorry, but we've gotta go. You boys should be getting back home now. You've got somebody to go to?"

"We'll be all right," Lionel said. But he wasn't all right, and he knew Ryan wasn't either.

Lionel realized that he and Ryan finally had something in common. Now they both had people they loved who were dead and gone, and not to heaven.

Lionel thought he should identify his uncle's body, but he didn't want to see André that way. He didn't really want to know how André killed himself either, if that was really the way he died. What difference did it make whether he had killed himself or was murdered? He was gone. There was no more hope for him. And Lionel had one more reason to grieve.

Lionel and Ryan rode back to Ryan's house in silence. The trip home took even longer than the trip to Chicago. Ryan seemed as starved as Lionel felt, and they stuffed crackers in their mouths and washed them down with soft drinks before stretching out in the tent. It was well after midnight by now, and Lionel heard Ryan whimpering in the dark. He was crying himself to sleep.

And Lionel did the same.

# 14

**JUDD** and Vicki reached the entrance road to O'Hare, just past Mannheim Road, late in the evening, about the time Lionel and Ryan were heading back to Mount Prospect from Chicago.

Judd had never seen anything like this in his life. He and Vicki found themselves wandering, along with hundreds, maybe thousands of others, who were coming to or going from the giant airport for a variety of reasons. Many, it was clear, had come to O'Hare hoping to find a friend or loved one alive. The people coming the other way, those exiting the airport, had either been unable to get their cars out of the parking garage or unable to find a taxi or limo to get them home.

It was hard for Judd to imagine how anyone could hope to get out of this place in a car. Traffic was jammed in and out of the place, and tempers ran short. All around them, Judd and Vicki could hear people shouting at each other. The occasional limo or cab would break from the pack and race along the grassy median and up onto Mannheim Road or another artery.

As they got closer and closer to the massive parking garage, Judd struck up conversations with others who were on missions similar to his. "Doesn't look like we're gonna be getting our cars out of here tonight," a middle-aged man groused to Judd.

"Nope," Judd said. "But I have to try anyway."

"I see lots of activity up there, cranes, tow trucks, cops. I don't know what they're doing."

"I don't either," Judd said. "I parked at the end of one row, so maybe I'll get lucky."

"Don't count on it."

At the parking garage, cops with bullhorns were stationed at the entrance. Judd heard one explain the process. "You're free to go sit in your car, if you wish," the cop said. "But don't start the engine until you see a clear pathway to the exit ramp. So far only those parked on levels one and two have even a chance of getting out into the traffic jam here, and you can see you're not going to get far anyway."

"I'm on level two," Judd told Vicki. "Maybe they've cleared the way for me."

The cop told everyone the elevators were not running, the pay booths were wide open, and that any looters or suspected car thieves would be shot on sight.

All over the multistory garage, workers labored to clear cars whose drivers had disappeared. Hundreds of cars had been coming into and leaving the garage when the Rapture had occurred. A little less than a quarter of those vehicles had been manned by people who were now gone. Their cars had continued until they struck other cars or walls, and there they sat, idling until they were out of gas.

Some of those cars had apparently had full tanks of gas, and if they were still running, workers were able to move them. The biggest job was finding a place for all those empty cars, just to get them out of the way. A long walkway snaked from the garage to the taxicab staging area, which was empty. All the cabs and cabbies swarmed the departure and arrival levels, seeking riders.

Of course, many of the cab drivers had disappeared as well. Fortunately, with so many others in the immediate area when that happened, this had resulted in just a bunch of fender benders. Other cabbies had grabbed those idling hacks and gotten them out of the way.

Judd shuddered as he and Vicki walked through the garage, passing cars with full suits of clothes in the driver's seat. He saw the occasional car with a stunned or weeping person who was sitting atop someone else's clothes, trying to maneuver the car out of the tangled mess.

Everywhere, workers were adding a gallon or two of gas to cars that had idled their fuel away. The workers all wore surgical gloves and masks, no one knowing what germs or diseases might have been left by whatever it was that had made these people disappear. Judd knew there was nothing to be afraid of, but he couldn't blame the emergency personnel for being careful.

At one end of the parking garage, a huge crane had been brought in, probably from a construction site at the airport. It was being used to lift cars over the guardrail and set them gently down in an area near the end of the garage.

When Judd found his father's car at the end of one row, he realized he was not in an advantageous position. Four cars blocked his, and in the row he would have to reach to get to the exit, workers were laboring over a gridlock of steel. A Chevy Blazer whose driver had disappeared had climbed one of the combination wood and steel parking guardrails and hung itself up. It was still idling.

Judd carefully surveyed the situation. Four cars were lined

up bumper to bumper from the wall at the end of the line where he had parked. They extended back past where he needed to back up.

"Vicki," he said, "do you think if we could get all four of those cars pushed back, I could get out of that parking spot?"

"I don't know," she said. "Let's walk it off and measure it."

There was a gap between the last of those four cars and a smashed up mess behind them. The question was, was the gap wide enough for all four cars? Measuring it with their steps, Judd and Vicki came to the conclusion that there was room for the four cars, but not much room for Judd to back out. He would have to do it in several moves if he could do it at all. They had to try.

"We'll just have to take them one at a time," Judd said. He peered into the window of the last car in line. There were no clothes on the seat. The engine was off, but the keys were still in the ignition. "This must have been someone who panicked and ran off," he said. "Lucky for us they left their keys."

Judd started the engine and backed the car up as far as possible. He slowly maneuvered it until it tapped the first car in its way.

"The next car is still running!" Vicki shouted.

"Back it up here," Judd said.

"I've never driven," Vicki said. "You'd better do it."

Judd jogged up and opened the door, quickly realizing why Vicki didn't even want to try. This car was full of empty clothes. In the driver's seat was a woman's suit. Her shoes were on the floor. Atop the clothes were her glasses, necklace, earrings, and something that appeared to have fallen from her hair. As usual, Judd found dental fillings. On the floor, near the shoes, were the woman's watch and rings.

Judd smelled perfume. He held his breath. Not wanting to

step on her belongings, he gathered them up and set them between the two front seats. On the passenger side, a man's suit and his belongings were draped where he had sat. Judd glanced in the backseat, where two people who had been sitting close had left everything but flesh and bone.

That gave Judd the willies, but he had to do what he had to do. He depressed the brake, shifted from drive into reverse, and backed the car out of the way.

The next car had its formerly lone occupant's clothes on the seat behind the wheel. Judd tossed these onto the passenger side and kicked the shoes out of the way. The car was in drive and the key was on, but it had run out of gas. "I'm gonna need your help here, Vicki," he said. "I'm going to shift this into neutral, then I'm gonna need you to steer it while I try to push it back into those other ones."

"I really don't want to be in that car with those clothes," Vicki said. "Anyway, I've never driven."

"This isn't driving," Judd said. "You'll just be keeping it straight until it touches that car back there."

"Please! I really don't want to do this."

"Well, what do you suggest? How are we going to get out of here if you don't help me?"

"Let me push," she said. "You steer."

"We can try," Judd said, "but I don't think you realize how heavy this car is."

"I'm pretty strong."

"Suit yourself. Try it."

Judd put the car in neutral, and Vicki climbed atop the hood. She put her feet on the trunk of the car ahead and wedged herself between the two cars. She pushed with all her might, trying to roll the car backward. It wouldn't budge. Judd opened the door and put his foot on the floor to help push that way. Nothing.

"I'm bigger than you are, Vicki. Let me try pushing while you steer."

"I told you I'm not getting in that car, and I'm not. Think of something else."

"There *is* nothing else. What are we supposed to do?"

"Just make sure the wheels are straight, Judd. Then we can both push. So what if it hits those cars back there? It's not going to move unless we both push it anyway."

Judd couldn't argue with that. Without the engine running, the power steering did not work. Straightening the wheels of that car was like driving a truck with no power steering at all. It took all of Judd's might to get the wheels to turn a couple of inches. He had to keep getting out to check whether they were lined up. When they were straight, he joined Vicki on the bumpers between the cars. With both of them putting their entire weight and muscle between the cars, the one finally began to slowly roll. Within seconds it had picked up a little speed, and Judd and Vicki dropped down from their perch on the second car. Judd ran to the driver's side and whipped open the door, feeling the tremendous weight and momentum of the vehicle. As it neared the car behind it, Judd jumped in. But before he could apply the brake or shift into park, the car smashed into the grille of the vehicle behind it.

Now there was barely enough room left between that car and the one pressed up against the wall near Judd's. What tricky problem might that offer?

Judd noticed that the front tires of the last car were turned sharply to the left. There were no clothes on the seat. No keys in the ignition. And the doors were locked. "This was obviously being driven by someone who had just started to turn left toward the exit when he was hit from behind by that other car."

"So he just left?" Vicki said.

"Wouldn't you have? You get hit by a car from behind and plow into the cement wall. You get out to see what happened and the car behind you gets hit and the car behind that one gets hit. There are no drivers in the middle two cars, only clothes. The driver of the last car runs off, leaving his keys in it. What would you do?"

"I guess I might turn mine off, take my keys, and lock my doors too," Vicki admitted.

"I'm going to have to break the window to get into this car," Judd said.

"I don't know much about cars," Vicki said, "but what good will it do you to get into that car if the keys aren't there?"

"Good point," Judd said. "But somehow I've got to get this car out of the way if we're going to get out of this parking lot."

Judd and Vicki stood there surveying the situation and sizing up the possibilities.

"There's no way you're going to be able to back out of your space without at least clipping the bumper of that car," Vicki said. "Do you think your car could push that one out of the way a little bit? You'd still have a tough time backing out and getting around it, but it may be your only chance."

"No harm in trying," Judd said. "I can't think of anything else."

Judd told Vicki to line herself up near the crashed car and try to guide him with hand signals so he would come as close to missing it as possible. If he had to hit it, he'd hit it. If he had to hit it hard, he'd do that too. Whatever it took to push it out of the way, that was what he had to do.

Judd got into his car and started the engine. He looked in his rearview mirror and didn't see Vicki. He looked at the mirror on the door and saw her standing there, motioning him to start backing out. He pretended to busy himself with something else in the car on the seat. He had to stall. It wasn't that he didn't want to do this, it was just that he was suddenly overcome with a feeling of such sadness and loneliness and grief that he could barely move.

What was it about merely being inside the car with Vicki outside that made him feel so alone? It was almost as if he was in a trance. He still longed for this to be just a bad dream, but he knew it wasn't. He was tired. He wanted to lean over and put his head on the passenger seat and close his eyes. He fought tears. He fought drowsiness. He heard Vicki call out, "OK! OK, Judd!"

He waved and shifted into reverse. Judd slowly began to back out, carefully watching Vicki's signals. She made a circular motion with her index finger, and he turned the wheel. It was the wrong way. She quickly reversed the motion. He felt his car nudge the one next to him. He pulled back in and straightened out, taking another shot at it. This time he turned the other way and she signaled him until he was within inches of the crashed car behind him. He rolled down his window. "No way to clear it?" he asked.

"No way," she said.

"Let me get a line on it, then," he said. "I want to have the straightest shot at that bumper I can get in this small space."

"Back straight up from where you are then," Vicki said.

When Judd did, the bumper of his car finally nudged the car in the way. "I'm gonna go back up to the guardrail now," he said. "Let me know if I get out of line."

Judd edged forward slowly. At one point Vicki said, "Right, right, right." Judd feathered the steering wheel to the right. "Perfect," Vicki said. "As soon as you touch the guardrail, you're right in line."

"You'd better get out of the way, then," Judd said. "I'm going to have to ram it."

He waited until Vicki was clear. With his seat belt fastened, Judd took a deep breath, grimaced, and closed his eyes. He floored the accelerator.

With a squeal of tires, a crash, and a scraping, the blocking car was driven out of the way. Vicki yelped, and Judd didn't know if it was out of fear or excitement. Whichever, their little plan had succeeded, at least for the moment.

She jumped into the passenger's side and buckled herself in. Judd was able to back out of his parking space behind the car he had just pushed and would have to keep bumping it to give him room to get around it and head toward the exit. Once he did that, it appeared he had a fairly clear shot past the pay booths and into the gridlock of traffic that appeared to have moved hardly an inch since this whole ordeal had begun.

Vicki put her hand on Judd's arm. He stopped about six feet back of where emergency crews were still trying to extricate the idling Blazer from the guardrail. "It looks clear," Judd said. "I'm sure we can get past."

"I know," she said. "I just thought maybe we should thank God for helping us get out of here."

Judd nodded and bowed his head, wondering if she meant he should pray aloud, or she was going to, or what? When she said nothing, he began. "Lord, thanks. We didn't know what to—"

A nearly deafening engine roar and high-pitched squeal made Judd jump, and he looked up just in time to see workers diving out of the way of the Blazer. It had been lodged into the guardrail at a crazy angle, and apparently someone decided to set something on the accelerator and shift it into gear while others attempted to rock it free.

Whatever they had lodged against the gas pedal had made the engine race at top speed. Three wheels spun crazily, causing the screeching, but the fourth bit deep into the rail. The Blazer shuddered and shook, appearing as if it might explode. The tires sent smelly smoke everywhere.

As Judd and Vicki watched, the stuck tire somehow dislodged and sent the Blazer nose first into the low concrete ceiling with a horrific crash. All four wheels now burning rubber, the empty Blazer hit the floor, bouncing and careening into the cars around it.

The four-wheel-drive vehicle lurched directly in front of Judd, slammed the next guardrail, and flipped over forward, landing atop the last car he had moved. It drove the roof of that car all the way to the seat and rested atop the wreckage, tires still racing. The workers sprinted to the crash, and one reached in to turn off the engine.

Judd sat there with his mouth open. He turned to look at Vicki, whose eyes were wide and unblinking. "We could have been killed," she said. "If that had happened a couple of minutes ago, we would be dead for sure."

"Just think if we had gotten here earlier," Judd said, "and hadn't received Christ yet."

Now Judd knew exactly how to pray, and there was no awkwardness or wondering how to begin.

There was a certain sense of freedom in being able to drive even those few yards from the tangled garage and into the stalled traffic, but Judd knew that they wouldn't be getting far very fast that night. To him, this traffic jam was just like his new life. He knew where he was going, but he had no idea how he was going to get there, or when.

**15**

**LIONEL** awoke, terribly uncomfortable, about an hour before dawn. Ryan had provided him with a sleeping bag, but the Daleys' backyard, despite its manicured appearance, was hard and bumpy anyway. His back was sore, his whole body ached from the long bike ride, and he was still sad.

Lionel tried to pray. When he had been a phony, a kid in a Christian family who pretended to be like everyone else in the clan, it never surprised him that God seemed distant. He couldn't remember when God had seemed close. He knew that was because he had never become a true Christian, and that was also why he had been left behind.

But now shouldn't it be different? He knew God was real. He knew the Bible was true. And he knew for sure that when he had finally prayed to receive Christ—even though it was too late for him to be "caught up together in the clouds" with his family to meet Christ, as the Bible put it—God truly heard him. He felt forgiven, and he was sure he was saved. But his grief over the loss of his parents—though they were in heaven and not dead—and his horror over what had happened to

137

Uncle André, plus the sheer exhaustion of trying to figure out what to do next, had caught up with him.

Whatever warm fuzzy feeling he might have hoped would go with his decision and his salvation had been covered over by his sense of regret and loss. And so he prayed. Just like before, it seemed his prayers were bouncing off the ceiling— or in this case, the canvas roof of the tent.

Lionel rolled onto his side and squinted at Ryan in the darkness. The little guy was sleeping soundly. At least he was sleeping deeply. Lionel had no idea whether it was really a sound sleep or not. What a horrible thing Ryan had been through. He didn't know what this was all about, but to him it had to look like something very spooky. It was one thing to be offered hope, to know you could still come to Christ and be saved for the future. But Ryan's parents had been killed and certainly didn't seem to have been Christians.

It was no wonder Ryan seemed angry, even angry with God. If all of what had happened was true, the way Bruce Barnes explained it—and Lionel knew it was—Ryan had to be drowning in confusion. What must he think of a God who would allow his parents to die and leave him behind while Christians disappeared into heaven?

Lionel's prayers to that point had been centered on himself. But now he found himself praying for other people. He knew it was hopeless to pray about something that had already happened, but he couldn't help pleading with God to assure him that maybe, just maybe, André had come to Christ before he was murdered or committed suicide. He even prayed the same thing for Ryan's parents. Was it possible someone could have been telling Mr. Daley about Christ just before the pilot of his plane disappeared, and could he have been saved just before they crashed?

Lionel knew that was a long shot, and he could never know anyway, but he could hope, couldn't he? And as long as he was hoping, maybe Mrs. Daley had had someone rush to her before she died and tell her about Jesus.

Lionel leaned on his elbow. He knew he was hoping for too much. Quietly, he rolled over and stood, ducking to keep from hitting the top of the tent. He wanted to groan like his father did after sitting or lying in the same position for too long. But Lionel didn't want to wake Ryan. And anyway, he wasn't a middle-aged man. He was thirteen years old. There was no need to groan. He had simply overdone it, that was all.

Lionel moved to the flap and began unzipping it. He heard Ryan grunt and move, so he stopped and waited. An inch at a time, he carefully opened the flap and moved outside into the cool dew. He wanted to go to the bathroom, and there was nothing about Ryan's house that scared him. In fact, he wished Ryan would get over his fear so they could enjoy a little more comfort. He knew he would sleep better in the house, whether Ryan would or not.

Lionel tiptoed inside. After using the bathroom, he sat in the kitchen, staring at the photographs stuck to the refrigerator. Lionel hadn't known too many only children. Almost everybody he knew had at least one brother or sister, and most had more than that.

Lionel decided he would not have wanted to be an only child. Sure, there had to be advantages, but he would have missed knowing his older sister Clarice, the one he usually just called Reece. If ever there was someone who really lived out her faith, it was Reece. His mother and dad had been good Christians too, but it's hard to see only the good sides of your parents. His little brother and sister, Ronnie and Talia, had been great kids too, though they usually had gotten on his nerves.

It was Clarice who had almost made him a believer in time to be ready for the Rapture. She hadn't known he wasn't a Christian, of course. No one had, except André. And where was André now?

Clarice, with her sweet spirit and her prayer life, and the way her smile had seemed to sum up her whole life—she had been the best example of a Christian he knew. Maybe she had been too good an example. There had been times he knew he couldn't live up to her example, even if he had been a Christian. Now he knew how dumb he had been. He knew better. He knew he wasn't supposed to live up to anything. He was just supposed to trust Christ and be thankful for the gift of salvation. But it was a gift he had never received.

Lionel noticed Mr. Ryan's sales awards. Those didn't mean much now. Ryan might have been proud of his dad, but whatever he had done and however he had been rewarded, that hadn't helped him when the end came.

Lionel moseyed back outside and began unzipping the tent flap again. He heard Ryan gasp. "Lionel! Someone's trying to get in!"

"It's just me, Ryan. I was inside."

"Oh! You scared me!"

"Sorry. It was just getting too close in here."

"I'm not going to be able to stand staying in this tent, Lionel. But I can't go into my house either. It's like a nightmare, like I can't even force myself to go through the door. Does your house feel that way to you?"

"Sort of, but I think I'll get over it. I mean, those clothes give me the creeps, but maybe if I just gathered 'em up and put 'em away, it wouldn't be so bad. I think one night in this tent is enough for me too. You wanna just go to my place now?"

"I was hoping you'd say that."

It was still dark when Ryan and Lionel packed their stuff in backpacks and rode off toward Lionel's. They both skidded to a stop two blocks from Lionel's house several minutes later, just as it came into view. A beat up old car was parked out front, next to a late-model van, and men were moving in and out of the house.

"Who are they?" Ryan asked.

"I have no idea," Lionel said, his heart thumping. "Let's get closer without letting them see us."

He and Ryan took a left and circled around the back way. "I wonder if they're looters," Lionel whispered when they dismounted and came toward the house from the back.

"Robbing your house?" Ryan said. "That's happening a lot."

"I can't let 'em do it," Lionel said.

"There are a lot of them and only one of you."

"There are two of us, Ryan."

"Don't get me in on this. This isn't my fight."

"What're you now, a chicken? I would have defended your house against looters. You want 'em to clean me out?"

"What do I care? It's not my place."

"Some kind of a friend you are."

"I never said I was your friend, Lionel."

Lionel stopped and stared at Ryan. What was this all of a sudden? "Oh, I get it," he said. "I'm fine as long as I'm keeping you company and giving you something to think about besides yourself and your parents. But as soon as I need you to help me a little, you're done with me."

"I'm only saying we just met, Lionel. Don't go thinking I'm your best friend who's going to be with you through everything."

"Believe me, Ryan, I'll never make that mistake again. Why don't you ride on home and stay in your tent until you're brave enough to go in the house."

"Stop it! That's not fair!"

"Face it, Ryan, you're a coward."

"What're you gonna do, Lionel? Take on these guys by yourself?"

"Looks like I might have to. This is my house. I can't let people walk off with our stuff."

"I'll stay here and be ready to call for help if you need it."

"Well, I sure hope no one sneaks up behind you and says *boo!*"

Ryan crouched in the alley, shaking his head. Lionel crept toward the house.

---

Just before dawn, Judd Thompson Jr. pulled into the trailer park where Vicki Byrne lived. It was a good thing they had talked all night in the heavy stop-and-go traffic all the way from O'Hare to Mount Prospect, because she was sleeping now. Judd didn't have to wake her after getting directions to her place.

He couldn't remember having been somewhere like this before. He had an uncle who had lived in a trailer when Judd was a very small boy, but his recollections of the place were vague. He remembered his uncle more than his uncle's trailer. He certainly didn't remember it being as run-down as the ones in this park, and he would have been a scared little kid if he had seen the rough characters then that he was seeing now. They were shirtless, tattooed, scowling bearded men and hard-looking women who appeared as if they would just as soon smack you as look at you.

One of the black leather–clad men stepped in front of Judd's car and slammed both palms on the hood. "Where do you think you're goin', boy!"

Judd hit the brake and rolled his window down a couple of
inches. He was so scared he could hardly speak. Fortunately,
he didn't have to. "Wait, Judd!" Vicki said, roused by the
noise. "I know this guy!" She leaned across Judd and rolled his
window all the way down. "What's going on, Vince?"

"What's going on?" he repeated. "You don't know what's
going on? Where you been?"

"With a friend. Now what's up?"

"Well, while we were sleeping, somebody came through
here and looted and burned all the trailers where nobody was
home. Some of the trailers are trashed, and some of 'em are
burned to the ground."

"What about ours?"

"You don't want to know."

"Yes I do! Now what?"

"Burned, Vick. I'm sorry. You know if we'd a seen anybody,
we'd a killed 'em."

"I know you would."

"So, where are your people?"

"Disappeared, Vince."

Vince stepped back and ran his hand through his hair.
"Wow! No kiddin'! What about your brother up north?"

"Gone too."

"You're sure?"

"Yup. Totally. I'm the only one left."

"What do you make of this, Vicki? You're not buyin' that
this is all God's doing, are you?"

"As a matter of fact I am, Vince. Look around. Look who's
missing. What else could it be?"

"I sure hope you're wrong."

"I hope I'm not. Can we get back there and see the trailer?"

"Probably. There's not much to see. You sure you want to?"

"I want to."

"Take it easy."

Vince backed out of the way and waved Judd on. "Let this guy through!" Vince hollered. "Leave this car alone! It's Vicki and a friend!"

As Judd carefully maneuvered his way through the water and mud and debris, people along the asphalt drive and walkways approached the car with sad faces and sorrowful comments to Vicki. "We're sorry, sweetheart," they said. "You can stay with us. Call us. Come for dinner. We'll help you."

Vicki waved her thanks at each person and showed Judd where to drive. When what was left of the Byrne family trailer came into view, she gasped. Judd couldn't even make out the color of the accents or the trim. The trailer was just a pile of twisted, smoking, blistered metal now. Its tires were flat and melted, only the stabilizing bar and bricks still recognizable.

Vicki lowered her head and sobbed as the crowd that had gathered around the trailer slowly moved away, seeming to Judd to want to leave Vicki to her own grief. He had heard her story. He knew she would not have felt any emotional attachment to this place before. But what must it now represent for her? She had grown up here, rebelled against her parents here, broken their curfew here.

She had learned to smoke and drink and run with a bad crowd. And though she had hated it, she had seen her parents and her brother and sister come to Christ in this little home. Now they were gone, she was alone, and the trailer was no more.

*At least,* Judd thought, *she knows the truth now.*

**16**

**LIONEL** Washington could barely breathe as he sneaked up to the driveway at the side of his own house. He peered into the basement window where he and his uncle André had shared the foldout couch just two nights before, the night of the vanishings all over the world.

Someone appeared to be setting up housekeeping down there. Lionel saw boxes of food, piles of strange clothes, a fan, a clock, a small bedside stand. Who thought they were free to move into his house, just because the rest of his family was gone? He thought he would find people taking stuff away, not moving stuff in.

Two men about Lionel's uncle's age burst from the door in a trot, heading toward the van. Lionel was startled but scampered back to behind the corner of the house before they noticed him. "This is going to be great," one of them said. "This is a good way for André to work off his debt."

"You gonna let him stay here?"

The other laughed. "He's the one who put us onto this place, man! 'Course he can stay here. Long as he behaves himself."

145

They were both laughing now as the door slapped shut behind them. While they were busy in the van, Lionel slipped into the house and up the stairs. Three or four other people were inside, but they ignored him. What was this, anyway?

Clearly, these people were moving in, taking over the house as if it were their own. The piles of clothes that had been the only remaining evidence of the other members of Lionel's family had already been gathered up and put somewhere. Lionel bounded down the stairs to see if his father's pajamas and robe and slippers were gone too.

At the bottom of the stairs he was met by the two who had gone out to the van. He recognized them as André's so-called friends, the ones he said he owed money. "Well, if it ain't the nephew!" the taller one said. "What's your name again?"

Lionel was not as brave as he tried to sound. "My name's Washington, and this is my house."

"Is it now? You own this place?"

"My family does."

"But your family is gone, ain't it?"

"So what?"

"So you need someone to look out for you and take care of the place, and that's what we're going to do for you. And no charge."

"Says who?"

"Says us, punk, so watch your mouth. André told us everybody but you disappeared from this place. He's got seniority in the family now."

"What's that mean?"

"That means of the only two people left who can claim this place, he's the oldest. I mean, he is older than you, ain't he?"

" 'Course."

"Well, there you go."

"So where *is* my uncle André?"

"He's around."

"How do you know?"

"He owes us money, that's how we know. He'll show up here, and he'll let us stay until he pays. We know he'll never pay. Why should he? This is the best deal for him and for us."

Lionel wanted to ask them what they would say if he told them André was dead. But he didn't want to give that away yet. When he said nothing, the shorter guy said, "Don't worry, little dude. You can stay here too. Just stay out of our way and keep your mouth shut."

"In my own house?"

"You'd better get used to the fact that this is not your house anymore, kid."

"What if I call the police?"

"You think the police have time to worry about you right now? We could kill you and bury you and leave a pile of your clothes on a chair, and they'd believe you were one of those people who disappeared. Trust me, boy, you're better off with a place to stay. We'll even let you eat, maybe teach you the business."

"The business?"

"The business of makin' money, son."

"Crime, you mean?"

"To some people. To us it's business. You can get in on the ground floor. What do you say?"

Lionel was afraid of what they might do if he tried to kick them out. He didn't want them to know he had no intention of staying with them. He just shrugged and trotted back upstairs. He filled his dad's old canvas duffel bag with everything—and more than—he thought he'd ever need, and he lugged it downstairs.

"Pick your own place to crash, dude," the taller one said. "After all, this *was* your house."

"It still is!" Lionel yelled as he ran past them and out the door. He was shocked that they ignored him. No one even tried to catch him as he raced down the driveway, into the alley, and back toward the bikes, where he hoped Ryan was standing guard. The bikes were there. Ryan wasn't.

---

"Wait here, please," Vicki Byrne told Judd. She stepped out of the car and stood staring at the pile of rubble that had once been her home. She was puzzled at her own reaction. How she had once hated this place! It was too small, too dingy. It told the world she was poor, that her family was of little account, that she was trailer trash.

That very trailer had made her resent people who lived in normal homes, let alone rich people who lived in large houses. She had assumed all kinds of evil things about people who seemed above her in society. She didn't know if it was true that they were mean and nasty and selfish, but it made her feel a little better to think they were not worthy of whatever they had and she didn't.

But now, as she stood in the cool of the morning, staring at the slowly rising smoke and smelling the acrid fumes, she was overcome with a longing for that little trailer house. She remembered how it looked, how it smelled, how it creaked when she walked through it. She had even learned where to step to keep from making noise when she tried to sneak in after curfew.

That seemed so long ago now, but it had been just two nights before that she thought she had gotten away with something. She had sneaked in late and thought her parents were asleep. Only later did she realize that they and her little sister and her big brother in Michigan had been among those who had disappeared before midnight Chicago time.

Was it only her realization that they had been right about God that made her feel sentimental toward a place she used to hate? Or was it just her fatigue and grief over the loss of her family that put them in a new light? She knew it was all that and more. She had finally come to see that she had been wrong about God. She knew she had been a sinner and that she needed him. And when she had committed her life to him, he began right away to change how she felt about things. She saw what a fool she had been, what an ungrateful rebel. How could she have been so blind? What had been her problem?

She had not wanted to admit that her parents had really changed, but it was obvious to everyone, herself included. She had been so determined to hang on, to control her own life, that she refused to let anyone know she even noticed the differ-ence. That was what hurt her the most as she gazed at the remains of everything she owned except the clothes she was wearing.

What a strange feeling that was, knowing she would have to start over from scratch. No clothes. No belongings. No nothing.

She turned slowly and moved back toward Judd's car. She had never hung with anyone who drove such a nice car, certainly not a sixteen-year-old. So far Judd had seemed to fit the rich-kid mold she had imagined, but there were good and nice and kind parts to him too. And like he had said, they were now brother and sister in Christ. She'd better learn to like and trust him, she decided. With not a possession to her name, she was probably going to have to depend on him for a while.

"Are you all right?" he asked when she slid back into the car.

She shrugged. "I guess. I'm not sure what else can go wrong."

"You're going to have to stay with me, you know," he said.

"Oh, Judd, I couldn't expect you to do that for me."

"I'd give you your privacy and everything. I mean, I wouldn't take advantage or do anything wrong or—"

"I know. But I just couldn't—"

"Sure you could. You have no choice."

"Someone here will give me a place to stay."

"No, no I insist. I have money and credit cards. My dad has some bank accounts, and I know he'd want me to use them to survive."

"Judd, it doesn't make sense."

"Of course it does. You need clothes, stuff, a place to live, food."

"But why should I expect that from you?"

"You think God is going to take care of you?"

"Now's the best time to find out," she said.

"Well, I'm how he's going to do it." Judd pulled slowly out of the trailer park.

"You're what? And where are you going?"

"I'm what God will use to take care of you. You're a Christian now, and he's going to watch over you and make sure you're taken care of. He's going to use me to do that."

"So you're God's guy now, his right hand man?"

"You could say that."

"So, where are we going?"

"To my house."

"Judd!"

"Just let me do this, Vicki. I really think God wants me to, and I'll feel like I'm letting him down if I don't."

Vicki found that hard to argue with. Maybe she *was* supposed to let Judd do this. Maybe this really *was* God's way of providing for her. "But if we stay in the same house, won't we get tired of each other and start hating each other?"

"I doubt it," Judd said, and Vicki was surprised. She really wasn't sure what she thought of this guy. He was not her type, and she probably never would have given him a second glance before. But he was being nice now. And that had been a nice thing to say, that he doubted he would get tired of her.

But he didn't know her either. He didn't know how she could be. She was independent and crabby and grouchy and self-centered. At least she *had* been that way. Could it be that those were things God would start to change in her? Or would she have the same personality and character, but just be a Christian now? She wasn't sure how it all worked, but she knew her parents had seemed different almost overnight.

She felt different; she knew that. Even with the fear and the dread of having lost everyone close to her in an instant, she found herself thinking of other people. Not every second, and not every time. But in just the few short hours she had lived since deciding to become a Christian, she noticed some changes.

"I'll check it out," she told Judd. "I'll see where you live and see if it would work for a short time. But I don't plan on being in your way for long. And I can't be sure it would work out at all."

Judd nodded. Vicki could tell he wanted it to work. But maybe he was just afraid to be alone. That was all right. So was she. It would be good to have someone to talk to.

"I'll tell you one thing," she said, as Judd drove toward his house, "I'm starving and I'm exhausted. If you've got any food and a place for me to sleep, I'll take it."

"Coming right up," Judd said.

———————————————

Ryan Daley had panicked. He had stayed close enough to keep an eye on Lionel until Lionel had sneaked into the house. Ryan was sure Lionel would get himself kidnapped or shot or something, and then what would Ryan do? He felt like such a coward, trying to get out of doing anything dangerous. But he had just lost his parents. How was he supposed to feel brave all of a sudden?

Ryan had crouched behind a neighbor's garage with his and Lionel's bikes. He didn't know what he would do if Lionel called for help, but he stayed out of sight and ready anyway. He was startled when Lionel went in the house when the two older guys came out to get something from the van. When they went back in, Ryan was sure Lionel was in big trouble. When he didn't come out for a while—and neither did the older two—Ryan was convinced something awful had happened.

Then there came Lionel, bounding out of the house with a big duffel bag over his shoulder. Ryan convinced himself that Lionel could be running only because someone was after him. A stranger. A bad guy. Someone with a knife or a gun. And Lionel was leading whoever that was right to Ryan. He didn't even take the time to mount his bike. He just ran off as fast as he could.

He had been doing a lot of that lately.

# 17

**VICKI** felt awkward when Judd pulled into the driveway of his big suburban home. She had been in a house that size only twice before, both times for parties. She hadn't felt comfortable then either. But this was different. There was no party here. There was no one here but the two of them. When was the last time she had been alone with a teenage boy without winding up drinking, smoking, doing dope, or worse?

Judd seemed nervous, showing her around, telling her she could stay in the guest bedroom downstairs while he would keep his room upstairs. "Doesn't it give you the creeps to stay so close to where the rest of your family used to be?" she asked.

"A little," he said. "But I have no choice. Where else would I go?"

Vicki had just been thinking the same thing. She didn't say so. All she said was, "I hate to ask, but do you have anything to eat around here?"

"Name it," Judd said. "We have anything and everything you want."

Vicki and Judd raided the refrigerator and ate well. She

noticed he was as heavy-eyed as she was. "I don't like to sleep during the day," she said. "But I'm going to pass out sitting here if I don't lie down."

Judd pointed to the guest room. "I'm going to sleep too," he said. "I wouldn't be surprised if I sleep all day and all night, but I've never done that before. More likely, I'll wake up after seven or eight hours, like I always do."

"Me too," she said. "But I don't remember ever being so exhausted."

"I'd say we've been through a lot, wouldn't you?" he said.

They both laughed for the first time since they'd known each other.

Vicki quickly grew serious. She said, "You know, Judd, I'm going to have to ask you to run me somewhere tomorrow so I can get some clothes. I'll keep track of whatever it costs and pay you back."

"No problem," he said, "but first you ought to check my mom's closet. She was about your size."

"Really? What size was she?"

"I don't know. She was about your size, that's all I know."

"Wow," Vicki said. "I hope I'm still thin when I'm her age."

"If you believe what Bruce Barnes believes, we haven't got much more than seven years to live anyway."

"Plenty of time to get fat," Vicki said, shrugging. What kind of a remark was that? She had never engaged in small talk with anyone before. In the past everything she talked about had been centered on what she liked or didn't like, what she was going to do or not do. She hated talking about normal things—"nothing" things, she always called them. This was the stuff adults and other boring types always talked about.

"You can have whatever you want of my mom's stuff,"

Judd said. "I mean, she's obviously not coming back. Will it make you feel weird?"

"Weird?"

"Wearing someone else's clothes, someone who disappeared."

"How will you feel seeing me in your mom's clothes?"

"I don't guess I'd mind. You'll probably wear them differently—I mean, tied up or cut off or tucked in or untucked or whatever."

"Yeah, and I hope it will be temporary anyway. I want to get a job and get myself some new stuff."

"Sure. But meanwhile . . ."

"Meanwhile I'll try to get by if there's anything that works, so I won't have to wear dirty clothes."

"Good. You want to look for some stuff now, in case you want to change when you get up? I mean, you don't have to. You look perfectly fine, but you might want some fresh . . . not that what you're wearing doesn't look fresh or anything, but—"

"It's all right, Judd. Yes, I would like to see if there's something I could wear when I wake up. Did your mother wear jeans, sweaters, that kind of stuff, or only dresses and old ladies' stuff?"

"Here's a picture of her."

Vicki studied the photograph of a very youthful, trim, and definitely petite woman. "Is this a recent picture?"

"Yeah."

"She looks very stylish."

"My friends said she was a babe."

"To her face?"

"No, to mine. I was proud of her."

Judd was talking about his mother as if she were dead. It seemed to Vicki his voice was about to break.

"I can see why you were proud of her," Vicki said. "If she has a lot of clothes like this, I'd be honored to wear them. Remember, Judd, she's not dead. If everything we believe is true, and we both know it is, she's in heaven."

"I know," he said, sitting on the couch and sighing. "But she might as well be dead. She's dead to me. I won't see her again."

"Not here, anyway," Vicki agreed, "but in heaven or when Jesus comes back."

"I guess I wouldn't want to see her in heaven," Judd said. "That would mean I'd have to die within the next seven years."

"Not necessarily," Vicki said, yawning. "Bruce says the seven last years don't actually begin until Israel signs some sort of a treaty with that Antichrist guy."

Again Vicki was stunned at what was coming out of her own mouth. Would she have heard of or known any of this a week ago? Would she have cared? Would she have talked about it? Hardly. She had never cared about politics, especially international politics. She didn't really care about much outside her own trailer park. Now not only was life in the park gone, but she also was talking about global affairs with a rich kid she had just met.

"Nobody even knows if the Antichrist is around yet," Judd said. "But Bruce said he already has his eye on somebody."

"I don't think I'd even want to know who it was," Vicki said.

"I sure do," Judd said. "I don't want to be sucked in by him and fooled."

"Well, that's true."

"You want to look at those clothes now?"

"Sure. Then I'm getting some sleep."

Judd directed her to his parents' bedroom and left Vicki to

look around in there for herself. She found it eerie. Not forty-
eight hours earlier, people were living here with no idea their
minutes were numbered. It was a neat room, but stuff was left
about, the way it is when people think they'll be back to tidy up.
A jewelry box was open. A drawer was half shut. One side of the
closet was open, the other shut. Books were on the nightstands;
half a glass of water was on the floor next to the bed.

Vicki was so tired she could barely keep her eyes open. She
checked the closet and wondered what it must be like to have the
money to live this way. Judd's mom's closet looked like a department store. Shoes, slacks, blouses, blazers, dresses, belts, you name
it. She had been serious when she'd said Judd's mom looked stylish, but these kinds of things had never been her style. She had
favored a hotter look, a street look, lots of black and leather.

Vicki pulled out a pantsuit that looked way too old for her,
but she imagined it with the top untucked and the blazer
open. She held it against her body and looked in the mirror on
the back of the bedroom door.

Vicki was startled by her own appearance. She took two
steps backward and sat on the bed, the hangered pantsuit still
pressed against her. She stared at her greasy hair, her makeupless
face, her puffy eyes. When was the last time she had paid attention to her face without a load of makeup and mascara? She
looked old and tired, yet her youthfulness peeked through too.
The girl in the mirror looked scared, tired, haggard. She had for
so long hidden that little girl, trying to make herself appear
older. Maybe it had worked, but she didn't want to appear older
now. She wanted to be who she was, a fourteen-year-old girl
who had finally come face-to-face with God. Finally she knew
who he was and what he was about. She had given herself to
him when she looked just like this, and she didn't want to
change.

Sure, she hoped she looked better when she had had a little sleep and a shower and clean hair. But she was finished trying to look like a woman in her twenties. No more hiding. No more pretending to be something she wasn't. She would wear an older woman's clothes, but she would wear them in such a way that she was honest with herself, with others, and with God. She was a teenager who had been left behind, but she was also one who had seen what was right and acted upon it. She belonged to God now, and she would present herself to him as she really was.

There was nothing wrong with looking nice, but she no longer felt the need to look hard, or sexy, or old. She lay back on the bed and stared at the ceiling, Mrs. Thompson's pantsuit draped over her. In a minute, she decided, she would get up and head for the guest room. But within seconds she had drifted into a deep, deep sleep.

---

Ryan Daley dove behind a hedge across the street and a block behind Lionel's house. Lionel came charging by, muttering, "Where are you, you little chicken?"

"I'm right here," Ryan answered.

Lionel skidded to a stop and glared at Ryan. "You *are* a chicken!" he said. "Look at you! Hiding there like a little scared rabbit."

"So, what am I, a chicken or a rabbit?"

Lionel shook his head, looking disgusted. Ryan found it hard to believe this boy was only a year older than he was. Lionel seemed so much older, so much more mature. He seemed like the kind of guy who could get along on his own, who would stand up to bad guys like he had apparently just done. Ryan couldn't imagine ever doing something like that.

"We've got to get back there and get our bikes," Lionel said. "Where'd you run off to, anyway?"

"What do you mean?" Ryan said. "You can see where I ran off to. I'm right here, aren't I?"

"I mean *why* did you run off?"

"Because I saw you being chased."

"No one was chasing me."

"Why were you running then?"

"I figured if I surprised them by bolting out of there, I'd have a big enough head start that they'd give up before they started. They must have."

"But, Lionel, they'll get us when we go back for the bikes."

"You want to walk all the way to your house?"

"My house? I thought we were going to stay here!"

Lionel sighed and told Ryan the story. "So I don't think we're staying here until I can get the police to throw them out."

"So call the police."

"Maybe I will. But don't you think they have enough to worry about right now, without trying to figure out who owns my house and who should be there or shouldn't? I mean, if the cops find out I'm thirteen and the only one left in my family, they'll try to put me in some orphanage or something."

"Orphanage?" Ryan repeated. No way. He had never heard anything good about an orphanage. Talk about a nightmare. Worst of all, when he thought about it, he realized that now he *was* an orphan. Being abandoned by his parents had always been his biggest fear, and he didn't think that was just because he was an only child. He was sure he would have felt that way even if he had had brothers and sisters, and that made him wonder if Lionel felt the same. He had to, didn't he? But he believed this was all about Jesus and heaven and everything, so maybe Lionel was handling it better. At least that's the way it seemed to Ryan.

Lionel also seemed more interested in getting their bikes. "I want my bike too," Ryan said, "but I'm still not going inside my house."

"Man, you've *got* to get over that," Lionel said. "You can't sleep in a tent the rest of your life, and I know *I'm* not going to."

"I just can't go in my house," Ryan said. "What are we going to do?"

"We're going to start by getting our bikes. Now come on."

Lionel left his duffel bag in the bushes, and Ryan followed him as he crept back toward his house. The two guys who knew André were still casually going in and coming out of the house, unloading stuff from their van. Lionel said, "Let's wait until they've just carried some stuff in, then we can run up, get our bikes, and speed away."

"And what if they see us and come after us in that car or that van?"

"What if Chicken Little was right and the sky falls in?" Lionel said. "You've got to learn to take some chances, man."

Ryan figured that was supposed to be funny, but he didn't laugh. Lionel was making him feel like a wuss. He had never felt that way before. He was an athlete, a tough guy. Kids looked up to him, respected him. What would they think of him now, running away and hiding?

But how was he supposed to act? The worst thing that could happen to a kid had happened to him. His parents were dead and gone, and he had no one left. Anytime anything bad had happened in his life before, his parents had been there for him. When his dad was gone to some sales training school for three months one time, his mother had been there. When she was in the hospital for back surgery, his dad had been there. Neither could do everything the other had always done with him and for him, but they tried. And they had made do until the other parent was home and back into the routine.

But what was he supposed to do now? Both parents were gone, and he couldn't talk to either of them about the loss of the other. He felt alone in the world. He really didn't want to irritate Lionel. If he lost this friend too, where would he be?

"OK," Ryan said finally. "When they go in the house, they've been staying inside for a couple minutes before they come back out. As soon as the screen door slams behind them, we go. That should give us enough time."

Lionel looked at him, and Ryan thought he actually detected admiration, or at least respect, on his face. "All right," Lionel said. "Now you're thinking. Let's go."

They crouched behind a corner of the house and peered at the door. The two came out, laughing and joking. "Too easy, man," one said. "This is too easy. Easy and sweet. Wait till André gets here."

From the front, Ryan heard the two grunting as they dragged something heavy from the van. "That's the last of it, then?" he heard.

"Yup, that's all. Set it down a second so I can kick that door shut."

Ryan heard the sound of the van door closing. Lionel and Ryan peeked out as the two lugged a small couch up to the door at the side of the house. The two fumbled with the door, finally hollering inside for "one of you lazy slobs to get this door for us!"

A young woman came running. "Just ask, you two. I'm here and I'm not lazy!"

They moved into the house with the couch, and the screen door slapped shut behind them. Lionel took off like a shot, and Ryan was right behind him. Fast as he had been for years, he couldn't keep up with Lionel. Lionel must have been really scared or really fast because he was moving like the wind.

They reached the bikes, and Lionel was quickly up on his and riding off in the direction of his hidden duffel bag. Ryan saw his own big bag on the ground next to his bike and considered leaving it right there. How would he handle it and ride fast too? But he couldn't leave it. He needed everything in there. And besides, those guys weren't even coming back out to the van, were they? Hadn't they said that was all of it?

Ryan bent to grab the bag and slowly mounted his bike, hoping to make no noise or draw any attention to himself. He had to keep one foot on the ground for balance as he slowly wobbled off, and once he had to come to a full stop to shift the weight of the bag. Just as he was starting to gain a little momentum, that scary, tingly feeling of fear raced up and down his back. Lionel was reaching down to grab his own bag from the bushes a block away, but Ryan was sure he heard footsteps and shouting behind him.

# 18

**JUDD** found himself shy and embarrassed about having a girl in his house when he was alone. He had dated before, of course, but his parents had put such restrictions on him that he had pretty much given up asking girls out. He saw them at school and after school, but he didn't have one special girl.

He was curious, of course, about who would be there and who would have disappeared when school began again. And who knew when that might be? A few days ago he wouldn't have cared if he never went to school again. Now he wondered, if Bruce Barnes was right about the Rapture signaling the end of the world in about seven years, whether school was worth anything. If it was true that the Antichrist, whomever that was, might soon sign some sort of an agreement with Israel, the seven years would begin, and Jesus would return again before Judd turned twenty-four.

While that might have convinced him that he didn't have a whole life and career to study for, he also realized how much time he had wasted in school already. For as old as he was and the grade he was in, he felt he hardly knew anything. Maybe it would be all right for school to start up again, once this traffic and fire and death mess had been cleaned up. Then he would try to learn as much as he could, at least about the basics, so he would be able to get along on his own for the rest of the time.

If all this was true, Judd felt obligated to serve God by telling others that they still had a chance. There was certainly no reason to pursue a big moneymaking career. He may have never before had a goal, a purpose, a reason for doing anything other than pleasing himself, but he sure did now. True, this had been thrust upon him. He'd had little choice. Of course, he could have chosen to ignore God, to thumb his nose at the Creator and continue living for himself. But he had been a rebel, not an ignoramus. Clearly, God had convinced him of the truth, and now Judd had made the decision himself. He had a lot of pain and grief and regret to work through, but from now on, it was he and God all the way.

Judd waited politely for Vicki to emerge from his parents' bedroom. He wanted to tell her she could feel free to use the shower in the master bath. When she shut the door almost all the way, he assumed she might be trying on something in front of the mirror. He didn't want to walk in on her.

But she didn't come out, and he heard no water running. He looked at his watch and decided that in five minutes he would discreetly knock, tell her about the shower, and finally be able to get upstairs to collapse in his own bed. He sat on the couch and clicked on the television to check the progress of the massive cleanup. Then he decided to call Bruce Barnes and see if he and Vicki could come by that evening or the next morning, whenever they woke up, to tell him some news. Judd was sure Bruce would be thrilled that they had made their decisions. Also, he wanted to know where he might find those other two kids, Lionel and Ryan. It seemed they were all in this together and that they should watch out for each other.

Judd muted the TV and dialed the church. He reached an answering machine with Bruce's voice on the greeting. Bruce sounded as shocked as anybody. This must've been a message he recorded within a couple of hours of the Rapture.

The message said: "You have reached New Hope Village Church. We are planning a weekly Bible study, but for the time being we will meet just once each Sunday at 10 A.M. While our entire staff, except me, and most of our congregation are gone, the few of us left are maintaining the building and distributing a videotape our senior pastor prepared for such a time as this. You may come by the church office anytime to pick up a free copy, and we look forward to seeing you Sunday morning."

Judd did not leave a message, figuring he'd call back after Vicki finished showering. He looked down the hall toward his parents' room. He heard nothing and the door was still nearly closed. He began to get up and head that way when he noticed bizarre images on the TV screen. He sat back down and turned the sound up.

Breathless CNN announcers told strange stories from around the world as they showed videotaped images of people disappearing right out of their clothes. A husband videotaping his wife about to give birth caught the nurse's uniform floating to the ground and his wife's huge stomach going suddenly flat. The baby had disappeared.

Local TV stations from around the world had submitted tapes of disappearances where the vanishings had occurred in time zones where it was daytime. Judd watched, fascinated, as a groom disappeared while placing the wedding ring on his bride's finger. A funeral home in Australia reported that nearly all the mourners and the corpse had disappeared from one funeral. At the same funeral home in another funeral at the same time, only a few mourners disappeared and the corpse remained.

A video cameraman caught the action at a cemetery as three pallbearers disappeared and the other three dropped the casket, which broke open to reveal it was empty. The video panned to several freshly opened graves with bodies suddenly missing. The CNN anchorman announced that morgues all over the world reported various numbers of bodies missing.

At a soccer game between two missionary schools in Indonesia, a parent had videotaped all but one player disappearing right from their uniforms during play. The announcer said that that one remaining player had reportedly taken his own life in his remorse over the loss of his friends. Judd knew better. Judd could have been that player. That suicide was the result of despair, not of remorse. That kid knew where his friends were and knew he had missed his chance. The problem was, no one had told him he had another chance.

When the TV moved on to more mundane reports of the cleanup, of a Romanian leader planning to visit the United Nations, and of a word of comfort and encouragement from United States President Gerald Fitzhugh, Judd fought to keep his eyes open. He lay on his side on the couch, wondering if he should call out for Vicki to see if she wanted to watch any of the disappearances if they were shown again. Within minutes, with the TV droning, Judd was out. He would sleep, motionless, for hours.

---

Ryan Daley had been wrong about hearing something behind him. His imagination was playing such tricks on him that he was sure he heard footsteps and shouting and was certain someone was gaining on him, someone who might yank him right off his bike.

He was already wrestling with his heavy bag in one hand and trying to steer with the other while keeping his balance. When he wrenched around to see who was about to nab him, the motion threw him completely off-kilter. He was relieved to see no one there, but as he turned back to face the front, he was wobbling and careening toward the corner of a garage. He frantically jerked the handlebars the other way, which pitched him and his bag off the bike and into the side of the garage. He bounced and rolled up and over the bike and onto his head. A pedal punched a deep bruise into his side, and his forehead was scraped.

Mostly, Ryan felt stupid. He had been knocked off his bike and injured by absolutely no one. He glanced back at Lionel's house. All those trespassing creeps were inside. They didn't care a whit about Ryan or Lionel or what they were up to.

Slowly, painfully, Ryan remounted his bike and pedaled off, looking for Lionel. Lionel was riding in a circle in the street a block away, waiting. "Why didn't you come for me, man?" Ryan complained. "They could have had me!"

"But they didn't, did they? I looked back just as you were looking back, and I saw what you saw. Nobody. Too bad you didn't learn to ride without running into garages."

Ryan figured Lionel was only teasing him, but he wasn't in the mood for it and it made him mad. In fact, he felt more angry than he had in a long time. Ryan had been known to be a bit of a hothead in sports when things didn't go his way. And he could scream and yell at Raymie Steele and his other friends once in a while. But he felt such a rage at Lionel that he could hardly contain himself. He wanted to kill this kid, despite the fact that right then Lionel was the last friend Ryan had in the world—at least that he knew of.

Ryan imagined himself jumping off his bike and charging Lionel, knocking him off his own bike and pounding him into the ground. He wondered if Lionel knew what he was thinking, because Lionel looked strangely at Ryan, as if he was worried about him.

"Are you OK, man?" Lionel asked.

"Of course I'm not OK!" Ryan shot back. "How could I be OK? My parents are dead, I don't believe in God—at least a God who would do this—and I have nowhere to live! How could I be OK?"

"You've got a place to live," Lionel said. "*I'm* the one without a house. You just have to get over your fear and talk yourself into going inside. What do you think, that death is contagious or something? You'll be safer in your own house than any other place I can think of."

"I just can't, Lionel. Now don't pressure me."

"Well, anyway, what I really meant was are you OK with that scrape on your forehead? You need to get that cleaned and bandaged."

"Where are we going to do that?"

"At your house. Follow me."

"Lionel!"

"You don't have to go in, you big baby. I'll get the stuff and do it in the driveway. But I might try to get you inside if you'll let me."

"I want to go inside, but I can't."

"Let's worry about that when we get there."

"Don't try to make me do something I'm not ready for, Lionel."

When they arrived several minutes later, Ryan waited in

the driveway while Lionel went in through the back. When he came out with a first-aid kit, Ryan thought he was strangely silent. "What's the matter?" Ryan asked.

"You don't wanna know."

" 'Course I do. What's up?"

"I'll never get you in there now."

"Why?"

"Just hush up and hold still. This is going to sting."

Ryan had to admit to himself that he was impressed with how Lionel was taking care of him and watching out for him, even if Lionel put him down and called him names some-times. This was clearly a kid who either had it in his personal-ity or character to help others, or he had really paid attention when his parents took care of him.

Lionel pulled several squares of gauze off a roll, drenched them in a solution that smelled like a doctor's office, and told Ryan, "Close your eyes, grit your teeth, and stand still. It'll sting, but I have to clean that wound, and it won't hurt long. The air will cool it, and the pain will go away quick."

"Wait! Don't! Let me do it!"

"Yeah, sure. No way. Now come on and let me. Hurry, this stuff evaporates faster than water. Now do what I say."

Ryan held his breath and shut his eyes. He forgot to grit his teeth, but that happened automatically when Lionel set down the first-aid kit and gently touched the alcohol-drenched gauze to his raw, scraped forehead. Lionel didn't even rub it but it felt like sandpaper on Ryan's wound. Ryan started to wrench away from the pain, but Lionel seemed prepared for that. He grabbed Ryan's arm with his free hand and hung on. Ryan wanted to squeal, but he resisted, his teeth pressed tightly together.

"OK," Lionel said. "Hang on. I'm through and I'm going to

let go. Just don't touch that spot. It's clean, and when it dries we can bandage it."

"Ooooh! Ooooh!" was all Ryan could say. It felt as if it would sting forever, and it took all he had in him to keep from pressing his hand over it. But, just as Lionel had promised, in a few minutes the stinging began to fade. Soon it felt cool, then cold, then numb. "I think it's dry, Lionel," Ryan managed.

"Hold still again," Lionel said, tearing a huge bandage out of its wrapper.

"Be careful," Ryan warned.

"You sayin' I wasn't careful cleaning it?"

"No, just that—"

"This'll be the easy part. Now be brave."

Lionel was right. There was nothing to applying the bandage. Lionel kept the sticky stuff on the outside of the sore and pressed it tight. But Ryan didn't feel brave. He was feeling more and more like a little kid, and that made him mad. The trouble was, he couldn't be mad at Lionel, who was trying to toughen him up. He didn't want to be mad at his parents, though he couldn't shake the feeling that they should not have left him. He knew they hadn't meant to or chosen to, but that didn't make him feel any better. It was hard to be mad at God when you didn't believe in God. So that left only himself to be mad at for being such a weakling.

He didn't like that much. Having been a good athlete for as long as he could remember, he had never been scared of bullies or shy of older kids, unless they were way older and a lot bigger. Lionel would not have bothered him a week ago. But Ryan felt so alone, so lost. He hated the feeling and wished it would go away. But he missed his mom and dad so much he couldn't imagine that he would ever feel any better. This was no way to live, but he had to.

Ryan was grateful for Lionel's help. It was almost like having a parent for those few moments. But he wanted to know why Lionel was so serious and seemed so bothered, and he wanted to know now. "Why would I not want to go in the house?" he said.

"I don't know. Do you? Let's be brave. Let's go in. You'll be glad you did."

"Not until you tell me why you don't think I'll ever want to go in."

"All right," Lionel said. "Someone's been in there."

"What?! How do you—"

"Don't get so excited. What did you expect with all the police busy with everything else? Bad guys take advantage of these kinds of situations all the time."

"There's never been a time like this before, Lionel."

"I know, but in my uncle's neighborhood, anytime something big is happening in the city or there's a fire or anything, people get their houses robbed or looted. You just have to watch and be careful, that's all. The robbers aren't out to hurt anybody. They're just trying to get something for nothing. You have to make it hard for them to get in or easy for them to get out, and if you happen upon them, be sure they're scared enough to run off before you try to hassle them. Just like cornered animals, if they feel trapped, they'll attack. You don't want that."

"How do you know someone was in my house?"

"Because the glass in the back door was broken, the door was open, and lots of stuff is missing."

"Oh, no! Stuff we're going to need if we're going to stay alive?"

"No. All the food and everything is still there. These guys must have known what they wanted and what was valuable. Your TVs are gone, your stereo; looks like some jewelry is gone from your mother's dresser. That kind of stuff."

Ryan shook his head and sat in the driveway. "You're right," he said. "I don't ever want to go in there again."

"Don't you see, Ryan? If we lived in there, robbers would be afraid to take the risk. They'd see the lights and they'd figure adults have to be in there. You never had anyone break in before, did you?"

"Never."

"There you go. This was a normal household, people coming and going. It was too risky to break into. Somebody just checked it out while we were gone and thought maybe the family had disappeared or were gone somewhere during the emergency. They got everything valuable there was to get, and they won't need to come back."

"But what about someone else?"

"You never know."

"Then I'm not going in."

"Can I?"

"You want to live in my house?"

"Where else am I gonna live?"

"In your own house."

"Where've you been, Ryan? My house has been taken over by my uncle's enemies, and until the police have time to mess with getting them out, I'm on the street. Now are you going to let me stay in your house awhile, or not?"

"You really want to, knowing someone's been in there? Aren't you scared?"

"I've got plenty to be scared about, Ryan, just like you. But if anything happens to me, I go to heaven to see my family. I'm not sayin' I want to die, but I've got a lot more to be afraid of than that some burglar is going to come back to a house he already cleaned out."

"You're going to make me stay by myself in the tent?"

"That's up to you."

"I want to be where you are, and I want that to be outside with me."

"Ryan, I can't stand sleeping on the ground or even in a sleeping bag. I'll be miserable. You've got nice beds in the house, food, drinks, bathrooms. Come on, man, get a clue."

"I can't help it if I'm scared. It's not like I'm being this way on purpose. How about we just sit in the tent now and keep an eye on the house. Then when it gets dark and we get tired, maybe I'll want to sleep in a real bed."

"That'll be the day."

"Well, I'm not promising, but if you can fix that broken window, I'd feel a lot better."

There was nothing to boarding up a broken window either, Lionel told Ryan. "You got some plywood and a hammer and nails?"

"Sure."

"Let me at 'em."

Ryan was amazed again at what Lionel could do. "Your dad teach you all this stuff?"

"Yeah, I guess. I never thought about it as him teaching me. He just let me do stuff with him and would tell me what to do. It's not hard. It's just logical. You want to nail this board all the way around the window in the door so it keeps air and water out. It'll let you lock the door and keep you safe until you can get someone out here who knows how to install windows."

"I figured you could do that too."

Lionel shook his head and smiled a tight-lipped grin. "Nah. Dad and I just took care of the basics. Nothing fancy."

By the time the door was finished and the boys had sat in the tent a few hours, talking and watching the house, it began to grow dark. "You thinking what I'm thinking?" Lionel said.

"What, that you'd like to go in the house?"

"Uh-huh."

"No, actually I was thinking that I hoped you would stay in the tent one more night."

Lionel looked exhausted as he shook his head sadly. "You stay in this tent tonight, man, and you'll be here alone. I mean, it's not my place to invite myself into your house, but you've got to let me stay there, Ryan. OK?"

"I don't know."

"Sure you do, now come on! The longer you put off doing something you're afraid of, the harder it is to ever do it."

"I know."

"Then let's go."

"My head's kind of still hurting, and I've got a bruise in my side."

"From what?"

"When I fell. I hit something on the bike."

"Let me see that," Lionel said. He turned on a flashlight and Ryan lifted his shirt. "Ouch," Lionel said. "That must hurt."

"Does it need a bandage?"

"No, just looks like a deep bruise. It'll hurt for a while, but it'll go away. Your forehead or your side are no reason to not go into the house. In fact, you'll probably get better faster if you do go in."

"Could we do something first?"

"Like what?"

"Ride around, go somewhere. I'm bored."

"You're stalling."

"Yeah, but if we do that I'll get more tired and maybe then I'll want to go inside."

"All right, but like I told you, Ryan, if you don't go in the house tonight, you're going to be out here by yourself.

I would think that would be scarier than being in your house with me."

Ryan believed that. He shrugged. "Maybe."

"So where do you want to go?"

"Maybe down to my friend Raymie's."

"You said he disappeared."

"Yeah, but I know his dad is home. And I want to know if his sister is all right. She's off at college in California, and she's cool. Raymie actually liked his big sister. I'd never heard of that before."

"Hey, I liked my big sister too. It's not so unusual, especially if they're enough older than you. So, what, you want to go talk to Raymie's dad?"

"That'd be OK. Maybe he'd let us stay with him."

"*That* would make you feel safe, wouldn't it?"

"Yeah. Maybe he misses Raymie so much he'd like to have a boy his age around."

"You *want* an adult in charge of you? Freedom is the only part of this I'm already getting used to."

"Just let's go, OK?"

"OK, but I'm not for talking to the guy. How far is it?"

"Just down the block."

# 19

IT WAS well past dark, and Vicki had been sleeping on her back for more than nine hours, her feet flat on the floor at the end of the bed. Her eyes popped open, and she stared at the ceiling, wondering where she was. It came to her quickly.

Her mouth felt thick and dry, her eyes still heavy, and yet she felt rested. A deep emptiness borne of loss and sorrow overtook her, yet she was comforted as well by her new faith.

From the living room came the sound of the television. Judd must be up. She tiptoed out, only to find him curled up on the couch, still sleeping. So, she thought, neither of them had slept where they planned. She gently pulled the remote control from his hands and turned off the TV. Judd did not stir. She would take advantage of the time to get cleaned up and changed.

The hot shower felt so good she could hardly pull herself away from it. She didn't know if hot water was limited in a big house like this the way it was in a trailer where family members had to schedule their showers carefully. She hoped she'd saved enough hot water for Judd.

Vicki put on one of Mrs. Thompson's silky robes and sat drying her hair, then brushing it. She felt so much better than she had, and she had to admit she looked better too. It was time for a new look. All her own clothes had been lost in the fire, and that was for the best. While she didn't care to look like a mother of teenagers, as Mrs. Thompson was, neither did she ever want to go back to her old look.

Vicki was grateful to find that her feet were roughly the same size as Mrs. Thompson's had been. She hung up the pantsuit that had served as her blanket when she fell asleep. And she found a sweater, jeans, white socks, and tennis shoes. Vicki had no idea whether she and Judd would be going anywhere that evening, but these were good hanging-around-the-house clothes too. She had not dressed this way since she was a little girl. Not so many hours ago she would have considered this her least likely choice for an outfit. Yet as she looked in the mirror now, she felt it was a good look for her.

Vicki knew she and Judd might both regret having caught up on their sleep during the day. No way would they be tired at a normal bedtime. But he had said something earlier about trying to hook up with Bruce Barnes again that evening.

She would like that. Bruce was an interesting guy. He seemed to care about them so much, and yet he hardly knew them. She wanted to see his reaction when he found out that not just one, but both of them had become believers. And what about those two younger kids, Lionel and Ryan? Lionel had already become a Christian, but the other one, the little blond kid, had run off angry. Vicki couldn't blame him. How would she have felt in his situation, losing both parents and knowing they probably weren't in heaven?

Vicki hoped Lionel had found Ryan and had had some influence on him. She had been acquainted with Judd and

Lionel and Ryan for such a short time, and yet she found herself already caring about what would become of them. These were all new emotions and feelings for her.

Vicki was hungry again. She moved into the living room to see if Judd was still asleep. He was gone, and she heard water running upstairs. If his shower felt as good as hers, he would feel a lot better. She rummaged in the kitchen for a snack for the two of them, set it up in front of the TV, and sat watching the news while waiting for him.

---

Lionel and Ryan had to stay on the other side of the street from the Steeles because a car was coming the other way and Lionel didn't want to risk crossing in front of it. He knew if he didn't, Ryan wouldn't. Lionel didn't understand why Ryan seemed so much younger when the difference in their ages was barely a year. But, if it was worth comparing their predicaments, he had to admit that Ryan was worse off than he was.

The headlights coming the other way did not pass the boys, however. They stopped in front of the Steele home, and Lionel noticed that the car was a cab.

"That's Raymie's sister, Chloe," Ryan said as a young woman emerged from the backseat. The cabby jumped out and pulled her huge suitcase from the trunk. He set it next to her as she dug in her purse for the fare. She was paying him when the front door of the house burst open and a tall dark man ran out in his stocking feet. As the cabby pulled away, Rayford Steele gathered his daughter into his arms.

"Oh, Daddy!" she wailed. "How's everybody?"

He backed away from her enough that she could see him shaking his head sadly.

"I don't want to hear this," she said, pulling away from him and looking to the house as if expecting to see her mother or brother.

"It's just you and me, Chloe," Mr. Steele said, and they stood together in the darkness, crying.

Lionel sensed Ryan getting ready to cross the street and greet them. "Not now," Lionel whispered. "There'll be plenty of time to talk to them. But not now."

As father and daughter made their way inside, Ryan said, "But I'm not ready to go back home yet."

"You wanna go to the church?" Lionel asked.

"What for?"

"To see if Bruce Barnes is still there."

"Why would I want to do that? I don't believe all that stuff he's saying, and even if it *is* true, it was mean of God to do that to us kids."

"We had our chances," Lionel said.

"*I* didn't."

"You said Raymie Steele told you about this a while ago."

"Yeah, well—"

"Yeah, well, I want to go see Bruce. You can wait here, go home alone, or whatever you want."

"I'll go, but I'm not coming in."

"Whatever."

---

Vicki felt a strange reaction when Judd came downstairs, cleaned up and dressed. He had shaved off his goatee, and he looked much younger. She still had no idea what she thought of him as a person. She was glad they might become friends, because she needed one and he seemed to know a lot about

God and the Bible because of how he had been raised. Vicki had no feelings for him or romantic interest in him. It was way too early for that, and because of what she had been through, she wasn't even thinking that way.

But Judd seemed so impressed with her new look that she wondered if he was allowing himself to become interested in her. She talked herself out of it, however. It was impossible. He had been through as great a trauma as she had, and he had to be suffering privately as much as she. Anyway, he had seen where she lived. No way a guy like him would be interested in her.

"Oh, good," he said. "Food. What's on TV?"

"Same as what's been on the whole time since the disappearances. News, news, and more news."

Judd asked if she had seen the strange videotapes he had seen on the news earlier. So far she hadn't. "All they're talking about now," she said, "is this guy with a funny name from some country in eastern Europe. He became president of his country recently and—"

"And now he's coming to speak at the UN, right? Yeah, I heard about him. Nicholas something. And his last name sounds like a mountain range."

"Nicolae, I think," Vicki said. She hadn't picked up the last name either, but just then the young leader's picture came on the news again. She turned it up. The announcer referred to him as Nicolae Carpathia, the new president of Romania.

"You're right," Judd said. "Nicolae. And he must have been named after the Carpathian Mountains."

"Hey," Vicki said, "I thought you said you didn't do well in school. How do you know about those mountains?"

Judd looked embarrassed. "That's about all I know," he said. "Really, you just reached the end of my information."

They ate and watched the news for several minutes. Finally

Vicki asked if he was still thinking about trying to see Bruce that night.

"Yeah, I was," he said. "You want to?"

"Sure."

"I'll call and make sure he's there."

---

Lionel and Ryan dragged their bikes inside the church and found Judd's bike there too. They poked around looking for Bruce, Lionel wondering if Judd was there or if he had just never taken his bike home. Lionel and Ryan found Bruce finishing up a session with several older people, but before he could greet them, Ryan said, "I'll be waiting by the bikes. I've heard all this before."

"C'mon, Ryan!"

"No!"

Lionel looked apologetically at Bruce when he approached. "Good to see you again, Lionel. Let me introduce you to these folks." Lionel couldn't keep track of the names except for one, Bruce's secretary, Loretta. She was old, had a southern accent, and seemed classy. Lionel knew if he was going to spend much time at this church, he ought to get to know her. Bruce whispered, "Ask her sometime to tell you her own story. It'll amaze you."

Lionel had been wondering how this handful of old people had been left behind. He figured anybody who had been around that long, especially churchgoers, would have learned the truth long ago. But then he had had time too and knew the truth. Like him, maybe, they simply didn't respond to it.

"Well, I found Ryan, as you can see."

182

"Yeah. Don't worry about him hanging back for a while. I'm sure he's embarrassed about bolting on us. If we don't scare him off, he'll come around and get curious and eventually join us again."

Lionel's look of doubt must have betrayed him.

"You don't agree?" Bruce said.

"I've been working on him," Lionel said. "And I know how important you say it is for him not to put this off."

"It is."

"But it's not like he's putting it off. It's more like he really doesn't understand or doesn't want to. Sometimes I think he understands fine but just doesn't believe in God."

Bruce shook his head and pulled up a chair for Lionel. Bruce sat on the corner of a table, took off his wire-rimmed glasses, and ran his hand through his curly hair. "He'll believe in God before long, if there's any truth to what I've been studying. Everybody is going to know God is in this when the seven-year tribulation begins. People are going to be dying right and left, and we'd better be prepared. I'm so glad you made your decision right away, like I did. I know you're sorry you missed out on the Rapture, but there was sure no sense in waiting once we knew what happened, right?"

Lionel nodded. "I saw Judd's bike out there. Did he come back?"

"No. He left that here. But I did just get a call from him. He and Vicki are coming by this evening. He sounded a little more upbeat. I didn't talk to her, but I'm sure worried about them. Both of them are where you and I were, and I don't want them to keep finding reasons to put off coming to Christ."

Lionel told Bruce about his and Ryan's day. He was impressed that Bruce, as tired as he had to be, seemed interested in every detail. Bruce offered to drive Lionel back to the morgue in Chicago so he could identify his uncle's body. He said he would call the police about the intruders in his house and ask them to check Ryan's house too.

"I don't want you to have to worry about all that stuff," Lionel said. "Everybody you know is going to have a lot of this kind of stuff going on, and you can't do this for them all."

"So, you caught me in a generous mood. Take advantage of it. I need to stay busy. For one thing, I'm making up for lost time. But you must know I've got reasons to not want to go home too."

Lionel nodded. Who was supposed to take care of Bruce when Bruce was taking care of everybody else? Bruce told him there were several small groups he was meeting with. "I can tell adults a little more of what I'm going through, and they're supporting me as much as I'm supporting them. We're getting more and more calls every day from people who have had some contact with this church in the past. I think we're going to have quite a crowd here Sunday. People are desperate for answers. And we have them."

Lionel sat wishing Ryan would come in from the foyer. He kept looking back that way. "Was there something specific you wanted, Lionel?" Bruce asked.

"Me? No. I just wanted to check in with you. I've been wondering about those other two, too, and I was hoping we could work on them and Ryan."

"Ryan's going to be the toughest," Bruce said. "This is newer to him, and his parents are dead."

---

Ryan traded off sitting on the floor and moseying around the front of the church, idly looking at literature in the foyer. He was bored, but he had no interest in meeting with Bruce again. He had just pulled a tract off a table and began reading it, not understanding a bit of it, when Judd and Vicki came in. He looked at them and then looked away, embarrassed. He hoped they wouldn't say anything about his crying and running out.

"Hey, Ryan!" Vicki said. "Glad you came back. Where's Bruce?"

Ryan shrugged. "Somewhere with Lionel."

"Is it private or can we join them?"

Ryan shrugged again, wishing she would stop asking him questions. He didn't know and he didn't care.

"Hey," Judd said, "where are you guys staying?"

Now *there* was a question Ryan wanted to answer. He gushed the whole story about being scared to go in his own house and how Lionel's place had been taken over by guys who might have murdered Lionel's uncle. He told them someone had broken into his house, just before he had almost talked himself into agreeing with Lionel that they *should* stay there.

"I've got plenty of room at my house," Judd said. "In fact—"

"You *do*?" Ryan said quickly. "That would be great. Can I stay with you even if Lionel doesn't want to?"

"Slow down there, little man," Judd said. "We can all talk about this together and see what Bruce thinks about it. Vicki and I have some news for all of you anyway. Come on, let's find Lionel and Bruce."

"I don't want to."

"Why not?"

"Same reason as the other night. I don't believe this stuff."

"Well, you probably will."

"No, I won't."

"Even if you don't, we're all in this thing together. We have to watch out for each other. We need each other."

185

"You just want to talk me into this."

"Nobody can do that, little man. It means nothing anyway unless you decide on your own."

"I want to stay out here."

Ryan was worried that he had disappointed Judd, who looked peeved.

"What if I said you could only stay with me if you come in and see Bruce?"

"I guess I'd have to then," Ryan muttered. "You're probably going to force me to become a Christian too."

"No, I won't do that. Nobody can do that."

"What about you guys? Are you Christians now too, like Lionel?"

Judd appeared to be about to answer when Vicki interrupted. "He can find out at our meeting with Bruce, Judd. I mean, if he'd really rather stay here, he can just wait to see what we talked about."

"Good idea," Judd said. "What's it going to be, Ryan?"

"Do you promise to quit calling me 'little man'?"

"Sure. Now quit stalling."

"I want to stay here," he said.

"It's your call," Judd said, turning to head into the sanctuary.

"I hope you don't regret it," Vicki said, not in a mean way. In fact, Ryan thought she seemed so nice, he wouldn't have minded going in with them.

They were almost out of sight when he muttered, "Wait up. I'm coming."

**JUDD** was glad Ryan Daley had followed Vicki and him to find Bruce and Lionel. He had a feeling this was going to be a good meeting, regardless of what Ryan decided. Still, despite his anticipation of telling Bruce his and Vicki's good news, Judd couldn't shake the turmoil deep inside him. He wondered whether, even if he survived the seven years of tribulation that was to come, he would ever forget his regret, his remorse, and the bitter loss of his family.

He tried to push that aside for now, knowing that everyone who had been left behind faced the same anxiety. Bruce opened their little meeting with prayer. Then he asked each person to bring the group up to date since the last time they had been together.

Judd was first, and he told of his and Vicki's talks, of their adventure at O'Hare, and added that he would leave it for Vicki to tell about what she found at her home and what spiritual decision she had come to. "As for me," he said, "I finally realized I was being stubborn and stupid to put off doing something I should have done years ago."

187

When Bruce realized what Judd was saying, he immediately stood and leaned down to embrace him. Judd felt awkward and embarrassed. His dad had not been much for hugging, especially after Judd got to be about twelve, but still he was glad Bruce seemed so genuinely happy for him. Bruce was on the verge of tears when he said, "Lionel and I welcome you to the family. We're all brothers in Christ."

Lionel reached out a congratulatory fist, and Judd met it with his own. Then it was Vicki's turn. "I'm going to keep this short, Bruce, because you look like you could use some sleep—"

"Oh, don't worry about me."

"—And I'm going to tell it in the order it happened." Her story was much like Judd's, of course, and when she got to the part where she prayed to receive Christ, Bruce embraced her too and welcomed her as a sister in the family. Lionel reached out his fist and she patted it, making him chuckle. Judd was too embarrassed to hug her, so he shook her hand. Meanwhile, it appeared Ryan was just taking this all in.

When Vicki told of finding the burned out shell of her trailer, Bruce looked startled. He did not appear pleased to hear that she seemed to be planning to stay with Judd for a while. Judd felt he had to explain.

"We're not going together or even interested in anything like that," he said. "And we would stay on different floors. We're more like brother and sister, like you said."

"I'd feel more comfortable if I could find you a woman from the church to stay with, like my secretary. She has a big home with lots of room. And she's by herself now."

"I don't think I want to do that," Vicki said. "This doesn't have to look bad, and if it does, it's only because people are assuming the wrong thing."

188

Bruce looked as if he wanted to talk about it some more, but instead he urged Vicki to continue with her story.

"That's all, really."

Bruce called on Lionel, who gave a rundown on all that he and Ryan had been through. Judd was surprised that he seemed to speak for Ryan, but it was also likely that Ryan didn't want to talk anyway. If Lionel didn't tell Ryan's part, no one would. Judd was amazed at all they had been through in such a short time. Was this what it was going to be like, then? Nothing but trouble around the clock? And how awful about Lionel's uncle! "I can take you to that high school where the morgue is," Judd offered.

"I've already got that covered," Bruce said. "I'll call to see where they're shipping the bodies, because surely no high school has the equipment to hold bodies for long. We'll find out where Lionel's uncle André is, and we'll get him over there to identify the body."

Bruce asked Ryan if he wanted to say anything. That was when Judd noticed that Ryan still had the tract he had taken from the foyer. He was pretending to study it, but he'd had time to read it over and over if he wanted. Ryan said nothing. He just shook his head.

"Fair enough," Bruce said. "No one's going to pressure you. You can be a part of this group as long as you want, regardless of what you decide to do. When you're ready, you make this decision on your own."

Finally, Ryan spoke. "And what if my decision is to say no?"

Bruce said, "Nobody can make the decision for you. You have to live with the consequences."

"Or die with them," Lionel said.

Now Ryan was mad. Judd thought he might bolt again. "He's been talking to me that way all day," Ryan said. "What kind of a Christian is that?"

"I've only been kidding. Kids our age crack on people all the time. Can't you take it?"

"This has to be a fragile time for him," Bruce said.

"It's that way for all of us," Lionel said. "But that doesn't mean we have to be so touchy."

"I just want you to quit hassling me, Lionel. OK?"

Lionel shrugged. "I guess. If it's bothering you that much."

"It is."

"So if I start talking nicer to you, will you—"

Bruce held up a hand. "No deals, no bribes, no pressure, remember?"

Lionel nodded. "Sorry."

Judd wanted to make his offer. "I'd like both of you guys to stay at my place too."

"I was hoping you'd say that," Ryan said.

"I'd feel better about Vicki staying there if the other two were there too," Bruce said.

Judd felt some of his old rebellion surfacing. He resented Bruce's implying that Judd was responsible to him. Maybe Bruce considered himself Judd's pastor already, and because he was older he thought he could boss him around. Judd thought maybe he *did* need somebody doing that, but his first reaction came from the person he used to be. He didn't like being told what to do. What kind of a Christian was he going to be? Well, Bruce seemed more comfortable with everybody staying in the same house, so maybe it wouldn't be an issue again. Judd hoped not.

After the meeting the kids filed into Bruce's office, where he began calling around to find out who in Chicago would know anything about Lionel's uncle André. The phones still gave everyone fits, and between busy signals, bad connections, and the usual runarounds and red tape everyone had to go

through, it appeared to Judd that Bruce was getting to the end
of his rope.

Finally someone was able to tell him that the bodies that
had been delivered to the high school in André's neighborhood would be available for identification at a city morgue in
a nearby precinct late Friday afternoon, two days away.

"I'll take you then," Bruce told Lionel. Then he helped load
Ryan's, Lionel's, and Judd's bikes into the trunk of Judd's car.
They took up so much room that Judd had to leave the trunk
open as the four of them clambered in for the ride to his house.

Judd rolled down his window and called out to Bruce.
"You sure you wouldn't rather stay with us too?"

"Only if you really need me," Bruce said. Judd was relieved.
He wished Bruce had a place to stay that wouldn't be so painful
for him. But the independent part of Judd also liked the idea
that he would be the oldest in the house, and the house was his,
after all. He didn't know if he was up to being in charge of three
people he hardly knew, but he was eager to find out.

---

Being in charge was not at all what Judd expected. For the next
few days it seemed all he did was worry what Vicki was thinking, referee arguments between Ryan and Lionel, and try to
explain why he and Vicki got the "good" rooms and the other
two got the leftovers. He had no say over when anybody came
and went. He wasn't their parent or their boss, as they reminded
him often. He suddenly realized how tough it would be to be a
parent whose kid or kids didn't respect him or listen to him or
obey him. He was getting a clear view of what a problem he had
been to his parents.

Judd spent a lot of time digging through his dad's papers,

finding out what bills had to be paid and when. He also found the documents that told him where his father had his money deposited and what accounts had balances. Judd was grateful to realize that his father was a good money manager and planner, and that there was more than enough there to last anyone ten years, let alone seven, if he was careful.

Judd gave Vicki cash to buy herself some clothes, and she proved to be very frugal. She told him that if she could really use his mother's stuff, she wouldn't need much more. And she kept insisting that she would get a job and pay him back. "You really don't need to," Judd said. "There's plenty more money."

"So I'm just supposed to become a bum and let someone else pay for everything for me? I don't think so, Judd. I mean, I appreciate it, but what kind of pride would I have if I let you do that?"

Judd didn't know what to say. Ryan said he would be happy to let Judd pay for everything, but Lionel shamed him into admitting that he would only feel good about himself too if he was earning some money to contribute to the pot.

Bruce phoned Judd's home during the middle of the afternoon that Friday. "Judd," he said, "I hate to do this to you, but I'm going to need you to bail me out. I've got people calling right and left and I'm meeting with them, counseling them, you name it. I've gotten nowhere in trying to prepare for Sunday, and it looks like we're going to be jam-packed."

"What do you need?" Judd asked.

"I need you to drive Lionel in to that morgue. It's not in a good part of town, and I know you have not dealt with Chicago authorities before, but if I tell you whom to ask for and what to say, can you handle it?"

"Sure."

"And you'll let me know as soon as you get back, so I'll know you're safe?"

Judd hesitated.

"Judd?"

"Well . . ."

"You don't want to do it? I understand. I'll get someone el—"

"No, it's not that. I just want to talk to you about checking in with you to let you know I'm safe and all that. I don't want to get into that trap."

"I'm only asking you this time because I'm asking you to do something as a favor for me—something I should be doing myself."

"Yeah, OK. I don't mind."

Bruce gave Judd all the information and directions. Surprisingly, not only did Ryan want to go along, but so did Vicki. Judd talked them out of it. "It's not a good part of town," he said. "I figure there'll be lots of cops there, and if they see a bunch of kids, they might have a lot of questions. Just let Lionel and me do this, and when we get back we'll tell you all about it."

———————————

Vicki found it strange to be alone in the house with Ryan. They had not talked much, and he didn't seem interested in starting. She tried to make small talk with him, but she didn't get far. He had already heard her life story and what had been happening to her lately. She tried to interest him in the news, then remembered that he had been watching the news when he learned of his father's death. She wanted to comfort him, encourage him, point him toward God, but she was at a loss. She had no idea how to reach him.

"I promised Bruce we would all be in church Sunday morning," she tried at one point.

"You didn't promise him for me, I hope," Ryan said. "Everybody's always deciding for me what I'm going to do."

"You don't want to go?"

" 'Course not. Haven't you figured that out yet?"

"I know you don't believe this stuff yet, but I'd think you'd want to check it out. Aren't you curious what Bruce is going to say to all the people who come looking for answers? I think it'll be cool just to see how many show up, what they're thinking, and how Bruce does. He says he's never really been a preacher, but he can't wait to tell these people about Jesus."

Ryan clammed up then.

"Well, I *did* tell Bruce I thought we would all be there," Vicki added. "But *you* made no promises, so it's up to you."

"I'll probably come," Ryan said, as if he had no choice. Vicki thought that showed progress. It was totally up to him, and he was pretending to reluctantly go along.

Ryan wandered up to his room, the one that used to belong to Judd's little brother, Marc. Vicki got out the Bible Bruce had given her and started reading in the New Testament where he had told her to begin. Who would have ever thought, she wondered, that she would want to read the Bible at all, let alone on her own when no one was making her?

---

Lionel wasn't comfortable with Judd yet. As they rode into Chicago, he found himself having to work at holding his end of the conversation. He was sort of amused at Judd. He had been a rich kid from a good home who had tried to blend in with the bad kids and the rebels. Lionel knew the type. He found Judd sort of plain and not at all a tough guy or street-wise. That made it funny to him that Judd had tried to be something he was not. In fact, he was so far from the image he had tried to project that it was laughable.

Lionel had to admit that Judd had changed pretty quickly. With the goatee gone and him no longer wearing all black, Judd started to look like a normal, suburban teen.

Lionel asked him about the details of the visit to the morgue. When Judd told him what Bruce had spelled out, Lionel said, "You know, I think I can handle this myself. Your car is not going to be safe down there, so you should probably stay with it. I won't be long."

Lionel thought Judd would put up a fuss, insisting on talking with the authorities himself. So far Judd had seemed to enjoy playing the big shot. But to Lionel's surprise, Judd seemed relieved. "Yeah, OK," he said quickly. "That's probably a good idea. I'll stay with the car, you do this stuff, and then we'll be out of there."

When Judd finally pulled in to the small, fenced lot behind the gray morgue building, he handed Lionel the sheet with the contact name. "I'll be right out," Lionel said.

He had prepared himself, he thought, for this moment. He had to be sure André was dead, and there was no better way than to see his body for himself. Lionel had always hated funerals, and he had been to his share for someone thirteen years old. What he hated most was the filing past the bodies. He always peeked at them, but he didn't stop and linger. He knew this would not be easy.

He had seen a lot of movies where someone had to identify a body. The coroner or medical examiner or whoever would dramatically yank the sheet away, and the identifier would collapse from the shock. Lionel didn't want that to happen. He knew André was in danger most of his life, and whether he really killed himself or had been murdered, it was no surprise that he had come to the end so soon. But he didn't want to be shocked by some horrible sight.

Lionel had stepped from the car with confidence, telling himself to just do his duty and get it over with. It made him feel grown up to handle this for his parents. He wished he could see them and his brother and sisters, but he was sure glad they weren't dead.

And yet as Lionel neared the front of the building, it was as if his legs had turned to jelly. He began to shudder and tremble, and he found it difficult to put one foot in front of the other. His breath came in short gasps, and he fought the urge to race back to the car and have Judd run him back to Mount Prospect. *I'm going to do this*, he thought. *I have to. Otherwise, I'll be a wuss, just like Ryan.*

Lionel put his hand on the brass handle of the front door and stopped. It was as if he was paralyzed, his legs heavy. The handle felt icy, though it was not that cold out. He forced himself to pull the heavy door open, and he was immediately struck with fear and dread by what he saw. This was nothing at all like he had assumed. The entire place had been turned into a storage area for white-sheeted bodies.

Lionel thought a morgue had one area for bodies in drawers. He knew that was true, but it shouldn't have surprised him to find this morgue overcrowded, what with everything that had gone on.

Lionel felt the cold rush from the air conditioners. This place, the whole building, was cold as a refrigerator. Covered bodies were lined up on stretchers down both sides of the hallway, and Lionel could only assume that's the way it was all through the building.

A bored receptionist in a winter coat said, "You can't be in here, son. What are you doing?"

"I'm here to identify a body," he said.

"All the bodies in here have been identified," she said.

Lionel dug the sheet of instructions from his pocket. "I'm looking for assistant medical examiner Ford," he said.

The receptionist paged him. "You'd better take a seat," she said. "No telling how long he'll be."

He was twenty minutes, time enough for Lionel to calm himself if he was able. But he was not able. All the wait did was to make him more upset. He wanted to be anywhere other than this creepy place. None of the dead bodies he had ever seen before were related to him. He had no idea how he would react.

Dr. Ford was a pudgy man in a hurry, and he was all business. "You're Washington? Where's Barnes?"

"Couldn't make it," Lionel said.

"This way, Washington."

Lionel followed the fast-walking doctor down the halls between the stretchers with bodies on them. He held his breath and looked neither right nor left. The doctor peeled a couple of sheets of paper back off his clipboard and studied a page. "André Dupree, right?"

"Yes, sir."

"Age 36, male, African-American, 5 foot 8, 155 pounds?"

"That's him."

"He's in the back. You OK?"

"Yeah, just a little out of breath."

"Almost there."

"Could you do it slow?"

"What, walking? Lots to do, son. Never seen this many deaths in so short a time. Never anything like it."

"No, I mean, will you show me his body slow?"

"Meaning?"

"Like, don't whip the sheet off."

"I never do that."

"Good."

When Dr. Ford got to the back, the place looked more like what Lionel expected. Six bodies were lined up next to each other. The doctor lifted the bottom of the sheets and read the tags on the toes of two in the middle. "Dupree," he said. "Here are his effects, if you want them. We threw away the jeans. They were, um, stained with blood."

"Lots of it?"

" 'Fraid so. This was a suicide, you know."

"I figured." Lionel was having trouble speaking loudly enough to be heard. He still wasn't sure he could keep from running out of there. The doctor handed him a manila envelope clasped by a red string. He unwound it with shaky fingers and saw his uncle's watch, bracelet, earring, ring, beeper, belt, and socks.

"He came in here with that and a pair of jeans and stocking feet."

Lionel nodded, dreading what was to come.

The doctor moved to the other end of the stretcher. "Ever done this before, son?"

Lionel shook his head.

"I'm just going to fold the sheet back to his chest and you can see his face."

"And then I identify him to you?"

"That's not necessary. Identity is not in question in this case. The personal effects were on the body and in the pockets. A neighbor identified him. He was in his own apartment. You can just look away for a moment if you'd like."

Lionel held the envelope in both hands, as if he were holding a hat in front of him. He heard the slow rustle of the sheet. "OK, son," Dr. Ford said.

Lionel stared, speechless, at the expressionless face, and his heart seemed to stop. He could hear himself breathing. He wanted to say something, but words would not come.

"All right?" the doctor said.

Lionel nodded, his lips quivering.

"Can you find your way out?" Dr. Ford said.

Lionel nodded again and hurried toward the door. He was afraid he was going to be sick. The corridors looked longer than ever, and he couldn't wait to get out to the warmth of the day. By the time he reached the receptionist's area he was running. He burst through the door and sprinted to the parking lot, jumping into the car.

"You look like you saw a ghost," Judd said, starting the car.

Lionel could only snort.

"Oh, sorry, man," Judd said. "I guess you sorta did, huh?"

Lionel nodded.

"That his stuff there?"

"Uh-huh." It was the first sound Lionel had emitted since seeing the body.

"Did he look like himself?" Judd asked.

"I wouldn't know," Lionel said. "He probably did. The only thing I know for sure is that that was *not* my uncle."

**21**

**JUDD** Thompson and the other three kids living in his otherwise abandoned suburban house sometimes felt as if it was just them against the world. Judd, at sixteen, was the oldest. Then came the redhead, Vicki Byrne, a year younger. Lionel Washington was thirteen, and Ryan Daley, twelve.

They were the only ones left from their families. Judd's parents and his twin younger brother and sister had disappeared right out of their clothes a few days before. Vicki Byrne, who had lived in a trailer park with her parents and little sister, had seen the same thing happen at her place. Her older brother, who had moved to Michigan, had disappeared too, according to one of his friends.

Lionel Washington had lost his parents, his older sister, and his little brother and sister. His uncle, the infamous André Dupree, was thought dead, but Lionel now knew he was alive somewhere—but where?

Ryan Daley had been an only child, and now he was an orphan. His parents had not disappeared. They had died in separate accidents related to the worldwide vanishings of millions of people—his father in a plane crash, his mother in an explosion while in her car.

The kids knew what had happened. At least the three older ones did. Ryan wasn't sure yet. All he knew was that he had been left alone in the world, and he didn't much like the explanation the other three had come to believe.

All three of the older kids had had parents who were Christians. They believed not only in God, but also in Christ. And they weren't just churchgoers. These were people who had believed that the way to God, the way to heaven, was through Christ. In other words, they did not agree with so many people who believed that if you just tried to live right and be good and treat other people fairly, you could earn your way to heaven and to favor with God.

As logical as all that may have sounded, the parents of Judd and Vicki and Lionel believed that the real truth, the basic teaching of the New Testament, was summarized in two verses in the book of Ephesians. Chapter 2, verses 8-9 said that a person is saved by grace through faith and that it is not as a result of anything we accomplished. It is the gift of God, not a result of good deeds, so nobody can brag about it.

They also believed that one day, as the Bible also foretold, Jesus would return and snatch true believers away in the twinkling of an eye, and they would immediately join him in heaven. That was what had happened, Judd, Vicki, and Lionel realized, since most of the people in their churches had disappeared too.

But what convinced them more than anything was that they themselves were still here. Judd had never received Christ, though he had grown up in church and knew the Bible. Vicki had hated it when her parents had become Christians two years before, and she didn't want anything to do with it, even though her older brother and younger sister had also believed. She had seen the changes in her family and realized there was some truth to what was going on. She had an idea they were onto something real, but she wasn't willing to give up her life-style or her freedom to join them in their faith.

Lionel had been more like Judd, having been raised by a Christian family and having gone to church every Sunday for years. He had not become a rebel as Judd did when he became a teenager. Rather, he had pretended all along to be a Christian. It was his and his uncle André's secret. They were not really Christians.

Those oldest three kids realized their tragic mistake immediately when the vanishings had taken place. In the midst of chaos, as cars crashed, planes fell from the sky, ships collided and sank, houses burned, and people panicked, they had to admit they had been wrong—as wrong as people could be. They were glad to find out there was a second chance for them, that they could still come to Christ. But though that gave them the assurance that they would one day see God and be reunited with their families, it didn't keep them from grieving over the loss of their loved ones. They were alone in the world until they had discovered each other and Bruce Barnes, the visitation pastor at New Hope Village Church who had agreed to help teach them the Bible. He had given them each a Bible and invited them to the first Sunday service following the disappearances, which the Bible predicted centuries ago.

But Ryan Daley was still a holdout. He was scared. He was sad. He was angry. And while he had been hanging with Lionel since they had met, Lionel made him feel like a wimp. Well, he didn't just *feel* like one. He *was* one. Lionel seemed brave. He confronted his uncle's enemies, he had been to the morgue to try to identify his uncle's body, and he had gone into Ryan's house after a burglary. Ryan couldn't force himself to do any of that stuff, and it made him feel terrible.

Judd had invited everybody to live at his place. Vicki didn't have any choice after her trailer had burned to the ground. Some of Lionel's uncle André's "associates" had virtually taken over Lionel's place, so he needed somewhere to crash too. Ryan could have stayed at his own house and Lionel would have stayed there with him, but Ryan couldn't make himself go inside. There were too many scary memories. It had been just him and his parents in that house, and now they were dead. And then there had been the burglary, so he wasn't about to set foot in the place. Lionel could make fun of him all he wanted, but Ryan was glad to take Judd up on his offer.

Judd's family had clearly been the wealthiest of the four. His house was a huge mansion. Well, almost a mansion. There were bigger and nicer homes around, but not many. In Judd's house, each kid could have his own bedroom and lots of privacy.

No one knew what the future held, at least among the kids. Bruce Barnes sure seemed to know. He had made it his business to become a student of Bible prophecy and must have been spending almost every spare minute buried in the Bible and reference books. He told the kids that it was time to be on the lookout for a man the Bible called the Antichrist. "He will come offering peace and harmony, and many people will be fooled, thinking he's a good man with their best interests at heart. He will make some sort of an agreement with the nation of Israel, but it will be a lie. The signing of that agreement will signal the beginning of the last seven years of tribulation before Christ returns again to set up his thousand-year kingdom on earth."

Bruce explained the Tribulation as a period of suffering for all the people of the world, more suffering even than they had endured when millions of people had disappeared all at the same time. Bruce promised to teach the kids all of the judgments that would come from heaven during those seven years, some twenty-one of them in three series of seven.

Judd had called the kids together one evening after they had all received their Bibles from Bruce. "I'm not trying to be the boss or anything," he began, "but I am the oldest and this is my house, and so there are going to be some rules. To stay in this house, we all have to agree to watch out for each other. Let each other know where you are all the time so we don't worry about you. Don't do anything stupid like getting in trouble, breaking the law, staying out all night, that kind of stuff. And I think we all ought to be reading what Bruce tells us to read every day and also going to whatever meetings he invites us to, besides church of course. I mean, we're going to church every Sunday to keep up with what's going on."

Vicki and Lionel nodded. "Of course," Vicki said. "Sounds fair."

"Not to me," Ryan said. "I'm not into this stuff, and you all know it."

"Guess you're going to have to live somewhere else then," Lionel said.

"That's not for you to say, Lionel!" Ryan said. "This isn't your house! Judd's not going to make me read the Bible and go to church meetings just to stay here. Are you, Judd?"

"Matter of fact, I am," Judd said.

"What?"

"I can hardly believe I'm saying this," Judd said, "because just last week it made me so mad when my parents said the same thing. But here goes. As long as you live under my roof, you follow my rules."

Ryan's face was red, and it appeared he might bolt out of there like he often did when he heard something he didn't like.

"I'm not going to force you to become a Christian," Judd said. "Nobody can do that. Even Vicki and I needed to decide that in our own time on our own terms. But I'm taking you in, man. You're staying here because I asked you to. The least you can do is to join in with what the rest of us are doing. It's all for one and one for all. We're going to look out for you and protect you and take care of you, even if you don't believe like we do, and we're going to expect you to do the same for us. I can't even make you read the Bible, but we're going to go to church and to Bruce's special little meetings, and we're going together. You can plug your ears or sleep through them, but you're going."

"And if I don't?"

"Then you can find someplace else to stay."

"He'll never do that," Lionel said. "He's too much of a scaredy-cat."

"Shut up!" Ryan said.

"Lay off him, Lionel," Vicki said. "You're not going to win him over that way."

"You're not going to win me over at all," Ryan said. "Just watch."

"Well," Judd said, "what's the deal. You in or out?"

"I have to decide right now?"

"We have a meeting with Bruce tonight and church tomorrow morning. You go with us tonight and you promise to go tomorrow, or you move out this afternoon."

"The man's drawing a line in the sand for you," Lionel said.

"Lionel!" Vicki scolded.

"I'm just sayin', the line has been drawn. You crossing the line, Ryan? Or are you with us?"

"I'll think about it," Ryan said, and he was gone. The others heard him banging around in the bedroom he had been assigned.

"We need to pray for him," Vicki said. "It's hard enough for us, but imagine what it's like for him. We know where our parents are. If he believes like we do that our parents were raptured and his weren't, he has to accept that his parents are in hell. Think about that. He's going to fight this a long time, because even if he wants to become a believer, that means he's accepting that his parents are lost forever."

"It sure would be nice if we could somehow find out his parents, or at least one of them, was actually a Christian or became one before they died," Lionel said.

"Get real," Judd said. "That rarely happens in real life."

"I know."

Lionel was dealing with his own dilemma. His uncle had left a long message on Lionel's answering machine, going on and on about killing himself and feeling so bad that he had influenced Lionel to not be a Christian. He was clearly drunk or high or both, and Lionel had been convinced that André had killed himself. When Lionel and Ryan had ridden their bikes all the way to André's neighborhood one night to investigate, the cops had told them André's body was at a nearby morgue. It had indeed been a suicide, they told Lionel. Because André, had had enemies to whom he owed money, and those guys had moved into Lionel's house and kicked him out, Lionel figured they had murdered André and made it look like suicide.

But when Judd had driven Lionel to the morgue a few days later so Lionel could identify the body, he had run into a shocker. While the victim was the same height and weight as André, and while he had carried André's wallet and wore André's clothes and jewelry, the body was clearly not André's.

Finding the truth about that mystery would be Lionel's mission over the next several days. Meanwhile, he was as eager as Judd and Vicki to learn more about what life was supposed to be like, now that Christ had raptured his church.

Judd agreed that they should pray for Ryan, and that in fact they should pray at the end of all their little house meetings, the way Bruce had them pray at the end of their meetings at church. But first he asked, "Is there anything else either of you needs to talk about now?"

"Yeah," Lionel said. "I just want to say that I'm not really trying to put down Ryan. I'm trying to toughen him up the way I did my little brother and sister and the way my sister did me. I don't want to make him mad or feel bad, but he's such a wuss. It's time for that boy to grow up."

"It's hard to grow up this way," Vicki said. "I don't know about you guys, but I'm having trouble. I have bad dreams, have trouble sleeping, find myself crying over my family as if they're all just dead and gone and not in heaven where I know I'll see them someday. I know we're all going to be called back to school one of these days, and I can't imagine sitting through class with all I know now. If this Antichrist guy shows up soon and does sign some sort of a contract with Israel, we're gonna have only seven more years to live."

Judd and Lionel sat nodding. "Anyway," Judd said, "Lionel, you do have to try to encourage Ryan. If he decides against becoming a Christian, I sure wouldn't want to have it on my conscience that I pushed him away. As much as you guys squabble, I still think he looks up to you."

"Really?"

"Oh, yeah," Vicki said. "I think that's obvious. He wants your approval."

"Wow."

"You might want to encourage him."

"Hold up," Lionel said. "I'll do it right now."

Lionel hurried to Ryan's room, trying to decide what to say. When he peeked in and knocked, Ryan whirled from what he was doing.

"Hey, little man," Lionel said.

"I thought I asked you to quit calling me that," Ryan said.

"Yeah, sorry. Listen, I just want to say that I'm sorry about getting on your case all the time."

Ryan didn't respond.

Lionel tried again. "I mean, uh, I'm just saying—"

Ryan approached the door, where Lionel stood, tongue-tied. "You're just saying you don't know what you're saying, right?"

Lionel did not respond.

"Are you finished?" Ryan asked, his hand on the door.

"No, I—"

"Yes, you are," Ryan said. And he pushed the door shut in Lionel's face.

Lionel returned to Judd and Vicki, clearly troubled. He told them what had happened.

"We do need to pray for that boy," Vicki said.

But before they did, Lionel said, "You need to know he was packing up."

"Really?" Judd said. "He's leaving?"

"I don't know," Lionel said, "but he was getting all his stuff together."

And they prayed for him.

# 22

**RYAN** was angry and confused. What else could he be? He had overheard Vicki trying to explain his situation, and she was exactly right. In truth, he wanted to believe exactly what these other kids believed. It all made sense. His friend, Raymie Steele, had warned him. And it seemed most of the people who had disappeared were known to be Christians. So many people from so many churches were gone that they must have known something.

But if all this was true, his parents had not made it. But still they were gone. Dead. The only nightmare worse than having your parents die, Ryan decided, was knowing that they had missed going to heaven. Was that fair? What kind of a God did something like that to people as nice as his parents? Or to someone like him?

He wasn't a bad kid. Sure, he had done a lot of things wrong, but who hadn't? Raymie Steele was a Christian, but he wasn't perfect.

The one thing Ryan couldn't get out of his mind was that if this was true and his parents knew it, they would have believed.

And for sure they would want him to believe before it was too late. But knowing it was probably true, even believing it, didn't mean Ryan was accepting it for himself. Because what Vicki Byrne had said was right. If he bought into it, it meant he was admitting that his parents had missed out and were in hell. That was too much to take in just now.

Ryan knew something the other kids didn't know. Well, except maybe Lionel. Lionel seemed to know Ryan better than Ryan knew himself. What only Ryan, and maybe Lionel, knew was that Ryan had no intention of doing anything that would cause him to leave Judd's house. He had never felt or been so alone in his life, and these kids were his new family. Whether or not he became a Christian, he was not about to leave them or let them abandon him.

Yeah, they treated him like a baby and used names for him that made him feel even smaller and younger. But he *had* been acting like a baby. He had a right. He was an orphan. The others were enduring the loss of their families too, but this was different. Ryan needed time away from the pressure, time to think, time to do something to take his mind off everything. He had to admit he was afraid to go out alone at night, so while it was still light, he headed out on his bike.

The others had seemed so concerned with his packing up his stuff that they would likely watch to see if he took it with him. They would be relieved, he hoped, to find everything still in his room. It was packed and stacked, though, so they could wonder if he was eventually going to leave, based on what decision he came to. But his decision, at least about staying at Judd's, was already made.

It made Ryan feel a little better to know that the others seemed to want him to stay regardless. He knew they wanted him to become a Christian, but that didn't seem to have anything to do with whether he stayed around. Was it because they really cared for him? Were they actually worried about him and looking out for him? He couldn't figure that one out. He had never cared about anybody else that much, except maybe Raymie.

Ryan wanted to work on his courage. Could he ride into his own neighborhood and past his own house? And if he could, could he also see what was happening at the Steeles'? He sure didn't want to ask them about Mrs. Steele or Raymie, because he knew both Mr. Steele and Raymie's big sister Chloe had to feel terrible about their vanishing. Maybe they'd be like his aunt was a few years ago, who seemed to want to do nothing more than talk about Ryan's uncle at his uncle's funeral. That seemed so strange. You'd think she would have been so upset she wouldn't want his name even mentioned. But she had talked about him nonstop. She even asked people to tell her their favorite stories about him.

"Sit here with me for a minute," she had said, taking Ryan's hand. "Tell me about that time your uncle Walter was trying to teach you to fish and he fell into the lake."

"Oh, Aunt Evelyn," Ryan had said, feeling sheepish and awkward. "You know Uncle Wally did that on purpose. I mean, I was only eight, but I knew that even then."

Aunt Evelyn had leaned back in her chair and laughed her hearty laugh, right there in the funeral home with people filing past the body of her husband. Many turned to stare at the insensitive person who would be guffawing at a time like that and were at first shocked, then pleased to find it was Aunt Evelyn herself.

"I saw the whole thing from the porch of the cottage," she had said, wiping away her tears of laughter. Ryan thought it funny that she usually cried when she laughed, but of course maybe this time she was covering her real tears of sadness. "I just knew what he was going to do because he had done it to me when we were first dating. He stepped on one side of the boat and then the other, and he kept saying, 'No problem. No problem. Shouldn't stand up in the boat, but don't you worry, I've got it all under control.' Right? Right? Didn't he say that in that big phony deep voice of his?"

"Yes, he did," Ryan had admitted.

"And then, pretending to adjust the fishing line or something, he just stepped back and flipped over the side in his shirt and pants and hat and everything. Didn't he?"

"Yeah, but he had put his glasses in the picnic basket first, and he even took out his hearing aid."

That just made Aunt Evelyn laugh all the more, and soon everyone in the room was waiting his turn to tell a favorite Uncle Walter story. Just thinking about that crazy funeral made Ryan pedal harder as he sped toward his own block. Aunt Evelyn herself had died not two years later. How he missed them both!

Why, he wondered, was he thinking about them now? Maybe because it reminded him that Raymie Steele had not been the first person to ever tell him about God. Ryan had been to Vacation Bible School a couple of times, but it was at Uncle Walter's funeral, when Ryan had worked up the courage to ask Aunt Evelyn why she wasn't more sad, that she had said that confusing thing to him.

"That's an excellent question, Ryan honey," she had said. She almost always would call him that, even in front of other people. "I'm sad and I'll have my bad days and nights, and I'll cry enough tears for the whole family. But you see, I know where Uncle Walter is, and it's where I'm going to be someday. He's in heaven."

214

"But how do you know?"

"The Bible says you can know," she had said.

But that was as far as the conversation had gone. Ryan had thought about that a long time and even asked his mom and dad about it. Uncle Walter was Mr. Daley's much older brother, and Aunt Evelyn was his second wife. "Your dad says your uncle Walter's wife has always been some kind of a religious nut, Ryan," his mother had said. "But she means well. She's been good for Walter."

"Good for him?" Mr. Daley had chimed in. "Took all the fun out of him, if you ask me. Got him the old-time religion, and he became a Holy Joe."

"He was still fun, Dad," Ryan had said. "He was always being funny."

"He kept telling us we need Jesus," Mr. Daley said. "But frankly, I don't feel the need for anything."

Ryan skidded to a stop in front of Raymie Steele's house. He couldn't tell whether Mr. Steele and Chloe were home. So that was it, he realized about his thoughts turning to his uncle Walter and aunt Evelyn. They had been Christians. They were in heaven. And they had tried to tell him and his parents about Christ. He wondered how many other chances his parents had had. His dad always had some comment when he saw a preacher on television. He thought they were all crooks, but he never kept the TV channel on any church program long enough to hear what they had to say.

Ryan sat straddling his bike, pawing the ground with his foot. What he wouldn't give to have it be just a week or so ago and to know that Raymie would come bounding out of this house for some fun. Man, they had good times. They squabbled and argued and had often been jealous of each other, but not a day went by when they didn't have more fun than any two kids deserved. They were best friends, blood brothers, and had pledged to always keep in touch—no matter where college or life took them. How Ryan wanted to see Raymie again!

He pedaled slowly to the end of the block, where his house came into view. There was a pile of newspapers on the stoop, and he knew he should get rid of them and call to cancel the paper. Making it obvious no one was home was an invitation to more burglaries. The drapes were all shut, too. And though there were lights on an automatic timer, all the power outages lately put them on a crazy schedule. The lights were on now and would go off early in the evening. Ryan thought about going in and resetting the timer and opening the drapes so it looked like the house was lived in. But as usual, he couldn't force himself to even move up the driveway by himself, let alone approach the front door. What in the world was he going to do when the lawn needed mowing?

Ryan headed off to the other side of town, where Lionel had lived. He would be scared to death to approach that house with all of André Dupree's so-called friends living there. But still, he wanted to see it, to spy on it. He couldn't figure out what was happening with Lionel's uncle André.

Ryan had been there when Lionel had played the answering machine message from André. He had to agree, the guy sounded ready to kill himself. Lionel was only kidding himself, Ryan thought, to think that someone André owed money to had killed him and made it look like suicide. The two guys Lionel said had threatened André once were the leaders of the bunch that had moved into Lionel's house, supposedly with André's permission. And they talked about how great it would be when André joined them. How did that make sense, especially now that Lionel had discovered that whoever had been killed in André's apartment, in André's clothes, wear-

ing André's jewelry, and carrying André's wallet, was not André
at all?

Ryan was as curious as he could be, but on the other hand,
he wasn't sure he wanted to know. What would he do with
that information?

He looked at his watch. He knew Judd Thompson had
been serious, and that if Ryan was not back at Judd's house
and ready to go to the meeting with Bruce that night, he would
no longer be welcome. He still had an hour. Ryan rode idly up
and down the sidewalk on the other side of the street from
Lionel's. There was little going on at the house across the
street, but the van was there and lights were on in the house.

At one side of the house was a wide driveway that served
the home next door. No one seemed to be home there. Ryan
wondered if he would be noticed if he parked his bike out of
sight and just moseyed over there, appearing to just be hanging around, playing. That would be a test of his courage,
wouldn't it? He didn't think anyone in Lionel's house would
recognize him as the one who had sped away from there on
bikes with Lionel. And if anyone didn't want him playing in
that area next to the house, he'd just move along.

The plan sounded reasonable to Ryan, but he found
himself petrified when he actually began walking across the
street. He wasn't sure why he was doing this, except that he
was hoping to take some bit of information back to Lionel.
Maybe Lionel would respect him if he actually did something
grown-up, something brave. Plus he really wanted to be help-
ful. He figured Lionel would rather live with the others at
Judd's anyway, but it wasn't right to be driven out of your own
home for no reason.

The police were too busy with all the other emergencies to
be worried about something like this, but what if he and

Lionel took them solid evidence on the fake suicide? It had obviously been a murder. If the police could be convinced of that, maybe Lionel's invaded house would wind up higher on their list of what needed to be investigated.

But what if it had been André who had committed the murder? Who else could have gotten into his place and put all his stuff on another person before killing him? Ryan was beginning to think he was in over his head.

Worse, he felt conspicuous walking across the street. He knew no one noticed or cared, but he felt as if every eye on the street was on him. Just putting one foot in front of the other took all the concentration he could muster. He tried to look casual, as if he were just strolling nowhere.

When he finally reached the driveway between the houses, he moved toward the back so he would be out of sight. He settled on the grass at the far back corner of Lionel's house, close to the neighbor's house and as far away from Lionel's garage as he could be and still be on Lionel's property. He was afraid someone might see him from the window, so he crept up to the wall and sat with his back to the foundation. The cold cement made him shiver, but he knew he was close enough now that if someone looked out a window, he wouldn't be seen.

What was he doing, he wondered? Putting himself in danger just to prove that he could? What good would he be to anyone if he was discovered? And what might these characters do to him? Would they hurt him? Kidnap him? Kill him? And if they did, where would he be then?

That was something he had to think about as he sat there in the grass, a couple of blades of it in his hands. He pulled the thin green strips apart and smelled the richness of the ground beneath him. It was one thing to hold out on his own decision about God because he didn't like what had happened to his parents. But what would they want for him if this was the truth?

How would he ever see Raymie again, or Aunt Evelyn and Uncle Walter? He knew he was still here because he had heard the truth and not acted on it. How long was he going to be stubborn, hoping everyone else was wrong when he knew full well they were right?

Maybe tonight, maybe at the meeting, he would ask to stay after and talk to Bruce. He didn't want to do something just because everybody wanted him to. He wouldn't be pressured into this. But he still had a lot of questions, and if anyone knew the answers, it would be Bruce.

Ryan froze when he heard footsteps above him in the house. He wasn't about to stand and peer into a window. He held his breath.

There was the squeak of a bedspring, as if someone had sat on the bed. He heard a mechanical sound he didn't recognize, but it came to him when he heard one end of a conversation. Someone had placed a phone call. It was a woman, sitting on the bed in the room just above him. He was able to hear her clearly if he kept his breathing shallow.

"André," she was saying, "you ought not to be drinkin' now. You got to keep yourself healthy, and you can surface sometime soon."

*Surface?* Ryan wondered. *What does that mean? He's hiding out somewhere but he can come out soon? Will he have a disguise? He'd have to have a new name. Did the police even suspect that he was still alive, that they had assumed the wrong dead man was André?*

"Now don't you go gettin' religious on me now, hon. You're just lonely. . . . Your cousin was over here the other day, and the guys offered to let him stay. But he wasn't too happy about us being here and he took off. . . . Yes, someone will try to find out where he is and check up on him. Or you can do that yourself in a few days. But you've got to be careful now, you hear? . . . No! Now don't be worrying about him. It wasn't your fault. He seems like a smart kid who can take care of himself. . . . Thirteen?! Are you sure? That big gangly boy? He looked sixteen if he was a minute. Well, he spoke well for himself—even stood up to the guys here. Don't worry about him. . . . Quit your crying now. This will all be over soon. . . . I love you, so shut up."

Ryan jumped to his feet and ran down the driveway and across the street to his bike. He had done his job. He had accomplished something. He had something to tell the others. André was alive. André was in hiding. André would be coming out into the open soon and might even come to Lionel's house.

But what was all that stuff about André getting religious and worrying about Lionel? His phone message that night must have been real. He must have really been worried about what his influence had meant to Lionel. That had to be good news, right?

Ryan began pedaling back toward Judd's when the door of Lionel's house burst open and a thin, young black woman raced at him across the lawn. Had she been the one on the phone? Had she seen him? What did she want?

Ryan tried to accelerate, but he couldn't do it fast enough. The woman overtook him and grabbed him by the shoulders. For as thin as she looked, she was wiry and muscular, much stronger than Ryan. The bike stopped beneath him, and it was all he could do to stay upright.

"What were you doing in our yard?" she demanded.

"*Your* yard?" Ryan said, barely able to catch his breath. His heart banged so hard in his chest that he worried his ribs would crack. "I thought it was my friend's yard."

"And who is your friend?"

Ryan knew better than to say. He kept his mouth shut.

"Maybe you'd like to tell one of the men in my house."

Ryan was petrified. "I'm not going to tell anybody anything," he said, amazed that had come out of his mouth. What he wanted to do, what he was afraid he would do, was break down and cry and tell everything. He was a friend of Lionel's, and Lionel wanted his house back, but that news would bring all kinds of trouble down on Ryan and his friends.

"We'll just see about that," the woman said. She strengthened her grip on Ryan's shoulders and began to yank him off his bike.

"You don't have to do that," Ryan lied. "I'll come with you. I'm not afraid of you or anyone in my friend's house."

"Then get off that bike and come in here."

She kept one hand on his arm as Ryan dismounted, and he noticed one of the men of the house coming out onto the front porch. If that guy joined her, he was in trouble.

As he climbed off his bike, she let go of his arm and the man on the porch hollered out, "You need help, Talia?"

"No! He's comin', and you're gonna talk to him!"

But with that, Ryan pulled away and began running with all his might, pushing his bike along. The woman yelled at him and took out after him, but Ryan was fast. He didn't want to jump on his bike until he knew he had enough speed to get away from her. She was yelling for the man on the porch. "LeRoy! Get him!"

"Get him?" LeRoy shouted back with a laugh. "I'll run him down!"

Ryan was sprinting as fast as he could and sensed he was

pulling away from Talia when he heard the old rattletrap van start up. He leapt onto his bike and pedaled with all his might. His only hope, he knew, was that his bike could go places that van couldn't. And Ryan knew this suburb.

It wasn't long before Talia had quit running because she fell too far behind. But Ryan could hear that old van engine growling, and he was scared to death.

He cut through yards, went down alleys, turned every which way as fast as he could. He thought he had gotten away from LeRoy a couple of times, and then he showed up, somehow guessing where Ryan would come out. LeRoy never got closer than a block or so, though, until Ryan got into his own neighborhood. LeRoy was about a block behind and closing fast when Ryan got near Raymie Steele's house. Raymie and Ryan had a route they always used when going between their houses, especially when they were trying to sneak somewhere or were trying to keep from being seen. It went through the side of Raymie's yard to the back and through the hedges in his yard to the hedges of the next one. That led into an alley that emptied out right near Ryan's house.

It put him right in plain sight unless he got there fast enough that no one was right behind him. If someone came out of that alley late enough and couldn't see him, he wouldn't know which way Ryan had turned. Actually, he didn't turn at all. Ryan just made a jog around the side of his own house and slipped through a small cutout in the fence. He usually ran through the shortcut, but on his bike he was really flying.

When he got to Raymie's side yard, his bike fishtailed in the grass, but he couldn't slow down. He just tried to stay up while still pedaling fast. He straightened out just in time to squeeze through those two hedges, but he could see LeRoy and his van heading for the alley. LeRoy had to slow down to make the turn, and by that time Ryan was through the hedges and clear. He could hear LeRoy but he couldn't see him, so he knew LeRoy couldn't see him either.

Ryan shot through the lawn at the side of his house, riding as fast as he ever had. His legs were burning, and he was gasping. He saw the headlights of the van just as he got to the fence and knew if he got off his bike and tried to slither through the fence on foot, LeRoy would see his bike and know where he was.

He had to take a chance. He was afraid he was going to tear himself up, but he remembered that he had gotten in trouble with his dad the last time he crawled through that opening in the chain-link fence—he had made the hole wider, and his dad had said Ryan was going to have to work with him when he fixed it. But they had never gotten around to it. He was going full speed next to that fence, hoping LeRoy would not find him with his headlights. Ryan put the bike down, and it slid through the grass, over to the fence, and right through the opening. Ryan felt the fence brush the back of his head, but it did not draw blood. The back wheel got hung up in the fence, and he tumbled off into the backyard. He dragged the bike far enough around the back so no one could see him, and ran into the house.

The last thing he wanted to do was go inside his own house, but what else could he do? All of a sudden that scary house looked like the safest place he knew. He didn't turn on any lights. He just lay on the floor in the kitchen in the dark and tried to catch his breath so he could hear which way the van went. He heard LeRoy racing up and down the street, as if he was sure Ryan had to be there somewhere. Luckily for Ryan, the light timer didn't kick on and give him away. LeRoy finally drove off.

Ryan shakily crept to the phone and called Bruce.

# 23

IT WAS time for Judd, Vicki, Lionel, and Ryan to drive to the church for their private meeting with Bruce Barnes. Judd kept looking at his watch, wondering how long he should wait for Ryan.

"Maybe he's not coming," Lionel said. "Maybe he's made his decision."

"You know him better than that," Vicki said. "You know he wouldn't even want to be out after dark."

"That means he found another place to stay," Lionel said. "Or he talked himself into going back to his own house."

"He'll go crazy there alone," Vicki said.

Judd couldn't believe how disappointed he was that Ryan was not back. He vowed he would wait five more minutes, and that would be it. "If he's not here when we leave," Judd said, "he's out."

"But what if he shows up at church?" Vicki said.

"Unlikely. But if he does, he'd better have a good story."

Judd broke his own vow and waited ten more minutes. He shook his head and pulled his jacket on. Vicki said, "Judd, I have a bad feeling about this."

"So do I, Vicki, but I made an ultimatum and I have to stick to it."

"No you don't. We're not about ultimatums. We're about mercy and grace, like Bruce always says."

Judd hesitated. At first he was angry that she was trying to correct him. Was she trying to take over? But then he thought, *Who cares who's in charge anyway, just because I'm older and it's my house?* Actually, he wanted a way out of this.

Vicki continued. "You said yourself that we were to watch out for each other. All for one and one for all. I mean, if he had come back here and told us to our faces that he wanted out, that he refused to play by our rules, then fine. He's never been afraid to speak his mind. He wouldn't leave and not say anything. Anyway, he has to come back sometime to get his stuff."

Judd knew she was right. "But why didn't he call? He knows he's risking getting kicked out of the house."

"I'm afraid he's in some kind of trouble," she said.

"I could be wrong," Lionel said, "but I think he's too chicken to get himself into trouble. That kid wouldn't go with me into his own house in broad daylight."

"He knows you think that too," Vicki said. "Maybe he went and did something foolish to try to prove himself to you."

"I doubt it," Lionel said. "I told you he just blew me off when I tried to apologize."

"So he doesn't know how to accept an apology. Is that a crime? He didn't have any brothers or sisters, and you can bet his parents didn't apologize to him much."

Judd was beginning to think Vicki was onto something. "So, if we're going to look out for him," he said, "where do we start? Where was he going?"

"I have no idea," Lionel said, and Vicki shrugged too.

"He was on his bike," Judd said. "Let's just drive around Mount Prospect and take the long way to the church."

"Should we call Bruce?" Vicki said. "Tell him we're going to be a little late?"

There she went again with suggestions, Judd thought. But again, she was probably right. He wasn't used to catering to adults like Bruce. Respecting people was something new for him, and, he knew, for her too. "My dad's car has a phone in it," he said. "That'll save us some time."

They piled into the car, and Judd dialed the church as he drove. Loretta, Bruce's secretary, answered in her southern accent. She said Bruce was on the phone. Judd told her his problem. "Why, young man, I believe Ryan is the one on the phone with Pastor Barnes right now."

"Where was he calling from?"

"I don't rightly know. Shall I have Bruce call you when he's free?"

"No, thanks. Just tell him we're on our way."

That was encouraging, at least. Judd hated the thought of Ryan having called his bluff and making him follow through on his ultimatum. Ryan reminded Judd so much of himself at that age. Judd had been in a church family, of course, but it was late in his twelfth year that he began to become rebellious. A rage had grown inside him that he didn't understand. He saw some of that in Ryan, and he didn't want him to run from the group. Ryan needed them. And they wanted him.

"I begged Ryan to tell me where he was," Bruce said a few minutes later. "He sounded really scared. All he said was to tell you, Judd, that he would get to the meeting as soon as the coast was clear."

" 'The coast was clear'?" Judd said. "What in the world is he talking about?"

"I told him I'd come and get him, wherever he is, but he said he doesn't want me leading anybody to him, whatever that means."

Judd could see from the looks on the others' faces that they were as dumbfounded as he was.

"I've got a lot I want to tell you tonight," Bruce said, "and I'd like Ryan to hear it. But I've had a long day and don't want to be up till all hours like I have been the last two nights. Should we get started, and then you can bring Ryan up-to-date when he gets here?"

That sounded good to Judd, but Vicki said, "I don't know if I can concentrate while I'm worrying about Ryan."

"I think he's safe," Bruce said, "as scared and mysterious as he sounded. Let's try to get something accomplished and not just spend our time worrying. Be praying for him, but let me teach you some things."

Bruce spent about half an hour going over the passages he had encouraged them to read since the last time he had seen them. "People are coming in here every day, hungry to read and learn what God has for them," he said. "We're planning a big service Sunday morning, and that's just one day from now, so I'm going to be swamped." He explained much of what they had been reading, about what was to come once the Antichrist signed a pact with Israel.

"But do we even know when the Antichrist will come on the scene?" Lionel asked.

"No, but many of the scholars I've read seem to think he would have already been here by the time of the Rapture."

"Then it might be someone we already like and trust?" Vicki said. "I never followed politics much, but I heard people saying they thought President Fitzhugh was a liar, and—"

"I'd be very surprised if it was President Fitzhugh," Bruce

said. "This week I want you to be reading the passages I have outlined on this sheet. It tells some of the characteristics of the Antichrist, and one of them is that he has some sort of blood ties with the Roman Empire."

"So he'll be an Italian?" Judd said.

"Not necessarily, but something in his ancestry will tie him to Rome. I don't believe that's true of our president, and after you have read these passages you may have other reasons why you agree with me that it's probably not him."

"Do you think he's here now?" Vicki asked. "Is there somebody you suspect?"

"I have my eye on an interesting world figure," Bruce said. "But it would be an awful mistake for me to try to identify the Antichrist before I was sure. Be watching and listening to the news. If the Antichrist is not a well-known world figure already, he probably soon will be. He's the one we're going to have to fight for at least seven years if we're going to survive until the Glorious Appearing."

"I want to survive," Lionel said. "But I remember my mother saying something about only a quarter of the people on earth after the Rapture still being alive at the end of the Tribulation."

"That's exactly what I believe the Bible teaches," Bruce said.

"Hold on a second," Judd said. "The population is already a lot less since the Rapture. Only one out of four of those will still be here when Jesus comes back again?"

"Because of the wars, plagues, famine, and disasters, yes," Bruce said. "I don't mean to scare you, but you don't have to be a rocket scientist to look around this room and see that there are four of us here."

"And you're saying," Vicki said, "that only one of us is likely to be still alive in seven years?"

"Seven years from the signing of the treaty between Antichrist and Israel, yes."

Vicki's shoulders sagged, and she said just what Judd was thinking. "What's the use then? What are we here for?"

"That's the exciting part," Bruce said. "Our job is to win as many converts as possible before the end. Because when Jesus comes back to set up his thousand-year reign on earth, we'll either be here waiting for him or we'll come from heaven with him. Only those who come to him between the Rapture and the Millennium will reign with him."

"How many will that be?"

"Some of the scholars I'm studying estimate that the multitude of believers the book of Revelation calls 'numberless' could be as high as a billion and a half."

"I want to stay alive and see that," Vicki said.

Bruce smiled a tired smile. "I want to stay alive and be part of winning them," he said. "I'll talk more about it Sunday. You'll all be here, right?"

"Right," Judd said. "All of us. All four of us."

They heard a commotion outside: a squealing of bike tires, the dropping of a bike, the banging open of a door. Ryan rushed into the room, flushed, sweating, and—it appeared to Judd— just a little proud of himself. "Whew!" he said. "I made it!"

Judd, in spite of how relieved he was, couldn't help saying, "You're late."

"I know, but I called Bruce. You told them, didn't you, Bruce?" Bruce nodded. "I still get to stay in the house, right?"

Judd nodded. "Just tell us what happened."

Judd was amazed as Ryan told where he had been and what he was up to. At first Judd wasn't even sure he could believe the story, but it had a ring of truth to it. Lionel's mouth dropped open when Ryan told of the phone conversation he had overheard between Talia and André. Lionel looked like he wanted to leave right then and track down his uncle.

Ryan brought the story all the way up to where he was racing away on his bike, with Talia running after him and the van starting in the distance. "What did you do?" Vicki demanded. "Where did you go?"

He told them the whole story.

"Why didn't you call us?" Judd said when Ryan finished.

"I didn't have the number! The church's number is still on the notepad by our phone from the first time I wrote it down."

Judd was as excited as Ryan had been. He had reason to be pleased with himself. Maybe what he had done, getting so close to those people at Lionel's house, had not been smart. But he had stood up to them until he could escape, and his escape was perfect.

"You wanted that bad to stick with us, huh?" Judd said.

"You have no idea," Ryan said.

"And you'll be here Sunday with the rest of your friends?" Bruce said.

Ryan nodded. "This is where I'm supposed to be, I guess."

"What are you saying?"

"I got to thinking when I was on Raymie's street, what happens if LeRoy catches me? Or what happens if I don't see some car and shoot out in front of it? I could die. Then where would I be? I made my decision and said my prayer while I was on that bike. Is that OK? I mean, I didn't even have the breath to say it out loud. Does it still count?"

Bruce stood and embraced Ryan. "It sure does, buddy," he said. "God heard you. Welcome to the family."

Later Bruce helped load Ryan's bike into the trunk of Judd's car. "See you tomorrow," he said, and Judd noticed that as happy as Bruce had to be, he wasn't smiling. There was happiness once in a while, Judd realized, when something turned out the way they hoped. And he was sure everyone was as thrilled as he was that all four of them were now believers. But looking and acting happy was something totally different now from what it had been just a week before. There was too much to think about, too much to get used to, too much to overcome to be too smiley.

Ryan let out a big sigh, sitting next to Lionel in the backseat. "Wow," he said. "I don't ever want to have to go through that again. You can fight your own battles from now on, Lionel. I'm getting tired of looking out for you."

That almost made Judd smile. For now he was as exhausted as Ryan sounded. He was ready to sleep. And already he could hardly wait for Sunday morning.

# 24

JUDD was awakened early Sunday morning by a phone call from Bruce Barnes. "I'm concerned about Ryan," Bruce said, "and I'd like you to help me check up on him."

"He's still upset about his parents, of course," Judd said. "But he seemed a lot happier last night. Why are you worried about him?"

"Well, I have no doubt his decision was real," Bruce said. "I just want to make sure it wasn't something done totally out of fear. He was afraid something might happen to him, that Lionel's uncle's friends or enemies might catch him and kill him."

"Yeah?" Judd said. He wasn't following Bruce. "Does it make a difference? I mean, a big part of my reason was fear too."

"Yes, Judd," Bruce said, "but you also understood, if I recall your story correctly, that you were a sinner and needed God's forgiveness."

"And you don't think Ryan thinks that?"

"I don't know. I'm just saying I didn't hear him say it. That doesn't mean his conversion didn't 'take,' but it's important to our faith and to our walk with Christ that we realize what he has saved us from. True guilt and sin have been washed away."

"You want me to ask him?"

"Not directly. I can probably do that better, being so much older than he is. I would have asked him last night, but I didn't have a chance to be alone with him, and I didn't want to embarrass him in front of you and the others."

Judd had to think about this. Maybe Ryan did have different reasons for finally making the decision he made, but not everyone came to Christ for the same reasons, did they? Of course, in the end they did. Everybody has the same problem—sin that keeps them from God. And it was by seeing and admitting that that Judd made his decision. But he also wanted to be with Christ and with his family when he died. And he wanted to avoid hell. Getting forgiven for being a sinner was a huge reason for him to do what he did, but the other stuff—being assured of heaven and staying out of hell—seemed almost as important. Did that mean his *own* decision had been based on fear? And was something wrong with that?

Bruce concluded by telling Judd that he was merely trying to be sure Ryan didn't think God was just some sort of a heavenly fire insurance salesman. Staying out of hell was one of the benefits of trusting him, but going from darkness to light, from death to life, from unforgiven sinner to sinner saved by grace, that was the crux of the decision.

On the way to the church that morning, Judd couldn't help prodding Ryan a little, just to see what he was thinking. Was he just the member of some new club with the only friends and "family" he had left? Or did he understand what had really happened to him? Maybe it was too much for someone his age to grasp. And yet, Judd reminded himself, when he was twelve, he knew the score. He simply had not acted on it and didn't really believe it was all that crucial. Needless to say, he did now.

"So, Ryan," Judd tried, "how does it feel to be part of the family?"

"Great," Ryan said. "I still miss my parents, and I know I always will. And I'm still hoping they somehow became Christians before they died. But I'm glad I'm going to heaven."

"Isn't it great to have our sins forgiven?" Judd said.

Vicki shot Judd a double take, which made him assume she sensed he was fishing for something. Lionel was not a morning person. He had leaned his head against the window in the backseat and seemed still to be sleeping.

"I guess," Ryan said. "I wasn't that much of a sinner, though."

"Oh, really?" Judd said. "You were the almost-perfect kid, huh?"

"No. But the only time I did bad stuff was when I was mad or something. I was never bad on purpose."

Now Vicki got into the discussion. "Never lied, never cheated, never stole, were never jealous of anybody or wanted revenge? Never gossiped?"

"Nothing that was really that bad," Ryan said. "Honest."

"But I'll bet you're glad that we don't get to heaven because of the good things we do."

"I don't know," Ryan said. "I might have made it. I was really a good kid."

"But you said yourself you weren't perfect, and only perfect people can get to God. And anyway, how can you say you might have made it? You *didn't* make it. Christ came and you were left behind, just like we were."

"I know," Ryan muttered, and he stopped talking. Judd was afraid he had scared Ryan off.

"I'm just saying," Judd said, "no matter how good or bad we are, no matter how much our good outweighs our bad, the whole point is that we fall short. We all need to be forgiven. That's what it means to be saved."

"So I'm not saved because I wasn't really a sinner? I mean, I guess I was a sinner the way everybody's a sinner, but because I didn't see myself that way?"

"How do you see yourself now?" Judd asked.

"Saved."

"From what?"

"Hell."

"But not from your sins?"

"Yeah, I guess."

"I'm telling you, man," Judd said. "We're all still sinners. But we're saved from our sins. Unless you're perfect—"

"I know I'm not perfect. But I was never that bad a guy."

"*I* was a bad person," Vicki said. "But my dad always said it was the people who don't see themselves as that bad who are the last ones to realize they need God."

"I knew I needed God because I didn't want to die and go to hell," Ryan said.

"And you would have gone to hell even as good a guy as you were, right?"

" 'Course."

Judd thought Ryan was actually getting it. He would leave Ryan's training to Bruce. Judd knew he himself had much to learn. He and Lionel were the only two of these four who had been raised in church and had heard it all before. But now, with new eyes and new understanding, and—needless to say— a whole new life situation, he still felt like a baby when it came to the Bible and stuff about God. He could only assume Lionel felt the same way.

It was as if Judd couldn't get enough of what Bruce had to teach, and he couldn't wait to see what Bruce would talk about that morning. He had to park several blocks from the church, though they arrived several minutes before ten o'clock. The church was packed. Lots of people looked desperate and scared.

The four kids found the last seats together in the balcony. Chairs were set up on either side of the center aisle right next to the pews, and hundreds of people stood in the back.

Right at ten o'clock, Bruce began. The big pulpit on the platform was empty, and no lights shone up there. Bruce had placed a microphone stand in front of the first pew and spoke from there, holding his Bible and notes.

"Normally we at this church would be thrilled to see a crowd like this," he said. "But I'm not about to tell you how great it is to see you here. I know you're here seeking to know what happened to your children and loved ones, and I believe I have the answer. Obviously, I didn't have it before, or I too would be gone."

Bruce then told the same story he had told the kids, and his voice was the only sound in the place. Many wept as he spoke of his wife and children disappearing right from their beds. He showed the videotape the senior pastor had left, and more than a hundred people prayed along with the prayer at the end. Bruce urged them and anyone else who was interested to begin coming to New Hope.

He added, "I know many of you may still be skeptical. You may believe what happened was of God, but you still don't like it and you resent him for it. If you would like to come back and ask questions this evening, I will be here. Rest assured, we will be open to any honest question.

"I do want to open the floor to anyone who received Christ

this morning and would like to confess it before us. The Bible tells us to do that, to make known our decision and our stand."

Judd leaned forward and peered down to the main part of the sanctuary, where the first to move was a tall, dark man, quickly followed to the microphone by dozens of others. "That's Raymie's dad!" Ryan whispered loudly.

The man introduced himself as Rayford Steele, an airline pilot, and Judd was captivated. As Rayford Steele told his story, of people disappearing off his plane over the Atlantic in the middle of the night on a flight to London, Judd's mouth dropped open. He had been on that very plane.

Most of the stories were the same as Captain Steele's. These people all seemed to have been on the edge of the truth because someone had warned them, but they had never fully accepted the truth about Christ.

Their stories were moving, and hardly anyone left, even when the clock swept past noon and forty or fifty more still stood in line. All seemed to need to tell of the ones who had been taken. Judd felt the same need, but he knew it would be a long, long time, even if he could get down to the main floor and get in line. Instead, he just listened.

At two o'clock, Judd's stomach was growling. Bruce finally interrupted, apologizing for having to bring the service to a close and teaching a simple chorus. Judd found himself overcome with emotion as he thought of the years when he had not enjoyed church at all. For how long had he ignored God, and how many times did he simply not sing when the congregation expressed its love for Christ? Now he sang through his tears, never meaning anything more in his life. And never did he miss his family as much as right then.

Judd and the other three returned that evening for the meeting of people who were still skeptical or had questions.

Though he was no longer a skeptic, he sure had lots of questions. He was sure he would learn something. Many of the people were angry, wondering why God did things the way he did them. Bruce told them he wouldn't begin to try to explain God or speak for him, but that he was convinced God had given everyone ample opportunity to have been ready for the Rapture.

Others had question after question, and what Bruce couldn't answer from his education and recent reading, he promised to study and report back on later. Bruce concluded the long evening meeting by urging everyone present who had not made a decision for Christ to not put it off. "We never know what the next day, the next hour, the next moment may bring. I confess I never liked preachers saying that, trying to scare people into becoming believers by convincing them they were about to walk in front of a bus. But in this day and in this situation, people are dying all over the place. People you know. People you love. Captain Rayford Steele, who told his own story this morning, got some news from one of his flight attendants today that I have asked him to share this evening, just to illustrate this point."

When Captain Steele stepped to the microphone, he admitted that his story was about a man he did not even remember. "He was on my flight to London, the one during which so many passengers disappeared right out of their clothes. His name was Cameron Williams, and he was a writer for *Global Weekly* magazine."

Judd flinched. He remembered that guy. He had been the one who had helped the old man with his luggage in first class, and then had gone off looking for the man when his wife discovered only his clothes in the seat beside her. He was also the first one to jump down the evacuation chute when the plane had landed. He had flipped over forward and done a somersault, scraping the back of his head.

"I found out today that he eventually made it to London, but that he was killed in a car bombing."

Judd shook his head. When would this end? People he knew and loved, people he had met or simply seen across the aisle on a plane—all dead. For whatever problems he had with his parents and his younger brother and sister, his life was tame compared to what the world had become. Who could keep up with it?

Captain Steele begged people to not wait. "You may have more questions," he said. "Ask them. Don't make a decision as important as this one without knowing for sure that you can believe with all your heart. But once your questions have been answered, don't risk your life and your afterlife by thinking you have all the time in the world. You don't."

---

The next day Vicki asked Judd to pick up a copy of *USA Today*. "I was sure never a news junkie before," she said. "But now I'm reading, watching, listening to everything. I want to know what's going on, who's who, and what's what. We have to be on the lookout for the Antichrist so we don't get fooled like so many people will."

Back at the house Vicki sat reading the paper while the television droned on. Every channel still carried news and emergency bulletins. No one complained that regular programming had not returned and likely wouldn't for a long time. The world was in chaos, and that was all anyone seemed to care about.

"Magazine Writer Assumed Dead," the *USA Today* headline read. "Cameron Williams, 30, the youngest senior writer of the

staff of any weekly newsmagazine, is feared dead after a mysterious car bombing outside a London pub Saturday night that
took the life of a Scotland Yard investigator."

"Judd!" Vicki called. "You'll want to see this."

Judd read the whole story over her shoulder. "Man, I can
still hardly believe it. I sat right near that guy on the plane."

Ryan watched the news on television. Lionel was also in
the room, but he was not watching. He was pacing, mumbling
about finding his uncle André if it was the last thing he ever
did. He ignored Judd and Vicki's talk about the dead writer.
Judd noticed Lionel perk up, however, when the news shifted
to the United Nations headquarters in New York.

"Even the press remains stunned this evening at the performance of Romanian President Nicolae Carpathia at the General
Assembly of the United Nations," the news anchor said. "Just
before Carpathia was scheduled to appear, the media was
shocked to learn that Cameron 'Buck' Williams of *Global Weekly*
was in attendance. Watch closely and you can see him, there, as
the camera pans the press gallery. Williams had been thought
dead in a car bombing in London last night. Investigation
continues into his involvement in that scene, but as you can see,
he is safe and sound now."

"What *is* this?" Judd said, his hand atop his head. "I can't
keep up with everything! So now he's *not* dead?"

"Shh!" Vicki said. "Look at this guy!"

CNN was replaying the afternoon appearance at the UN of
Nicolae Carpathia. He entered the assembly with a half dozen
aides. He stood tall and dignified, yet he didn't seem cocky. He
appeared an inch or two over six feet tall, broad shouldered,
thick chested, trim, athletic, tanned, and blond. His shock of
hair was trimmed neatly around the ears, sideburns, and neck,
and he wore a navy blue business suit with a matching tie.

Even on television, the man seemed to carry himself with a sense of humility and purpose. He dominated the room, and yet he did not seem impressed with himself. His jaw and nose were broad and prominent, and his blue eyes were set deep under thick brows.

First to speak was UN Secretary-General Mwangati Ngumo of Botswana. He announced that the assemblage was privileged to hear from the new president of Romania and that an Israeli dignitary would formally introduce him. A little old man with a heavy accent introduced Carpathia as "a young man I respect and admire as much as anyone I've ever met."

With courtly manners, Carpathia remained at the side of the lectern until the older man was seated, then stood relaxed and smiling before speaking without notes. Judd was astounded to notice that he never hesitated, misspoke, or took his eyes off his audience.

Judd was impressed that Carpathia spoke earnestly and with passion. He mentioned that he was aware that it had not been a full week yet since the disappearance of millions all over the world, including many who would have been "in this very room." Carpathia spoke in perfect English with only a hint of a Romanian accent. Occasionally he used one of the nine languages in which he was fluent, each time translating himself into English. He was articulate, carefully enunciating every syllable.

Judd realized how strange it was that he was watching news like this. He would have cared nothing for this kind of thing a week before. Now he was fascinated. Here was a man with confidence and maybe some answers. He sure seemed like a great guy.

Carpathia began by announcing that he was humbled and moved to visit "for the first time this historic site, where nation after nation has set its sights. One by one they have come from all over the globe on pilgrimages as sacred as any to the Holy Lands, exposing their faces to the heat of the rising sun. Here they have taken their stand for peace in a once-and-for-all, rock-solid commitment to putting behind them the insanity of war and bloodshed. These nations, great and small, have had their fill of the death and maiming of their most promising citizens in the prime of their youth.

"From lands distant and near they have come: from Afghanistan, Albania, Algeria. . . ." He continued, his voice rising and falling dramatically with the careful pronunciation of the name of each member country of the United Nations. Judd heard a passion in his voice, a love for these countries and the ideals of the UN. Carpathia was clearly moved as he plunged on, listing country by country in alphabetical order by memory.

Judd noticed the other three kids were as riveted by this as he was. At the UN, people began standing and clapping with the mention of each new country name. More than five minutes into the recitation, Carpathia had not missed a beat. He had never once hesitated, stammered, or mispronounced a syllable. When he got to the *U*'s and came to "The United States of America," Judd applauded, Vicki smacked her hands together once, Lionel raised a fist, and Ryan said, "Yes!"

By the end of his list of nearly two hundred nations, Nicolae Carpathia was at an emotional, fevered pitch. Delegates and even the press stood and cheered. The tape ended and TV viewers were switched back to CNN news where the anchorman sat shaking his head in amazement. "Talk about a man taking a city by storm," he said. "They're already calling him Saint Nick, and he's the toast of New York."

"The Antichrist, whoever he is, will have to face this guy sometime," Vicki said. "I'd like to see that."

"Me too," Judd said. "Wonder how he missed the Rapture. He sure seems like a Christian."

"I never cared about politics before," Lionel said. "But this man is something else. Just hearing him makes me want to find my uncle, and right now."

"I'll help," Ryan said.

"We all will," Judd said.

# 25

**LIONEL** Washington didn't really want everyone else's help, and he told them that. "Talia is André's old fiancée. I didn't know they were back together, but if they are, maybe she'll tell me something."

"You don't want us to go with you?" Judd asked. "I could drive you."

"I'm going to ride my bike. You guys don't need to get in trouble with these people."

"Why don't you go during the day?" Vicki said.

"Yeah," Judd said. "It's dark. How do we know when to come looking for you?"

"I'll be fine."

"Don't even say that," Vicki said. "You heard what almost happened to Ryan."

"If we don't hear from you by eleven," Judd said, "we'll come after you."

"I have no idea where I'll be. André's not going to be at my house."

"What are we supposed to do if we don't hear from you?"

"I'll be fine, all right?"

"No," Judd said. "We agreed to look out for each other. We're going to have to follow you, that's all."

"I don't like this," Lionel said.

"You won't even see us," Judd said. "We'll worry about you, but you won't have to worry about us. Now get going."

Lionel jogged out to his bike and rode directly home. Judd had been right. Lionel was not aware of Judd following him. He was still certain he would be safe, but it did make him feel better to know that the others cared about him.

Lights were on, but no cars were in the driveway. Who was there? Lionel stepped to the door and raised his hand to knock, suddenly realizing how silly that was. *This is my own house,* he thought. He walked in and went straight upstairs to his room. He heard quick footsteps from a back room downstairs. They came across the hardwood floors in the living room, into the dining room, and up the stairs.

"LeRoy?" Talia called out. "I didn't see you guys pull in."

Lionel stepped into the hall and could tell he had startled her. "Hey, Talia," he said simply. "I need you to take me to André."

"Yeah, right," she said. "Like I know where he is."

"I know you know where he is," Lionel said. "And if you don't take me to him, he's going to be upset."

"I heard he was dead," she said.

"Cut the baloney," Lionel said. "We both know you chased off a friend of mine today. He heard you talking to André on the phone, and it was obvious he was worried about me."

"If I hear from him," she said, "I'll tell him you're fine."

"Is there a car in the garage?"

She hesitated. "No. There's not. Why?"

Lionel sensed she was lying. "I know there is," he said. "C'mon and take me."

"That's LeRoy's two-seat roadster. He'll kill me if I take it."

"You're not takin' it," Lionel said. "You're borrowing it. You'll probably be back before LeRoy is."

Talia appeared to be thinking it over. "I wouldn't mind seein' André myself," she said. "LeRoy and them haven't been getting back before one or two in the morning the last coupla nights anyway."

"Let's go," Lionel said.

"I'd better call him first."

"Who? LeRoy?"

"No! André!"

"We both know he's hiding out. He's not going anywhere."

"You think of everything, you little brat. And there's no way you're only thirteen."

Lionel ignored her, taking both comments as compliments.

The roadster was a cool car, Lionel thought, and had it not been for the disappearances of his family and the danger in which he now found himself, he might have been impressed enough to really check it out. He had been interested in unusual cars since he was a small child. But now this was just a way to get to André. Something to ride in.

Talia seemed unable to concentrate even on where she was going. All she could say, over and over, was "Ooh, LeRoy's gonna kill me if he finds out about this!"

Lionel tried to talk to her, mostly to simply change the subject. "So, Talia," he said, "where were you when the disappearances happened?"

"What?" she said, as if demanding to know what in the world he was talking about. "Where *was* I?"

"Yeah. Simple question. Everybody remembers where they were. I was sleeping in my basement with André. Where were you?"

"I was at a party André shoulda been at. So he was with you?"

"He didn't tell you where he was?"

"No! I told you! He's usually at all the parties, but he owed these guys some money, so I figured he was laying low."

"I thought he was hanging with us because we're family."

"Oh, yeah," Talia said. "That's André. Big family man."

"He could be, at times."

"I know. Whenever he really needed something, he played you guys like banjos. When he needed cash or a place to crash, he'd run back to the family and get religion. Am I right? Huh? Am I right?"

Lionel shook his head and looked out the window. Talia was driving toward Chicago. It didn't seem to slip past her that Lionel had ignored her question. "Tell me," she said. "Isn't that what André pulled on your family every time?"

Lionel nodded, but she must not have seen him. "Isn't it?" she pressed.

"Yeah," Lionel muttered. "So, what did you think when people disappeared?"

"Nobody disappeared from *that* party, honey. Made me start believin' it was only Jesus' people who flew away."

"You believe that?"

"No! I'm just sayin' . . ."

"That's what I believe, Talia."

She whirled to face him. "No lie?"

"No lie," Lionel assured her, nodding toward the road where another car was signaling to move into Talia's lane. Lionel hated when she took her eyes from the road. She was an erratic enough driver when she was paying attention.

"So," she said, "how'd you miss out then, comin' from a family like yours? André says they're all gone but him and you."

"Right," Lionel said, and for the next several minutes and most of the ride to Chicago, he told her his story.

Lionel almost wished he hadn't started on the subject. Within minutes, Talia was wiping her eyes with her fingers while still trying to maneuver LeRoy's roadster through Chicago traffic. Lionel was eager to reconnect with André, but he didn't want Talia crying and driving at the same time. He was relieved when she finally pulled to the side of a street about six blocks south of where the police found the body they thought was André's.

Talia shifted into park and buried her face in her hands. "My mama's gone too," she wailed. "I knew the truth. I always knew the truth. I was raised the same way you were. Well, maybe not the same, but Mama warned me and warned me about this!"

"It's not too late, Talia," Lionel said. "I'm a believer now, and so are three of my friends and lots of other people—"

"No! No! It's too late. When Jesus took the Christians away, the Holy Ghost left and nobody can be saved anymore!"

"That's not in the Bible," Lionel said. "You need to talk to our pastor."

"Your pastor was left behind?" Talia said.

Lionel told Bruce's story. "And he told us the Bible talks about a great harvest of souls during the last seven years of the world. Something like a billion and a half people will get saved, and there'll be like 144,000 Jewish evangelists."

"Even if what you're saying is true, Lionel," Talia said, "I know I'm too far gone. If there really is a second chance, I don't deserve one, I know that."

"Nobody deserves a *first* chance. If we had to deserve it, nobody would make it."

To Lionel it appeared that Talia suddenly realized she was

pouring her heart out to a thirteen-year-old boy. She quickly wiped her eyes again, turned the rearview mirror so she could check her face, and quit crying. "André is close by," she said, "but I'm gonna have to let him know you're here and find out if he wants to see you."

"Never mind," Lionel said, reaching for his door handle. "He does."

"You can't just barge in there with me," she said.

"Yes, I can, and you know it. You know he wants to see me."

Talia hesitated. She snorted. "True enough," she said. "He probably wants to see you more than he wants to see me."

Lionel got out of the car, prepared to follow Talia. As he fell into step behind her, he said, "You two not getting along?"

"I'd still marry him, messed up as he is."

"He doesn't want to?"

"Obviously! But I'm scared to death to be facin' the future alone."

"But André is *really* messed up," Lionel said.

"Not as much as me," she said.

Lionel wondered what kind of a couple those two would make.

Talia led Lionel around the back of a three-story brick apartment building in a bad neighborhood. Lionel wondered if Judd and the others were still keeping track of him. In a way he hoped they were, but he also wondered what three white kids would do to protect him in *this* neighborhood.

As they approached the rear entrance, Lionel noticed the lights went off in the apartment at that end on the top floor. As they climbed the square staircase, Lionel was quickly enveloped in odors and noise. People were apparently cooking, arguing, and fighting.

As they reached the third floor, where the lights at the end of the building had gone out, Talia put a finger to her lips and knocked four times at the door. Silence.

She knocked four times again. "Open up, André!" she called out. "It's jes' me."

"Somebody's with you!" André hissed from just inside the door. "Who is that?"

"It's your nephew! Now open up!"

Before the words were out of her mouth, André had begun the process of unlocking, unbolting, unchaining, and opening the door. He peered out from the dark apartment, then grabbed Talia and Lionel and yanked them inside. He shut, locked, bolted, and chained the door in the dark. "Now," he said finally. "Let's get a look at you."

Lionel couldn't help but chuckle. His uncle had always been a little crazy, but—

"It'll be a long time before my eyes get used to the darkness and I can see you," Lionel said. "Get a light on in here."

Lionel heard André feeling along the wall for a switch. When a single, bare bulb came on above them, Lionel was stunned to see his wasted uncle. André was barefoot and wore a pair of old, shiny suit pants and a sleeveless T-shirt with food stains down the front. He appeared to not have bathed for days. His hair was matted, his facial hair patchy. His breath smelled of alcohol, and his dark eyes were bloodshot. It was all Lionel could do to keep from gasping and telling his uncle how bad he looked. Lionel assumed André knew that and didn't care.

"Oh, André!" was all Talia seemed to be able to say, and when he approached her, she stiffened. Whatever relationship was there or had been there or was trying to be rekindled, Lionel knew André's present condition wasn't helping.

"Ain't there no shower in this place?" she finally managed.

André shrugged. "Yeah, I guess."

"Get your stinking self in there and get cleaned up," she said. "Shave and brush your teeth too, and don't be comin' back out here until you do."

André squinted at her and looked as if he were about to burst into tears, but his shoulders sagged and he skulked away like a little boy who'd been ordered about by his mother. "Oh, man!" he whined.

"Hey," Lionel said. "I haven't got all night. I got people who worry about me when I get in late."

"That's more than I can say," Talia said, collapsing into a plastic chair at the Formica-topped dinette table. A heavy, glass ashtray full of butts and a nearly empty bottle of cheap wine graced the table. Talia noticed them as if an ugly insect had just landed before her.

"Oh, for the love of all things . . . ," she said, never finishing the thought. She had just used her foot to slide out another chair for Lionel when she stood and grabbed the wine bottle in one hand and the ashtray in the other. She tossed the bottle into a wastebasket nearly full of beer cans, where it settled at a crazy angle. She held the ashtray at eye level, looked resolutely at Lionel, and let it drop. It smashed the wine bottle, and Lionel heard the last of the wine drip to the bottom of the basket. The contents of the ashtray, however, scattered on the floor. Talia swore.

Steam poured from under the door of the nearby bathroom. Over the sound of the cascading water, André hollered, "What's goin' on out there?"

"I'm just clearin' the table," Talia answered. "What you been doin' for food, just drinkin'?"

"That's all the food I need!" André said. "Don't be messin' with my hooch."

Lionel was disgusted. He was relieved to know that André was still alive, if you could call this living. There was always a chance for André if he didn't kill himself or get himself killed first.

Was this the life André thought was better than what the rest of the family enjoyed? There had never been cigarettes or booze in Lionel's house. When guests asked his mother if she minded if they smoked, she always said kindly, "Of course not. I have an air-conditioned facility for you just beyond that door." It was the door to the driveway. And when Mrs. Washington's colleagues at *Global Weekly* magazine forgot themselves and showed up at dinner parties with gifts of expensive liquor or wine, or if they sent the same as Christmas gifts, she thanked them politely. She did not serve the stuff, of course, but the next day sold it to the manager of the beverage department at the corner store and gave the entire amount to the church. "The devil used that money long enough," she would tell her husband sweetly, winking at Lionel. "It's time the Lord got it back."

How Lionel missed his mama at times like this! What had he been thinking when he considered being a rebel with André better than being part of the family of God?

The only things André had to change into were brightly colored and way-too-big workout shorts and a T-shirt that had been left in the apartment. Lionel could only wonder whose place this was and whose clothes those were. André padded out, keeping the shorts up with one hand.

"You look better," Talia said, smiling. "But not much."

André did not smile. "Man," he said, "it's good to see you both."

Lionel was frustrated. This was no family reunion. This was the only family he had left. "André," Lionel said, "I want to know what happened after you left that crazy message on my answering machine."

But the phone rang. André jumped, then stared at Talia. "How'd you get here?" he asked.

"I borrowed LeRoy's roadster."

"What? He doesn't loan that out!"

"He doesn't exactly know."

"Oh, man!"

André answered the phone and immediately glared at Talia. "LeRoy!" he mouthed silently. "And he's not happy."

# 26

**ANDRÉ** stood and paced, stretching the phone cord to its limit. He whined, cried, begged, explained, and tried to cover for Talia. "It was my fault, man," he told LeRoy. "I called and begged her to come here and see me. . . . Anyone with her? No, why do you ask? . . . No, you don't need to come here! She'll be right back. . . . I just needed to see her, that's all. I want to get out of here! When can I live with you guys? . . . I did my part! . . . I'm not telling you what to do. I'm just askin'."

Lionel had no idea what LeRoy was saying, but André was as scared as Lionel had ever seen him. "I'll send her right home, LeRoy," André said, "but remember, this was all my idea. Don't take it out on her."

André hung up. "LeRoy's mad," he said.

"No kidding," Talia said. "And you were a lying wuss. Don't you ever get tired of being a coward?"

"I was just trying to protect you, girl. You ought to be grateful."

"You were protectin' yourself, André! And I don't need your help."

"LeRoy will kill you and never think twice about it. You'd better get back there."

"We're going," she said. "Come on, Lionel."

"I'm not going anywhere," Lionel said. "I need some answers, and I'll find my own way back."

"Yeah, right," Talia said. "Let's go."

"I'm not going," Lionel insisted. "Go if you want to."

"Well, I've got to go. If you want to find your own way back—"

"If you don't get back soon, Talia," André said, "LeRoy will come looking for you, and we don't want that."

"This bus is pullin' out, Lionel," Talia said. "Last call, all aboard."

He waved her off.

"Suit yourself," she said, as if he had made the dumbest decision ever. She went through the whole unlocking routine to let herself out, and then André had to lock up again.

"What is all this about?" Lionel demanded. "Talk to me!"

But André had turned out the lights and crept to the window to keep track of Talia on her way to the car. "Ooh, that *is* LeRoy's roadster! Oh, man!"

"What'd you think, we were lying? Now, c'mon, André! I've been worried about you for days!"

"Shh!" André said, still peering out the window. "You don't know what kind of trouble I'm in, and if you're not out of here soon, you're gonna be right in it with me."

Lionel turned the light on, and André ducked away from the window, crashing into a chair. "Don't do that!" he said. "Somebody'll see me!"

"Who are you afraid of? LeRoy isn't even around here."

"How do you know? He wasn't at your house, or he never would have let Talia leave with you."

"Is he coming here?"

"He might. Not too many other people know where I am."

"What's it all about, André? You make that crazy call and leave a long message on our machine that sounds like you're going to kill yourself, and when I get to your place to check on you, the cops tell me you committed suicide and where I can identify the body. So I go to the place and there you are, but it's not you. Who killed himself or got himself murdered wearing your clothes and carrying your identification?"

André sat and buried his head in his hands. "I didn't mean it to come to all this," he wailed. He was interrupted yet again, this time by another knock on the door. He looked up with a start and motioned frantically for Lionel to turn off the light. Lionel did, but then turned it back on when he heard Talia's voice.

"It's just me," she whispered loudly through the door. "Don't open up. I just wanted to tell you there's an expensive car full of white kids down the block. Looks like they're up to no good, but they're in the wrong neighborhood. They're going to get that nice car stole. If you pulled that off, André, you might be back in good with LeRoy."

"I ought to already be back in good with LeRoy," André said, but Lionel was beginning to unlock the door.

"Don't be openin' up now," Talia insisted. "I'm going."

"No!" Lionel said. "Wait!" He got the door open. "Those are my friends down there. Tell 'em I'm all right and that they should wait for me. They're my ride home."

Talia rolled her eyes and shrugged. "Whatever. But that car would sure get LeRoy's attention."

"You and LeRoy already hassled one of the kids in that car," Lionel said. "One more deal like that and you'll be out of my house sooner than you think."

"Ooh, tough guy," she said. "I'll tell your chauffeur you're on your way."

André and Lionel fell silent, listening to Talia's footsteps all the way down the stairs and out into the alley, where she fired up the roadster. Lionel turned out the light, and they watched out the window as she pulled down the street and stopped next to Judd's car. Lionel only hoped the others would believe her and not come charging in to rescue him. Who knew what Ryan would do after having been chased by her and LeRoy earlier?

Lionel was mad. "Turn the light on, Uncle André," he said. The word *uncle* nearly stuck in his throat because he sure had seen a new and unattractive side of André. He didn't seem older or wiser or worthy of any respect like he sometimes used to. Now it seemed as if Lionel was the one who should be in charge. Maybe André was in trouble, but did that justify his acting like such a wimp? What was wrong with him?

They both knew that the faith they had turned their backs on before was right and true and could save them now, so why was it only Lionel, the younger of them, who had seen the light?

André turned the light on and sat down, as if expecting a lecture. But a lecture was not what Lionel had in mind. He had a lot of questions, and he wanted answers.

"When you called my house, drinking and crying and slobbering and talking about killing yourself, were you serious or were you put up to that?"

"Both."

"What do you mean? Part of that was just acting?"

"Part of it," André said, staring at the floor.

"I was worried to death about you. I didn't want you to go to hell. Anyway, we're family, man. We're all we've got left. We've got to watch out for each other."

258

"Listen, Lionel, I'm going to hell whether you want me to or not."

"You want to?"

" 'Course not! But that's where people like me go!"

"I'm not going there!" Lionel said. "And I used to be like you."

"You were just a kid. I was afraid I was the one who made you what you were. I'm so glad you're a Christian now."

"Then why aren't you?"

"It's too late for me."

"You know better than that! You know the truth. You just have to act on it now, André."

"You have no idea."

"Then tell me! What's going on? I want to know!"

André stood, paced, then sat again. He let out a huge sigh. "All right," he said finally. "That guy found in my apartment was one of the guys I owed money to."

"Really? He wasn't one of the two I met that one time, was he? He sure didn't look like them. They were both a lot bigger."

"Those two just worked for him. They were his collection guys. When they couldn't get any money out of me, he came lookin' for me. It was pay up or be killed. I had held out on him way too long. Well, I had no money, and LeRoy wasn't about to advance me any, so it came down to kill or be killed. That's when I called you. I didn't want to die. If I was going to go, I was going to go on my own terms. I'd rather kill myself than die that way."

"So you were serious."

"Well, mostly. LeRoy had come up with a plan. He knew this guy I owed the money to, see, and he was the one who reminded me that the guy was my size. It was LeRoy's idea to get him to come to my place for the money. He told me to leave some message somewhere that would make it look like I killed myself. I called your machine, left that message, talked about how guilty I felt about you and all that, and then even wrote a suicide note.

"After the guy showed up, LeRoy's friends had his people outnumbered and ran them off. While the guy thinks he's got his bodyguards protecting him from the hallway, LeRoy pops out of the closet and gets the drop on the guy. He makes him put on my clothes and put my wallet and stuff in his pocket. He put on my rings and watch and everything. Then LeRoy told me to off him."

"Kill him?"

"Yeah. But I couldn't do it. I had the blade and everything to make it look like a suicide. I was afraid the guy would fight and make it look obvious that someone had done it to him, but LeRoy had thought of that too. He tells the guy he's going to die anyway and gets the guy crying and begging and starts loading him up with whiskey. This is real strong stuff now, the good stuff, not like I'm used to drinking. He gets the guy so mellow and out of it that he didn't even struggle. I was supposed to cut him, but I couldn't even do that."

"Of course you couldn't kill someone, André. You know better than that."

"Oh, don't be makin' me out as some kind of saint now, Lionel. Fact is, I wish I could have done it. LeRoy was setting me up, don't you see? I had told him all about your house and how I knew you would let us stay there and everything. But once he set up this fake suicide and murdered the guy, he made sure he had something on me."

"What does he have on you? You owe him money too?"

"No! Think, boy! We never expected you to go identify the body. We figured you'd get the word and believe it was me, and that would be the end of it. But now that you told the cops it wasn't me, it won't be long before they figure out who the victim was, and guess who looks guilty? I mean, the guy was found in my place in my clothes. If it's not me, it has to be someone I murdered and made to look like me, right?"

Lionel nodded slowly. "So, you're hiding out from everybody. The dead guy's men. The cops. Anybody who might know you and spread the word you're alive."

"Exactly."

"André, I never told the cops it wasn't your body I saw."

André stood quickly. "What? You didn't? Are you sure?"

" 'Course I'm sure. I was spooked by that place, and I was so shocked it wasn't you that I just left."

"You didn't even tell the coroner?"

"The only people who know are my friends and my pastor."

André clapped and danced. "Oh, man!" he shouted. "I love you!"

Lionel sat and put both hands atop his head. "I don't know what you're so happy about. No matter how you look at it, you were there when a guy was murdered. You're in on it. You're as guilty as LeRoy."

"Technically, legally, yeah, I guess," André said, and the full realization hit Lionel how far gone his uncle truly was. "But don't you see? LeRoy's really got nothing hanging over my head! I can go live in your house with those guys. My debt is gone because the guy I owed is dead. LeRoy can't keep me hidden away because there's no need. I can just use a new name, get new papers, and nobody's the wiser."

Lionel suddenly felt very old. André was more than twice his age, and as usual, André seemed to know less than he did. How long could he get by after coming out of hiding before someone who knew him put the word out that he wasn't dead after all? Sure, the cops had a lot of other stuff to do with all the chaos that had come from the disappearances. But no one was going to look the other way when there had been an obvious murder. An apparent suicide victim is in the morgue, and yet people see him on the streets? Lionel was amazed at the shortsightedness, the stupidity of his uncle. More, though, he was heartbroken at André's complete lack of guilt or sense of responsibility for what had happened. Maybe the guy who died was a bad guy who deserved it. He had probably killed people himself. But that didn't make his death any less of a murder, and André, was in it up to his ears.

Lionel stood and moved to the door. "Tell LeRoy what you told me," André said. "I mean, I'll call him, but he won't believe me unless you tell him too. Then I'll be back at your house before you know it."

Lionel just shook his head as he began the unlocking routine again. "Uncle André," he said, turning to face him, "you have only one chance. You have to tell what you know about the murder, admit you were part of it."

André laughed. "Yeah, good plan. I don't go to heaven when Jesus comes back, I have to live through the Tribulation, I'm on my way to hell, and you want me to spend what's left of my miserable life in prison."

"What I want is for you to do what's right."

"I've never done what's right," André said. And for the first time that evening, Lionel thought André was right on the money.

# 27

IT WAS getting late. Judd was tired and knew the others had to be too. He had sat in that idling car for more than an hour, including when the young black woman showed up alone and told Judd that Lionel would be down soon.

"Is he all right?" Judd asked her as Ryan slid off the backseat and crouched on the floor.

"Yeah," Talia said. "He's all right as long as he's with his uncle. André ain't gonna do nothin' to his own blood. And you can tell your little spy in the back there that he can come out of hiding. Next time LeRoy sees him on our property, though, he's going to be in deep dirt."

Vicki laughed.

Talia leaned in past Judd, who backed up to make room. "What's your problem, little wench?"

"I'm not the one with the problem," Vicki said, and Judd was stunned at her casual tone. She must have had a lot of experience talking tough to older people. "You're the one referring to Lionel's house as your property. What a joke."

"You don't see me laughin'," Talia said.

"How long do you guys think you can get away with just moving into a person's house without his permission?"

"Long as you mind your own business," Talia said. "I wouldn't be messin' with stuff that's none of your concern."

"As long as Lionel's our friend, his trouble *is* our business."

Talia had waved them off and hurried back to her car. That's when Judd began to worry. He kept an eye on the clock, and time seemed to drag.

"Is she gone?" Ryan asked from the floor of the backseat.

"Yes," Vicki said, turning to talk to him. "You don't have to be afraid of her."

"You didn't see this LeRoy guy. He looks like he could whip anybody. I'm afraid of all of 'em."

"Not me," Vicki said.

"That was obvious," Judd said. "Why not?"

"It wasn't that long ago I was a brat and didn't care what I said to adults. They hardly ever follow through on their threats, and what are they going to do anyway? I mean, these people may be the real thing, but they aren't going to waste their time hassling kids like us."

"Except they have to worry that Lionel is eventually going to go to the police."

"That's why they keep trying to intimidate him. That stuff doesn't work on me. I don't want to be mean, but she didn't scare me at all."

"You'd be scared if LeRoy was chasin' you," Ryan said.

"That is probably true," Vicki said.

Judd grew tenser as the night wore on. "We said we were going to come looking for Lionel if we didn't hear from him by eleven," he said.

"But we heard from him through the woman," Vicki said.

"She could have been lying. Why should we trust her?"

"That message had to come from Lionel. Otherwise, how would she know we were his friends?"

"You have to admit, Vick, we look a little out of place here."

Vicki shot Judd a double take. "Why did you call me 'Vick'?"

Judd shrugged. "Just a nickname. Sorry."

"I don't mind," she said. "It's just that my big brother always called me that. I miss him so much." She turned away and covered her eyes with her hand.

"Sorry," Judd said again.

"It's all right," she managed. "I like remembering him."

"I'm really tired," Ryan said. "If this wasn't such a scary place, I'd be sleeping right now."

"I wouldn't be able to sleep here either, partner," Judd said.

"Oh, man!" Ryan said, falling to the floor again. "That van that just turned into the alley! That's got to be LeRoy!"

"Are you sure?"

"How could I forget that ugly thing chasing me all through the neighborhood?"

"Oh, great," Judd said, glancing at Vicki, who quickly wiped her eyes and turned to look around the area.

"We've got to get Lionel out of there," she said, reaching for the door handle. "Let's go."

"Just a minute," Judd said. "We don't know what we're walking into. What if LeRoy's armed, or not alone? And where exactly *is* Lionel? And is there more than one way out of that alley?"

"Let's just go home," Ryan whined.

A figure appeared in the rearview mirror. Judd whispered, "Uh-oh," and put the car in gear. When the figure reached for the back door, Judd floored the accelerator, and the car screeched away from the curb.

The figure slapped the car and shouted, "Hey!"

"Oh, no!" Ryan shouted. "Go! Go!"

Judd was going all right, until Vicki whirled around and stared behind them. "That's Lionel!" she said. "Go back! Go back!"

Judd slid to a stop and threw the car into reverse. He wasn't used to speeding backwards and twice veered into the curb. That must have made Lionel wonder about his safety because Judd saw him skip up onto the sidewalk. When Judd finally stopped near Lionel, he was stunned to see Lionel chuckling.

"What did I do, scare you guys?" he said, as he slid into the backseat. "And what're you doin' on the floor, Ryan?"

Judd floored the gas pedal again, but he had forgotten to shift into drive, and the car jumped back and over the curb, narrowly missing a light pole and stopping inches from a brick wall. "Hey! Whoa!" Lionel said, laughing. "You're safe in this neighborhood, now that you've got a brother in the car."

Judd was relieved he had not hit Lionel or the wall but was also embarrassed at being such a klutz. He was soon speeding away, only to have to stop quickly at a red light a few blocks away. "Didn't you see LeRoy?" Judd demanded.

"LeRoy? No, Talia brought me to see André. They've got him holed up in—"

"I mean didn't you just see LeRoy pull into that alley?"

Lionel turned around in his seat. "Are you sure?"

"We're sure," Ryan muttered from the floor.

"Get up here, will you?" Lionel said. "You're safe now."

Ryan clambered into the seat. "He was drivin' that ugly old brown and yellow van," he said.

"Must've been him all right," Lionel said. "We'd better go back."

"Right," Judd said sarcastically. "I'm gonna go back there and face LeRoy in the middle of the night."

"Yes," Vicki said. "Let's."

"No!" Ryan wailed. "I've been brave enough for one day."

"Yeah," Lionel said. "You're brave as long as you can camp out on the floor out of sight."

Judd didn't know what to do. He felt responsible for Lionel, but was André his problem too? He pulled to the side of the street after getting a green light.

"We're not going back, are we?" Ryan said.

"Just let me think," Judd said.

"We have to," Vicki said.

"If you don't go back, I'm going to have to go on my own," Lionel said. "He's my uncle, and I have to make sure LeRoy doesn't do something stupid. Once LeRoy figures out that I'm onto him and that my friends know, André is as good as dead."

"Well," Judd said, "I can't let you go back alone, but I don't think we all need to go either."

"I don't want to go at all," Ryan said.

"We got that message," Lionel said.

"I don't want to get this car down in there and not be able to get out," Judd said.

"C'mon," Vicki said, "let's just walk back with Lionel and see what we can see."

"You can't leave the car here either," Lionel said. "You'll come back to a pile of trash or maybe to a pile of nothing."

Judd sighed. He felt responsible for everyone. It wasn't fair to make Ryan face LeRoy again. And how could Judd ensure his safety? He breathed a silent prayer. He didn't know how to tell yet when God was leading him directly. He decided to use his best judgment and assume that was from God.

"Vicki," he said, "Lionel and I will go back and be sure André's all right. You and Ryan stay here with the car—"

"Oh, I wanted to go," Vicki said. "I'm not afraid of—"

"Just do this for me," Judd said. "I don't have time to argue about it, but I'm not leaving the car here or Ryan here alone."

"Thank you!" Ryan shouted.

Vicki shook her head. "OK," she muttered.

"I hate to leave you out of it," Judd said. "But I don't know what else—"

"Just go," she said. "I understand."

It didn't seem like she understood or agreed, but Judd didn't have the time to persuade her. He took her word for the fact that she was all right with his decision, and he and Lionel headed back. "Keep the doors locked and the engine running," Lionel said as they left. "And don't talk to anyone but a cop."

It appeared to Judd that he and Lionel were the only ones on the street at that time of the night. He followed Lionel, who loped down the sidewalk and cut in to the first alley he could find. Half a block in that direction he took a right and was headed directly back to where he had visited André. He pointed and said, "Three blocks up. That three-story building."

The words were barely out of Lionel's mouth when Judd heard what sounded like a firecracker. Lionel stopped and Judd ran into him, knocking him flat on his face. Lionel sat up and groaned as Judd apologized. Lionel pulled up his jeans to display scrapes on both knees. His hands and elbows were scraped raw too.

"I'm sorry, man," Judd said over and over. "I heard that pop, but I didn't see you stop."

"I'm all right," Lionel said through clenched teeth. "Let's keep going." But as he stood, a huge shock wave and then a deafening explosion rocked the alleyway. It knocked Lionel back onto his seat and made Judd cover his ringing ears.

"Oh no, oh no!" Lionel said, scrambling to his feet and

running toward André's building. As they closed the gap, Judd saw flames leaping from the top-story window. Within seconds, flames engulfed the third floor. Judd stared at the fire as he ran and was startled when Lionel slowed and turned around, catching him and flinging him up against a building in the alley.

"What—?" he began, then noticed headlights coming fast and furious. He and Lionel plastered themselves back against the wall as the careening vehicle bore down on them. The alley was barely wide enough for them and the truck, or whatever it was. As it scraped the wall across from them on its way by, Judd saw it was a brown and yellow van. Crazily, he noticed the vertical row of decals running down the passenger side of the front windshield.

"That's got to be LeRoy!" Lionel shouted, and ran on. Judd stood staring at the back of the van as it darted from side to side and scraped buildings, hit garbage cans, and nearly rolled over as it shot left out of the alley and onto the street. He worried that LeRoy would see Vicki and Ryan in his car as he raced by.

When Judd turned back, Lionel was long gone. Judd raced toward the burning building, making out Lionel's silhouette ahead of him as he ran. He hoped against hope Lionel wouldn't try to get into that place, but he knew he would do the same if *his* last living relative were trapped in there.

Lionel didn't hesitate. He blasted through the door on the first floor as other people were making their way out, screaming and hollering. The entire third floor was enveloped in fire, and Judd saw a burly man in just his undershorts and T-shirt trying to keep Lionel from getting all the way in. Lionel quickly evaded him, and soon Judd was near the entrance himself and faced a decision.

269

Everything in him wanted to run the other way. He knew it wouldn't be long before the fire began dropping embers to the other floors. This building would not be saved. Dozens of tenants hurried from the place, gathering in clusters as far as they could get from the fire.

Judd stood on the walkway leading to the back door, squinting against the orange light of the flames and holding an arm before his face to shield his cheeks from the searing heat. He could hardly believe a fire still thirty feet above him could radiate like that. Judd reached the door and peeked around the people who streamed out. He caught sight of Lionel bobbing and weaving and darting up the stairs between, around, and sometimes over the escapees. Some tried to restrain him, but he fought them off, clearly not willing to be held back.

Surely he would retreat when he reached the wall of flame that filled the third floor, wouldn't he? But what if he didn't? Judd felt a huge and terrible responsibility for his new friend and brother. He couldn't afford to lose Lionel. He would never forgive himself. He charged into that building like a crazy man, not knowing whether he was there to drag Lionel out or help him find his uncle André. All he knew was that he was on his way.

People tried to stop Judd just as they had tried to stop Lionel. But the roar of the fire grew, and soon people worried only about themselves. To Judd it seemed the heat and noise intensified with every step up the stairs. On the second-floor landing he ran into a family who seemed to be moving in slow motion. The man was huge and heavy. He waddled across the landing, his big belly leading the way, with an old woman straddling his neck and a frail, elderly man in each arm. The men howled and the woman sobbed. The man merely looked resolute, as if the only thing on his mind was saving every member of his family. Judd hesitated and watched them go.

The man stumbled on the first step leading to the lower floor and had to run awkwardly downstairs to remain upright. He turned at the last moment and his shoulder crashed against the wall, making his wife scream, but he somehow kept any of the three he carried from getting hurt.

Judd turned back in time to see Lionel barging up to the third floor, where the heat and flames were so oppressive Judd couldn't imagine how anyone could breathe, let alone survive. His instincts screamed at him to turn back, but he would not let Lionel do this alone.

When Judd finally caught up with him on the third-floor landing, Lionel had stopped at last. The fire billowed, flames devouring the ceiling, popping bulbs and melting fixtures. Old drywall and slats burned and fell around them. "We can't go any further!" Judd hollered, but Lionel either didn't hear or refused to pay attention.

"He's right through there!" Lionel screamed, pointing at the first door across the hall. The door seemed the only thing above floor level not on fire. "LeRoy would never have had time to lock him in!"

"That knob will be hot!" Judd said, but Lionel was ahead of him, pulling off his shirt and wrapping his hand in it. He ducked and scampered to the door, turning the knob while Judd kicked at the door.

The knob was so hot it started Lionel's shirt afire. He beat it out on his thigh as the door swung open and banged against the wall. There was no doubt the fire had begun in this room, and LeRoy—if he had done it—had not even tried to hide the evidence. A five-gallon gas can lay in a corner, sending flames licking to the ceiling.

Judd had never felt such heat, and it seemed as if his skin were blistering and might slide right off his face.

"Here he is!" Lionel shouted from the bathroom. "He's bleeding!"

Judd caught himself just in time to keep from telling Lionel not to try to move André. How absurd would that be? No matter what André's injuries, even tossing him out the window would be preferable to letting him roast to death in this room.

Judd made his way to the bathroom door, where Lionel had already begun dragging his uncle out by his shoulders. Judd was bigger and stronger than Lionel, so he told Lionel to grab André's feet. Judd thrust his fists under André's arms from behind and began scooting backward out of the bathroom and toward the door.

Praying they would have time to get the man down the stairs before the whole building came crashing around them, Judd heard sirens and people screaming. He was suddenly aware that his left forearm was being drenched anew with every beat of André's heart.

"At least he's still alive!" Judd shouted.

**28**

**THOUGH** André was not a big man, he was barely conscious and unable to help Lionel and Judd get him down two flights of stairs. Judd thought André was trying to talk, but all he could hear was a gurgle above the roar of the flames and the crashing of his own heart.

Judd tried to keep his eyes closed because the heat and smoke grated on them. He peeked each time he felt Lionel backing into another turn, and once he saw a burning wood slat drop onto Lionel's shoulder. Lionel flinched when it hit him, but when it stuck and kept burning, he had to drop one of André's legs to brush it away. That made Judd lose his grip, and he fought to hang on. André's weight carried Judd down toward André, and he found himself nearly stumbling over the wounded man.

As the boys struggled to get a new hold on André, a great roar and crash came from above them, and Judd knew the top floor was giving way. Would it take the second floor with it and crush them beneath a fiery load? They didn't have time to wonder. With his skin blistering and his lungs desperate for clear air, Judd thrust his hands deeper under André's arms, lifted, and began moving as quickly as he knew how. He tried to keep as much weight as possible off Lionel, who was lighter and lower on the stairs, trying to guide their cargo to safety.

André thrashed and screamed, and Judd wondered if he would have to punch him in the face to protect him from himself, the way he had seen in movies. But there was no time, and he didn't know if he was strong enough to knock out a grown man anyway.

Fire surrounded the boys, and Judd heard the walls and ceiling dropping behind him. The whole staircase shuddered beneath their weight, and as the last of the other tenants pushed through the front door and out into the night, three firemen swept in, axes in hand, and surveyed the scene.

They apparently didn't see Judd and Lionel and André at first. They studied the crumbling holocaust, looked at each other, shook their heads, and turned to head back out.

"Hey!" Judd shrieked. "Help us!"

The three whirled as one, tossed their axes out through the glass doors, and rushed up the stairs. "You boys get out now!" the first said. "We've got this guy!"

Judd let go of André, who now rested awkwardly with his head upstairs and his feet in Lionel's hands. Lionel refused to let go. Judd kept the front door in sight, fearing he would pass out if he didn't get fresh air, and right now. He grabbed Lionel on the way past and was amazed at how strong the younger boy was. Judd could barely budge him at first, but with his weight heading down, he got enough leverage and yanked Lionel away from his uncle.

Just as the first fireman lifted André and threw him over his shoulder, the whole staircase dropped three feet. That made the firemen and the boys fall onto the burning floor, and André dropped onto his back. "Get out! Get out!" the first fireman yelled. "All of you!"

He lifted André again and used his knees and shoulders to herd the boys the last few feet to the door. At a dead run now, the big man carried the thrashing André on his back. He charged through what was left of the glass, Judd and Lionel a step ahead of him. The four of them tumbled and rolled out into the night air, landing in a heap in the grass. Judd sucked in the sweet air for his very life.

The fireman dragged André thirty feet from the inferno and laid him on his back, barking into his radio for paramedics. He whirled to face the building and, not seeing his coworkers, sprinted back, grabbing his axe on the way. Judd watched him call for support, frantic to get to the two firemen still trapped inside.

As more firemen donned oxygen masks and began the dangerous journey into the fire, Judd turned back to see Lionel sprawled nearly atop his uncle, who appeared to be breathing his last. Blood still spurted from the right side of his neck, but his heartbeat had slowed and weakened. "No! No!" Lionel screamed. "God, don't let him die! André!"

Judd covered with his hand the deep wound in André's neck as the man tried to talk. "This is what hell will be like," he rasped. "I deserve it, Lionel."

"No! We all deserve it, André! But you don't have to go! Don't go!"

"It's too late for me. I'm not gonna make it, boy."

"André! You can still go to heaven! Pray! Pray!"

"It's too late."

"It wasn't too late for the thief on the cross! Please, André!"

Judd's fingers were directly on the carotid artery, which is where Judd assumed André had been shot before the apartment was set afire. He felt precisely when André's heart stopped. André thrashed a bit more, shaking his head. "Can't breathe," he whispered. And suddenly he went rigid.

Lionel sobbed while using his shirttail to wipe André's face and his own mouth. He leaned over and began mouth-to-mouth resuscitation, but Judd knew the heartbeat was as important as the breathing. Judd began rhythmically pushing on André's chest, and with each thrust a tiny rivulet of blood eked from André's neck.

"It's no use, Lionel," Judd said. "He's gone."

"No! Don't give up!"

Two medics arrived and pulled the boys off André. "Let me get in here, guys," one said. "I can do more than you can."

He slapped an oxygen mask on André as his partner felt for a pulse in the neck. "What happened to this guy?" he said.

"I think he was shot," Judd said.

"Keep him alive!" Lionel insisted.

"It's too late, son. I'm sorry."

"Try!"

"Son, this man is gone. Now we have firemen to attend to. I'm sorry."

Lionel was inconsolable. He would not leave André's body, even when the medics came back and covered it with a sheet and told Lionel someone would be there soon for the body. Judd tried to get Lionel to come with him back to the car, but he would not budge. He didn't talk, didn't pray, didn't do anything but kneel next to André, rocking and shaking his head as he wept.

"I'm going to go tell Vicki and Ryan what happened and bring the car back to get you," Judd said. Lionel didn't respond. "I'll be back as soon as I can, but I'm probably not going to be able to park very close. You don't have to come until someone comes for André, OK?" Judd got no reaction from Lionel. "I'll be right back," he said.

Judd planned to jog back to the car, but when he rose, he could barely walk. He didn't know what he had done to strain his ankles, his knees, his hips, even his shoulders. He felt like an old man, slowly making his way past the tenants, the onlookers, and the emergency vehicles. The cool night air felt good in his lungs, but it stung his face, which he was afraid to touch. He knew he would have blisters and burns, but he was sure he had not been seriously or permanently injured.

The farther Judd got from the burning building, the stranger the experience seemed. Was this a dream? Had it really happened? He couldn't imagine anything as traumatic as losing his family to the Rapture and being left behind, but neither had he ever been through something like this. The sounds of the blaze faded more with each step, and though he saw the shadows of the flames in the darkness, he had to turn and look once more to let the reality set in.

Judd began to pray. He felt sobs rising in his chest as he thanked God that LeRoy, or whoever had done this, had not arrived while Lionel was still in that apartment. Surely he too would have been shot and burned to death.

Lionel had tried so hard to reach his uncle for God. Judd could only hope that Lionel would eventually accept that these decisions were personal. After all, that was why both he and Lionel had been left behind in the first place. No one could make the decision for them.

The police had already barricaded several streets leading to the apartment fire. Gawkers seemed to come from everywhere. Judd finally decided he couldn't cater to his fatigue and pain anymore. He owed it to Vicki and to Ryan to get to them and tell them how much longer he would be.

But when he got to where he had left them in the car, he found nothing. Now what? Neither of them was old enough to drive. Had someone stolen the car? If so, where were Vicki and Ryan? Had LeRoy come by here?

Judd spun around in the street, his eyes landing on a cop directing traffic away from the fire. The cop was short and husky with thick, wavy blond hair. "Someone stole my car!" Judd shouted. "And two of my friends were in it!"

"So *they* stole it," the cop said. "Find them, you find your car."

"They're both too young to drive."

"Then find 'em quick. I'm kinda busy here."

"I have no idea where to look."

The cop talked without looking at Judd, keeping his attention on the traffic. "What kind of a car was it?"

"A BMW."

The cop laughed. "Daddy's car, hmm?"

"Yup."

"And what was a nice boy like you doing in a neighborhood like this with a car like that?"

"Looking out for a friend."

"Another rich kid with no business here?"

"Not exactly."

"Can't help you, son. 'Fraid lost or even stolen cars are pretty low priority these days. We barely had enough guys to handle this fire."

"If I tell you who firebombed that building and murdered a guy, will you help me find my car?"

The cop suddenly focused on Judd. "You're serious, aren't you?"

"I couldn't be more serious," he said.

"Wait right there," the cop said. He hurried to the side of

the street and dragged into the intersection an oversized, blue wooden construction horse with "Police Line. Do Not Cross" painted on it in white. He stepped to his squad car and spoke into his radio. Then he waved Judd over. His nameplate read Sgt. Thomas Fogarty.

"That'll take care of the traffic until I get some backup," he said. "Now, listen—whew, you smell like you were in that fire."

"I was," Judd said, eager to tell his story.

Sergeant Fogarty grabbed Judd by the shirt and pushed him up against a light pole. "You listen to me, kid. This has nothing to do with you, but I was in the homicide division until I got busted back down to traffic detail for reasons you don't need to know. I tell you that only so you'll know that I understand murder. I'm not lookin' to crack some new case to get back into homicide, but that wouldn't be bad either. The thing is, if you know anything about this fire and it really involves a murder, I'll know whether you're lying or if there's a ring of truth to it. Now what's your name?"

Judd told him and showed him his driver's license. "How long you been drivin'?" Fogarty asked.

"Not that long," Judd said.

Fogarty directed Judd to the squad car, where they sat in the front seat. The cop radioed in a request for an APB (all points bulletin) on Judd's car. Then Judd told him the whole story. He began with losing his family in the vanishings ("I lost a few relatives myself," Fogarty said) and told how he and Lionel had met. He told the cop about the phony suicide/murder, the invasion of Lionel's home, Ryan's close call, Lionel's visit to André that evening, and everything that followed.

"So you're guessing this LeRoy is the shooter because your friend, what's his name—?"

"Ryan."

"Right, Ryan ID'd the yellow and brown van."

"Right."

"Let's get you back over to the scene and see if we can help your friend and be sure the body is taken care of."

As Sergeant Fogarty pulled out into traffic his radio squawked to life with the news that a cruiser had just pulled over the BMW that was the subject of the APB. "Who's the driver?" Fogarty asked.

"Female Caucasian, Byrne, Victoria, underage, no license. Other occupant male Caucasian, Daley, Ryan, age twelve."

"Ten-four. What's their story?"

"She says they were awaiting two other friends, the driver, male Caucasian, Thompson, Judd Jr., sixteen, and male African-American, Washington, Lionel, thirteen. Long story, Sarge. She thought they were safe with the doors locked and engine idling. Claims they were nearly hit by a van."

"Let me guess. It was yellow and brown."

"Ten-four."

"That checks out. Don't cite her unless there's some obvious violation."

"She wasn't moving when I found her. Nothing to cite."

"Give me your ten-twenty, and I'll bring the driver within the hour."

André's body was being loaded into an ambulance when Sergeant Fogarty pulled up to the scene. He asked a paramedic to check for a carotid artery wound. "Already checked, sir. In our opinion, it was the cause of death. That'll have to be confirmed by the coroner, of course, but this man bled to death. No ID on him, by the way."

"Let me give you one," Fogarty said. He got the information from Judd and Lionel, who sat sullenly in the backseat of the squad car, and the medic pinned the identification to the body.

"It'll be like looking for a needle in a haystack," Fogarty told the boys as he drove them back to Judd's car, "but we'll use heavy duty metal detectors to try to find the bullet, and maybe the weapon, in the rubble."

Judd sighed heavily, feeling every ache and pain and grieving with Lionel, who cried softly in the backseat.

## 29

EARLY the next morning, Judd stood gingerly in the shower, his scalp and face and neck and hands stinging from the spray on his tender flesh. If everybody else in his house had slept like he did, they had been dead to the world. What a night that had been!

All the way home, Ryan and Vicki had told and retold their harrowing escape from LeRoy and his brown and yellow van. Lionel had listened but did not respond at first. "Are you sure it was LeRoy?" Judd had asked.

"Positive," Vicki said. "Ryan got a clear look at him. We were just sitting there when we heard someone race up behind us. I was sitting behind the wheel, just to see what it felt like, and the engine was running. I had driven my friends' cars before, you know, like in an empty parking lot late at night, so I knew the basics. Anyway, we see this van come barreling past us, and we both lean up against the window for a closer look."

"Which was really stupid," Ryan said. "Especially for me. I mean, LeRoy doesn't know this car or Vicki, but he must have seen me staring at him out of the backseat. He slides to a stop and lowers the window and stares right at me. I slid off the seat and onto the floor. I said, 'Vicki, get me outta here!' "

Vicki picked up the story. "I shifted into drive and floored it, but I forgot to turn. We were on the side of the street, so I had to slam on the brakes to keep from hitting one of those, you know, utility poles. LeRoy pulled right in behind me to pin me in, but when he got out of the van, I just shifted into reverse and backed into the van. That's why your taillights are both smashed. Sorry. Anyway, he jumped back and screamed and swore at us, and I just yanked the wheel to the left, shifted again, and took off. He chased us all over the place, but I finally lost him. I was scared to death."

"He knew you could put him in that neighborhood where the murder and the arson happened," Judd said. "He *wanted* you dead. Probably still does."

"If I'd known that," Vicki said, "I probably would have been too scared to move."

"And you wouldn't be here right now," Lionel said finally. "LeRoy's a murdering scumbag. I know he'll kill me as soon as he finds me."

"He won't find you," Judd said. "He has no idea where I live, and we're keeping this car in the garage once we get home."

"I don't much care anymore," Lionel said.

Vicki turned in her seat to face him. "What do you mean?"

"I failed André," he said.

"So you want to die too?"

"Why not?"

"Because we love you," she said. "That's why. We need you in this family. I feel awful for you and sorry for your uncle, but from what you tell me, he knew the truth and had every chance to accept Christ."

As Judd stood in the shower now, he recalled Lionel's shrugging and turning away. But Judd hoped the truth of what Vicki said would settle in on Lionel this morning and that he would realize that Judd and Ryan—yes, even Ryan—felt the same way about Lionel.

Toweling off was an ordeal, because his raw burns stung. He applied petroleum jelly as Sergeant Fogarty had suggested. Judd looked forward to their ten o'clock appointment. The officer was coming to his house to talk to all of them about the next step.

"I don't feel like meeting with the cop," Lionel told Judd in the kitchen a few minutes later.

"Why not? You're going to be the key to whatever he wants to do. You're the one who knows who these people are and what's really happened."

"I don't know," Lionel said, hunched over a bowl of cereal he had not touched. "I don't feel like much of anything right now."

"You want to call Bruce? I can run you over to the church."

"Nah. I got to work this out for myself. I think I've had enough of talking with adults. First it was André, then Bruce, then LeRoy and the other guy, then Talia, then André again, and now this cop."

"Fogarty."

"Yeah."

"You shouldn't really put André or Talia in the same category as Bruce, should you?"

"I don't know what I think anymore. To tell you the truth, Judd, this makes no sense to me. Why did both André and me get second chances, but I was the only one who did anything about it?"

Judd shrugged. "You're askin' the wrong guy, Lionel. I never

285

thought about stuff like this until last week. You're asking now like you wish André had been saved and you hadn't."

"That's sort of how I feel."

"That sounds pretty biblical to me."

"Biblical?"

"Like the way Jesus feels."

"He wants to be dead?"

"He was willing to die so we wouldn't have to die for our sins. Sounds like you wish you could have died in André's place."

"Yeah, but mostly I want to die because I messed up and André missed his chance."

"You didn't mess up, Lionel. I hate to say it, but André messed up. There was nothing more you could do. You explained. You pleaded with him. Plus, he knew all this from the beginning. He was raised the same way you were."

Lionel sat before his full bowl, hands in his lap, head down. Silent.

---

Sergeant Thomas Fogarty of the Chicago Police Department showed up that morning in a late-model sports car and street clothes. "We have a bit of a problem," he said as Judd showed him to a chair in the living room. Judd sat across from him, Vicki on the couch, Lionel on the floor against the wall, Ryan stretched out on the carpet.

Fogarty turned to Lionel. "Son, ironically, your uncle's body was taken to the same morgue the first murder victim was taken to. Of course the identification you gave me, and which we put with the body, ran into a duplicate record on their computer. I explained the situation to the medical examiner's office, so they have André Dupree correctly identified this time. But now they want to exhume the body of the first André Dupree. You know what that means?"

"Dig him up?"

"Right, to do another autopsy, this time with murder in mind."

"Why is that a problem?" Judd asked.

"That's not the problem. I don't know when or how they'll do that or what they'll do with any new evidence they uncover. Our problem is caseload and jurisdiction."

"What's that?" Ryan asked.

"Because we're still trying to dig out from all the problems associated with the disappearances, everybody on the police force is already working overtime every day. We have to set priorities."

"And murder isn't a priority?" Judd said.

Sergeant Fogarty looked uncomfortable. "This is not easy to say," he said, "especially in this day and age. But we have to face the facts. Prejudice is still alive and well, even among the police. Sometimes especially among the police."

"What are you saying?" Vicki asked.

"Here's the thing. I spent most of last night talking to my old boss in Homicide. I told him the whole story, and he thinks there's a good chance we can nail this LeRoy Banks for both murders—André and the André look-alike. As long as LeRoy is living here in Mount Prospect, that's where the jurisdiction problem comes in. The Chicago PD often cooperates—in a manner of speaking—with suburban departments, but here's where, unfortunately, the racism surfaces.

"My boss claims he was speaking for *his* bosses, but I think I know him better than that. He was speaking his own mind and pretending he wasn't."

Lionel leaned forward. "What'd he say?"

Fogarty pursed his lips and shook his head, as if he could hardly bring himself to repeat it. "He said to me, 'Tommy, with everything we've got on our plates right now, everybody overworked and all, people are asking themselves what do they care about this element killing each other off.' "

"I have no idea what you just said," Ryan said, sitting up.

"I do," Lionel said. "Nobody cares if blacks kill blacks. Especially if they're lowlifes like LeRoy and my uncle and whoever that first victim was."

"That's exactly right," Fogarty said.

"So, you're not going to help us?" Lionel said.

"If I wasn't going to try, I wouldn't be here," the cop said. "I'm a police officer because I'm a justice freak. The problem is, I represent the Chicago PD, and LeRoy Banks is living too far from home right now. I'd have to somehow get Banks back into Chicago."

"Because otherwise, your people don't care enough," Lionel said.

"I'm afraid that's right."

"So what do we do now?"

"You understand I can only advise you," Fogarty said. "I can't do anything for you or with you, and I have no official capacity outside Chicago."

Judd and Vicki nodded. Lionel turned his face away. Ryan still seemed puzzled.

"Our people know of Banks and think we can link him to other killings. But as long as he's holed up this far from Chicago—"

"And nobody down there cares enough," Lionel interrupted.

"—Right, that too. I think your best chance is to scare him

288

out of your house and get him to set up shop back in Chicago where he belongs. Then he's out of your hair, and he becomes Chicago's problem."

"But they don't care," Lionel said, "and when he finds out I've moved back home, he comes back and wipes me out."

"Oh, I wouldn't move back there if I were you," Fogarty said. "Even if you get him to move out. At least until you hear he's been caught and charged."

"So until then, he wins."

"Exactly."

"I'm for trying to run him off," Lionel said. "But how do we do that?"

"That I cannot tell you," Fogarty said. "I have some ideas about how someone might, how shall we say it, persuade someone to move on. But one thing I must caution you: Don't ever confront him in person. You know already that he's armed and dangerous. He'd just as soon kill you as to look at you. He's done it, and he'd do it again. You already know he knows Lionel was with André just before he got there. And he knows Ryan and Vicki were in the neighborhood."

"I'm the only one who's never seen him or been seen by him," Judd said.

"Unless he saw you when he came racing out of the alley last night," Lionel said.

"I doubt it," Judd said.

"I wouldn't risk it," Lionel said.

"Neither would I," Fogarty said. "But I'll tell you what I will do. I'm going to investigate this story and these two murders on my own time. When I get enough evidence on LeRoy, I'm going to be looking for him in his old neighborhood. If you can spook him to the point where he will retreat to there, even one more time, I'll stop him for any reason I can think of. If he so much as has a broken taillight or a loud muffler, I'll pull him over and find a reason to take him to the precinct station house. Once there, I'll find a way to fingerprint him, interview him about two mysterious deaths, and start working on getting him off the streets."

"I believe he's already murdered the guy André told me about and, of course, André," Lionel said.

"Assuming you're right on those, that makes at least four."

"Four?"

"Didn't you see the paper today? Two of the firemen who went into that building last night never made it out. If that was arson—and they found the source of the fire, a gas can, in an apartment rented under the name Cornelius Grey—deaths related to it can be considered homicides. Mr. Grey hasn't been seen there for a long time, and we know he was not the murder victim. But Grey *is* a known associate of LeRoy Banks."

"Connie Grey is an associate of LeRoy's all right," Lionel said, sounding angry. "He's livin' in my house with his sister, Talia."

Fogarty was speedily taking notes. "So LeRoy Banks and Cornelius Grey are the two kingpins of the little group that moved into your house."

Lionel nodded.

"And Talia is Grey's sister."

Lionel nodded again.

"Grey hasn't been tied into any of this before," Fogarty said. "Wonder what's become of him?"

"He's the quiet one of those two," Lionel said. "I don't know if it means anything, but André always kind of liked him. André hated LeRoy. Said he was a bully, a big mouth, a know-it-all. Liked to intimidate people."

"Liked to do more than that to them," Fogarty said. "Now

let me just think out loud here about how I might encourage illegal squatters—you know what that means?"

"People who move into a place they don't own?"

"Yeah. Here's what a person might do to get them to move on. . . ."

For the next hour, Judd took notes. Tom Fogarty told story after story of pranks, ruses, and tricks that had worked on stubborn cases. His favorite was the time the police sent notices to several known felons, informing them they had won expensive gifts, prizes, and trips in a special sweepstakes. All they had to do was come to the ballroom of a swanky downtown hotel to claim them. About 80 percent of the targets of the sting showed up and, at the appropriate and surprising instant, were arrested on their outstanding warrants.

That wasn't something Judd and his friends could pull off without a lot of money and help, but several others of Fogarty's suggestions seemed right up their alley.

# 30

IT FELL to Judd, who believed he was the only one of the four kids who had never been seen by LeRoy Banks, to keep an eye on Lionel's house. Fortunately, his mother's minivan was also in the garage, and he was able to use that and not risk LeRoy recognizing the car that had backed into his brown and yellow monstrosity a few nights before.

The first couple of days Judd tooled around the neighborhood, occasionally passing Lionel's house. The only thing he noticed was that nothing seemed to be going on. He saw neither the old van nor the roadster Lionel had told him about. Maybe LeRoy was lying low for a while, more concerned about keeping out of sight than trying to eliminate the one person who could implicate him in the arson and murders: Lionel.

Finally, though, Judd caught a break. He saw the old brown and yellow van, only it didn't look so old anymore, and it wasn't brown and yellow. It had been spruced up, the rust spots filled and the whole thing painted a muted cream. It looked pretty good. Judd checked in with Sergeant Fogarty, who found out that LeRoy had ordered new plates too. They were for an off-white van in Talia Grey's name, but Fogarty said the van had the same vehicle ID number as LeRoy's. What had not changed, however, were all the city stickers on the far right side of the front windshield. That was the one thing Judd remembered from the van that flashed so close to him in the alley the weekend before. At first all he had seen were the headlights. At the last moment that windshield came into view for the shortest instant, and Judd remembered wondering where in the world they would put another sticker.

When he saw the "new" van, it all came back to him. Someone had had the nerve to park the thing right in front of Lionel's house, as usual. Eventually they would have to get a Mount Prospect city sticker. On the other hand, Judd knew, that would be the last priority of the local police department. If the Chicago PD didn't even care to investigate suspicious deaths in the black community, Mount Prospect might let a few delinquent city stickers slide during a season of international chaos.

Judd could only wonder what type of trouble Talia had been in with LeRoy when LeRoy found out she had borrowed his roadster and taken Lionel, of all people, to see André. Clearly, it seemed LeRoy was intent on doing away with anyone who knew anything about the first murder. That likely included Lionel.

Judd hadn't seen Talia while staking out the area, but one day something showed up on the front porch that made Judd squint, shake his head, and wonder. It was a duffel bag with Lionel's name on it, plain as day. Someone had set it on the top step. To normal passersby, perhaps it wouldn't even catch their attention. But to Judd, and to anyone who knew Lionel and his situation, this seemed some kind of a signal.

Judd drove to a nearby elementary school, closed since the

disappearances, and parked in the deserted staff lot. He then walked idly through the neighborhood, passing Lionel's house on the other side of the street. He still had seen no occupants of the home in all the time he had spent spying on it, but that bag and that repainted van meant someone had to be there.

That evening he mentioned the bag to Lionel.

"That's the bag I used to take on my sports and Y trips," he said. "I thought it was stuffed way deep in my closet. I have no idea what it means. I want to see it."

"I suppose if we go at night we'll be safe," Judd said. "Anybody else want to go?"

"Not me," Ryan said.

"I thought you were getting brave on us all of a sudden," Lionel said. "Don't fall back to being a chicken now."

"I'm not! But I don't care if I never get chased by a van again—I don't care what color it is—as long as I live."

"I'm not afraid of the van," Lionel said. "But I wouldn't want to run into LeRoy right now."

"I want to go," Vicki said, "but I want to stay out of sight until we know no one is watching us."

"Promise," Judd said. "That'll go for you too, Lionel."

"Yeah, I guess I'd be pretty conspicuous in my own neighborhood when everyone knows I don't live there anymore."

"I'm stayin' here," Ryan repeated.

"It's all right with me," Judd said. "As long as you think you'll be all right alone."

"I'll feel safer here. Anyway, like I said, I'm not a chicken anymore. I just don't want to push my luck too far with those murderers."

"I can't blame you," Judd said. "Let's go."

Judd left Ryan with the car phone number, just in case. Several minutes later, with Vicki ducking down in the front passenger seat and Lionel lying out of sight across the backseat of the minivan, Judd drove past Lionel's house. "What do you see?" Lionel wanted to know.

"Nothing. Not a thing. I mean nothing on the porch anyway. The cream van is out front, and there's a light on in a back room."

"That's where Ryan said he heard Talia talking on the phone the other day," Lionel said. "I wonder how she feels about André."

"Wait," Judd said. "I just saw someone! It's a woman, and she's coming from that back room into the hall. The light just went out in that room and on in the hall."

"Park somewhere!" Lionel said. "I want to see if it's Talia."

Judd pulled off to the side, several houses past Lionel's. "You see anybody on the street?" Lionel asked. "Can I sit up?"

"Yeah, but don't do anything stupid."

Lionel sat up. "What, like jumping out of the car and telling everyone in the neighborhood I've come home? Whoa! I can't see anything from here. Back up closer to my house."

"I don't think that's smart," Judd said. "We're going to start drawing attention to ourselves if we do a lot of moving back and forth."

"Then I'm going to sneak up closer and get a look through the window."

"No you're not!" Vicki said, sitting up herself. "We came close enough to losing you the other night. What if LeRoy or Cornelius or whatever his name is in there?"

"Why don't we find out?" Lionel said.

"Not by going up to the house!" Judd said.

"Let's call 'em," Lionel said.

Judd and Vicki looked at each other. "We need to keep this phone open for Ryan," Judd said.

"Ryan will be fine for a few minutes," Vicki said. "No one there will recognize my voice. How about I call?"

"Do it!" Lionel said.

Judd showed her how to dial.

"What if they have caller ID?" Vicki said.

"They don't," Lionel said. "It's my phone, and we don't have it. Unless they added it, and why would they?"

"Even if they do, it's going to trace to this mobile phone," Judd said. "And there's no way the mobile phone company will give out any information on the number. Even if they did, it's listed under my mom's name. Those guys wouldn't have a clue."

"Shh!" Vicki said. "It's ringing."

Judd told her to leave the phone in the cradle so the speakerphone would come on. A female voice answered.

"Who am I speaking to?" Vicki asked.

"Who's askin'?"

"That's Talia!" Lionel mouthed.

"A friend," Vicki said.

"A friend of who?"

"André."

"Oh, oh!" Talia wailed. "Who is this? You know he's dead, don't you? Started a fire, shot himself, and burned himself up in a fire the other night."

"Who told you that?" Vicki said.

"A friend of his."

"The same friend who gave him the gasoline?"

"What're you talking about? Who is this?"

"Someone who knows you were with André before he died." Silence.

"Are you there, Talia?"

"How do you know my name?"

"I told you. I'm a friend. A friend of a friend. A friend you've been looking for and trying to communicate with."

"I'm going to hang up now."

"Wait! Don't! Don't you want to talk to Lionel?"

"Yes! Put him on."

"I'm here, Talia. What'd you put my duffel bag out for?"

"You saw that? Oh, thank God! Ooh, boy, I got in trouble for that. Connie come flyin' in here in LeRoy's roadster and saw that bag before I got a chance to get rid of it, and he told LeRoy. My own brother, tellin' on me. LeRoy liked to kill me."

"The way he did André."

"LeRoy didn't kill André!"

" 'Course he did, Talia. You were there with me. You know André didn't have any five gallons of gas. And if he wanted to kill himself, why did he have to set a fire?"

"LeRoy went to see him later that night, Lionel. Said he found him shot and his place burning."

"It's a lie and you know it. LeRoy did it, don't you see? My friend and I heard a shot and an explosion. We saw the fire and went back. LeRoy almost ran us over in the van. Why do you think he got it painted? Huh? My friend and I dragged André out of there, but it was too late. LeRoy shot him in the neck, blew open some kind of artery—"

"Carotid," Judd whispered.

"Yeah, the carotid artery."

"I don't want to hear this."

" 'Course you don't. Truth hurts. You loved André. I know you did. I loved him too. That's why we have to face the truth."

Judd and the others heard Talia crying. "Why did you want me to see my duffel bag?" Lionel asked.

"I just wanted you not to come around here for a while. LeRoy's been blamin' you for André, shootin' himself. Says it must've been something you said when you saw him. He knew I wouldn't upset André, but he was mad at me for goin' anyway, and especially for taking you."

"You've got to get away from LeRoy," Lionel said. "He's bad news."

"I know," she said. "You know what LeRoy wants to do now? He wants to see if there's any insurance on Connie's apartment that burned, or any life insurance on André."

"You're kidding."

"It's true. They're acting all sad about André and all, but LeRoy and Connie both are talking about checking into some kind of insurance payoff."

"That's sick. Anyway, André never had any life insurance, as far as I knew."

"LeRoy thought he might have had some through his work, you know, before he got laid off from the city."

"Why didn't he try to get that when it looked like André had killed himself before?"

"He was going to. Said he was gonna split it with André and the rest of us. But then he found out you were nosing around and he figured you told somebody that that wasn't André's body."

"I didn't."

"I know. But he didn't know that then. But that was for sure André the other night, wasn't it?"

"For sure."

"So, LeRoy's going after the money."

"How's he going to do that?"

"Call the landlord I guess. Or the city about the life insurance."

"Sick."

"I know. Anyway, stay away from here for a while. I'm sure

glad you saw my message. And I sure hope you're wrong about LeRoy."

Lionel shook his head and said his good-byes. Judd called Sergeant Fogarty on the way home. There had to be a way to use LeRoy Banks' greed against himself.

"I have an idea," Judd told Fogarty. "I want to come downtown and tell you about it."

"I'll meet you halfway," Fogarty said, and he set the meeting at an all-night restaurant in Des Plaines.

By the end of their meeting, it was clear to Judd that Fogarty liked what he heard. "I took you for a sharp kid," the cop said, "but who knew you had a mind like that? Let's hope you always use it for the right side of the law."

"Oh, I will," Judd said. They laid their plans, and on the way back home to Mount Prospect, Judd smiled at the thought that, just a few weeks before, he was using for his own gain the brain Tom Fogarty admired so much.

———————————

The next day, while Judd coached Vicki on what to say over the phone, he knew what Tom Fogarty was doing. After assuring his bosses that he would deliver a known killer right into their hands within a block of the precinct station house, Tom would run a few errands. He would rent a storefront office, move in some rented furniture, have his name painted on the window, "Thomas M. Fogarty, Attorney at Law," and would wait there for one LeRoy Banks to present himself.

When Judd got the call from Sergeant Fogarty that everything was in place, the cop told him of his own bit of creativity. "I set up a messy secretary's desk all covered with work and a cardboard sign that says, 'In the law library. Back in 30 minutes.' "

"Perfect," Judd said. "Talia tells us LeRoy will be home late morning. I'll let you know when to expect him."

At eleven-thirty the four kids finished a prayer meeting, piled into Judd's minivan, and drove to Ryan's house. The plan was to call LeRoy from there, just in case he grew suspicious and tried to trace the call.

Ryan let them in, and he and Lionel and Judd sat quietly while Vicki dialed. She threw on a very adult-sounding voice. Cornelius Grey answered the phone.

"Mr. Grey, this is Maria Diablo from the law offices of Thomas Fogarty in Chicago. Mr. Fogarty is representing the insurance company handling the settlements in the destruction by fire of your apartment building last week."

"Yeah, what do we get?"

"Well, sir, I'm not at liberty to discuss the amount over the phone, but I can tell you it is substantial. Unfortunately, the payout must go to the payer of the rent over the last several months, and our records indicate that it has not been you."

"No, the rent's been paid lately by a friend of mine, helpin' me out. Name is LeRoy Banks."

"Would I be able to speak to him?"

"Sure!"

Judd and the others heard Cornelius Grey quickly filling in LeRoy on their huge stroke of luck. "Let me have that phone," LeRoy said, clearly doubtful.

"Who is this?" he demanded.

Vicki went through the same routine with him, in its entirety, just the way Judd had scripted it. Rather than let LeRoy build on his doubts, she made the prize a little harder to get.

"Of course, sir, we would not be able to issue a check of this magnitude unless you were able to prove to us that you are the same LeRoy Banks who has been paying the rent on Cornelius Grey's apartment."

"Oh, I'll be able to prove it all right. What time did you say Mr. Fogarty could see me?"

---

On the way back to Judd's house, Lionel and Ryan congratulated Judd for his idea and Vicki for her performance. When they arrived, Judd went to call Sergeant Fogarty to fill him in on how things went. Not only did he want to tell Fogarty when to expect to see LeRoy Banks and Cornelius Grey, but he also wanted to beg to be there himself to see the big arrest. It was only fair that Vicki be allowed to be there too, but he couldn't imagine the Chicago Police Department risking having civilians so close to what could become a dangerous situation.

Still, he would ask. He wanted above anything to see the look on LeRoy's face when he found out he was not getting a check but rather getting arrested for murder. When he reached for the phone, however, it rang.

"Are you watching channel nine?" Bruce Barnes asked Judd.

"No, we're in the middle of—"

"Turn on nine," Bruce insisted. "I've got a hunch the guy they're interviewing could be the one we're supposed to watch out for."

"You mean the Antichrist?" Judd asked, grabbing the remote control. He wanted to tell Bruce the story of the sting, but that would have to wait until he talked to Fogarty.

He thanked Bruce and turned on the television, watching in fascination. "You'd better call the sergeant," Vicki suggested.

"Yeah!" he said, turning down the volume and dialing the number.

Fogarty was ecstatic, and he wasn't closed to the idea of Judd and Vicki being there when it all happened. "We have a one-way mirror at the back where my backups will be. That's where they'll come from to surprise these two when I give the signal. I think if you two agree to stay there until it's all over, you could have a great view and stay safe. I think it'd be too risky to have your young friend there, and we don't want the murder victim's nephew in the neighborhood at all that day, just in case."

"But Vicki and I can come, really?"

"Sure. Just be sure you're an hour early and park far away."

Judd couldn't wait. As he hung up he looked at his watch and decided he and Vicki would have to leave within the hour to be downtown in time to be in place. He turned up the TV and watched more of the interview with the man Bruce now suspected could be the Antichrist.

Boy, would he and Bruce have a lot to talk about the next time they got together!

**31**

**JUDD** felt a tingle down his spine as he and Vicki got in the car. He'd had enough excitement for a lifetime the last couple of weeks, but he had never been involved in anything like this. He had been a rebel, a difficult, stubborn, self-centered teen. Lying to his parents and running with the wrong crowd had been the extent of his adventure—at least until the Rapture.

His world had been turned upside down. Meeting three other instant orphans, having them move in, and all four of them coming to Christ within a few days made his previous life seem eons ago. Was it possible that just a few weeks ago he thought he knew everything there was to know about just about everything? Now, strange as it seemed, he knew he was more mature and grown-up than ever, mostly because he realized how little he knew about anything.

Everything important to him before now seemed childish and stupid. What he cared about now was God. People. Truth. Justice. Survival. In a way, he missed the carefree youth he had been squandering by playing the tough guy. Rascal though he was, his parents were always there to bail him out. And while they may have wondered what would ever become of him, he knew down deep they would have even forgiven him for stealing his dad's credit card and running away to Europe. Always, there had been that escape hatch. They loved him, wanted the best for him, and would eventually forgive him and welcome him back. They had modeled God to him, but he had been too self-centered to realize it.

Here he was, on his own now, wondering when or if school would ever start up again. How would they notify the kids when it was time to come back? How many had disappeared? How many teachers? Would school ever seem normal again? And should he go to school? If Bruce was right and Nicolae Carpathia, who had just become the new secretary-general of the United Nations, could be the Antichrist, how long would it be before he signed some sort of an agreement with Israel?

If that came soon, there would be only seven more years of life on earth as they knew it. Did Judd need an education, or would he be wasting time in class while the world hurtled out of control? These were things he and the others were going to have to discuss with Bruce. But that would be later. Now it was time to get to Chicago and to watch the police sting LeRoy Banks and Cornelius Grey. It was a trap he had devised, which had impressed Sergeant Tom Fogarty.

Vicki had done a great job on the phone, pretending to be Maria Diablo, secretary to Tom Fogarty, "the attorney." Judd had thought of the fake name for her.

"Where did you come up with that name, anyway?" she said.

"*Diablo* means 'devil' in Spanish."

Vicki shot him a double take. "You think I'm a devil?"

"Hardly," Judd said, carefully picking his way through traffic. He wanted to look at Vicki, but there was still enough

306

rubble and construction going on that he didn't dare take his eyes from the road.

Judd's grades had tumbled during the last year, but he had always been a good memorizer, probably from all the years he had spent in Bible memory clubs as a kid. That memory told him *diablo* was from the word *diabolical*, which meant "tricky" or "devious." That was what his plan was.

How many times had Judd's mother complained, "But you've got a good brain"? She used to say, "Use it like you used to, and your grades will shoot up."

He knew she was right, but because he had not been controlled by God back then, he had used the gift God had given him, that sharp mind, for his own purposes. He had devised a runaway plan, saved cash he got from the stolen credit card, and made his own plane reservations. Fittingly, God chose the middle of Judd's escape from his "awful" home life to send Christ and rapture the church.

If it hadn't been so devastating, Judd might have found humor in it. Though he knew the truth and what he had to do—receive Christ after all—still he found himself facing the despair of the loss of his family. Sometimes he caught himself in such a dark hole of sadness, despite finally settling things with God, that he wondered if he could go on.

Maybe, he thought, that was why God had, in essence, left him in charge of these other three kids. Without that responsibility, he wondered what would have become of him. Keeping track of Ryan and Lionel alone kept his mind occupied much of the time. Then there was reading his Bible and studying what Bruce believed was crucial for him to know. Vicki didn't take any work. It was good to have someone close to his age to talk to, someone who seemed to understand him.

Judd pulled onto the expressway and found himself in that

crazy traffic that had seemed to double since the Rapture. Where was everyone going? With so many having disappeared, it seemed strange that rush hour lasted all day and half the night now. People were desperate, frantic to see how this would all sort itself out. What would happen to their jobs, their companies, their careers, their plans?

It would be months, Judd figured, before the roadways were cleared of all the crashed cars and debris. It seemed all he and the others heard or saw on the news was crime and mayhem. Bad people took advantage of bad times, and times had never been as bad as this.

Judd was grateful Vicki was with him. On the one hand, he thought she was the type of girl he could get interested in, but on the other he realized that, had it not been for the crisis they found themselves in, they would never have even met. In fact, with him being from the ritzier part of Mount Prospect and her being from the trailer park, he wondered if they would have ever had anything to do with each other.

That all seemed so petty now. What was so important about how people looked and acted and dressed, or how much money their parents made, had nothing to do with their personal worth. Maybe some people would have been embarrassed to date someone from a lower class than themselves, but Judd had already seen how shallow that was.

When he talked to Vicki and spent time with her, he realized she was the same person whether she wore his mother's clothes or whether she wore her own. With or without makeup, with or without jewelry, who she was came through. At first her grammar was lazy and she used a lot of slang. But she knew better. It was clear she had a good mind. She had been even more rebellious than Judd, and it was clear she had seen how wrong she had been too.

Judd wanted to talk about the sting they were about to
witness, but there was nothing to say. It had all been planned
and laid out, and as far as they knew, neither LeRoy nor
Cornelius suspected a thing. The only question was whether
Talia had figured out what was happening. She had told Vicki
that her brother and LeRoy were looking to cash in on insurance money. That had given him the idea of how to trap them.
Would Talia catch on to that? And if she tipped the two guys
off, would they avoid the sting or come in shooting?

For sure they would come armed. Both had enough
enemies to make them look over their shoulders no matter
where they went. That was why Sergeant Fogarty insisted that,
while Judd and Vicki could come and watch, they had to be
behind the protective one-way mirror, out of the way if
anything bad happened.

Vicki wasn't sure yet what she thought of Judd. She had heard
his story enough that she felt she knew it as well as her own.
She was surprised at how similar they were, both having been
rebellious kids. But she couldn't imagine why a rich kid would
rebel against a setup like he had: his own room in a huge,
expensive home, permission to drive his parents' cars, the
latest clothes, the best gadgets, and never having to work.
What was to rebel against? While she had always told herself
she hated her parents' religion and rules, it was really where
they lived that she hated.

Vicki never would have admitted that to a rich kid. In fact,
she would have defended the trailer park and its people over
the phonies who lived in the big houses and didn't seem to
care about anyone. Sure, her neighbors could be loud and
destructive, but look what kind of lives they led. No one could
get ahead. They were all working to just get by. Vicki had

wanted to get out of that environment, and she had the sinking feeling it would never happen.

Now, here she was, trying to convince herself she could fit into a different culture. But was it just living in a rich kid's home that made her look and think and act and even talk differently? She knew better than that. She had grown up overnight, and like Judd often said, the things they used to think were so important weren't so important after all. Her biggest change, though she looked different, was inside. She didn't have to apologize for being a trailer-park girl.

She certainly didn't feel as if she were somehow from a lower class of people than Judd was. He had treated her nicely from the beginning, and she didn't get the impression he was just condescending to her. He seemed like a good kid, and he sure was smart. She was too, if she could believe her teachers. They had constantly told her she could do better and that she wasn't working up to her potential. But the idea of sitting up late at night studying instead of running with her friends almost made her gag.

Now she felt like a fool. Like Judd, she missed the family she had squabbled with. She wished she had followed her teachers' advice. If she ever got the chance again, she would. Everything was different now. What a difference a few weeks made. More than that, she realized, the difference had come in an instant. Everything she ever thought or cared about changed when her perspective changed. And nothing could have changed her perspective more dramatically than millions of people—including her whole family—disappearing, just like they said they might someday.

Vicki shook her head as she thought about it. *When you're wrong, you're wrong,* she told herself.

"What?" Judd asked, startling her.

"What what?" she said.

"Out of the corner of my eye, I saw you shaking your head."

"I was just thinking," she said. "How different you and I are from who we thought we were not that long ago."

"I was just thinking the same thing."

"Are you scared?" Vicki asked, suddenly changing the subject.

"About this? Today, you mean?"

"Yeah."

" 'Course. Aren't you?"

"Yeah," she said, "but it's kind of fun, and there's no way I'd miss it. It's like being in a TV show or a movie—only it's real."

---

Several minutes later Judd found the street he was looking for and parked three blocks away and around the corner. "We've got to hurry," he said. "Fogarty doesn't want us to be around here in case LeRoy or Cornelius comes early to check out the area."

# 32

**LIONEL** had the same fear Judd had, and at about the same time. As he sat at Judd's house with Ryan, waiting to hear how everything would turn out, he suddenly wondered whether Talia might figure this all out and spill the beans to her brother and LeRoy. She was not a dumb woman.

Lionel stood quickly. "I gotta get going," he said.

"What do you mean?" Ryan said. "You're not leaving me here alone."

"I have to, but just for a little while."

"No!"

"Yes! Now just wait here for me."

"Tell me what you're doing."

"If you have to know, I'm going to my house."

"What for? What if LeRoy and Cornelius are still there?"

"They won't be."

"You don't know that, Lionel. You're going to spook them!"

Lionel hesitated. "I think they'll be gone by now."

313

"You'd better check. Why not call them?"

Lionel thought a minute. "Good idea," he said. And he saw Ryan beam. Talia answered the phone. "Hey, Talia," he said.

"Lionel?"

"Yeah."

"What's up?"

"Thought I'd come and talk to you."

"Come on ahead. Nobody here but me."

"Really?"

Now Lionel didn't know what to do. He hadn't really wanted to talk to her. He had just wanted to distract her, to keep her from saying anything to LeRoy and Cornelius in case she had realized that they were being set up. It sounded as if she had never given that a thought.

"Yeah, come on over. I'm real sorry about André. You and your friends think LeRoy killed him."

"What do you think, Talia?"

"I don't want to think about it. I couldn't stand it if I thought LeRoy did something like that."

"You think LeRoy's never killed somebody before?"

"Not unless it was self-defense," she said. "Anyway, I was in love with André, and LeRoy knew that."

"Did André know it?"

"I hope so."

"I don't think he did," Lionel said. "You did a good job of hiding it."

Now she was crying. "Don't remind me," she said. "I was tryin' to control him, that's all. I figured if I made everything too easy for him, he would never do the right thing. André was a wild man, you know."

"I know."

"I wanted him to behave, to act right, to grow up, for me."

"He was tryin', I think. There at the end, I mean. Only somebody murdered him."

"Oh, no," she said. "He just died in that fire, that's all."

"Haven't you seen the news, Talia? He was found with a bullet hole in his neck, and he wound up bleeding to death. The fire would have killed him, but we pulled him out of there. We knew he was bleeding, but we didn't know why or where from. If we knew, we might have been able to stop the bleeding and save him."

"I'm sorry, Lionel."

"That LeRoy did this?"

"I'm not sayin' that."

"I am. How come you're alone there anyway?"

"LeRoy and Connie are in Chicago."

"What for?"

"I don't know. Some insurance thing. We're gonna be rich, so they tell me."

"I can't come over then, because I wouldn't want to be there when they get back."

"I think they're going to let you live here with us when they get a little money."

"And how are they getting this money?"

"Insurance, like I told you. It was Connie's apartment that burned, you know."

"How does that work? The insurance, I mean."

"I have no idea. All I know is that my brother was insured and he lost his apartment, so that's that."

"How much is it worth?"

"I don't know. Enough for them to risk going back into Chicago when lots of people, and the cops, are looking for them there."

"Why are the cops looking for them?"

"Lots of reasons. I wish they wouldn't go down there for a while, but when they smell money . . ."

"But you don't know how much?"

"All I know is that it's a lot, because they have to come there in person."

Lionel realized how strange this conversation was. Talia would be looking for some place to live tomorrow. Should he let her stay in his home, where she was now? No, that wouldn't be good. She had moved in with her brother and his friend, knowing they were up to no good, knowing it was wrong, and knowing it couldn't last. She would probably be arrested and held until the police determined whether she was in on any of the illegal stuff. Lionel didn't think she was.

"Well, I'll see you, Talia."

"You're not coming over?"

"Not tonight," he said. "Maybe I'll see you soon."

Lionel knew he would.

---

As soon as Judd and Vicki walked in the door of the storefront with "Thomas Fogarty, Attorney at Law" painted on the window, Tom Fogarty took them to the back, out of sight. He had the answering machine with him. "Here," he said to Vicki, pointing to a chair. "I need you to record a message."

As Fogarty was writing it out, Vicki asked what it was all about.

"It's important in a sting to play hard to get," the sergeant said. "If everything looks too easy for the mark—that's what we call the victim of the sting—he gets suspicious and might be scared off. We have to get these guys to come to us and keep after us until we arrest them."

Vicki recorded the script. "You have reached the law offices of Thomas Fogarty. We will be back in the office tomorrow. Please leave a message after the tone. Thank you."

"Won't this just make them mad and make them not show up?" she asked.

"The opposite. I'll be listening in. If they just seem mad and ready to hang up, I'll pick up and tell them I was just in for a second and heard their call. If they threaten to come and break in if no one's here, I'll let 'em. Once they get here, I'll pretend to be unable to find their file or their check, and you can bet I'll make them identify themselves thoroughly. They'll be working so hard to convince me they are who they say they are that they'll forget about any doubts they've had."

The other police officers came through the back, and Fogarty briefed everyone on where to be and what to do. Judd was so excited he could hardly stand it. The answering machine was hooked back up to the phone, and Fogarty turned around the Open/Closed sign in the window to indicate his office was closed. The phony secretary's desk was just messy enough to look real, and, of course, the chair was empty.

When everyone was in place, they waited.

"What makes you think they'll call?" Vicki asked.

"They're eager. They want to make sure we're here and that everything is ready for them. If they don't call, that's OK too."

But they did.

Sergeant Fogarty set the answering machine to pick up on the fourth ring, only prolonging their agony. As soon as the message started to play, Fogarty, the other cops, and Judd and Vicki heard LeRoy and Cornelius whining in the background.

LeRoy swore. "Oh, man, Connie! They can't be closed! What is this?"

At the tone, LeRoy yelled into the phone, "My name is

317

Banks, and I had an appointment, so you better be in there when I get there!"

Judd was afraid Fogarty would be disappointed because he couldn't get on in time to tell LeRoy he would be there. But Fogarty apparently felt things were going perfectly. "He said 'when I get there,' " Fogarty said. "They're still coming. He'll probably call one more time when they get close."

They waited several more minutes, and sure enough, the phone rang again. Same message. Same anger.

"If you ain't there when we get there, we gon' trash your office!" LeRoy shouted. "Now you should be expecting us! Don't make us break in there!"

Fogarty smiled.

Not long later, with everyone hidden, they heard the road-ster slide up to the curb. LeRoy and Cornelius climbed out, looking enraged. They came up to the window and peered inside, and Judd heard LeRoy shouting and swearing all the way from inside. Cornelius had his hand in his belt, as if on a weapon.

LeRoy hurried to the car and popped the trunk, pulling out a long metal rod. He approached the storefront with it in two hands, like a baseball bat. With that, Tom Fogarty grabbed a file folder and walked out from the back room into the front office, not looking up, as if he was unaware anyone was even there.

LeRoy saw him and quickly held the rod out of sight behind his back. "Hey!" he hollered. "You open?"

Fogarty approached the locked door. "No! Sorry! Tomor-row!"

"I had an appointment!" LeRoy shouted.

"Today?"

"Yes! Today! Now let me in!"

Tom went to the secretary's desk and looked at the calendar, then slapped himself in the head, looking embarrassed and apologetic, and hurried to the door. Cornelius stepped in front of LeRoy as LeRoy skipped back to the car and tossed the metal rod in the backseat. "Now we're in business," Cornelius said.

Sergeant Fogarty had LeRoy and Cornelius right where he wanted them.

# 33

**RYAN** Daley was glad Lionel had decided not to go to his own home, where Talia Grey was alone. Ryan knew Lionel had intended to go without him, and Ryan had been left alone enough. It wasn't just that he was afraid, though that was a large part. But there was nothing to be afraid of at Judd's house. As far as he knew, none of the people who had invaded Lionel's house even knew about Judd or his place. Ryan felt safe enough there.

But also, Ryan had no brothers or sisters. He and his parents had been the extent of his family, and he'd had enough alone time when they were alive. That's why he had spent so much time with Raymie Steele, who had also disappeared in the vanishings.

Ryan was slowly adjusting to the fact that his parents were gone. They were still on his mind almost every minute of the day, and he often woke up between midnight and dawn, wishing this were all just a bad dream from which he would soon wake up. He had cried until he was sure there were no more tears, and then cried some more. He was embarrassed about that, being the youngest and noticing that the others didn't seem to cry much. But one night he had woken up with his sad thoughts and heard two of the others—he guessed Vicki and Lionel—sobbing in their beds too.

There was nothing wrong with that. What could be worse than losing your parents? Only missing out on going to heaven with them, Ryan figured. He put out of his mind the fact that his parents had not been Christians and that unless something very strange and very quick had happened before they died, it was likely they weren't in heaven now.

Ryan wandered into the kitchen, where he found Lionel eating a sandwich. "Want something?" Lionel asked, his mouth full.

"Nah. Just bored."

"Wish we were down there for the sting," Lionel said. "I want to see LeRoy get his."

Ryan nodded, and the phone rang. It was Talia. "For you," Ryan said. Lionel had given her his number the night she had driven him to see André.

Lionel pointed at the rest of his sandwich and nodded, and Ryan decided he was hungry after all. He finished the sandwich while Lionel talked with Talia.

———————————————

Vicki Byrne had been involved in a lot of mischief in her young life, but she decided this was about as exciting and scary as anything she had ever done. She was crouched behind a low table next to Judd. They were in a perfect position to peek over the top and through a huge one-way mirror that gave them a view of the entire storefront and front door. They could hear perfectly because the whole meeting was being taped in that same room by the police. The storefront was full of hidden microphones so Sergeant Fogarty wouldn't have to wear a wire, as the police called it. In case the bad guys got suspicious and searched him, he would be clean.

Vicki watched as Fogarty unlocked the front door but opened it only a few inches.

"You can see there that we had an appointment," LeRoy said, attempting to come in.

"I'm sorry, gentlemen. It does say that on the calendar, if you are . . . ?"

"Banks. Banks and Grey."

"Yes, but Miss Diablo must have made a mistake. She knew I was off today."

"But you're here and we're here, so let's get this done."

"Well, I'd like to, but I have to be in court in half an hour and—"

"This ain't gonna take no half hour. We were told you had a check for us, and that's all we need."

"Really, gentlemen," Fogarty said, still standing inside the slightly opened door, "this would be much more convenient tomorrow or next week—"

"No!" LeRoy said. "Now we're here and you're here and we know you've got a check for us, so let's do this." He pushed his way past Fogarty, and he and Cornelius planted themselves in chairs at the side of the secretary's desk.

Fogarty was playing his part to the hilt. "To tell you the truth, gentlemen, I'm going to need you to refresh me on what this is all about."

LeRoy let his head roll back and he sighed as he stared at the ceiling. "Connie here, that's Cornelius Grey, he rents an apartment, well, he did anyway, on Halsted. It burned down."

"Oh yes, and this is about the insurance settlement then," Fogarty said.

"Exactly."

"And what is your stake in this, Mr., ah . . . ?"

"Banks. LeRoy Banks. I've been paying the rent for Mr. Grey here for several months, so—"

"And why was that?"

"What business is that of yours?"

"Oh, none, I guess. Proceed."

"Proceed? *You* proceed. Your secretary said she had a big check for us, so let's have it."

"Oh, I'm sorry, sir. Were you expecting the check itself today?"

"Of course! That's why we're here!"

"Well, this initial meeting was just for paperwork, signatures, identification, that type of a thing."

"So, we'll sign some papers. Let's get on with it."

"Well, the documents have to be forwarded to the home office for verification, and then the check can be released."

"So you're saying the check hasn't even been written yet? It's not here, like she said?"

"Oh, it's here, but if it's released before everything is verified by the home office, then I'm in trouble."

"You know what, Mr. Fogarty," LeRoy said, his face clouded with rage, "you're gonna be in trouble with somebody when we leave here, and you better hope it's the home office."

"But I can't—"

"Yes, you can. You give us that check based on our word that we are who we say we are, and you deal with the home office yourself."

"I'm afraid I can't—"

"You don't understand, Mr. Lawyer Man. We're not negotiatin'. We're walkin' out of here with the check."

Fogarty gulped and looked for the file. Vicki was impressed that there was an actual check in the folder. "OK," he said, "just let me see some ID so I'm covered."

Banks and Grey reached for their wallets and produced driver's licenses. Fogarty made a big show of meticulously copying down every detail. "Now, the check," LeRoy demanded.

"This is really highly irregular," Fogarty said.

LeRoy closed his eyes as if struggling for a last sliver of patience. "Just hand it over," he said.

Fogarty handed it to him, and LeRoy glanced at the figure. He smiled and showed it to Cornelius, then began folding it. Vicki noticed three cops a few feet from her, guns drawn, preparing to burst from the back room. "Hey," Cornelius Grey said, "wait a minute. What's that say?"

LeRoy had stood and was shoving the folded check into his pocket when he pulled it back out and studied it. Where his or Grey's name was supposed to be were the words *You're under arrest.*

"What?"

Fogarty flashed a badge from his pocket, "LeRoy Banks, you're under arrest for the murder of André Dupree and for arson in the case of—"

LeRoy and Cornelius were reaching for their weapons when the cops rushed in. "Don't even think about it!" one shouted, and the two were disarmed, handcuffed, and led away. Vicki decided it was one of the coolest things she had ever seen.

While Banks and Grey were being read their rights, Vicki heard another police officer on a walkie-talkie telling someone else to "move on Talia Grey."

---

Lionel stood in the kitchen of Judd Thompson's house, watching Ryan finish the rest of his sandwich. Lionel talked with Talia Grey on the phone, wondering what in the world she was so excited about.

"This is the weirdest thing," she said. "You have to see this. Maybe you've already seen it."

"What, what?"

"It's a videotape. Connie said it was in the VCR he ripped off from a house not too far from here. Guy on the tape says he's pastor of New Hope Church or somethin' and that if we're watchin' this, it's because he's gone. He's tellin' all the stuff we must be going through, and he's explainin' what happened, just like what my mamma used to tell me. This is so cool!"

"Yeah, I *have* seen it," Lionel said. "Like I told you before, I was the only person in my family who wasn't a believer. That's why I was left behind."

"Me too, I guess," Talia said sadly.

"You can do something about that, you know," Lionel said.

"Um-hm," she said, but from the background Lionel heard a doorbell and a loud knock. He recognized the doorbell as the one at his house, where Talia was. "Jes' a minute, Lionel," she said, and he heard rustling, as if she had slid the cellular telephone into a pocket. She had left it on.

As Lionel heard her walk through the house toward the door, he heard the shout, from a woman police officer. "Police, ma'am, open up!"

"I'm coming!" Talia managed. "Did something happen to—?" But her question was drowned out by louder banging on the door. "All right!" she said.

Lionel stood transfixed on the phone, listening as she opened the door.

"Talia Grey?" the policewoman asked.

"Yes! What—?"

"Miss Grey, you're under arrest for—"

"What? Under arrest? What'd I—?"

"For home invasion, burglary, accessory to murder . . ."

"What? No! I don't know anything about—"

She grabbed her phone. "Lionel! Help! I'm being arrested."

Lionel wanted to tell her there was nothing he could do for her and that actually he was glad she was being dragged from his house. Maybe he could go home soon. But someone grabbed her phone and said, "Who's this?"

"Lionel Washington," he said. "You're at my house."

"Does Talia Grey have permission to be here?"

"No."

"And you're working with Fogarty?"

"Sort of."

"Thank you, son."

"Thank *you!*" Lionel said. And he decided life was crazy.

---

Judd was fascinated with how cops celebrated a sting that had worked well. They seemed unable to stop grinning. Fogarty and two others he had apparently known from his days in Homicide took Vicki and Judd to a coffee shop, where they sat reminiscing and congratulating each other. Everyone was impressed with the plan Judd had come up with, the performance by Vicki on the phone, and especially Fogarty's acting. "You sucked them right in," the older of his cohorts said. "You'll be back in Homicide in no time."

"That's what I want," Fogarty said. "But the way I hear it, most of you guys have been working double shifts, just like the rest of us working stiffs."

The cops sympathized with each other about how much work they'd all had to do since the vanishings. "What do you make of it?" Judd blurted, wondering if he should interrupt an adult conversation. But they had treated him almost like an equal up to now.

"Make of what?" Fogarty said, and Judd felt his face redden as everyone's eyes seemed focused on him.

"The disappearances. Where'd everybody go, I mean, in your opinion?"

Fogarty shook his head. "I've heard every opinion from space aliens to Jesus," he said. "One's as good as the other, I guess."

Judd was at a loss for words. What an opening! Bruce had told them to watch for opportunities to talk about the truth, and he predicted that at a time as dark and scary as this, there would be plenty of chances.

The younger detective said, "Seems like all we do is sit around asking each other if we lost anybody in the disappearances. Did you, by the way?"

"Me?" Fogarty said. "Yeah. Two elderly aunts. It was the strangest thing, something that would make you believe God *did* have something to do with this."

Something in the way he said that made the others laugh, and Judd wondered why. Was it a joke? Did Fogarty pray that he'd lose the two old aunts? He didn't get the humor.

"Why do you say that?" Judd asked.

"Oh, it's just that nobody in our family has ever been religious, except on holidays, you know. Going to church on Easter and Christmas was all part of the routine, but none of us claimed to be church people. But those two aunts of mine all of a sudden changed."

Judd thought the young cop looked particularly interested. Fogarty kept talking. "They started showing up to family reunions with their Bibles. That was kind of strange. We all had Bibles somewhere. The wife and I have one stashed in a

328

drawer. It was a wedding gift, I think. That was weird, because this is a second marriage for each of us, and we didn't even get married in a church this time. But one of the aunts gave us that Bible. It was real pretty but it didn't look right sitting out, so we put it away."

Judd noticed the young cop lean forward, ignoring his dessert. He had blond hair and wore his side arm in a shoulder holster. "But what about these aunts?" he said. "What's their story?"

"Well, one of 'em had a husband die, and she kept living in their big old house for six or seven years. Then the other became a widow, and she didn't want to live in the same house she and her husband had lived in for so many years. So she moved in with the other. They were still young enough to be healthy, and they got out and about quite a bit. Somebody invited them to some kind of a religious meeting. It wasn't at a church. More like at an auditorium or something. Anyway, they started talking about getting saved and all that. They got religion, that's all I know. Started going to church and everything."

The young one, whom Judd thought he had heard Fogarty call Eddie, was still listening intently. Judd didn't want to admit he had forgotten the man's name already, so he asked if he had a card. The cop pulled one from his pocket. Judd studied it. His name was Archibald Edwards. No wonder he went by Eddie.

"But these aunts," Edwards pressed, "they disappeared, didn't they?"

"Yup."

"You ever consider maybe they *had* been saved? I mean, anybody else in your family vanish?"

Fogarty shook his head. "Well, my first wife. And I can't say I was sorry to see her go."

The others chuckled, all except Edwards. He was on the trail of something, Judd decided. "She was religious too, right?" Edwards asked.

Fogarty's body language made it appear he wanted to move on to something else, but he said, "Yeah, matter of fact she was. I think that's why we split. That and the job."

"Tell me about it," Eddie said. "This job's the enemy of marriage."

Fogarty nodded. "I was no saint. Gone all the time. I used to drink a good bit, you know."

The older homicide detective, a balding man with a huge belly, laughed. "That's an understatement," he said. "But it was what you did when you were drinkin' that cost you your first wife."

"All right," Fogarty said. "Enough said."

But Eddie the bloodhound was still on the scent. "So your wife and your two aunts—"

"My first wife."

"OK, your first wife and your two aunts are the only people in your whole family who were religious, and they're also the only ones who disappeared. Anybody else see a trend here?"

"We've heard and read all about the various theories," Fogarty said dismissively. "For all I know they were the only left-handers or redheads in the family too."

"Jeannie?" The old cop said. "Your Jeannie? She wasn't either one!"

"I'm just sayin'," Fogarty began.

"I'm telling you," Eddie said, "there were guys on the job who told me about God and everything, and those guys are gone. It's got me thinking."

"That's dangerous," the old cop said. Fogarty laughed.

"Yeah," Eddie said. "You guys laugh it off. What if it's true?

330

What if this *was* something God pulled off? Where does that leave us?"

Judd turned to see if Fogarty had an answer for that one. Eddie must have taken Judd's look as agreement. "You brought this up, kid. What's your take on the vanishings? What do you make of it?"

# 34

**HOMICIDE** detective Archibald (Eddie) Edwards had posed the question. The ball was in Judd's court. Nervous and dry-mouthed as he was, he stepped and swung hard.

Judd told Sergeant Fogarty and the two detectives his whole story, from being raised in the church, to rebelling, to running away, to the Rapture, to getting home, connecting with Bruce Barnes, meeting the other kids, praying to receive Christ, and moving in together.

"So, you buy the whole package," Eddie summarized, reaching for his wallet and sliding his portion of the restaurant bill over to Fogarty.

Judd nodded, but it was the older detective who spoke. "'Buy' is right. Man, have you been sold a bill of goods, kid."

In his peripheral vision, Judd noticed Fogarty nodding. Next to Judd on his other side, however, Vicki gently pressed her elbow against Judd's. He took that to mean she was with him, supported him, was glad he'd said what he said and that he shouldn't worry what anybody else thought.

Judd had hoped for more reaction than that from these

guys. He didn't expect them all to fall to their knees or ask him to pray with them, but he wanted more than sarcasm or amusement. They were standing now and paying up. Tom Fogarty paid for Judd and Vicki. As they made their way out, Eddie got between Fogarty and Judd and put his arm around Judd. "You know what, Tom," he said, "this boy and his girl-friend and those other two kids ought to meet Josey."

The big detective, the older one, wheeled around and pointed in Fogarty's face. "Now, that's a good idea, Tom, and you know it. These kids ought to meet your wife."

"Excuse me," Vicki said, as quietly as Judd had ever heard her. He decided these guys must have intimidated her. "First of all, I'm not his girlfriend, and—"

"Ooh, ho!" the older detective said. "Touchy area, hm?"

"Second of all," Vicki continued, apparently unfazed, "why should we meet Sergeant Fogarty's wife? I mean, I'd like to and all that, but I was just wondering what made you think of that, Mr. Edwards."

"Call me Eddie. Well, first off, I know she'd love you and you'd love her. She's real warm and friendly. But ever since we've known her, she's been talking about stuff like this. We were surprised Tom even married her, she seemed so religious, and his first wife was way overboard. So, we figured—"

"And yet she disappeared, right?" Vicki said. "Along with Sergeant Fogarty's two aunts and the other people you used to work with who you thought were too religious."

"Yeah," Eddie said, pausing between the cars parked at the curb. "And I think there might be something to that. But Judd here himself said this pastor was left behind. And what about Josey Fogarty? She was all into angels and crystals and chan-neling and stuff."

"What they used to call New Age," Fogarty said. "Most of

334

those people think the people who disappeared had bad vibes or something, so all the good people were left."

"We know from personal experience that ain't true," the big cop said, laughing loud.

Fogarty grinned and nodded. "Yeah. If we're the good people, the world's in a sorry state."

"The world's in a sorry state anyway," Eddie said. "But I still think Josey and these kids ought to get together. I'm tellin' ya, you'd love her. But hasn't she been talking like this lately, Tom?"

Fogarty shrugged and looked away.

"C'mon, Tom," Eddie pressed. "You know it's true. Isn't she trying to drag you to some kind of a Bible study or something?"

"Better that than those channeling sessions she used to like," Big Man said, getting into his unmarked squad car.

Eddie got into the same car on the passenger's side, and Fogarty opened the door of his own squad car, prepared to take Judd and Vicki back to Judd's car. Judd suddenly felt overcome with an urge to not let Eddie get away without talking to him first. He asked Tom to wait a second and stepped to Eddie's window. "It was really great to meet you both," Judd said, reaching in and shaking both their hands. "Sometime I'd like to talk to you some more about those other cops who disappeared, Eddie."

Eddie met his gaze. "Yeah, let's do that. Seriously, I'd like that too."

Judd was certain that Eddie was curious and interested.

---

Lionel and Ryan sat watching television at Judd's house, waiting for news of the sting. More than an hour after it was supposed to have happened, they still had heard nothing. Lionel was worried. How long did it take to get to a phone and report in? He tried to make sense of what he was watching on TV, but it was all about the new head of the United Nations, Nicolae Carpathia. Bruce would have to explain this stuff to him. All Lionel knew was that since the Rapture there had been nothing on television except news, and he had never cared much for that before.

Finally, the phone rang, but it wasn't Judd. It was Talia Grey.

"Talia!" Lionel said. "I thought you got busted!"

"I did, fool. I get one phone call."

"And you call me? Shouldn't you call a lawyer?"

"A lawyer won't do me any good now, Lionel. I know we hardly know each other, but I got nobody else. My brother and LeRoy are in deep trouble, and LeRoy is going to think I set him up."

"Why?"

"He's always accusin' me of stuff like that. And Connie's no kind of brother. He'd just as soon get me in trouble with LeRoy than help me out."

"Well, I can't help you, Talia. I don't have money for bail or anything like that."

"I'm not worried about bail, Lionel. I'm better off in here than on the street, where LeRoy or Connie can have me killed."

"Your own brother wouldn't have you—"

"You don't know my brother. He's tried to kill me before. And he told LeRoy about my tryin' to signal you with your gym bag that one time."

"But they're both going to be in jail for years."

"I know. But they also know everybody on the street. They'll just have someone get rid of me, I know they will."

"What can I do?" Lionel said. "I can't let you stay in my

house again if you get out. That's the first place someone would come looking."

"Don't you see, Lionel? I don't want to get out. I don't want to be anywhere where they can get to me. I don't care if I die in here. I might just kill myself."

"Don't be talking like that."

"I'm just sayin' I could die in here as easy as I could out there, and I know I'm not ready to die. You gotta help me get ready to die."

Lionel was speechless. She was flat out asking him to help her come to God. He had never helped anyone do that before, and while he thought he had an idea what to say, he wasn't sure he could do it right then, right there on the phone. He would need to be sure he was doing it right, knew what to say, what verses to use, and how to be certain Talia understood and was being genuine. "Where are you?" he asked finally.

She told him what precinct station-house jail she was in.

"Can you have visitors?"

"Yes, come and see me."

"I'll try to get there tonight."

"Hurry."

"I will. I promise. Now can you tell me something?"

"What?"

"Do you have any idea what happened with your brother and LeRoy today?"

"All I know is what they told me here, that they were busted in a sting operation and they're at Cook County Jail."

"And everything went OK with the sting and all that?"

"Well, it didn't go OK with Connie and LeRoy, did it?"

"I mean, nobody was hurt or shot or anything."

"Not that I know of. Why? What'd you hear? You hear somethin' different? How'd you know about this, anyway?"

Lionel guessed there would be no harm in telling her now. "Two of my friends were there. We helped set them up."

Someone said something to Talia about her time being up. "I gotta go, Lionel, but you have to tell me. Did they get the idea for this because I said LeRoy and Connie were tryin' to see about insurance money?"

Lionel's silence apparently told her what she needed to know. "Ooh," she whined, as she was hanging up. "I'm a dead woman."

———————————

"Still busy," Vicki said in Judd's car, after redialing Judd's home phone for the tenth time.

"Humph," Judd grunted. "You'd think they'd stay off the phone to wait for our call."

"We should have called them before we went out and celebrated with the cops," Vicki said. "Lionel probably got worried and is calling around to see if anyone knows what happened."

"Who would he call? He doesn't know any other cops that I know of. And Talia won't be reachable. Well, we'll be home soon enough. You know who you should call? Josey Fogarty."

"Why?"

"Invite them to my house."

"For when?"

"Tonight."

"Why not? You still have Fogarty's home number?"

Judd dug it from his wallet.

———————————

Lionel sat by the phone for five minutes after he had hung up from Talia. Finally he located Judd's car phone number and punched it in. Busy. He shook his head and called Bruce. He knew he wasn't supposed to tell anyone outside the case about what had happened, so he just asked for advice on what to say to Talia and how to say it.

---

"Mrs. Fogarty?" Vicki began. "You don't know me, but my name is Vicki Byrne and—"

"I know who you are, hon," came the friendly, husky voice. "I surely do. Tom just called to tell me everything went down fine and you kids were great. He thinks we ought to meet, you guys and me."

"We were thinking the same thing. How about tonight at Judd Thompson's house?"

"Tom's been there, right?"

"Right."

"I think tonight's wide open, Vicki."

When Vicki hung up she turned to Judd. "What a neat-sounding lady," she said.

When Judd got back into Mount Prospect, he went to the other end of town first and cruised slowly past Lionel's house. Two police paddy wagons were there, and a half-dozen or so uniformed cops were loading them with stuff from the house. Judd had no idea how they were going to tell what belonged to LeRoy's gang and what belonged to Lionel's family. Clearly, though, they were gathering evidence and trying to put the house back the way LeRoy and his cohorts had found it.

As Judd was finally pulling into his own driveway, the car phone rang. It was Lionel. "Where *are* you guys?" he demanded.

"Look out the window in the driveway," Judd said. "Be in in a minute."

When Judd traded stories with Lionel, he was as amazed as Lionel seemed. "So, you're going to see Talia at the jail tonight?"

Lionel nodded. "I'll see if Bruce can take me. He wants to meet with all of us sometime tomorrow, by the way. Big news. He said that guy my mom knew from the magazine, the one who called me once looking for her, has interviewed that United Nations guy."

"Carpathia? The one who was president of Romania?"

"Yeah, I think."

"What's the deal with him?"

"Bruce wants to tell us all together."

"What's the news guy's name?"

"Cameron Williams," Lionel said.

"Really? That was the *Global Weekly* guy I saw on the plane. But he's not from here. I wonder how he knows Bruce. He must know Captain Steele."

Lionel shrugged. "So, anyway, I won't be here when the cop and his wife come. I'll have to meet her some other time."

---

Lionel overheard Judd call Bruce later and fill him in on everything that had happened that day. Bruce stopped by to pick up Lionel about half an hour before the Fogartys were to arrive and asked if he could talk to the four of them briefly.

Lionel followed him inside and was reminded why they liked Bruce so much. He was so earnest, so focused, and busy as he was, he seemed to care about everybody. Bruce gathered them in the living room. "We need to thank God for Judd's and Vicki's safety today, for Judd's chance to share his faith with the police officers, for Lionel's opportunity with Talia this evening, and for the rest of you with the couple coming over."

The five of them huddled, arms around each other's shoulders, as Bruce prayed. Lionel couldn't hold back the tears. This reminded him of Sunday nights with his family after a week of school and work and play and a whole day of church. His parents would bring everyone home and they would have some sort of a snack. It might be ice cream or popcorn or some special concoction his mother came up with. Then, before bed, they would gather, just like this. His dad or his mom, sometimes both, would pray for everybody in the family.

Even during the last few years, when Lionel kept to himself the terrible secret that he wasn't a believer, he had to admit he liked those family huddles. He wasn't rebelling against his parents, and he knew they cared for him. He had simply resisted God, and it had cost him everything. Thinking about that warm, loving family he would not see until he died or Christ set up his kingdom on Earth made him weep now.

When Bruce finished praying, Lionel was relieved to see that everyone else was emotional too. Even Bruce, who clapped him on the back. "Let's go, Lionel," he said, and Bruce led the way out of the house.

---

Vicki had a sudden thought as the kids were doing a quick cleanup before their company arrived. "Isn't this going to be, like, dinnertime?" she asked Judd. "Do we have anything planned?"

"Not unless they like TV dinners or fish sticks or something," he said. "Maybe we should order out for pizza or Chinese."

"Yeah," Ryan said. "Pizza!"

"That sounds kind of tacky," Vicki said. "Oops, too late. They're pulling in."

Vicki was very nearly blown away by Josey Fogarty. The woman appeared to be in her late thirties, was of average height and trim. She had pale blue eyes that reminded Vicki of a summer sky, and she wore no makeup or even lipstick. Her face was pale and cutely freckled, her hair was a sandy blonde, and there was plenty of it. She had a huge, easy smile that couldn't cover a certain sadness behind those eyes. But what got to Vicki most was Josey's forceful personality. She didn't hold back, but immediately took the initiative and took over, but in an appealing, inoffensive way.

"Why look at you all," she said, beaming. She took both of Judd's hands in hers and held them up to her cheeks. "You must be Judd, the great brain."

Vicki was amused at Judd's red face.

"And here's Vicki the redhead," she said, embracing Vicki. "Tom always calls you that as if it's one word."

"This must be Ryan!" She took his face in her hands and bent down so she could speak to him on his level. "You're only twelve? Why, you'll be tall as me inside a year!"

Vicki liked this woman already. "We, um, didn't really plan anything for dinner," Vicki said. "Did you already eat?"

"No," Tom said. "That's all right."

"No! It isn't!" Josey said. "We're starving and we're going to eat! What have you got around here?"

Vicki turned to Judd. He shrugged. "We could order out. . . ."

"No way!" Josey said. "Come on, now, there must be something somewhere in this big ol' place. You got a freezer?"

"You mean a big one?"

" 'Course! We don't want TV dinners and ice-cream sandwiches! C'mon, son, show me the big freezer. Where is it? In the garage? The basement? Where?"

It had been a while since Vicki had seen Judd flustered. "Well, ah," he said, "the big one's in the utility room downstairs."

"Well, la-di-da!" Josey Fogarty sang out. "This here house has its own utility room. I'm just in from outer space, Judd. Take me to your freezer!"

Vicki shook her head. Outer space was right. She was going to love this woman.

## 35

**LIONEL** liked having Bruce to himself for a while. If there was one thing frustrating about living with the three other kids, it was that he didn't get much time with Bruce, and when he did, it was usually shared with someone else.

Trouble was, Lionel couldn't think of much to say, now that they were on their way to Chicago to visit Talia in jail. All he did was fill Bruce in on the whole situation and tell him what Talia had said about her own spiritual life. "Her mother disappeared at the Rapture, and Talia says her mother tried to warn her. Now she thinks she has no chance because someone taught her that when Jesus raptured the church, the Holy Spirit was taken away."

"So she thinks no one can be saved now?"

Lionel nodded.

"We can counter that argument fairly easily, I think," Bruce said. And they lapsed into silence again.

Lionel wondered how Bruce found time to do everything he had to do. But he was afraid to ask. Lionel figured the answer would have something to do with Bruce's not having a wife and kids anymore, and who would want to be reminded of that?

Bruce found a parking place several blocks from the precinct station house. "If there's any problem with your getting in to see her," Bruce said, "let me try a few angles."

---

Josey Fogarty had impressed Judd, too. From several items she had found in a freezer, Josey had cooked up some sort of a ground beef casserole with noodles and vegetables and cheese and all kinds of other good things that everyone seemed to enjoy.

Judd was also taken aback by Josey's beauty. He had never seen someone so pretty who was dressed and made-up so plainly (or, he should say, not made-up at all). Mostly, though, Judd simply loved being in her presence. She was warm and friendly, interested in everyone. If she made the others feel as warm and special as she made him feel, he assumed they all felt the same about her as he did.

---

"I'm here to see Talia Grey," Lionel said at the desk of the station house.

"She's not up for bail yet, son. Anyway, how old are you?"

"His age is not relevant," Bruce interrupted. "He's related to her former fiancé, who has died."

"I thought it was her former fiancé she was accused of murderin'," the desk sergeant said.

"She's not been accused of murder," Bruce said. "Now—"

"He'd have to be accompanied by an adult. Would that be you, Mr. Attorney?"

"I'm not an attorney. I'm clergy."

"Oh, why didn't you tell me, Father?"

"I'm not a pr—"

"Right this way. You weren't wearin' your collar, so I didn't even . . . I mean, you know. . . ."

The desk sergeant asked someone to cover for him while he led Lionel and Bruce into the bowels of the tiny jailhouse. "I don't know if you've been here before, Father, but we have only three men's cells and two women's."

"Thank you, Sergeant. So, is there a meeting room or . . . ?"

"Nothing sophisticated like Plexiglas walls or nothin', no. Just this little room over here, and we'll have a guy hanging around outside the door if you need anything. Now, I'm sorry but I have to pat you down for weapons and contraband. Rules, you know."

As helpless and panicky as Talia sounded on the phone, Lionel was surprised to see that she had slipped back into her more normal sassy and sarcastic tones. As she was led out of her cell by the matron and delivered to the desk sergeant, who walked her down the hall to the interview room, she said, "You all won't be seeing me much more in here, I'll tell you that right now! I got my people coming to get me out!"

The matron must have smiled or shook her head or something, because Talia immediately responded with, "Don't you be looking at me that way now! You just watch me! I'll be out of here soon!"

The desk sergeant told her to watch her mouth and manners and to behave herself in front of her company. Talia just cackled. "You don't have to be telling me what to do. Just mind your business."

Talia maintained her attitude until the desk sergeant left and someone else was assigned to stand in the hall. The door was shut behind her, and she quickly sat down and acted like a schoolgirl again. "I'm so glad you came," she said. "I had no one else to call. And this here, who's he?"

"This is my pastor, Bruce Barnes," Lionel said. "I think you should talk to him about your questions about heaven and all that."

"I already told you, Lionel, I don't have any more questions about heaven."

"Why don't we sit down, Lionel?" Bruce said.

Once they were seated, Talia started right in again. "I'm going to need you to find me a lawyer, preacher man," she said.

"I'll do what I can," Bruce said, "but mostly I'm here to support Lionel and to answer any questions you might have."

"And what makes Lionel think I have questions?" she said.

"You said you thought your mother was in heaven," Lionel said. "But you were afraid you had no more hope for some reason."

"I was always told that after the church got raptured, the Holy Ghost would be gone. No Holy Ghost, no salvation."

Bruce pulled a small New Testament from his pocket and opened it on the table before them. "Did you ever hear of a teaching from Revelation that says that during the time of the seven-year Tribulation God would raise up 144,000 witnesses who would go about the world evangelizing?"

"Yes," Talia said, "I think I did hear something about that somewhere along the line. Yes."

"Let me ask you something, Talia. What need would there be for evangelizing during the Tribulation if no one could come to Christ?"

Talia looked up and raised her eyebrows. "I never thought

of that," she said. "How do these people get saved if the Holy Spirit is no longer here?"

"I'm not sure I agree that the Holy Spirit is gone," Bruce said. "I don't see that in Scripture, but even if it's true, apparently God finds another way to bring men and women to salvation, doesn't he? Otherwise, those 144,000 witnesses are out of business, aren't they?"

"I guess they are!" Talia said.

Bruce stood. "I'll tell you what, Talia," he said, "I know we don't have much time here, so I'm going to leave you and Lionel alone for a few minutes. Lionel, as you already know, is a new believer after growing up in a Christian home. It sounds to me like you are in a similar position to where he was not that long ago. It's important for Lionel to learn to tell others about his faith and how to come to Christ. I don't know how interested you are right now, but even if you are not, you would be doing Lionel a great service to simply listen to him and maybe even critique his approach. Perhaps you could help him learn to do this better. Could you do that for us?"

"Sure," Talia said.

---

Vicki was amused to see that even when they were finished with dinner at Judd's house, Josey Fogarty was still in charge. While her husband sat seeming bored or at least not surprised at her outgoing nature, Mrs. Fogarty began clearing the table and barking assignments. As usual, she was not in the least offensive. She had Ryan organizing the dishes, Vicki washing, and Judd drying, while she wiped everything down and even had her husband sweep the kitchen floor. "Make yourself useful, Tom," she said, smiling.

Vicki got the feeling that Josey was on a mission, had something to accomplish, something she wanted to do. That soon became clear. When the dishes were done and the place was spotless, she said, "So what do you want to do now, talk? That's what I want to do, talk. Where can we do that?"

"OK, Josey," Tom Fogarty said. "We can talk anywhere. Just slow up and sit down. We're not going anywhere until you get off your chest whatever it is you want to talk about."

For the first time, Josey looked slightly embarrassed. "Your friends thought I would enjoy talking to these kids, that's all," she said. "And I think I just might."

Vicki caught Ryan's eye and nodded toward a chair in the living room. Judd seemed to have already caught on that this woman was not going to be happy until she had nothing else to do but talk to everyone. Tom sat in an easy chair, Vicki in a wing chair, Judd and Ryan on the couch. Josey slid the footstool over from in front of her husband and sat on it, facing everyone.

"So you kids think the disappearances were what, something God did?"

Vicki blinked. Now there was an example of getting to the point! Vicki looked at Judd, who appeared at least temporarily speechless. He had been the one doing the talking to Sergeant Fogarty's coworkers after the sting. Vicki figured it was her turn now.

"That's exactly what we think," Vicki said. "Everybody we know and loved who disappeared had told us about this and warned us. It happened just like they said it would, in a split second. They were gone, and we were left."

"But where are all the children?" Josey said. "The little ones, I mean. The babies, the toddlers, the . . . the . . ." She broke down and couldn't continue. She didn't hide her face or cover her eyes. She simply sat there open-faced, those beautiful blue eyes streaming.

Vicki glanced at Judd again, wishing Bruce was there. Judd appeared content to let Vicki have the floor. "We don't totally understand that either," she said. "Bruce Barnes, that's our pastor, says it has to do with something called the age of accountability. He says no one knows for sure about this, but it seems that God holds people accountable for what they know about him only if they're old enough to understand. We don't know how young a kid could be and still be held accountable, but, like you, we haven't seen too many kids left behind who are younger than Ryan."

Josey took a labored breath. "Did you know I lost two boys?"

Vicki shook her head. Why wouldn't Tom have said something?

"They were from my first marriage, and I didn't see them as much as I wanted to. I've always been curious about God, and I tried all kinds of religions and belief systems. Unfortunately, I was into some kind of strange stuff when my husband Steve left me for someone else. Even though he was living with another woman long before we were divorced, he got custody of Ben and Brad. I couldn't keep him from moving out of state, and I've been able to see the boys only about one weekend a month for more than two years."

"And your first husband?" Vicki said.

"What about him?"

"Was he left behind?"

Josey nodded. "Bless his heart, Steve blames himself. His young wife has already left him, so he has no one. But the boys, they were just gone from their beds the next day. He tried to file a missing person's report and was laughed off.

Someone told him that if they filed missing person reports now, the cops would never get anything else done. Poor Steve had to swallow his pride and call Tom for advice. He wanted to know how he could get somebody somewhere to help him look for his kidnapped kids. Tom told him he'd maybe be a little more sympathetic if he didn't have a grieving mother to take care of too and if Steve would quit being so naïve as to think someone kidnapped millions of kids all at the same time."

"Basically," Tom interjected, "I just reminded him that he wasn't the only father to lose children that day. I mean, that may not have sounded too sensitive, but did he really think law enforcement was going to help him find his two kids when the whole world was grieving the loss of millions? Even Josey was realistic enough to know there was no future in driving six hundred miles to look for her boys."

"But don't think I didn't consider it," she said.

Vicki couldn't imagine the pain of losing your own child. It was hard enough for her to miss her big brother and little sister, and she felt guilty every day for the way she had treated her parents, right up until the time they disappeared. It was no wonder the world was in such chaos. There were millions of grieving mothers all over the world, hoping against hope that whatever these disappearances were, wherever their children had gone, it was not painful or frightening for them. The hardest part for parents whose children have been victims of crime, she knew from a mother in the trailer park, is imagining the fear and pain and loneliness of their last minutes alive. Vicki's neighbor, whose daughter had been kidnapped, said her worst nightmare was her complete inability to do anything for her child in the moment of her greatest need.

Vicki felt a flash of inspiration, a question crossing her

mind that surprised even her. She hesitated, wondering if she should actually say it aloud. Before she could talk herself out of it, it talked itself out of her. "So, is that why you're so interested in knowing whether these people are in heaven? Because of your sons?"

"Of course," Josey said. "If I thought this was some kind of an alien invasion or attack from some foreign power, I'd rather die than think my boys are scared to death and suffering, or that they've been killed. They're dead to me unless they come back anyway, but I have to know they're all right."

"Nobody can tell you that for sure," Tom said.

"He's been saying that all along," Josey said, "and I know he means well. But someone must know. I'm not asking you to say something just to make me feel good, but—"

Vicki was glad when Judd finally decided to chime in. "If they disappeared right out of their pajamas in the middle of the night of the Rapture, then they're in heaven. You don't have to believe that, but that's the only explanation that makes sense to me."

"Well," Josey said, "thank you for that, anyway."

---

Lionel was talking straight with Talia Grey. He had run through all the verses Talia had heard in church from childhood. He started with the fact that "all have sinned and fall short of the glory of God" (Romans 3:23) and that "the wages of sin is death" (Romans 6:23). He said there is no other name under heaven by which we must be saved. He reminded her that she could not earn her salvation, that it is "not by works of righteousness which we have done, but according to His mercy" that God saves us. He added that Ephesians 2:8-9 makes it clear that we're saved by grace and that not of ourselves, not of works "lest anyone should boast."

With Bruce out in the hall, Lionel said, "You've got to be honest with me, Talia. I don't know what you and your brother and LeRoy were running out of my house, but if it was a burglary ring or dope selling or whatever, you're gonna wind up in jail for a long time, just like them. They're going to try to get you in on André's murder too, and—"

"There's no way! I loved him! I knew nothing about that! I would have tried to stop LeRoy if I'd known he was gonna do that."

"I'm saying that LeRoy and Cornelius will try to say you were in on it."

"How could they?"

"Criminals turn on each other all the time. André told me that."

"But Connie's my brother, and me and LeRoy go way back!"

"You know them better than I do. But didn't you tell me that Connie has already tried to kill you?"

Talia slapped a palm on the table, rousing the attention of the guard, who asked if everything was all right. "We're all right," Talia snapped. "Mind your business."

Lionel knew she was upset because she realized he was right. The only people she had left in the world would leave her high and dry if they thought it would do them any good. "Don't you think you ought to make sure about you and God before you go to trial or even to county jail? You never know what's going to happen to you."

"That's why I asked you to come here," she said. "I'll think about it."

"What's to think about? You grew up with this just like I

did, and your mother was raptured just like she warned you
about."

"I know."

"It takes more than knowing."

"I want to do this. But I'm not going to be pushed into it.
I have to do this on my own."

"Fine. Then do it."

"Who do you think you are, talkin' to me like this? You're
what, thirteen?"

"Talia, that has nothing to do with anything, and you
know it. I'm being straight with you because you talk that way
to people. I wish someone had talked to me this way before it
was too late."

"Let me talk to the preacher man a second."

"Time's up," the guard said.

"No it ain't!" Talia exploded. "Not yet!"

"Yes, it is," the cop said, entering.

"I'm 'bout to get saved, so let that preacher in here now."

"You're what?"

"You heard me, now give me a minute."

The cop hesitated, looking at the glaring Talia and then at
Lionel, who responded with a pleading look of his own.

"Awright, you trade places with the preacher man, and he's
got two minutes."

# 36

"**HERE'S** the thing," Josey was saying, crying openly. "I knew all that channeling, crystal, New Age stuff had nothing for me, but I was desperate. I had not been to church since I was a little girl, but I remembered there was supposed to be a God who loved me."

"Why didn't you go back to church?" Vicki asked.

"I believed what everyone else was saying. People said the church was full of hypocrites, that institutionalized religion caused more problems than it solved, that God was in all of us and that we could find him within ourselves. In fact, if some could be believed, we could be gods ourselves. It just seemed to me that the closer I got to finding the god within me, the farther I felt from a real God, if there was one. Then someone invited me to a Bible study. That wasn't scary. It didn't sound like church. It was just a place to read the Bible and talk about it."

"What have you learned so far?" Vicki asked.

"That's just it. I think I've got all the basics. If I can just accept the fact that there's nothing I can do to make this happen, I'll—"

"Make what happen?" Tom Fogarty said, suddenly interested. "What is it exactly that you want to happen, hon? You want to make sure there's pie in the sky by and by for you, or do you just want to cover all your bases so you'll get to see your boys again, in case they're in heaven?"

Josey turned to face him, and Vicki wondered if she was angry. She didn't appear to be, though she may have had a right to be. "No, Tom. I don't know. I want to be sure, and I want to know God. I have no idea where my boys are, but I have this feeling that if I can know God, I can know that too."

"I just worry," Tom said, "that this is simply another short-term interest of yours, something with an ulterior motive. Seeing your boys again is a worthy goal, of course, but you see what I'm saying."

"I'll tell you one thing, Tom," Josey said, "this is no phase, no novelty. I'm desperate for God, and I won't stop searching till I find him. It's about the boys, yes, and it's about heaven, yes, and it's about fear over being left behind. But forgetting all that, I have to believe God knows me, knows about me, cares about me. If he loves me, I want to know it and know him."

Ryan surprised Vicki by talking directly to Tom. "What do you think, Sergeant Fogarty? Do you think we're all wrong about the disappearances?"

"I don't know what to think, Ryan. One of my detective partners, Eddie Edwards, I think he's really intrigued by all this. He thinks he has it figured out because so many people who talked about the Rapture were among those who disappeared. But there are also a lot of people missing who never talked about it. What about them?"

"You don't have to talk about it to believe it," Judd said.

"My dad wasn't real big about telling other people, but he's gone."

"But if he knew, why didn't he say so? Why didn't people tell everyone about this before it was too late, if that is really what this was?"

"They're telling us now," Josey said.

Tom Fogarty's beeper sounded. "Excuse me," he said, glancing at it and then looking for a phone. He looked at Judd, who pointed to one on the wall in the kitchen. A minute later Tom came back with an apology. "I have to run," he said. "I can come back for you, Josey, or you can come along."

"I'll stay if you don't mind, hon," she said. "What's up?"

"Banks and Grey attempted a jailbreak while Eddie and two uniforms were escorting them to a deposition. Grey and Eddie were wounded. Grey's not serious. Eddie might be in trouble."

Vicki glanced at Judd, who had seemed so eager to talk to Eddie. Judd was pale, and he stood. "Can I come with you?" he asked.

"Sure."

---

Bruce was quiet on their way out of the jail. Lionel asked him what had happened with Talia, but he just put a finger to his lips. "Tell you in the car," he said.

After starting the car and putting on his seat belt, Bruce let his head fall back, and he sighed. He shook his head. Lionel waited, knowing Bruce would tell him when he was good and ready. "Well," Bruce said finally, "she prayed the prayer, as they say, and she said the right words, but I don't know."

"Don't know what?"

"Her motives or her sincerity. I think she's mostly scared of her brother and LeRoy. She might be scared of going to hell too, but there's nothing wrong with that. Who wouldn't be? Lots of people become believers based on that kind of fear. But I'm afraid what Talia really wants, why she wanted to pray with me instead of with you, is for me to get her a lawyer."

"Are you going to?"

"Oh, sure. I'll make a few calls. We have lawyers attending the church. But if she was sincere about her faith, I'd like to see her get serious about Bible study, get a chaplain to counsel her, get into a church even in jail. I assume she's not into this crime spree and the murders as deeply as her brother and LeRoy are—at least I hope she's not—but still she could be in jail a long time. She'd better not wait till she's free to start exercising her faith. You remember the parable of the seed that falls on the different kinds of soil? I can't think of anything or any place worse for new seed than prison. She could come out of there hard as a rock, where the seed can't grab hold and sprout."

---

Judd noticed that Tom Fogarty's own car was the same size as his squad car but a lot roomier. There was no radio, no shotgun, no computer screen, none of the stuff that crowds the dashboard of a police cruiser. Tom looked worried and drove fast. Judd was buckled in, but he also braced himself and tried to engage Tom in conversation.

"What'd they tell you about Eddie? How bad is it?"

"Not good," he said. "You know officers don't carry weapons inside the jail, because if a prisoner jumps you and disarms you, you've got trouble. So Eddie and whoever else he was with would have checked their guns with the jailer, then escorted the handcuffed prisoners down the hall and into the parking garage for a ride to the courthouse or wherever they had to go."

"So where would Grey and Banks have gotten guns?"

"Probably from a cop either in the garage, the elevator, or even one of the vehicles."

"Those jailbreaks never work, do they?"

"Not usually. A guy jumped a woman officer in the elevator downtown once and disarmed her, killed her, killed a guard, and wasn't shot himself until he had gotten free and was out on the ramp. I hope he enjoyed his freedom. It lasted maybe fifteen to twenty seconds."

"What kind of a shoot-out was this one with Grey and Banks?"

"Quick, I guess. They usually are, but sometimes they get to be drawn-out things. They tell me one of them, probably Banks, grabbed someone's gun and shot Eddie in the face before he had a chance to respond. Three cops fired at the prisoners, apparently blowing off Grey's ear. Banks immediately surrendered."

"Sounds like the whole thing took just seconds."

"Probably, but depending on where Eddie was hit, it could last him a lifetime."

"You don't know how serious it was?"

"He's unconscious, that's all I know. And that's not a good sign. Sometimes these facial wounds are bloody but don't do much structural or organ damage unless they lodge in the eye or the nasal passage. If he's unconscious because of the wound, it could be brain penetration. That would be bad. He might never regain consciousness."

"Could he die?"

"I don't even want to think about that. He's the youngest guy in Homicide, but I worked with him for years. Met him when he first came over. Energetic, smart, good team guy. A cop's cop. You know what the worse thing is? I got a call earlier today from downtown, congratulating me on the Banks bust. Said I was next in line to get back into Homicide but that they didn't have a spot for me just yet. They said to be patient and I'd get my chance again."

"And you wanted that?"

"More than anything, but I sure don't want it this way."

It took Tom just minutes to get onto the expressway, and he wasn't afraid to take chances, to ride on the shoulder even without an emergency light. If he got stopped, Judd assumed, he would just let the officer know he was on the job, and he would be waved on.

Judd wanted to find out why Fogarty seemed so uninterested in God when his wife seemed so eager to learn everything she could. But Judd didn't know how to ask. "You know, Mr. Edwards seemed really interested in talking with me about the Rapture and stuff."

"I noticed that."

"Was he just being polite, teasing me?"

"I don't think so. He's not that kind of a guy."

"But even though your wife is interested, you don't seem to be."

"I'm not."

Well, Judd thought, at least that was honest. Tom was a straightforward kind of a guy. He liked directness and wasn't afraid of disagreement. "Why not?" Judd asked.

"You really want to know?" Fogarty asked.

"Yeah, I do."

"It might offend you. I can see you're really into this. I

wouldn't want to be the one responsible for changing your mind."

"You couldn't."

"Fair enough," Fogarty said. "I'll tell you exactly why. I was raised in a church where I was taught that God was love, but also that if you died with one sin on your soul, you went to hell. I couldn't make that compute. I quit the church as soon as I was old enough to make my own decisions. I still carried around in my head the belief that there was a God, but that he was a God of love. Not an angry judge, not a crabby parent. Not someone who would create a person and burn him up later."

Judd wanted to argue. Bruce had taught the kids that hell was a judgment for sin and that it had to do with justice. But God didn't want anyone to die and go to hell. He had given the world so many chances to be saved that there was no reason anybody had to go to hell. Judd sat silent, but Fogarty had just warmed up. As he wheeled around traffic and went as fast as the jam would allow him, he continued.

"I was OK with that view of God for a lot of years, even after I became a cop. But then stuff started to not add up. When I got into Homicide I saw stuff nobody should ever have to see."

"But you like it. You want to get back into it."

"It's where the action is, and I'm good at it. I feel I'm accomplishing something and helping people when I solve a case and put bad guys away. But I sure grew up in Homicide. I quit thinking of God as someone who made sense. In fact, I don't know if I believe there's a God at all anymore. How could there be a God, in charge of everything, who would allow the things I've seen? People bludgeoned and mutilated, usually by someone they love and trust. I've seen parents murder their own children, children murder their own parents. I've seen people go through things that no one should ever have to endure. Where is God in that?"

Judd had had the same questions, and he wasn't sure of all the answers. But he knew what Bruce would say. He didn't know the exact words and didn't know if he could back up those words anyway without being a Bible student like Bruce. But he had learned that just because God allowed something didn't mean he was for it. God truly was a God of love, and seeing people murder each other had to make him sad. But he had temporarily given control of the world to Satan. God would win in the end, but in the meantime, things were going to get only worse.

Judd knew if he said that, he would sound like some idealistic young kid who believed everything he heard. He had not seen the things Tom Fogarty had seen. He didn't know what he would think if he did see them.

"I'm glad for you that you have something you believe in," Fogarty said. "If it works for you, fine. If it works for Josey, I'll be thrilled. Nobody that wonderful should have to go through what she's going through. It's been a long time since I've seen her come to life the way she did around you kids today. She rarely smiles anymore, but the way you saw her today, that's the way she used to be all the time. But parents are not supposed to outlive their kids. It's too much to ask of a mother to have her children disappear. And it's happened all over the world. And you want to tell me the loving God of the universe did this on purpose? For what?"

"To convince you once and for all," Judd said.

"Convince me of what?"

"That he's real. That he was willing to give up his Son and that he will give you chance after chance to believe that he is who he says he is. He said he would rapture his church, and he did. He's going to come back again in seven years or so, and that will be the last chance of all for anyone who will still be alive."

"Good. I'll wait until I'm convinced."

"But very few people are going to still be alive by then. Bruce Barnes thinks only a quarter of the world's population will still be alive when Jesus gets here."

"This is your loving God doing this? Wiping out three-fourths of the world after already taking away the believers? I don't get it."

"He's not doing it. He's allowing it to get our attention."

"Call it whatever you want. It sounds crazy to me."

Judd was frustrated. He knew he wasn't explaining it well. On the other hand, Bruce had told him and the others that it wasn't up to them to convince people. They were just supposed to lovingly tell them the truth. Changing people's minds and hearts and getting them to come to Christ was God's work. We do our part and God does the rest. It seemed to Judd that neither he nor God was getting through to Tom Fogarty.

A few minutes later they pulled into the front circle of a huge hospital in the Loop. A uniformed cop hurried over to tell them to move the car, but he backed off when he saw Fogarty's badge. "Here to see Eddie?" the cop said. "He's out of Emergency, but he's in Intensive Care. Fourth floor, south wing."

As Judd and Fogarty hurried to the elevator, Fogarty said, "Unfortunately, I know exactly where ICU is. Been there many times."

Desk personnel tried to stop them in the lobby, but again, Fogarty just flashed his badge and kept moving. When the elevator doors opened on the fourth floor, Judd followed Tom down the hall past dozens of uniformed cops lined up on either side of the corridor. "Everybody on the clock?" Tom said, kidding them. "Nobody out serving and protecting while they're making their money?"

"We're standing behind your buddy, Tommy. Show a little respect."

"How's he doin'?" Fogarty asked, not slowing to listen.

"Not so good," another said. "If he don't make it, I know two bad guys who are never gonna get out of the can alive."

"Now you know better than that," Fogarty said. "I'd be right in there with ya if that was the answer, but you know Eddie wouldn't want that."

"Just the same . . . ," someone grumbled, leaving the end of the thought unspoken.

They reached the door of the ICU room with "Edwards, Archibald" on the nameplate.

"What's happening?" Fogarty asked the cop at the door.

"They're telling us nothing. He's still unconscious. No promises."

"Where'd he take the bullet?"

"Through the cheekbone."

"Ouch. Brain damage?"

"They're not saying, but what else can it be, Tommy? Point-blank range."

Fogarty swore, then glanced at Judd and apologized.

"Excuse me, gentlemen," a doctor said, trailed by a nurse and what looked like an intern, a young woman. He pushed his way through, and the three slipped inside the door.

Before the big door swung shut, Judd peeked in and saw a male nurse on a stool, studying a printout as it came from a machine near the bed. Judd would not have recognized Eddie.

He lay still, on his back, hands at his sides, tubes running to both arms, oxygen mask in place. His chest did not seem to be moving. His eyes were closed. No movement. Worse, just before the door eclipsed the view, Judd saw the nurse look directly into the doctor's eyes and shake his head.

---

Vicki wished Bruce and Lionel would get back soon. Besides wanting to know what went on with Talia Grey, she wanted help with this lovely troubled woman. Josey Fogarty sat there with Vicki and Ryan, pouring her heart out and virtually pleading with them to lead her to Christ. Vicki decided she could not and should not wait any longer. Using the same verses Bruce had taught Lionel, and starting with the basics, she asked Josey if she saw herself as a sinner in need of someone to forgive her and save her.

"I surely do," Josey said. "I surely do."

# 37

**VICKI** had listened intently during Bruce's training sessions with his new young charges, and she had wondered if she was up to a task like this. She was not prepared to lead someone to Christ just yet, though she agreed with Bruce that there could be no higher privilege for a Christian.

She was brand-new in the faith, and she had already been grounded in the basics, but she really hoped Bruce would arrive soon and take over with Josey Fogarty. Silently, Vicki prayed earnestly. Her major request was that Bruce bail her out. But short of that, she pleaded with God to remind her of the verses, to give her the words to say, to assure that she would say whatever she was supposed to say and avoid whatever she was not supposed to say. The last thing she wanted was to somehow mislead this precious woman who so desperately wanted to come to God. Vicki didn't know what all that New Age stuff was that Josey had talked about, but she sure knew it was not part of the true gospel as she knew it.

Vicki didn't want to stall any longer when it was obvious how ready Josey was. So once she had established that Josey knew her position before God and how it could change, she plunged ahead. When she was finished explaining how to pray and receive Christ and Josey bowed her head and closed her eyes, Vicki glanced at Ryan. She was encouraged to see a look on his face of wonder, of emotion, of encouragement to her. It was as if he told her with his eyes that he felt privileged to be there.

Vicki asked Josey if she wanted her to lead her in the prayer of acceptance of Christ, and Josey surprised her. "You know, hon, I don't think so. I think this is somethin' I got to do for myself. If God loves me and cares about me personally, like you say, I want to talk to him myself. So I think I'll just start in."

Vicki lowered her head and listened.

"God," Josey whispered, her voice thick with emotion, "you know I've been looking for you for years, and I'm glad to hear you've been looking for me too. I know I'm supposed to start by telling you I know I'm a sinner and that I need you. Part of me always wanted to do good and be known as a nice person, but I knew myself then and I know myself now. I've never been able to be the kind of person I know you would want me to be. Thank you for dying for my sins and for forgiving me. Forgive me for not being ready when you came for your people. If you will accept me, and I believe that you will, I offer you the rest of my life."

Vicki wept as she heard Josey go on to pray for Steve and Tom. And for her sons. She prayed for Eddie. She prayed for "these three kids I've just met and for the one I haven't met. And for their pastor."

Vicki thought it the most impressive prayer she'd ever heard, especially coming from someone who was taking her first step as a believer. Josey ended by saying, "I don't even know how to sign off, so I'll just say good-bye and I'll be talking to you again soon. Amen."

Vicki looked up through her tears as Josey sat there, her cheeks wet too. "Was that all right?" she asked, timidly.

"That was perfect," Vicki said, and they hugged each other. Ryan looked on, appearing to be fighting tears too.

"C'mere, Ryan!" Josey said, opening her arms wide. He rushed to her, and the three of them embraced.

---

Judd wondered how long Tom Fogarty would wait for the doctor to emerge from Eddie Edwards's hospital room. He was worried Tom would just barge in. Instead Tom approached the nurses' station around the corner. "Is there some reason we're getting no hard information from the doctors about Detective Edwards?" he asked.

The woman in charge looked sternly at him. "And you are . . . ?"

Tom showed her his badge and told her. She glanced down the hall and removed a chart from a rack. She motioned him closer with a nod and glared at Judd as he also approached, but Tom said, "He's with me."

She flipped open the chart. "We're talking about Edwards, Archibald, are we not?" she whispered.

Tom nodded.

"We are off the record, sir, and nothing you hear from me should be considered official or final or quotable. Is that understood?" Tom saluted her. "You're not related, are you?"

"No, why?"

"Because a next of kin would not want to hear this. I'm not a doctor, you understand, but I've been an R.N. for thirty-five years and I can read a chart. This man is not going to regain consciousness, and that's the kindest thing God can do for him at this point, short of just taking him."

"Ma'am?"

"You sounded like you wanted the truth, young man. I'm giving it to you. This patient took—" she began reading—" 'a high-speed, hollow-point, nine-millimeter shell to the cheek-bone from less than six feet away, fired from a Beretta service revolver.' "

"A Beretta is not a revolver," Fogarty said, "but otherwise I'm following you."

"I'm just tellin' you what it says. I'm no firearms expert. What I understand is that this bullet is made that way for maximum speed and shattering ability upon impact."

Tom nodded, looking glum.

She read again. " 'The bullet entered at an acute, nearly vertical angle, passing just under the right cheekbone and bursting into fragments that destroyed the olfactory canal, the entire right eye socket, and extending into the frontal lobe of the brain before exiting through the top of the skull.' "

She let her reading glasses slip off and dangle at the end of the strap around her neck. "Need I be more specific?"

Fogarty shook his head. "It'll be more merciful, as you say, if he passes. Am I right?"

"I'm afraid so, son. I'm sorry."

Tom thanked her and turned away, and Judd noticed he walked stiffly, as if he had to plot each step. "You want something to pray about, Holy Joe?" he said. "You pray Eddie Edwards dies before his family has to see him like that."

Judd didn't want to pray for that at all. He wanted a mira-cle. He wanted that man who had just hours before seemed so interested in the things of God to regain consciousness, to know how close he came to death, to be spurred to take action now and receive Christ.

As he and Fogarty went back around the corner, the doctors and the nurse emerged from Edwards's room. They were met by the same heavyset detective who had been in on the sting that day and had been with them in the diner. "There's Willis," Fogarty said. He looked grave.

"I'm the ranking officer here," Willis told the doctor. "And I want to tell these cops something concrete."

"Is there a next of kin?" the doctor said quietly.

"Oh, no," Willis said.

"Come on, sir, we've all been through this before. I can't be making statements the next of kin have not heard."

"Tell me and I will tell the next of kin."

The doctor pulled a notepad from his pocket. He spoke so softly that only Willis, Fogarty, and Judd could have heard him. "Time of death, 8:55 p.m."

The doctor moved away, and the sea of cops surged toward Detective Willis. "You people are to be back on the street immediately. We will broadcast an update in fifteen minutes. Be somewhere where you can hear it."

"Is he dead?" someone called out.

"Don't start acting like the press," Willis growled. "Now get going!"

---

Lionel and Bruce were near Judd's home when the report came over the radio about the jailbreak attempt a few hours before. "An update on that story," the newsman said, "is that the police officer wounded in the brief shoot-out fights for his life at this hour."

Lionel and Bruce looked at each other. "Unbelievable," Bruce muttered. He asked Lionel to call Judd's house and tell them to turn on the news.

"Lionel!" Ryan said, blurting all the news at once. "Judd and Tom went to see the cop shot in the escape thing, and Tom's wife is here and she just prayed to accept Jesus, and—"

"We're on our way, Ryan," Lionel said.

---

Judd sat stunned in the quiet car as Tom drove him back from Chicago. Judd was frustrated that he had not been able to talk to Eddie about God when he had seemed so interested. How many other ways did God have to use to show him that no one was guaranteed any time anymore? They had driven almost an hour before Tom spoke.

"Explain that one to me," he said, "if you know the mind of God so well."

"I never claimed that, Mr. Fogarty, but it's sure a lesson, isn't it?"

"Yeah? What's the moral of this story?"

"Don't wait. If you're curious about God, don't put off finding out about him."

"So a great young cop dies to warn me to find God? I don't think so."

Judd knew Fogarty was in too much pain to be reasoned with just then, so he fell silent. Tom turned on the radio when they reached the suburbs and soon heard the news they had known before anyone else. When they pulled into the driveway at Judd's, Bruce's car was in the driveway. "I want you to meet this guy," Judd said, assuming Tom would at least come in to get his wife.

"I really don't feel like seeing anyone right now," Tom said. "Would you mind just sending Josey out?"

Judd hesitated, then said, "Sure."

As he was getting out of the car, Tom called out to him. "Judd, I'm sorry if I took this out on you a little. I don't want you to lose your faith or anything."

Judd didn't know what to say, so he just nodded and ran into the house. There he found everyone beaming and was quickly filled in on what had happened to Josey. She was sitting with an arm around Lionel, whom she had finally met and who was looking pleased but uncomfortable with her attention.

"I hate to be the one with the bad news, Mrs. Fogarty and everyone," Judd said, "but your husband's waiting for you in the car, and he's pretty upset over Eddie's death."

Josey's smile faded as fast as it had come. "Oh, no," she said, over and over. And she hurried toward the door.

"Take a minute and let us pray for you," Bruce said, and he and the kids huddled again, this time with her in the middle of them, and prayed for her in her new faith. Bruce prayed for her husband and for the Edwards family.

A minute later Josey was gone, and Judd and his friends sat with Bruce, exhausted and silent. "I've got to get going," Bruce said finally. "Big day tomorrow. And then the next night we're meeting, just the five of us. I have so many things to tell you. Huge news about the Antichrist and the Tribulation and other things in prophecy. You learned today that not everything in the Christian life is neat and tidy. Things happen that we don't understand, we don't like, and we can't explain. God's ways are not our ways, and his thoughts are not our thoughts.

"Not that long ago I never knew anyone who had been the victim of a violent crime. I never knew anyone who had been killed, murdered, or even threatened. Now Ryan has had his parents both die, Lionel has lost an uncle to murder, and Judd has lost a new acquaintance. It's as if God is using this period in history as a crash course in life and death. We tell people they don't have a lot of time to be deciding what they will do about Jesus, and then it is proven to us every day."

Judd collapsed into bed that night with mixed emotions. He missed his family, but he was grateful for his new friends, for Bruce, and for his own assurance of heaven. He wished he knew the mind of God better and could understand why things happened the way they did—either that or to be able to somehow explain them to people like Tom Fogarty.

Judd was fascinated by prophecy and the fact that he and his friends were living right in the middle of it every day. He knew Bruce's teaching on the Antichrist would be troubling and scary, but he would sure rather know than not know what was coming.

**38**

**THE** following Sunday, Judd had the idea Bruce was holding back with the congregation that packed the pews at New Hope Village Church. Oh, Bruce was as earnest as ever. But he had told Judd and the other kids that he suspected Nicolae Carpathia, the new head of the United Nations, was the Antichrist. Bruce swore them to secrecy and said the only others who knew how he felt were four adults who formed a sort of inner circle within the church.

When Judd heard Bruce's message that Sunday, he realized the point of all the secrecy. Bruce outlined from Scripture what he believed were the characteristics of the Antichrist, and anybody with a brain could see he was talking about Carpathia. But Bruce was careful not to use his name or the name of the organization he ran. Judd decided that Bruce had big plans and that he wanted to survive in order to carry them out. He wanted to expand his ministry, to branch out and teach small groups in homes all over America and maybe the rest of the world. If he said from the pulpit of a big church exactly who he thought was the Antichrist—and if he were right—his life would be worthless.

Bruce had promised the kids that he would show them tapes from the big news shows, tapes he had been gathering for days. Somewhere in the middle of all his study and ministry, Bruce had found the time to edit and put the tapes in order. He told Judd that with just a little of his own explaining, he believed Judd and the other three would know for sure what to make of Carpathia.

Monday afternoon the kids met with Bruce, and only Bruce. At other times there were a few other adults or Bruce's secretary in with them. But not this time. Bruce had rigged up a TV set and a VCR, and he sat with a pile of notes on a yellow legal pad, and of course his Bible.

After they brought each other up-to-date on their lives, their study, and their prayer requests, they prayed. Then Bruce began with a tape from *Nightline* the night after Carpathia appeared at the United Nations. "It shows this guy as a master communicator. I know you all saw his address to the United Nations. Remember, he was just a guest. That speech and the way he carried himself made them beg him to take over. Watch now, and see how well coached he is. Either that, or he's a natural, born for television."

Carpathia looked directly into the camera whenever possible and seemed to be looking right at the viewer. Judd couldn't take his eyes from the handsome, engaging, often smiling face. He found himself wishing such a nice, well-spoken, and seemingly kind man didn't have to be a bad guy. And he even found himself wondering if Bruce could be wrong. He hoped so, but Bruce hadn't been wrong about much so far.

The interviewer was a newsman named Wallace Theodore. He began, "Your speech at the United Nations, which was sandwiched between two press conferences today, seems to have electrified New York, and because so much of it has been aired on both early-evening and late-night local newscasts, you've become a popular man in this country seemingly all at once."

Carpathia smiled. "Like anyone from Europe, particularly Eastern Europe, I am amazed at your technology. I—"

"But isn't it true, sir, that your roots are actually in Western Europe? Though you were born in Romania, are you not by heritage actually Italian?"

Bruce pointed the remote control at the TV and paused the tape. "Remember what I taught you about the Antichrist?" he said. "That he would have Roman blood?"

The kids nodded, and Bruce turned the tape back on.

"That is true," Carpathia was saying, "as is true of many native Romanians. Thus the name of our country. But as I was saying about your technology. It is amazing, but I confess I did not come to your country to become or to be made into a celebrity. I have a goal, a mission, a message, and it has nothing to do with my popularity or my personal—"

Bruce fast-forwarded the tape, explaining that Carpathia was defending his submitting to an interview with *People* magazine. Bruce started the tape again as Carpathia was saying, "I am on a crusade to see the peoples of the world come together. I do not seek a position of power or authority. I simply ask to be heard. I hope my message comes through in the article in the magazine as well."

Vicki interrupted by raising her hand. "Now, see?" she said. "What's so wrong with that? Isn't that what we want to hear someone say at a time like this?"

"Sure," Bruce said, "but keep listening carefully."

Mr. Theodore said, "You already have a position of both power and authority, Mr. Carpathia."

"Well, our little country asked me to serve, and I was willing."

"How do you respond to those who say you skirted proto-col and that your elevation to the presidency in Romania was partially effected by strong-arm tactics?"

"Whoa!" Lionel blurted, shaking his head. "Pause that. He totally lost me. What is he asking?"

Bruce chuckled. "Let me interpret. Protocol is the standard and accepted way of doing things. Romania had a democratic election, but some people say that Carpathia somehow got around that by getting himself put in as president, even though it was in the middle of another man's term in office. Carpathia was just a member of the lower house of govern-ment there before that."

Lionel nodded and the tape began again.

Carpathia responded, "I would say that that is the perfect way to attack a pacifist, one who is committed to disarmament not only in Romania and the rest of Europe but also globally."

"In other words," Bruce interjected quickly, "he says he doesn't believe in war and weaponry."

"So you deny," the newsman came back, "having a busi-ness rival murdered seven years ago and using intimidation and powerful friends in America to usurp the president's authority in Romania?"

"The so-called murdered rival was one of my dearest friends, and I mourn him bitterly to this day. The few American friends I have may be influential here, but they could not have any bearing on Romanian politics. You must know that our former president asked me to replace him for personal reasons."

"But that completely ignores your constitution's procedure for succession to power."

"How they elect a president," Bruce explained.

"That was voted upon by the people and by the govern-ment and ratified with a huge majority," Carpathia said.

380

"After the fact."

"In a way, yes. But in another way, had they not ratified it, both popularly and within the houses of government, I would have been the briefest reigning president in our nation's history."

Theodore asked him, "Why the United Nations? Some say you would have more impact and get more mileage out of an appearance before our Senate and House of Representatives."

"I would not even dream of such a privilege," Carpathia said. "But, you see, I was not looking for mileage. The U.N. was envisioned originally as a peacekeeping effort. It must return to that role."

"You hinted today, and I hear it in your voice even now, that you have a specific plan for the U.N. that would make it better and which would be of some help during this unusually horrific season in history."

"I do. I do not feel it was my place to suggest such changes when I was a guest; however, I have no hesitation in this context. I am a proponent of disarmament. That is no secret. While I am impressed with the wide-ranging capabilities, plans, and programs of the United Nations, I do believe, with a few minor adjustments and the cooperation of its members, it can be all it was meant to be. We can truly become a global community."

"Can you briefly outline that in a few seconds?"

Carpathia's laugh appeared deep and genuine. "That is always dangerous," he said, "but I will try. As you know, the Security Council of the United Nations has five permanent members: the United States, the Russian Federation, Britain, France, and China. I propose choosing another five, just one each from the five different regions of the world. Then you would have ten permanent members of the Security Council, but the rest of my plan is revolutionary. Currently the five permanent members have veto power. Votes on procedure require a nine-vote majority; votes on substance require a majority, including all five permanent members. I propose a tougher system. I proposed unanimity."

"I beg your pardon?"

"Select carefully the representative ten permanent members. They must get input from and support from all the countries in their respective regions."

"It sounds like a nightmare."

"But it would work, and here is why. A nightmare is what happened to us last week. The time is right for the peoples of the world to rise up and insist that their governments disarm and destroy all but ten percent of their weapons. That ten percent would be, in effect, donated to the United Nations so it could return to its rightful place as a global peacekeeping body, with the authority and power in the equipment to do the job."

Bruce paused the tape yet again and apologized to the kids. "I'm sorry to make you listen to all that discussing of the ins and outs of the United Nations, but I think you can catch the drift there. Does anyone hear anything that sounds suspicious, based on what we've been studying in the book of Revelation?"

Judd took a breath to speak, but Vicki beat him to the punch. "There's all kinds of stuff in Revelation about the ten kings! You think Carpathia's idea of ten rulers matches up with that?"

"What do you think?" Bruce said.

"I guess it's pretty hard to argue with," Vicki said.

"Let me just play another couple of moments from this tape, which I find more than alarming." Bruce started the tape.

"What is your personal goal?" Theodore was asking. "A leadership role in the European Common Market?"

"Romania is not even a member, as you know. But no, I have no personal goal of leadership, except as a voice. We must disarm, we must empower the United Nations, we must move to one currency, and we must become a global village."

Bruce turned the tape off and removed it from the VCR. "Would you believe that several adults who have talked to me found Nicolae Carpathia a very impressive guy?"

"That doesn't surprise me at all," Vicki said. "He's a *very* impressive guy. He seems so sincere and humble."

"If this man is the Antichrist," Bruce said, "he will be attractive, charming, and a great deceiver. Of course, if he were for real, he would also be attractive and charming. We must be, as the Bible says, wise as serpents and gentle as doves as we study this. But think with me for a moment. If this man is the Antichrist—and we already know that since these tapes were recorded he has been installed as secretary-general of the U.N.—think what the world is doing if it does what he says."

The kids sat silent for a moment. Judd looked at the others. They looked puzzled. He had already thought of it. "He calls himself a pacifist," Judd said. "But what if he's not? What if he's a dictator? He's talked everyone else into giving up their weapons, destroying most of them and giving the rest to him. He'll have all the firepower. We'd better *hope* he's a pacifist!"

Bruce nodded. "Now let me show you this tape I recorded from CNN. It was shot in Israel, and it's the strangest report. What you'll see first is a mob in front of the famous Wailing Wall in Jerusalem. They're surrounding two men who seem to be shouting. Watch and listen."

"No one knows the two men," said the CNN reporter on the scene, "who refer to each other as Eli and Moishe. They have stood here before the Wailing Wall since just before dawn, preaching in a style frankly reminiscent of the old American evangelists. Of course, the Orthodox Jews here are in an uproar, charging the two with desecrating this holy place by proclaiming that Jesus Christ of the New Testament is the fulfillment of the Torah's prophecy of a messiah.

"Thus far there has been no violence, though tempers are flaring, and authorities keep a watchful eye. Israeli police and military personnel have always been loath to enter this area, leaving religious zealots here to handle their own problems. This is the most explosive situation in the Holy Land since the destruction of the Russian air force, and this newly prosperous nation has been concerned almost primarily with outside threats.

"For CNN, this is Dan Bennett in Jerusalem."

Judd noticed Bruce was particularly excited now. "I know you've already seen some of these reports, but you must recognize those two men preaching at the Wailing Wall as the two witnesses prophesied in Scripture. The Bible says that those two men will be safe from harm and will have power over even the rainfall in Israel for the first half of the Tribulation period. They have the power to keep it from raining, the power to turn water into blood, and the power to breathe fire on people who try to harm them before the due time. What will be really incredible is that when they are finally assassinated, the Scripture says they will lie in the street for three days before the eyes of the entire world. Before technology as we know it, most biblical experts considered this to be figurative or symbolic language. How could the whole world see two men lying in the streets for three days? Well, now we know. Most will likely watch this on CNN.

"The people who have hated these two men will wildly

celebrate their deaths. But after three days, God will audibly call them into heaven by simply saying, 'Come up here.' "

Lionel leaned forward and shook his head, laughing. "That ought to change a few minds real quick!"

"Remember what I said about God raising up 144,000 Jews who would believe in Christ and begin to evangelize around the world?" Bruce said. "I believe these two will be leading the way."

Bruce turned the tape on again. A CNN anchorwoman had turned to national news. "New York is still abuzz following several appearances today by new Romanian president Nicolae Carpathia. The thirty-three-year-old leader wowed the media at a small press conference this morning, followed by a masterful speech to the United Nations General Assembly in which he had the entire crowd standing and cheering, including the press. Associates of Carpathia have announced that he has already extended his schedule to include addresses to several international meetings in New York over the next two weeks and that he has been invited by President Fitzhugh to speak to a joint session of Congress and spend a night at the White House.

"At a press conference this afternoon the president voiced support for the new leader."

The president's image filled the screen. He said, "At this difficult hour in world history, it's crucial that lovers of peace and unity step forward to remind us that we're part of the global community. Any friend of peace is a friend of the United States, and Mr. Carpathia is a friend of peace."

CNN broadcast a question asked of the president. "Sir, what do you think of Carpathia's ideas for the U.N.?"

"Let me just say this: I don't believe I've ever heard anybody, inside or outside the U.N., show such a total grasp of the history and organization and direction of the place. He's

done his homework, and he has a plan. I was listening. I hope
the respective ambassadors and Secretary-General Ngumo
were, too. No one should see a fresh vision as a threat. I'm sure
every leader in the world shares my view that we need all the
help we can get at this hour."

The anchorwoman continued: "Out of New York late this
evening comes a report that a *Global Weekly* writer has been
cleared of all charges and suspicion in the death of a Scotland
Yard investigator. Cameron Williams, award-winning senior
writer at the *Weekly*, had been feared dead in a car bombing
that took the life of the investigator, Alan Tompkins, who was
also an acquaintance of Williams."

"I need to tell you about this young man, Williams," Bruce
said.

"I know who he is," Lionel said. "He called me on the
phone once, looking for my mother."

"And he was on the plane with me the night of the
Rapture," Judd said.

"Well," Bruce said, "he's a friend of Captain Steele, and he
has spoken directly to Carpathia. He says Carpathia told him
that Israel needs protection the United Nations can provide.
Israel has a formula that makes the desert bloom. In exchange
for that formula, Carpathia says the world will be content to
grant them peace. If the other nations disarm and surrender a
tenth of their weapons to the U.N., only the U.N. will have to
sign a peace accord with Israel. If Cameron Williams is right,
the agreement with Israel, in my mind, would signal the start
of the seven-year tribulation period.

"Our time is up for this evening, but next time I want to
start teaching you what I have been teaching a small adult
group. I have drawn out a time line from several different
sources that should give us a rough outline of what to expect

during this, the most difficult period that will ever be recorded in the annals of time."

Judd, for one, couldn't wait to return and learn more. As he drove home that night, he could hardly get a word in edgewise. The other three were chattering away about what they had heard from Bruce. Finally, Ryan said, "Judd, what do you think Bruce expects us to do with all this stuff? I mean, we can't go to New York and fight this Carpathia guy, can we?"

"Of course not," Judd said. "I think Bruce just believes we'll be better off knowing our enemy than not knowing him. Our job is to bring as many people to Christ as possible over the next seven years, and you know that's not going to make us popular with any of God's enemies, especially the Antichrist."

# 39

**THE** next morning, Judd had two problems on his mind, and they both had to do with females. He had wrestled in the night with an idea for Talia Grey. And just after he thought he had the perfect plan to bounce off Bruce, he was awakened by the telephone.

Of all things, the call came from inside the house. Judd's father had had two phone lines, so he could run his computer and fax machine when he worked at home. "I'm sorry to bother you, Judd," Vicki said, and it was obvious to him that she was crying.

Judd rolled up on one elbow and cradled the phone while glancing at the alarm clock. It was after three in the morning. He had just dozed off after coming up with his Talia Grey idea. "It's no bother, Vicki," he said. "What's up?"

"I was just wondering if I could talk to you for a while?"

"Sure. You mean on the phone right now, or . . . ?"

"I thought maybe face-to-face, like in the kitchen. That is if you think it would be OK."

"Is it an emergency, Vicki?"

"No," she said sadly. "I guess it can wait until tomorrow."

"No!" he said. "If it was worth calling in the middle of the night, it's worth talking about now. I'll meet you in five minutes."

Judd changed into jeans and a sweatshirt, splashed cold water on his face, and headed down to the kitchen.

A few minutes later he and Vicki sat sipping milk while she unburdened herself. "I just feel guilty, I guess," she said. "I mean, I love Bruce just like we all do, and his arguments are really convincing."

"I'm not following you," Judd said. "What is it you're feeling guilty about?"

"I don't believe him, that's all!" she blurted.

"Don't believe him about what?"

"The Antichrist!"

Judd slid his chair back and looked at her, brows raised. "After all Bruce has told us and explained to us about prophecy and the characteristics of the Antichrist, you don't think Nicolae Carpathia is the guy?"

Vicki was fighting tears. "Don't put me down about it, Judd, please!"

"I'm not! I'm just stunned. Tell me why."

"I don't know, and I'm afraid to tell Bruce. I see this Carpathia guy on TV, and he's so charming and smooth and convincing—I guess I'm one of the deceived. I can't seem to get into my mind that he's a bad guy."

"You know what Bruce would say, Vicki. He would say that that alone almost proves that Carpathia *is* the Antichrist."

Vicki nodded miserably. "I know," she said. "I feel like such a fool. But I can't just decide something is true only because the people I know and love and respect say it is. I want to agree with Bruce and all of you, but that's why I feel so guilty. I guess I need to be convinced."

"Are you looking to me to convince you? It's true I agree with Bruce on this, but I'm no more of a student of it than you are. If Bruce can't convince you, I sure can't."

"I know," Vicki said. "I guess what I'm looking for is just some sympathy and someone to talk to."

"I can do that," Judd said. "But what do you think it will take to convince you?"

"I don't know, but I sure wouldn't mind talking to that *Global Weekly* writer."

"Cameron Williams?"

"Yes."

"I thought he was based in New York," Judd said, "but he must have been around here. He talked to Bruce, and Bruce says he's a friend of the Steeles."

"If he has actually talked to Carpathia," Vicki said, "I think it would be fantastic for him to come and talk to us. In fact, I think it would be great if he came and talked to the whole church."

"Slow down there, Vicki. Bruce hasn't even said whether or not Williams is a Christian. And if he is, he sure can't be talking about Carpathia in public, especially if he believes Carpathia is the Antichrist."

Vicki slumped in the kitchen chair, her arms folded. She looked down. "I know," she whispered.

"But, hey, it sure wouldn't hurt to ask Bruce about him. You want me to?"

"I can ask him myself," Vicki said. "I just don't want to tell Bruce yet that I am not convinced about Carpathia."

Judd rinsed their glasses in the sink. He turned and looked expectantly at Vicki, who still sat there, staring at the floor. "You think I'm awful?" she asked.

"Hardly," he said. "The truth is, I think you're pretty special."

She looked up at him shyly. "I wasn't looking for a compliment," she said. "But I appreciate that."

Judd had not planned to say anything like that, and he had nothing to follow it with. "I'm good at keeping secrets," he said, "if that means anything to you."

"Of course it does, Judd. It means a lot to me that I can talk to you without the fear of being quoted."

Judd had trouble getting back to sleep, and early in the morning he felt the need to talk directly with Bruce. He would not betray Vicki's confidence, but he agreed that getting a chance to meet Cameron Williams would be a great thing for him and his friends. Also, he wanted to talk about his idea for Talia Grey.

When Judd called, Bruce told him he had another appointment in half an hour, but that he could see Judd right away, if he was available. "If I'm available?" Judd said. "It seems all I have is time. If they don't reopen our high school soon, what else am I going to do but talk to you?"

"Frankly, Judd," Bruce said, "time is something I wish I had more of."

Judd hurried to the church. Bruce's secretary, Loretta, ushered him into Bruce's office, where he found Bruce hunched over his Bible and several commentaries. "I know you don't have much time, so let me get right to it. I was wondering if you've already found a lawyer to help Talia Grey."

"As a matter of fact, I have. That's my next appointment."

"I don't suppose it would be possible for me to talk to him."

"Sure it would. Why not? But why are you assuming it's a *him*?"

"Oh, it's not?"

"Her name is Beth Murray. If you can hang around, you'll meet her in a few minutes. What else was on your mind?"

"This one might be tougher, Bruce. When you said you spoke with Cameron Williams, was that on the phone, or was he at the church here?"

"He was here," Bruce said. Bruce sat studying Judd, his eyes narrowing. "Why do you ask?"

"Is he a Christian?"

"As a matter of fact, he is. And he just happens to have one of the most incredible stories I've ever heard. The only problem is, I'm not sure he's at liberty to share it widely."

"Will he be back? Would he be able to meet with us? I think we'd all love to hear his experiences, especially if he's actually talked with Carpathia."

"Let me think about this for a minute," Bruce said. He stood, turned his back, and strode to the window. He peered into the parking lot for several seconds. When he turned back to face Judd, he appeared to have come to a decision. "You know what?" he said. "This is going to be totally up to Mr. Williams, of course, but I think I'm going to give the Junior Tribulation Force the true test."

"I hope you know I have no idea what you're talking about," Judd said.

Bruce sat on the edge of his desk and looked down kindly at Judd. "It just so happens that Cameron Williams has been reassigned to Chicago. He had been headquartered in New York for several years, but he will be living in this area now for a while."

"And he'll be coming to this church?"

Bruce nodded. "He's become the fourth member of the Tribulation Force, along with the Steeles and me."

"And what's this about some sort of a test?"

"Yes, a true test for you kids."

"By the way, Bruce, we don't mind being referred to as

kids, because that's what we are. But I don't think any of us would be excited about the term *Junior Tribulation Force,* or whatever."

"Sorry. It's just that your adult counterparts, the four people who make up the inner core of serious Bible students here, as I've told you, refer to themselves as the Tribulation Force."

"Call us the Kids Tribulation Force then," Judd suggested.

"Fair enough," Bruce said.

"And this big test . . . ?"

"No promises now," Bruce cautioned, "but I think I'm going to ask Cameron Williams to tell you kids his story. The reason I call that a big test is that if you are going to be called the younger version of the Tribulation Force, it requires keeping life-and-death secrets. Buck Williams—"

"Buck?"

"That's his nickname, yes. Buck Williams is privileged to have personal access to Nicolae Carpathia himself. As a new Christian, that puts him in a very dangerous situation. All I can do is ask him to tell you his story. If he chooses not to, we'll all have to accept that. If, however, he does decide to entrust you with the story, it must never be repeated to anyone anywhere without Buck's express permission. Is that understood?"

Judd nodded, his pulse quickening. *What in the world might the story be?* "Can I ask you something else, Bruce?"

"Of course."

"You did say that Williams believes Nicolae Carpathia is the Antichrist?"

"The fact is, Judd, Buck believed Nicolae Carpathia was the Antichrist even before Buck became a believer. In fact, I believe his coming to that conclusion helped persuade Buck to come to Christ."

"Wow! Do you think Buck would have any trouble convincing someone that Carpathia is the Antichrist?"

"Absolutely none," Bruce said. "Why? You know someone who needs convincing?"

"I didn't say that."

"But I asked you that."

"Let's just say I could use some more convincing myself," Judd said. "It seems this is an important enough deal that we should all be very sure about it. You have to admit, we could sure use somebody like Carpathia, I mean if he was for real."

"He appears as an angel of light," Bruce said, sighing. "Don't ever forget that."

Loretta poked her head into Bruce's office. "Excuse me, gentlemen," she said. "Pastor Barnes, your next appointment is here."

**JUDD** appreciated Bruce's custom of having strangers tell their stories immediately after being introduced. Everyone now attending New Hope had, of course, been left behind at the Rapture, and so each had a story to tell. Where were they when it happened? How had they missed out? Whom had they lost? How did they find the truth? And what were they doing now?

The lawyer, Beth Murray, was an extremely tall, dark-haired woman with sharp features but a soft smile. When she and Bruce and Judd were seated, Bruce asked Judd to tell his story first. As many times as he had told it, it never grew old for him. There were sad parts, of course. Regrets. Fear. Even terror. There were parts he didn't much enjoy rehashing—discovering his family was gone, realizing he was alone in the world.

And yet Judd loved to get to the grace part. He never grew tired of telling the wonderful news that he had been given a second chance. God's grace extended to him despite his rebellion and failure the first time around. He realized he had been more than fortunate. He could easily have been killed in an accident during the Rapture, as so many others had. His voice grew quavery when he told how he had learned from Bruce that the Christian life was a series of new beginnings.

Judd became quickly aware that Beth Murray had learned well the listening part of her craft. She leaned forward, rested her chin on her fist, and locked in to his gaze. She made him feel as if he were the most important person in her world just then. It seemed she didn't want to miss a word. It nearly made Judd uncomfortable, but soon he realized it was her way of encouraging him, and he plunged ahead.

Ms. Murray grew emotional along with Judd as he recounted how he had met the other three kids and had invited them to live with him. She particularly enjoyed the brief stories of how each had come to Christ. "I can't wait to meet each of them and hear them tell of their own journeys."

Her story was a new one to Judd. She said she had been an atheist, "but in actuality, describing myself as an agnostic would have been more precise. I worshiped at the altar of education, achievement, and materialism. I married a nonpracticing Jewish man ten years ago, and we got along fine until about eighteen months ago. I believed I was the most open-minded and tolerant person in the world until Isaiah converted to Christianity and began attending a messianic synagogue. I was mortified. I was angry. I refused to discuss it. I would not attend with him. Our marriage was nearly on the rocks, and yet I could not deny the change in him. No matter how I treated him, he loved me and forgave me and treated me kindly.

"I was not happy in a marriage with a man I respected but whose belief system I could not respect. Much as I love children, I'm so grateful Isaiah and I decided not to have any. I was on the brink of an affair when the Rapture occurred. Isaiah had warned me of that, and so I was speeding toward that messianic synagogue within ten minutes of the disappearances. No one was there. Every person associated with that fellowship was gone. I stumbled across New Hope. I simply drove past and saw it here, a church with a few people milling about. I met Pastor Barnes, I watched the videotape that had been prepared for people just like me, and I joined the kingdom."

With their stories—which Bruce sometimes referred to as "testimonies"—out of the way, they got down to the reason for their meeting. Beth Murray told Judd that Bruce had brought her up-to-date on Talia Grey's case. "I have studied her file, and it doesn't look good for her at this point. She was much more deeply involved than you might have assumed in many of the crimes committed by her brother and his friend. The best thing we have going for us is that court dockets are jammed and only getting worse. I have a few ideas, but Bruce tells me you have one too."

"If you don't mind," Judd said.

"Let's hear it," she said.

Judd told her of the idea that had come to him in the middle of the night. "I don't claim to know much about the law, and I guess I thought of this because of the things I've seen on TV. But I was just wondering whether she might be able to help herself by agreeing to testify against LeRoy and Cornelius."

"That's an excellent idea, Judd," she said. "I had been thinking of something along those lines as well. If she is willing and brave enough to withstand the threats of LeRoy's and her brother's associates, she just may be able to do herself a lot of good. Good thinking."

"Actually," Judd said, "now that I have met you and think about it a little, I see one more big advantage to having you working with Talia."

"And what's that?" Ms. Murray said.

"You'll have to interview Sergeant Tom Fogarty, won't you?"

"Yes. In fact, I already have."

"And did you meet his wife?"

"Just briefly. It was long enough, however, for me to sense that there's some tension there."

Judd and Bruce filled her in, and the three of them agreed to be praying for just the right opening for Beth to support Mrs. Fogarty in her new faith and to perhaps reach Tom for Christ.

---

Judd drove home that day feeling better than he had in a long time. He was glad he had met Beth Murray, and he was optimistic about the futures of his new acquaintances. He knew there were no guarantees. He knew that in real life, not everyone made decisions or took the actions one might want them to.

He enjoyed being able to tell Vicki that he had not only kept her confidence but that she would also get her wish to meet Cameron Williams and hear of his experiences with Nicolae Carpathia. That meeting came one momentous afternoon the following week, when Mr. Williams was able to get away from the Chicago bureau office of *Global Weekly* magazine and join the Kids Tribulation Force and Bruce for a highly secret meeting.

---

To Vicki, the ruggedly handsome thirtyish Buck Williams seemed like a man more comfortable with adults than with teenagers. He greeted them warmly enough, but he was a bit formal and quiet, something she knew he couldn't be normally with a job like his. He joined them in their prayer time, but then he sat behind the kids.

Bruce began the meeting by finishing his promised lesson on the time chart of the seven-year tribulation. "It looks to me," he said, "and to many of the experts who came before us, like this period of history we're in right now will last for the first twenty-one months of the Tribulation. They encompass what the Bible calls the seven Seal Judgments, or the judgments of the seven-sealed scroll. Then comes another twenty-one-month period in which we will see the seven Trumpet Judgments. In the last forty-two months of the seven years, if we have survived, we will endure the most severe test, the seven Vial Judgments. The last half of the seven years is called the Great Tribulation, and if we are alive at the end of it, we will be rewarded by seeing the glorious appearing of Christ.

"These judgments get progressively worse, and they will be harder and harder to survive. If we die, we will be in heaven with Christ and our loved ones. But we may suffer horrible deaths. If we somehow make it through the seven terrible years, especially the last half, the Glorious Appearing will be all that more glorious. Christ will come back to set up his thousand-year reign on Earth, the Millennium.

"Let me just briefly outline the seven-sealed scroll from Revelation 5 and 6, and then we'll hear from Mr. Williams. On the one hand, I don't want to give you a spirit of fear, but we all know we're still here because we neglected salvation before the Rapture. I know we're all grateful for the second chance, but we cannot expect to escape the trials that are coming."

Bruce explained that the first four seals in this scroll were described as men on four horses: a white horse, a red horse, a black horse, and a pale horse. "The white horseman apparently is the Antichrist, who ushers in one to three months of diplomacy while getting organized and promising peace.

"The red horse signifies war. Three rulers from the south will oppose the Antichrist, and millions will be killed."

Bruce turned a sheet on his flip chart. "All that killing will likely come within the next eighteen months. Immediately following that, which will take only three to six months because of the nuclear weaponry available, the Bible predicts inflation and famine—the black horse. As the rich get richer, the poor starve to death. More millions will die that way. Sad to say, it gets worse. That killer famine could be as short as two or three months before the arrival of the fourth Seal Judgment, the fourth horseman on a pale horse—the symbol of death. Besides the postwar famine, a plague will sweep the entire world. Before the fifth Seal Judgment a quarter of the world's current population will be dead. You're going to recognize this judgment, because we've talked about it before. Remember my telling you about 144,000 Jewish witnesses who evangelize the world for Christ? The world leader and the harlot, which is the name for the one-world religion that denies Christ, will murder many of the converts, perhaps millions.

"The sixth Seal Judgment consists of God pouring out his wrath against the killing of his saints. This will come in the form of a worldwide earthquake so devastating that no instruments will be able to measure it. It will be so bad that people will cry out for rocks to fall on them and put them out of their misery. The seventh seal introduces the seven Trumpet Judgments, which will take place in the second quarter of the seven years. That's the second twenty-one months."

Bruce concluded, "Most believers will be murdered or die from war, famine, plagues, or earthquakes."

Vicki was depressed. She found herself actually looking

forward to Mr. Williams's presentation. She knew times would
be rough, and she didn't expect any better. But this was devastating. Whatever Cameron Williams had to say had to be better
than this.

"First," Mr. Williams said, "I go by *Buck*. Calling me *Mr.
Williams* makes me feel too old, and calling me *Cameron*
makes me think you're making fun of me the way kids did in
grade school years ago."

Vicki couldn't help but smile. There wasn't much to smile
about these days, but Buck Williams's rapid-fire delivery was
fun to listen to. Her mind had been changed about him immediately. He proved to be an intense, impassioned guy. And he
was a natural-born teacher.

"Remember your vow of confidentiality," Buck said, "and
here we go. My assignment, as I understand it, is to use my
own experience and conversations with Nicolae Carpathia to
convince you he is who Bruce fears he is. Let me run this down
quickly. As you may have seen on the news, he's asked for
resolutions from the U.N. supporting some of the things he
wants to do. These include a seven-year peace treaty with Israel
in exchange for his ability to broker the desert-fertilizer
formula. He's moving the U.N. to New Babylon. He's establishing a one-world religion, probably headquartered in Italy.
Though he might have trouble with the Jews on that one, he
has promised to help them rebuild their temple during the
years of the peace treaty. He believes they deserve special treatment. All those things are predicted in the Bible."

Buck Williams had been standing. Now he pulled up a
chair and sat with the kids. "Let me tell you a story that I
wouldn't believe myself if I had not lived it. I have gained the
attention and respect of Nicolae Carpathia. My former boss
has become his public relations man. Because of that, I got

invited to a private meeting at the U.N. immediately before
Carpathia was to introduce to the world his ten new international ambassadors.

"I knew well the characteristics of the Antichrist, mostly
based on a lengthy conversation I'd had with Bruce. I was not
at that time a believer. When I got to Carpathia's private meeting, I felt such an intense presence of evil and foreboding that
I hurried from the room and got alone where I could receive
Christ. I went back to the meeting, where I witnessed something so astounding that, had I not received Christ and he had
not been in control of my mind and spirit, I know I would
have been brainwashed like everyone else in that room.

"You heard what happened there. The world, the press—
in fact, everyone else in that room that day except Nicolae
Carpathia and me—believe that one of those ambassadors
grabbed a security guard's gun and shot himself. In the process
he killed Carpathia's biggest supporter."

*Yes*, Vicki thought, *that's exactly the way we've heard it
happened.* "Not true?" she asked.

"Not true at all. After Carpathia went around the room,
shaking hands and welcoming each new ambassador to his
team, he borrowed a huge, powerful handgun from the guard
and asked his financial supporter, a man named Jonathan
Stonagal, to kneel before him.

"Stonagal did not want to do it. He was humiliated at the
request. Carpathia pleaded with him to trust him, calling him
his best friend in the world. Once Stonagal was on his knees,
Carpathia was in no hurry. He spoke calmly and quietly, and I
will remember every word he said for as long as I live. He said,
'I am going to kill Mr. Stonagal with a painless hollow-point
round to the brain, which he will neither hear nor feel. The rest
of us will experience some ringing in our ears. This will be

instructive for you all. You will understand cognitively that I am in charge, that I fear no man, and that no one can oppose me.'

"Carpathia went on to say, 'When Mr. Stonagal is dead, I will tell you what you will remember. And lest anyone feel I have not been fair, let me not neglect to add that a high-velocity bullet at this range will also kill Mr. Todd-Cothran.'"

*This is preposterous*, Vicki thought. *How could anyone let a man get away with something like that?*

"I was so shocked and scared," Buck said, "I could not move.

"With his so-called dear friend kneeling there, Carpathia murdered both Stonagal and Todd-Cothran with one shot. I just stared, my mouth hanging open, as others pushed back from the table and covered their heads in fear. Carpathia placed the gun in Stonagal's limp right hand and twisted his finger around the trigger. Carpathia said kindly, as if speaking to children, 'What we have just witnessed here was a horrible, tragic end to two otherwise extravagantly productive lives. These men were two I respected and admired more than any others in the world. What compelled Mr. Stonagal to rush the guard, disarm him, take his own life and that of his British colleague, I do not know and may never fully understand.'

"Carpathia then went around the room, asking each person what he had seen. Every one of them told the story exactly the way Carpathia had described it. When he got to me, God told me to say nothing. Carpathia assumed I was speechless from shock or because he was controlling my mind. And I had no idea whether he knew or not that I knew the truth. When the police arrived and began taking eyewitness accounts, I rushed back to my office and began writing the story. My boss burst in and demanded to know why I had not been at the meeting. I could not convince him I had been there. No one I have talked to in the room remembers I was ever even there.

"You kids don't know me from Adam. You don't have to believe a word I say. But I swear to you as a new brother in Christ that this is the truth. Nicolae Carpathia is evil personified, and if he is not the Antichrist, I don't know who is."

Vicki knew the others were as impressed as she. Buck looked spent. Vicki knew what he had said had a ring of truth to it. She believed him instinctively. And she had the same thought the others had at the same time. As one, they reached out and gently touched Buck's shoulders. Then they knelt around him and prayed for him.

---

Judd, for one, was proud to be a part of this little group, in this church, under this pastor, and alongside people like Buck Williams. He and his friends were just kids to some people, but their task, just like that of the adult Tribulation Force, was clear. Their goal was nothing less than to stand against and fight the enemies of God during the seven most chaotic years the planet would ever see.

# ABOUT THE AUTHORS

**Dr. Tim LaHaye** (www.timlahaye.com), who conceived and created the idea of fictionalizing an account of the Rapture and the Tribulation, is a noted author, minister, and nationally recognized speaker on Bible prophecy. He is the founder of both Tim LaHaye Ministries and the Pre-Trib Research Center. He also recently cofounded the Tim LaHaye School of Prophecy at Liberty University. Presently Dr. LaHaye speaks at many Bible prophecy conferences in the US and Canada, where his current prophecy books are very popular.

Dr. LaHaye holds a doctor of ministry degree from Western Theological Seminary and a doctor of literature degree from Liberty University. For twenty-five years he pastored one of the nation's outstanding churches in San Diego, which grew to three locations. It was during that time that he founded two accredited Christian high schools, a Christian school system of ten schools, and San Diego Christian College (formerly known as Christian Heritage College).

Dr. LaHaye has written over fifty nonfiction books and coauthored more than twenty-five fiction books, many of which have been translated into thirty-four languages. He has written books on a wide variety of subjects, such as family life, temperaments, and Bible prophecy. His most popular fiction works—the Left Behind books, written with Jerry B. Jenkins—have appeared on the bestseller lists of the Christian Booksellers Association, *Publishers Weekly*, the *Wall Street Journal*, *USA Today*, and the *New York Times*.

Another popular series by LaHaye and Jenkins is the Jesus Chronicles. This four-book fiction series gives readers a rich first-century experience as *John*, *Mark*, *Luke*, and *Matthew* narrate thrilling accounts of the life of Jesus. LaHaye's other prophetic novels include the Babylon Rising series and The End series. These are suspense thrillers with thought-provoking messages.

407

**Jerry B. Jenkins**, former vice president for publishing at Moody Bible Institute of Chicago and currently chairman of the board of trustees, is the author of more than 175 books, including the bestselling Left Behind series. Twenty of his books have reached the *New York Times* Best Sellers List (seven in the number one spot) and have also appeared on the *USA Today*, *Publishers Weekly*, and *Wall Street Journal* bestseller lists. *Desecration*, book nine in the Left Behind series, was the bestselling book in the world in 2001. His books have sold nearly seventy million copies.

Also the former editor of *Moody* magazine, Jenkins has contributed writing to *Time*, *Reader's Digest*, *Parade*, *Guideposts*, *Christianity Today*, and dozens of other periodicals. He was featured on the cover of *Newsweek* magazine in 2004.

His nonfiction books include as-told-to biographies with Hank Aaron, Bill Gaither, Orel Hershiser, Luis Palau, Joe Gibbs, Walter Payton, and Nolan Ryan, among many others. The Hershiser and Ryan books reached the *New York Times* Best Sellers List.

Jenkins assisted Dr. Billy Graham with his autobiography, *Just As I Am*, also a *New York Times* bestseller. Jerry spent thirteen months working with Dr. Graham, which he considers the privilege of a lifetime.

Jerry owns Jenkins Entertainment, a filmmaking company in Los Angeles, which produced the critically acclaimed movie *Midnight Clear*, based on his book of the same name. See www.jenkins-entertainment.com.

Jerry Jenkins also owned the Christian Writers Guild, whose aim was to train tomorrow's professional Christian writers. Under Jerry's leadership, the guild expanded to include college-credit courses, a critique service, literary registration services, and writing contests, as well as an annual conference. After fourteen years of ministry, Jerry has recently chosen to close the Guild.

As a marriage-and-family author, Jerry has been a frequent guest on Dr. James Dobson's *Focus on the Family* radio program and is a sought-after speaker and humorist. See www.ambassadorspeakers.com.

Jerry has been awarded four honorary doctorates. He and his wife, Dianna, have three grown sons and eight grandchildren.

Check out Jerry's blog at www.jerry-jenkins.com.